Thomas William Shafto Robertson

Principal dramatic works

With memoir by his son. Vol. II

Thomas William Shafto Robertson

Principal dramatic works
With memoir by his son. Vol. II

ISBN/EAN: 9783744749121

Printed in Europe, USA, Canada, Australia, Japan

Cover: Foto ©Andreas Hilbeck / pixelio.de

More available books at **www.hansebooks.com**

THE PRINCIPAL

DRAMATIC WORKS

OF

THOMAS WILLIAM ROBERTSON

With Memoir

BY HIS SON

VOL. II.

LONDON

SAMPSON LOW, MARSTON, SEARLE & RIVINGTON, Limited

St. Dunstan's House

FETTER LANE, FLEET STREET

SAMUEL FRENCH, DRAMATIC PUBLISHER

89 STRAND

1889

CONTENTS.

VOL. II.

PORTRAITS.

VOL. II.

THE NIGHTINGALE.

A NEW AND ORIGINAL DRAMA,

IN FIVE ACTS.

BY

T. W. ROBERTSON,

AUTHOR OF

"Caste," "A Breach of Promise," "School," "M.P.,"
"Birth," "David Garrick," "The Ladies' Battle," "Ours,"
"Play," "Progress," "Row in the House," "Society,"
"Dreams," "War," "Home," "Faust and Marguerite," "My
Wife's Diary," "Noemie," "Two Gay Deceivers," "Jocrisse
the Juggler," "Not at all Jealous," "Star of the North,"
"Birds of Prey," "Peace at any Price," "Half Caste,"
"Ernestine," "Chevalier de St. George," "Cantab," "Clock-
maker's Hat," "Duke's Daughter," "Sea of Ice," &c,, &c.

LONDON:
SAMUEL FRENCH,
PUBLISHER,
89, STRAND.

NEW YORK:
SAMUEL FRENCH & SON,
PUBLISHERS,
28, WEST 23RD STREET.
C C

THE NIGHTINGALE.

DRAMA IN FIVE ACTS.

(Produced at the Adelphi Theatre, London, January 15th, 1870.)

CAST OF CHARACTERS.

Harold Fane	MR. ARTHUR STIRLING.
Ismael-al-Moolah	MR. BEN WEBSTER.
Chepstowe.	MRS. ALFRED MELLON.
William Waye	MR. J. D. BEVERIDGE.
Major Pomeroy	
Joe	
Willie	MASTER BLANCHARD.
Mary	MISS FURTADO.
Kesiah	MISS ELIZA JOHNSTONE.
Mrs. Minns.	MRS. CAUTFIELD.

ACT. I.—THE ENGLISH HOME, 1863.—*Room in a Cottage.*

ACT II.—THE ITALIAN INN, 1865.—*Room in an Italian Hotel.*

ACT III.—THE LODGINGS, PORTSMOUTH, 1867.—*Meanly furnished Room. Mechanical Change to River Scene.*

ACT IV.—THE SQUARE, LONDON, 1868.—*A Square in London.*

ACT V.—THE VILLAGE CHURCH, 1869.—*A Country Churchyard Modern Costumes. Time of Representation, three hours.*

THE NIGHTINGALE.

ACT I.

SCENE.—*Room in a cottage ornée, elegantly furnished. Door* R. *and* L. *Window* C. *Scene enclosed. Piano covered with music,* L. H. *The window looks into garden ; at back of garden, wall looking on to road ; garden wall about 7ft. high ; flower-stands and flowers everywhere ; all bright and cheery. A tap heard at door.* KEZIAH *crosses from* L. H. *and opens* R. H. *door.*

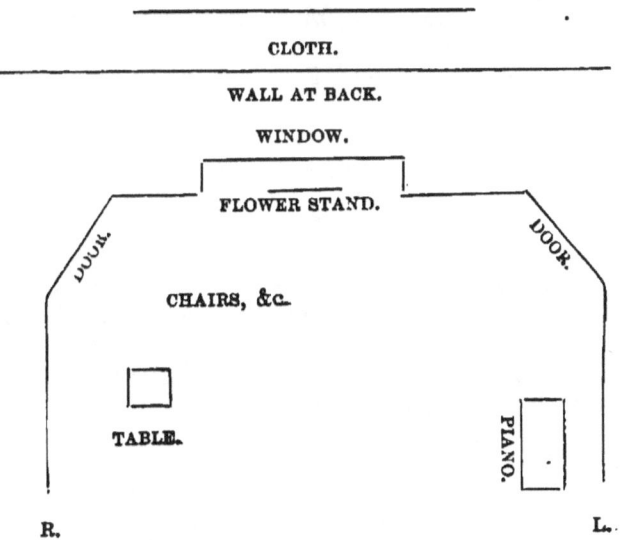

CLOTH.

WALL AT BACK.

WINDOW.

FLOWER STAND.

DOOR

DOOR

CHAIRS, &c.

TABLE.

PIANO.

R.

L.

JOE. (*outside*) I beg your pardon, miss, but I was told there was a short-cut to the village : is it that footpath just opposite ?

KEZ. Yes ; are you going to the village ?

JOE. Yes, miss.

KEZ. Where do you come from ?

JOE. I've walked this morning from Cambridge.

KEZ. Come in and sit down.

JOE. Thank ye, miss.   (JOE *enters*)

KEZ. Do you belong to Cambridge ?   (*with dialect*)

JOE. No, miss.

KEZ. But you don't belong here?

JOE. No, miss.

KEZ. I do.

JOE. I should ha' thought so.

KEZ. Why?

JOE. 'Cos all the young ladies about here seem so nice!

KEZ. (*flattered*) Ha! ha! ha! ha! Do you think so?

JOE. Sure on it. I suppose this pretty place (*looking round*) is yours, miss?

KEZ. Mine! no. La bless you, sir—I'm only the servant.

JOE. (*surprised*) Oh! I should ha' thought you was the missus.

KEZ. No. Mrs. Bransom is the missus, but she's gone to London on law business—but she ain't my missus—No! My missus is Miss Waye. Do you know her?

JOE. No.

KEZ. She is a young lady—an orphan.

JOE. Dear! dear! dear! No father nor mother, then?

KEZ. No—not living. Had both, but they died, leaving her a lot of money.

JOE. How nice of 'em! But they all seem to be real ladies and gentlemen about here.

KEZ. But missus won't stop here long.

JOE. Won't she though!

KEZ. No. She's going to be married to her cousin, Mr. William. He's got a lot o' money, too.

JOE. Has he though!

KEZ. At least he had; but he's spent some. But now he's going to reform, because he's going to marry. He's saving by the advice of his great friend Ismael.

JOE. Ismael! What a funny name!

KEZ. Yes—he's a Turkey.

JOE. A Turkey?

KEZ. Yes. I mean, he comes from Turkey, or somewhere there. I know it's in America. He's a sort of tutor to Mr. Waye. They've been all over the world together. My missus and Mr. William have been engaged almost ever since they was babies. That was long before Mr. William used to get so drunk as he does now. But he was always fond of liquor from a child. He was weaned on liquor.

JOE. Lor!

KEZ. Yes, Mr. Ismael never drinks anything.

JOE. Don't he?

KEZ. No.

JOE. That's nasty.

KEZ. It's the way with them. foreigners. I don't like him.

JOE. Why not?

KEZ. 'Cos he's a Turkey, and I don't think it's right to like any but English.

JOE. No. Britannia rules the waves!

KEZ. (*who throughout has talked very quickly*) And charges for it in the taxes! Why should she rule 'em for nothing? I wouldn't! But I know somebody else who is in love with my missus—young Mr. Harold! Yes—he's got a little money, too, and in two years' time, he's going to be a parson. He's going back to Cambridge to learn how. That's where they make parsons; but I don't think he cares much about it—I don't mean about Cambridge, but about being a parson—but I know he's fond of my missus, who is a very sweet young lady, and got the loveliest voice for singing you ever heard. They call her about here the nightingale, and Mr. Ismael says that with such a voice she ought to come out upon the stage, and she'd make her fortune, but Mr. Waye won't hear of that. That's her piano—pretty piano, ain't it? Such a nice piano to dust. My missus is out for a walk. She'll be back directly. You must feel very thirsty after so much talking?

JOE. Well, miss (*wiping his mouth*)——

KEZ. Come into the kitchen and have some beer. Do you like beer?

JOE. Very!

KEZ. That's right. (*aside*) Nice young man this. So much conversation. This way.

(*Exeunt* KEZIAH *and* JOE, D.L.)

HAROLD *looks in at window.* HAROLD, *a young country gentleman with a cross of the parson in his manner, a black paletôt, white cravat, wide-awake, and drab trousers. All plain and unpretentious.*

HAR. No one here! I suppose she is still in her room. (*looks at watch*) By the next vacation she may be married to her cousin. Ay! ay! I suppose life is so to all of us, and it is no use my loving her. No use! As if I could help it! as if I could help it! And my day-dreams of the life we might have passed together in some sequestered parsonage, with the villagers to take care of, and the

fulfilment of our peaceful, honest duties day by day;
Why, the thought of her made me a poet. (*entering* R.D.
and looking at music) The last new song, and the last time
my eyes shall rest on these inanimate surroundings. The
flowers she looks on, the instrument her touch makes
harmony. The last time! the last time! (*seats himself*)

CHEPSTOWE *appears on wall at back.*

CHEP. Harold! Harold!   (HAROLD *rises*)
HAR. Chepstowe!
CHEP. Then it was you. I saw you before me on the
road.
HAR. How is it you are here?
CHEP. Drove over half an hour ago. Called at your
place; they told me they thought you'd come on here, so I
came after you. Miss Waye at home?
HAR. No; but you can come in. (CHEPSTOWE *gets over
wall*) There's the gate.
CHEP. I prefer the wall. I'm more used to it. (*gets
over, disappears, and enters* R.D.) How are you, Harold?
You look just the same as when we were at Rugby. By
the way, you don't know why I'm here?
HAR. (*throughout scene distrait*) No.
CHEP. Huzza! Then I shall have the pleasure of
telling you. Ask me, ask me—I can't tell you if you
don't ask me.
HAR. (*smiling*) My dear Jack, what unknown cause
gives me the happiness of seeing you here?
CHEP. I'm *en route* for London—*en route*. I go by the
coach at three to Cambridge.
HAR. So do I.
CHEP. Bravo! Then we shall be comrades—I mean
fellow-passengers. Now ask me why I am *en route* for
London.

CHEPSTOWE *to be very young, in high spirits, and to
flourish a cane.*

HAR. My dear Jack, why are you *en route* for London?
CHEP. I—I—I can't tell you—I'm so pleased. Look
here—read that. (*gives* HAROLD "*Gazette*," *and goes up
singing the march from* "*Faust*," *and flourishing cane*)
HAR. (*reading*) "John Chepstowe, Esq., to be ensign, by
purchase." What!
CHEP. Yes; I'm a soldier—I mean I'm an officer, I shall
be a soldier by-and-bye. All in good time—officer first—

soldier afterwards. (*sings march*) Ensign Chepstowe—
Lieutenant Chepstowe—Captain Chepstowe—Major Chepstowe—Lieutenant-Colonel Chepstowe—General Chepstowe
—Field-Marshal the Duke of Chepstowe, K.C.B. Congratulate me Harold.

HAR. I do, my dear Jack.

CHEP. Thank you ; I know you do. Hurrah !

HAR. But I thought——

CHEP. Yes ; so did I. I was to have gone to Cambridge
—like you, and to have taken orders ; but I didn't like the
notion of taking orders any more than of taking pills ; so
the governor said to me, "Jack, you're such a thundering
fool that you're fit for nothing but a soldier." I said,
"Governor, you're right ; if you made me into a parson I
should only be a nuisance in the parish." So I should.
So I'm off to the depôt, and I shall soon have to carry the
colours.   (*sings, and imitates carrying colours*)

HAR. You are a lucky fellow, Jack, to have a father
and a mother, and——

CHEP. To get a commission ; you're right. *Chacun à
son*—coat. You shall be a Bishop—I shall be a F.M.
"F.M. the Duke of Chepstowe presents his compliments to
the Bishop of—any see—and hopes to have the honour of
seeing his—Reverence—Lordship—Grace—which is it ?—
to dinner at Chepstowe Castle, at seven, on Wednesday, the
17th day of the month after next. N.B.—Grace before
meat as per usual."

HAR. What different lives lie before us !

CHEP. Yes ; when I shall be saying—(*commands*)—you
will be saying "Dearly beloved" ; when I'm rolling out
"Cha-r-r-rge," you'll be intoning "Amen !" and when you're
burying the dead I shall be potting the living.
                                   (*sings march*)

ISMAEL *looks in at window*, C. CHEPSTOWE R HAROLD L.

ISM. Ah ! good morning, my young friend, good morning !
A golden day, is it not ? Fresh, warm, and glorious as
youth itself.   Our sweet cousins still out walking, eh ?

> ISMAEL *to be a man about forty-five, he wears a
> frock-coat and red fez ; his beard half grey, half
> black ; his manner amiable and agreeable, per-
> petually smiling. (no Iago-glances at the pit, and
> private information to the audience, that he is a
> villain, and that they shall see what they shall see)
> A suave, bland Oriental, with the old Oriental
> dignity.*

HAR. (*coldly*) I believe so.

ISM. How lovely these flowers ! (*looking at piano*) and the music—but the music is dumb till it is evoked, and the flowers need no fairy touch to spread their perfume.   Oh, Nature! oh, Art! You should be twin-sisters—one the exact counterpart of the other—and you are hardly tenth cousins, and have no mutual resemblance.   (*disappears*)

CHEP. Who's he?

HAR. Ismael-al-Moolah !

CHEP. What is he?

HAR. I don't know.

CHEP. He looks like an acrobat—baked.

Enter ISMAEL, *at door* R.

ISM. The room smells like a conservatory. (*seeing* CHEPSTOWE) Pardon me, Signor. (*to* HAROLD) You don't introduce me to your friend.

HAR. Mr.——

CHEP. Ensign John Chepstowe.   I'll introduce myself.

ISM. Ah ! a soldier.   My heart warms to a soldier.   I, too, have been a soldier.

CHEP. Indeed! What service?

ISM. Many.   (*shows decorations and ribbons*)

CHEP. Then you have been under fire?

ISM. How else could I show these?

CHEP. Did you ever kill a man?

ISM. You mean in battle?

HAR. How else could he mean?

ISM. (*sighs*) I fear many.   Does that surprise you?

CHEP. Not a bit.   You look the sort of fellow who could kill a fellow—and not care a damn !

ISM. And eat him afterwards, eh?   You think that because I come from the rich East, and have brown blood, and a brown skin, and black eyes and yellow eyeballs, and my tongue is strange.   I speak English like a Frenchman, because I have lived many years in France.   You have a strong prejudice against foreigners, you English, and it is hard on me, for I love Europe ; I am a European in education, thought and feeling.   But I have the gift of tongues and that makes many suspect me.   I look like a man in the " Arabian Nights "—like one of the Forty Thieves, don't I?

CHEP. Yes, exactly like Forty Thieves ; but I should like to hear you talk about the battles you've been in.

ISM. Talk! Ha! Speech is the index and mirror of the soul.   I have many indices and mirrors, though only one soul. In what language will you that I converse with you? Italian?

CHEP. No!

ISM. Spanish?

CHEP. No!

ISM. German?

CHEP. No!

ISM. Latin?

CHEP. No?

ISM. Greek?

CHEP. No!

ISM. Hebrew!

CHEP. No!

ISM. Coptic?

CHEP. No!

ISM. Turkish?

CHEP. No!

ISM. Arabic?

CHEP. No!

ISM. What then?

CHEP. English! English! English!

ISM. Ah, English! Please to pass then on the other side, for I use this ear only for foreign and scientific tongues, and the other for the vulgar maternal and vernacular.

CHEP. (*surprised*) Eh?

ISM. Ha! You've never read Molière's "Mariage Forcé?"

CHEP. No; but I've read Pierce Egan's "Boxiana"!

ISM. And yet you've been quoting him unconsciously for the last five minutes. Oh! divine Molière!

CHEP. But about these battles you've fought in?

HAR. (*rising*) We have no time. If you'll go and help me to finish packing up, we can return here to bid Miss Waye good-bye.

ISM. (*to* HAROLD) You are going away to-day? I am so sorry!   (*shaking hands with* HAROLD)

CHEP. And I'm so glad!

ISM. I shall see you again before you start?

HAR. Perhaps.

(*they salute.* CHEPSTOWE *à la militaire*)

Exeunt HAROLD *and* CHEPSTOWE. CHEPSTOWE, R.D., *singing.*

"How happy's the soldier," &c.

ISM. (*watching them from window*) Poor young Fane!

He's in love with Mary.   I know it, I feel it, but he's not in love with me.   I feel that, too.

Enter WAYE, R.D.   (WAYE *to be a fresh-coloured, fair-haired, weak, vacillating young man, self-indulgent, one who cannot deny any man a favour*)

WAYE. Good morning, governor !

ISM. (*turning*) Ah ! my young pupil ! (*tapping him on the shoulder*) How goes it ?

WAYE. Somewhat seedy—(*looking round*)—and——

ISM. Ah ! A dram of brandy would——

WAYE. (*showing empty flask*) My flask is out.

ISM. (*producing flask*) And mine is full.   (WAYE *drinks*) Wonderful how you can swallow such fire, and so much of it ! Would my temperate Eastern constitution were like yours ! but you overdo it ; you drink too much ; it must tell on you in time.   You know I always warn you against it ?

WAYE. You do ; but don't preach.   Don't consider me a little boy of ten years old !

ISM. A boy of ten years old ! Why, you're a lover ; shortly, I hope, to be a husband ! Eh ? Oh, divine youth ! Divine power to love, and still diviner power to inspire it. My time is gone, and my heart can never stir again save at the sight of the happiness of others.   And when's the marriage ?

WAYE. I've never asked her.

ISM. What a sluggish boy ! If it were my case ! Ah ! But you must ask, and soon.   If not to solace the impatience of your own heart, for a more material and worldly reason—a reason that in this atmosphere of sentiment and flowers I blush to name—that is, I would blush but that my brown skin forbids me.   Our company in Hungary——

WAYE. The Limited Asiatic and European Association for Supplying Preserved Fresh Meat to over-populated countries at one-third the present market price.

ISM. Yes. Our company in Hungary wants money.

WAYE. The devil it does ! It has already swallowed up such a lot.

ISM. It has—but if we would reap we must sow.   We will sow—sovereigns that shall come up hundreds.

WAYE. When ?

ISM. In three years—perhaps two—who knows ? It must come.   So the sooner you put your wife's money into the speculation the sooner you do your duty to her as well as to yourself.

WAYE. If you think it's my duty.

ISM. It is.

WAYE. You're sure?

ISM. I swear it, by the beard of the prophet— I mean by Our Lady of Loretto.

WAYE. And to embark Mary's money in it too, when she's my wife?

ISM. When she's your wife—and *apropos*—when you are married you must insure your life for her,

WAYE. For how much?

ISA. Umph—say for four thousand.

WAYE. Is that my duty too?

ISM. I swear it, by the holy Ganges—I mean by the holy Jordan! (*searching for papers*) And, by the way, here's your cheque-book. The company wants £300.

WAYE. Three!

ISM. Yes.

WAYE. Is there as much balance left?

ISM. I think so. If not, they will let you overdraw.

WAYE. I don't know that.

ISM. Then my purse must make it up.

WAYE. But you have no money: it's all embarked in our Preserved Fresh Beef.

ISM. (*affectionately*) I'll pawn my jewels rather than your cheque should be dishonoured.

WAYE. What a good fellow you are!

ISM. Not half so good as I seem. Here's pen and ink.

WAYE *writes cheque and gives it to* ISMAEL. *As soon as* ISMAEL *has got it, enter* MARY, L.D.

MARY. Good morning.

ISM. (*hiding cheque behind his back*) Good morning—as the morning cannot help being when it shines on you. Don't be impatient—I'm going.

MARY. Going! Why?

ISM. That I may not interrupt you.

MARY. Oh, you may stay. Willie is not a very ardent lover, and he's been out with me an hour and a half.

WAYE. But I was very happy all the time, Mary.

MARY. (*sitting down to piano and playing*) Now, that is so kind of you to say so. I wonder if you really do care about me.

WAYE. You know I do—ever so much.

Ism. A charming sentiment.

MARY. (*playing throughout dialogue*) So you ought, considering how long we've been engaged—ever since we were children. If it were not for that, I don't think I would have you.

Ism. Oh, don't say that! (*aside to* WAYE) Ask her not to say that.

WAYE. (*mechanically*) Don't say so!

Ism. No, don't. Ah! you young people, why play with your happiness while youth gilds your affection with its roseate glow? If I were you——

MARY. Well, if you were me?

Ism. If I were both of you—(*as with a sudden thought*) —I *will* be both of you. (*acting the two parts*) Then, I, William Waye, loving and beloved of Mary Waye, should draw near unto her who was to me as both my breath and the beating of my heart, and I should say, "Mary, we have loved each other from childhood—from the days when we lisped in infancy together, and walked out into the green fields and wove chaplets of alternate violets and daisies."

MARY. (*laughing*) But we never did weave chaplets of violets and daisies.

Ism. Then you should have done. Don't interrupt me. "The time draws nigh, love, which should make you mine in the sight of Allah—I mean of Heaven and of men. Come unto me, Mary, my wife—for my soul yearns for thee. I love thee as the waters of the rivers love the sun, and the sight of thee floods me with light, and warmth, and rapture —even as with the glory of thy face, the majesty of thy step, and the intoxicating perfume of thy presence. Name the day, and that day to be within a month from this that I may take thee to the mosque—to the church—and bid the priest unite us now, for ever and for ever."

MARY. (*half frightened*) I never thought there was all that in marriage.

WAYE. Nor I.

Ism. Then I, Mary, so gentle and so sweet, so beautiful and bashful, should place my hand in that of my betrothed —(*suiting action to word*)—and looking full into his eyes, that I might there read his inmost thoughts, I would say, "The heart I gave you when a child, I now, a woman, give to you again. Take me! I am thine for ever! In joy, triumph, sickness, sorrow, in the bloom of life, in the hour of death, I am thine!"

MARY. (*impressed*) You frighten me!

Ism. And our wedding-day shall be Wednesday, this day month.

Waye. Done! On Wednesday, then——

Ism. (*with pocket-book*) July 27.

Waye. I shall be the happiest of men!

Ism. There! you are betrothed! (Waye *kisses her*)

Mary. Oh!

> *Disengaging herself and crossing to mirror, which she touches, the mirror falls to the ground.* Keziah *enters* l.d. *at the same moment.*

Kez. (*in consternation*) Oh, Miss Mary!

Mary. Keziah!

Kez. Who broke it?

Mary. I did.

Kez. Then you'll have no luck for seven long years!

Ism. Psha! 'Twas not worth a guinea. I'll replace it.

Mary. My grandmamma's favourite old mirror. I would not have broken it for worlds!

Waye. Never mind, Mary, forget it.

Mary. I can't.

Waye. Sit down and sing us a song.

Mary. Not now.

Kez. Yes, miss, do. They say music has a charm to keep off spells.

Mary. Has it? (*seats herself at piano, out of spirits*) What shall I play?

Waye. And sing? This. (*pointing to song*)

Kez. May I stop and hear it?

Waye. Yes.

Mary. That broken glass! (*she sings song*)

> *During song* Harold *looks in at window. He remains there till song is over.*

Kez. Here's Mr. Harold. (*they all turn*)

Ism. He arrives most *apropos.*

Mary. Won't you come in, Harold?

(Harold *disappears from window*)

Waye. Yes, come in. (Harold *enters at door* r.)

Ism. You have arrived most opportunely. Come and give us joy.

Har. Joy!

Ism. Yes. Let me present you to two young hearts that have long beaten apart, but will soon throb side by side. In a month these two will be one. (*a pause*)

HAR. You are—so soon to be—married?

WAYE. Yes.

KEZ. Isn't that nice?

ISM. And I claim the first kiss of the bride.

(kisses MARY)

KEZ. And isn't that nasty?

ISM. You see I understand your English manners.

KEZ. Those Turkeys always look as if they could gobble you up!

MARY. Yes, Harold. It seems strange—I don't know why it should—but it does seem strange that I should have to tell you—but I have given my word.

HAR. I congratulate you, and wish you every happiness.

KEZ. Oh, they're sure to have that. People who are married are always happy!

MARY. But you seem out of spirits, Harold?

WAYE. What's the matter?

HAR. I am not in the best mood, for I come to bid you good-bye.

MARY. } Good-bye?
WAYE. }

HAR. Yes; I go back to Cambridge to-day. The coach will take me up as it passes. (KEZIAH *begins to cry* O—oh!)

MARY. What are you crying for Keziah?

KEZ. 'Cos he's going away. I like people to go as far as church together, but no further.

HAR. *(aside)* And she will be the only one that mourns me.

MARY. I am very sorry that we are to lose you.

HAR. Thank you.

WAYE. So am I.

HAR. Thank you.

ISM. And I. (HAROLD *bows*)

WAYE. If you'd been a parson, Harold, as you will be some day, you might have married us.

HAR. Yes—I might have married you.

ISM. Even now you could give away the bride.

HAR. Yes—even now I could give away the bride. (*to* MARY) Though I did not think your marriage was to take place so soon, I thought that the next time I saw you I might have to call you—no longer Mary, but—Mrs. Waye. I had brought you, as a gift from an old friend, this ring— (*producing it in case*)—which I now, in presence of your future husband, ask you to accept. (*mastering his emotion as she takes ring. Music; song in orchestra, piano*) In a .

few days there will be another ring upon this finger—
a pledge of mutual love to last till death. Should this little
gem be honoured by a place beside it, let their emblematic
circles remind you of the affection of your chosen husband,
and of the unalterable esteem of your true absent friend.
God bless you !

> *Horn of coach heard. Music. He kisses her on the
> forehead. The roof of the coach appears in sight.*
> CHEPSTOWE *on the box.*

CHEP. (*from roof*) Now, Harold ! Here we are, off
for London. Good-bye, Miss Waye—good-bye, Waye—
good-bye everybody ! For-r-r-r-ward !

> HAROLD *goes off* R.D. WAYE *and* MARY *watch
> him from window* C. WAYE'S *arm round* MARY'S
> *waist.* KEZIAH *cries near piano.* ISMAEL *takes
> out book and is absorbed in calculation.*

END OF ACT I.

ACT II.

SCENE.—*A Salon in the principal hotel in a small town in Italy. (2nd grooves) Door* R. *and* L. *The apartments supposed to be en suite. Window* C., *showing street* L.C., *opposite. The rooms supposed to be on the second-floor. The fittings and furniture shabby magnificent. All decayed grandeur. Chairs, sofa, easy-chair, footstool. Table* L.C. *with writing materials. Cradle. Scene enclosed.*

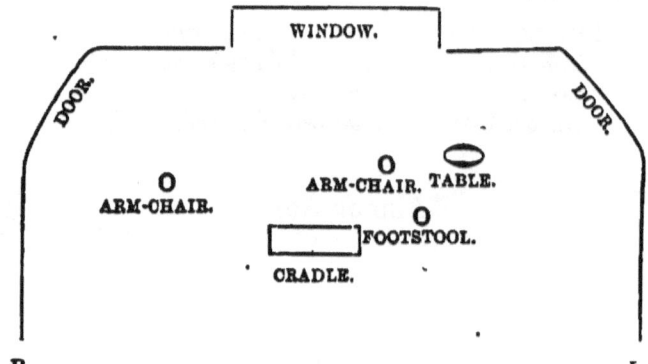

*Discovered—*KEZIAH *asleep in arm-chair.* MARY *singing the song of the 1st Act to the baby in the cradle, which she is rocking. At end of song* ISMAEL *appears at* L.D. *He remains on the threshold. He wears a long dressing-gown.*

ISM. (*in a whisper*) Keziah !

MARY. Can I——   (KEZIAH *wakes*)

ISM. No. (*to* KEZIAH) The fresh medicine—some more water ?   (KEZIAH *gives it him from table*)

MARY. Is he any better ? (ISMAEL *shakes his head*) Shall I take your place ?

ISM. Not just yet. I expect that after this he will sleep.   *Exit* ISMAEL, L.D.

KEZ. I've been asleep. It was sitting up all last night. (*looking at watch*) It's eight o'clock.

MARY. And William has not slept the whole night. I fear that he gets worse and worse.

KEZ. So do I. Sometimes when I look at him I'm

afraid he'll never get over it. I wish we were in England.
I don't like these foreign doctors. I like a real regular
doctor with a white neck.

MARY. But Ismael has studied medicine, and he is
wonderfully skilful.

KEZ. He believes too much in change of air for me.
First we go to France, then to Germany, then to the south
of France again, then to Italy—across such hills as
Government shouldn't allow to be, and wouldn't in my
country where there's freedom and beer on draught—and
here we are!

MARY. And here we have been four months—and here
baby was born.

KEZ. Poor little thing! To be born in Italy, where
there's no registration, nor vaccination, nor any other
Christian comforts—and as soon as you get better, master,
who was ill before, gets worse, and we're forced to stop
here. I hate Italy; it's a nasty place, nothing in it but
grapes and public buildings—every one out of repair.
Talk about beauty!—a lot of tumble-down old ruins!—a
few hods of brick and mortar, and a pail or two of white-
wash would make 'em worth looking at, and they should
have it if I had my way; but I don't believe the people
here have got the money to do it, nor the brains. Talking
of bricks makes me think of poor Mr. Harold—where was
it you heard he was, in that letter that was forwarded to
you from Paris?

MARY. In India, at Secunderabad.

KEZ. Secunderabad! another Italian sort of name.
Only to think now, just after you got married, of his giving
up the notion of being a parson and turning officer, and
buying a regiment of soldiers that he might command them,
having previously taken his degree at Cambridge that he
might know how—but la! a clever Cambridge man can
turn his degree to anything. (*looking into cradle*) Why I
declare baby's wide awake, and quite quiet—which ain't
usual with him—and lately he's been in India, fighting with
the negroes—Mr. Harold I mean, and not the baby. Dear!
dear! dear! slashing and cutting—cutting his teeth will
make him suffer, I know—but perhaps he'll get promoted
for it, and grow up to be a general, and a blessing to you—
I mean the baby, not Mr. Harold——(*knock*, R.D.)—That's
Catterina. Come in—I mean *entrate*. (*Enter* CATTERINA,
an Italian nurse-girl, with cloak and hood for child) Bong
journey, comati to take outi baby for a promenadi. (*taking*

up cradle behind table) Put on coati—mantilly. I go tooty. Do you know, missus, I used to think Mr. Harold was in love with you?

MARY. In love!—oh, no; he cared for me as a friend—nothing more.

KEZ. Oh, if he only cared for you as a friend, that isn't much. I once lent a chap—Joe Petherick by name—four pound eight, and when I asked him when he was going to put up the banns, he said he only cared for me as a friend; but his friendly feeling did not go so far as to make him pay me back my four pound eight. Just an hour's walk, missus, and we'll be home again. Ah! talking to me of old times makes you feel quite comfortable, don't it? A good gossip about what is past and gone relieves your mind—I know it does—Avia, Catterina! La, her eyes are as black as sloes, and her skin is like a bath brick! These here Italian foreign women always look to me like Napoleon Buonaparte in petticoats; and they say - he was only an Italian by rights.

    Exeunt KEZIAH, *and* CATTERINA *and child*, R.D. *At the same moment* ISMAEL *appears at* L.D.

ISM. (*aside*) 'Twill soon be over now.

MARY. (*seeing him*) How is my husband?

ISM. Asleep—at last.

MARY. Is there any hope?

ISM. None—at least, I fear none.

                              (MARY *sinks in chair*)

MARY. Oh, my child! my child! my child! My boy who will never know his father's face.

ISM. Mary—dearest Mary—remember Providence is still with you—I am still with you.

MARY. My husband!

ISM. I fear that medical or any human aid will not much longer avail him. His strength seems going. You know how I have watched him.

MARY. (*giving him her hand*) You have indeed been like a father.

ISM. I fear that when the inevitable blow shall fall, that you will find yourself in some pecuniary embarrassment.

MARY. (*surprised*) No; my husband is rich.

ISM. He was rich, but speculated in the affairs of the company in which he had so largely invested.

MARY. Poor Willie! He was not prudent, I know; but

his good, kind heart, and your shrewd worldly knowledge made him insure his life heavily.

Ism. Yes—but the debts will swallow it.

Mary. Debts!

Ism. (*shaking his head*) Speculation—the company—the company.

Mary. Then there will be only left my money—the portion that I brought him when we married.

Ism. That also, I regret to say, has gone.

Mary. (*astonished*) Gone! How?

Ism. Debts—speculation—the company.

Mary. My portion too?

Ism. Alas! I urged him to settle it on you when he was solvent, but you know—he would not take hints—my poor suffering friend—delicacy forbade me from pressing the subject.

Mary. (*falling into chair, her head resting on the table*) Then I and my baby are both beggars?

Ism. Alas! Yes!

Mary. My child! my husband!

Ism. Still you have resources.

Mary. Where?

Ism. In your voice. At the opera you would make a fortune.

Mary. My voice! Could I sing with the thought of a dead husband and a beggared child weighing on my heart?

Ism. Time is a great consoler. Heaven has willed it should be so. (*lowering his voice*) And Mary I am always at your feet. · Affection for my poor friend stilled my tongue, when I first beheld you, three years ago; but then, and since then, I have loved you. (Mary *starts*) I am rich —I have knowledge—I can protect you from the cruel frown of the world. Give me but the right to do so. Make me a second father to your child.

Mary. (*rising. After a pause*) And is it when a husband lies dying, that you dare ask his wife to forget her vows, and plight herself to you? Coward! I see through you now!

Ism. (*seating himself*) Mary, you mistake, you misunderstand me. I am your friend.

Mary. Friend!

Ism. You have no knowledge of the world, and my proposal——

Mary. Is base as its proposer. (*goes to* L.D., *opens it, and addresses herself to the inmate, whispering*) Oh! my darling ! my husband and my love ! I see you lie there, with death marked on your pale face ; and could I—(*with horror*)—Oh ! I shudder at the thought ! (ISMAEL *rises and approaches*) Do not touch me ! I cannot breathe ; let me go from hence, for your villainy poisons the air.

Exit MARY, R.D.

ISMAEL *goes to* L.D. *and watches, then closes it.*

ISM. Ah, woman ! woman !—divine but dangerous ! 'Tis thus they repulse their best friends. Poor, tender, helpless,—'tis useless to struggle,—what has she to rely on but me ? (*takes out letters and calculations*) 100—108—240 —312—506—800—9—Ah ! this must be met, and by this post. Poor Willie ! It will be better that he should not know the state that his affairs will be found in at his death. Perhaps, after all, we quarrel with the decrees of Providence unwisely. Had he lived, he might have had to meet this dreadful charge, which what I now do can shake off but a month or two. I will spare him the pain and shame of ranking among criminals. (*feels in the pocket of dressing-gown, and produces cheques, tracing-paper, &c.; then sits down to table*) Poor Mary—alone and with her child. This for 135. 135. (*writing*) Good ! Ah, William Waye !—ah, William Waye !—you have gone much—much too fast. A short life and a merry one—that was your device. Your life will be short. Has it been merry ? I fear not. 210 —345. He and the company will have a race which shall expire first. Then the discovery and—more debts—more fraud—more——

> *During this* WAYE, *thin, cadaverous, and weak, has appeared at door* L. 2 E. ; *he staggers towards door in flat, then seeing* ISMAEL *engaged in writing, he listens, overlooks him, and places his hand on the forged papers. Picture.* WAYE *secures the papers.*

WAYE. (*in a weak, dying voice*) No, villain ! No more ! No more !

ISM. My friend !

WAYE. I see it all ! The money which has been raised as you told me by speculation—all forged—all forged. (*looking at cheque*) And in my name.

ISM. My friend, you are delirious !

WAYE. Mary ! Keziah ! Where are you ? This shall be known ! I will at once accuse you !

(*going to bell.* ISMAEL *holds him down in chair*)

Ism. My friend, do not ring the bell, you are not strong enough. I will ring it for you.

Waye. Monster! Thus to abuse your strength.

Ism. But for your good, William—but for your good.

Waye. Oh, I am dying! *(leaning back)*

Ism. Alas! my friend, you look as if you were dying!

Waye. I shall see the sun no more! In these last few moments my mental vision clears, and I see all! I am dying by poison!

Ism. Poison! Allah!—I should say blessed Virgin!

Waye. Mary, my wife, come to me!

Ism. Your wife! Do you suspect her?

Waye. No, villain, you!

Ism. You are delirious!

Waye. You shall not escape! Mary!

Ism. My friend, consider. If we should unhappily lose you, you may rely on me—*(the triumph on his face)*—to take care of your wife and child when you are gone.

Waye. Villain!

Ism. Your pecuniary affairs are in confusion. Be it my task to show the world how you managed them.

Waye. This pain!—the poison!

Ism. You know, how I have tended you during your long sickness.

Waye. And hurried me from place to place to hide your guilt. *(rising)* Help!

Ism. My poor friend, death is on your face. *(letting him go)* Have you strength to reach the bell?

Waye. I will try. I will not die alone with you. *(rises)* My sight is gone. I—I——

(falls in chair. Ismael's face expresses triumph)

Enter Mary *and* Keziah *with the child, followed by* Officer *and two Italians and* Catterina.

Mary. A gentleman wishes to see my husband, I have told him he is too ill.

Off. My business is with William Waye.

Ism. He is here.

Mary. *(going round to chair)* He has fainted!

Off. You are my prisoner. *(arresting* Waye *in chair)* I hold in my hand a warrant to arrest him for forgery.

(Waye rises)

Mary. What! *(Waye falls dead in chair)*

Ism. Alas! my poor friend—he is dead.

(coming from before the arm-chair)

MARY. }
KEZ. } Dead !

MARY. (*takes his hand and gets the papers which were grasped in it*) My husband !

ISM. Quite dead. Your prisoner has escaped you, sir. No human law can touch him !

Picture.

END OF ACT II.

ACT III.

SCENE I.—MARY'S *lodgings in Portsmouth. Meanly furnished chambers—(in 2nd grooves) Scene enclosed. Doors* R. 1. E. *and* L. 1 E. *Large window at back looking on to river. The opposite shore painted on cloth. Outside window is a boat and pair of oars, not seen at the commencement of Act. As the Act progresses the tide rises, bringing boat to the level of stage. Table on strip of carpet and chairs,* R.C. *Chest of drawers, &c. Discovered,* KEZIAH *and* LITTLE WILLIE. KEZIAH *is dressing the child for a walk.* MRS. MINNS *standing looking on.*

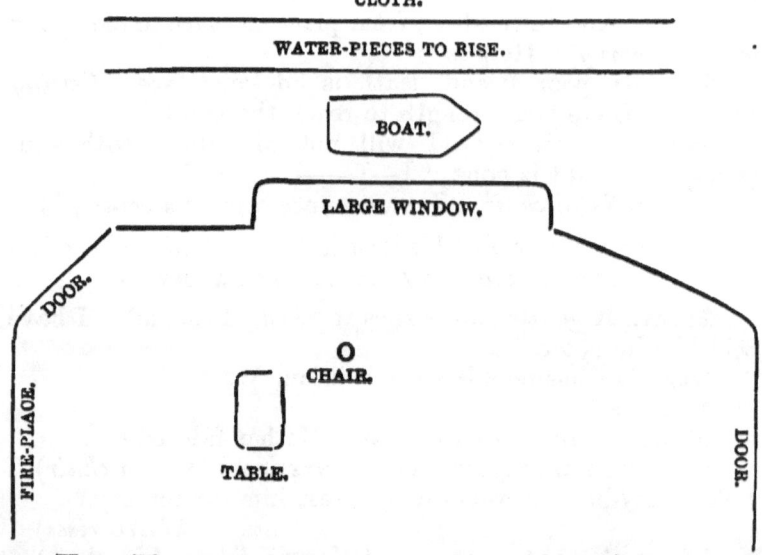

KEZ. There he is, and he looks a perfect picture, don't he, Mrs. Minns?

Mrs. M. He do, indeed !

Kez. And he loves his own Keziah, don't he ? (*boy assents*) He never won't love nobody better than his own Keziah, will he ? He'll never let nobody else wash him and dress him and love him, will he ? He'll never scratch nobody else's face, nor kick nobody else's shins, but always remain true to his Keziah, won't he ? (*child assents;* Keziah *comes down*) Ah, he says so now, but he'll grow out of it like all the rest of his sex, won't he ?

Mrs. M. Most likely.

Kez. Boys never remain good after they get into knickerbockers. I suppose there must be some charm in the petticoats, for directly they leave them off they grow up into trousers and deceivers.

Mrs. M. (*shaking her head*) Ah, they do. When you talk like that you make me think of my poor old man as is gone fourteen year ago.

Kez. Was he a deceiver ?

Mrs. M. (*proudly*) Oh, very much so indeed! In that respect he was quite a gentleman, I assure you.

Kez. Deceiver ! ah !—I suppose they all are—the same as the dogs in the hymn-book, becos' "it is their nature to." I've had seventeen sweethearts.

Mrs. M. Seventeen ? What luck !

Kez. I'm thirty-four years old—that's one sweetheart for every two years. Seventeen I've had, and they all deceived me.

Mrs. M. What a misfortune !

Kez. I'd like to try the eighteenth, though.

Mrs. M. Better luck next time.

Kez. But I never would have a sweetheart as was a gentleman—no ; I don't think it's right for a servant-gal. As the proverb says, "the pitcher as goes too often to the swell is sure to get broken." Look at my missus !

Mrs. M. Ah, indeed ! Whenever I look at her it reminds me of my poor old man.

Kez. She got married—lots o' money—he spent it all. When he died, not a penny left—or what there was was made away with by that rascal Ismael.

Mrs. M. Him as I read about in the paper the other day, who has been over in India lately, and made himself so useful to the English Government during the mutiny ?

Kez. Him !—as big a villain as never walked on two legs like a man, but ought to have been a serpent, crawling on his stomach.

Mrs. M. Dear, dear!

Kez. Well, there was my missus, in a forcign land—where they don't speak English—a low, ignorant set, only Italians, dear, the best on 'em. There she was, left without a penny, or anything to wear, or to eat, or to drink—except the baby, who was a great comfort to her—he was so tiresome, and that turned her attention from her grief. But she had a lovely voice, and she was advised to turn her attention to singing; so the last few pounds she had, she spent in going to Milan, and learning, la! la! la! (*runs a scale*) only she did it better than that, you know; then she came to England, and came out at the opera—and what d'ye think? At the opera they made her sing in Italian, and I heard that all the great singers was Italians—such rubbish! as if the English couldn't sing better than the Italians, let alone being more easy to understand.

Mrs. M. Ah! that reminds me of my poor——

Kez. Old man? I knew it would—'cos everything else does. Do let me get a word in now and then, and I'll listen to you by-and-bye. Well she made a great hit——

Mrs. M. What's that?

Kez. I'll tell you, if you'll let me. When a lady singer becomes a favourite—that is, when she becomes "a great miss"—they always call her "a great hit." Well, she made such a name that they called her "The Nightingale," and the nights she sang used to be called the "night's nights." There were only fourteen of them altogether.

Mrs. M. Fourteen! just the same number of years as my poor old man——

Kez. Just so. Well, then she fell ill; the excitement had been too much for her; six months she lay upon a bed of sickness, and when she got well, her voice—that is, the best part of it—had gone.

Mrs. M. Couldn't she get it back again?

Kez. Dear me, Mrs. Minns, what a funny question! You can't get back a lost voice by advertising for it in the papers as if it were a lost dog! So they gave her a second part at the opera, and then she failed.

Mrs. M. Poor thing. Then I suppose she went through the Bankruptcy Court?

Kez. (*irritated*) No; failed as a singer. Then, as we hadn't a penny to buy the baby anything with, she was forced to go into the chorus.

Mrs. M. Ah! poor thing! such a long way off.

Kez. (*gulping down her annoyance*) Went into the

chorus for two pounds a week ; and here we are in Portsmouth, in lodgings at nine shillings a week.

MRS. M. Which does not include washing, though that doesn't come to much here.

KEZ. (*looking round*) I should think not. And this being Saturday, she always takes out Willie for a walk before she goes for her money.

(the child is near window)

Enter MARY. She is much altered, older, &c.,
dressed shabbily in light dress and shawl.

MARY. Mind ! Willie might fall out of the window !

MRS. M. The window is fastened. (*going up and looking down*) The tide is just turning.

MARY. (*to* WILLIE) My darling shall go out with his mamma. Mamma is going to get some money, and buy him a new hat, and some toys. (*guns outside ; cheers ; drum ; march played by military band, behind the scenes*) What's that ?

KEZ. (*opening window*) Boats and soldiers.

MRS. M. I know what it is. It's the troops landing. They're the heroes of India—the men who've been fighting there, and putting down the Mutiny.

MARY. The heroes of India !

KEZ. (*holding child*) Look at the pretty soldiers, dear, who go out to fight and die in cold weather and hot weather, that pretty babies like you may lie soft and warm, and have no fear of nasty foreigners.

MRS. M. They're marching down the street.

(quick-step outside ; cheers)

MARY. Let's go and see them, Willie.

KEZ. (*taking up child*) Come, darling, whenever I see a red coat it always reminds me of Mr. Harold, and of that ugly, horrid——(*looking at* MARY) But I mustn't mention him. Say go on, mamma, we'll follow. (*Exit* MARY, L.D.) Isn't he a beauty, Mrs. Minns? Don't he remind you of your——

MRS. M. Of my——

MRS. M. } together. Poor old man !
KEZ. }

KEZ. I thought so.

Exit KEZIAH and child, L.D. Military music and
cheers nearer.

MRS. M. (*at door* L.) Poor fellows ! How glad they

must be after all that fighting abroad to get home and have
some tea.   There's some of them at the corner.   (*noise of
manœuvres without as she describes them*)   It's wonderful
to see all their legs going together ; its like machinery—like
steam engines in boots and trousers.   Now they've stopped,
all at once, like the kitchen-clock.   I wonder they ain't
afraid of handling those guns.   Now they're turning
towards the barracks.   Eh!   Why, here's two of 'em looking
at this house.   (*knock* L.)   Why they're in the passage !

HAR. (*appearing at door* L.)   Is there a young woman
living here by the name of Keziah ?

HAROLD *and* CHEPSTOWE *enter* L.D., *both in regimentals.*

MRS. M. I beg your pardon, sir.   Who did you want ?

CHEP. Allow me to explain.   This gentleman has just
disembarked from a long sea voyage, and he wishes to see
a young lady.

HAR. Will you be quiet ?   I saw a young woman pass
up the street, whom I knew before I left England.

CHEP. No confessions now.   If the old lady isn't
modest, I am.

HAR. Do keep silent.

MRS. M. There is a young woman lodging here, called
Keziah—but she is out.

HAR. That I know.   When will she be back ?

MRS. M. In about an hour.

HAR. I can't wait an hour.

CHEP. My friend is so impatient.

HAR. (*seeing pen and ink on mantel-piece*) May I write
a line to her ?

MRS. M. Yes, sir (*getting materials*)   She shall have it
directly she comes in.

HAR. Thanks.

CHEP. Dearest K.—I've been away—come back to-day
—Oh don't say nay—Love and honour and obey. (*sings*)

> " List to me, fairest she,
>   I'll ne'er love any other than thee,
>   Oh will you be as true ?
>   No, said she, I'll be blowed if I do."

MRS. M. I beg your pardon, gentlemen, but haven't
you just come from India ?

HAR. Yes.

MRS. M. And you've been fighting the black heathens
there.   Serjeant Higgins was telling me all about it
yesterday.   A very gentlemanly man, Sergeant Higgins

—been in the Artillery, and much respected there. He told me of one young gentleman who was taken prisoner by one of the nasty leaders of the heathens.

HAR. Bahauder Khan.

MRS. M. Yes, that's his ugly name. Well, sir, this Porter-can took a young gentleman prisoner, and wanted him to send false information to the English soldiers so as to lead them into a barricade—no, not a barri—but an ambuscade—it was some cade or other—and he, that is the young gentleman said No, he'd see Porter-can (something he made use of in improper language) first. Then Porter-can showed him all the tortures—and threatened to burn him—and to grind him to powder—and to cut his eyelids off—and all sorts of things—but all he got out from the young English gentleman was that he would see him (improper language) first.

HAR. Yes, all that happened—and that is the young gentleman to whom it happened.

MRS. M. Lor!—this! (*curtseying to* CHEPSTOWE)

CHEP. And this is the young gentleman who came with two companies and rescued me and the other prisoners.

MRS. M. Lor! What two nice young fellows! They do so remind me of my poor old man as I lost. (*military music outside*) More heroes! You'll find the pen and ink all here, sir. *Exit* MRS. MINNS, L.D.

CHEP. Lovely woman, eh, Harold? Plenty of her—nice thick waist, and fine large hands and feet. With a wife like that, what more could the heart of man——Keziah?

> CHEPSTOWE *goes up to window* C., *opens it, and looks out. It begins to grow foggy on the river. The fog accumulates during* CHEPSTOWE'S *speech.*

HAR. (*at table*) If I am not compelled to go to London to-morrow, I will call and see Keziah. She can, no doubt, give me news of Mary. What can have become of her? Since her husband died in Italy, I have lost all trace. In the village they know nothing. It would have been better had she married me, and shared the poor fortunes of a soldier. Keziah has, of course, left her, but perhaps she may know of her whereabouts. Why can I not forget her? Why does her voice still linger in my ears, as if the past had not been? I may think of her now—she is no longer another's wife. (*he writes*)

(fog on the river gathers during the following)

CHEP. (*at window*) The tide's coming in at a slashing pace! Why, here's a boat below! When the tide is up, I should think it must come flush with the window. By Jove, Harold—(*at open window*)—isn't it fine to be again in England? Don't all the men you meet look fat, and don't the women look beautiful? Isn't it fine to hear the fellows in the street swear so boldly, and to know that if you gave them a crack with your cane, instead of crouching and getting out of your way, like those Indian hounds, they'd let out with their left, and hit you smack between the eyes; to know that your men will come into barracks drunk, not with filthy raki, but with honest adulterated beer. Isn't it charming to see that nobody salaams to you, or treats you with the slightest politeness, not like those brutes abroad, who are eternally civil and obliging, cuss 'em. Then look at the climate! What a lovely clouded sky—none of your beastly blue—and a fine thick fog rolling down from the river! It's beautiful! It's natural! It's poetical! It's jolly! It's home! It's England!

(he leaves window open)

Re-enter MRS. MINNS, L.D.

HAR. There is the note, Mrs.——

MRS. M. Minns, sir, widow of Matthew Minns. (HAROLD *gives her money*) Thank you, sir. Shall I say you'll call to-morrow, sir?

HAR. If I can, yes; but I may have to go to London. If not——

MRS. M. You'll call. Very good, sir.

CHEP. (*coming down*) And you're a widow, are you, Mrs——

MRS. M. Minns, sir. Yes, sir.

CHEP. Do you ever intend to enter the happy state again?

MRS. M. Lord, sir!—no. An old woman like me!

CHEP. If I were you I wouldn't.

HAR. Come Chepstowe. *Exit* HAROLD, L.D.

MRS. M. Why not, sir, if I may be so bold?

CHEP. Men are so deceitful, and the next offer you receive, Mrs.——

MRS. M. Minns, sir.

CHEP. Minns, sir. Remember my advice and follow it.

Exit CHEPSTOWE, L.D.

MRS. M. Two very nice young gentlemen; but the other seems the steadier. (*during this speech the boat,*

attached to the shore by a chain, comes flush up to window)
The other seems to me to be a flirt. I wonder what he can
want with Keziah! (ISMAEL, *in a boat passes the window
swiftly*) What is that? Oh, a boat! La! how foggy
it's getting. *(closing window)* And I've to do all my
marketing. I'll ask Mrs. Alsop to keep an eye on the
front door while I'm out. *Exit* MRS. MINNS. *Music.*

> ISMAEL *opens window and enters. A second boat is
> seen moored close to the other.*

ISM. Yes, this is it. I saw Mary leave the house before
I took the boat. Oh, human suffering how terrible; but
how beautiful thou art! The love I feel is not the hot and
selfish passion that passes in the sunny East for love. No
'tis the purer feeling painted by the poets of this cloudier
clime. I will it, and you shall be mine. My hand shall
draw you from the slough of poverty, and lift you to wealth
—to power—to me. Where is the child? It was not with
its mother. *(goes to door, R.)* The bedroom—no, empty—
void as my poor old friend Mrs. Legrant's heart. She
would adopt a child, and, in her simplicity, she advertised
for it, *(takes out a newspaper slip and reads)* "Wanted
to adopt, a child—a boy preferred—by a lady." Ah, poor
old lady! she shall have her wish, and she shall also insure
her life heavily for the child, whose guardian I will be.

> *During this speech he reads letters on table and
> pockets them.*

MARY. *(without)* I can carry him myself, Keziah.
ISM. Her voice! *(he drops newspaper slip)* And
with the boy.   *(conceals himself)*

> *Enter* MARY *with child sleeping in her arms.*

MARY. I'll fetch the toys, and you can carry the basket.
(whispering as she enters) Fast asleep! The fresh sea-air
has overcome him. Lie there, my darling. *(placing the
child in the arm-chair and covering him with shawl;
whispering to him)* And when you wake you shall find
your playthings all around you, and your mother watching
your joy.   *(leaves him and goes off, L.D.)*
ISM. *(coming forward)* A pretty boy—a very pretty
boy! And fast asleep. Lest the cold should wake him, and
he should be distressed at finding himself among strangers,
this will prolong his slumber. Luckily, the fog is getting

thicker. (*places phial under child's nostrils. Music continued at intervals, until end of Act*) Now for the boat!

      ISMAEL *wraps child in a shawl that he has brought with him, leaving the shawl left by* MARY *still on the chair, and carries him to the boat, then shuts window.*

      Enter MARY *and* KEZIAH, *both carrying toys—a waggon, a hoop, a gun, &c. They place them on the table.*

MARY. Now, my boy, when he wakes—(*turns, sees chair empty*) Why, where is he? I left him on the chair, sleeping.

KEZ. He's woke up, and toddled into the bed-room (*goes into bed-room,* R.H.) Oh! you bad boy. Come out! come out!

MARY. To think of his falling . asleep just as we got to the toy-shop. Such a silly little fellow!

        KEZIAH *re-enters.*

KEZ. He's not in the room.

MARY. Not in the room? Impossible!

             (*rushes by her into bed-room*)

KEZ. He can't have passed us nohow—oh, no! (*opening casement*) He couldn't have opened this big window. Oh! if anything should have happened to him!

      MARY *shrieks outside, then rushes on, and throws herself into* KEZIAH'S *arms.*

MARY. He's gone! gone! My boy—where—oh! I shall die. Hold me, I—I—I. My boy, Willie, they shall not keep us apart. .

    (*she sinks on stage,* KEZIAH *on her knees with her*)

KEZ. For Heaven's sake, bear up! He's only missing for a moment. Perhaps he's with the old woman. (*lying on the floor beside her*) Mary! Mary, my love! speak to me! Let us go together and find him. My dear! my love! (*feeling her hands*) She's quite cold! I—I—The child cannot be lost! Lost! No. And if he were I'd find him, if I sought out every hole and corner upon earth. (*sees slip of newspaper dropped by* ISMAEL) What's this? (*reads*) Eh! Who's been here? Who's dropped this? This means something! Mary, my love! (*she lifts* MARY *so that her face is seen by the audience. She is mad. With sudden conviction*) Great heavens! She is mad! I must find help. Stay here, dearest! Don't you know me? No

—no! Dare I trust her by herself? I must for a moment.

Exit KEZIAH, L.D.

MARY. (*her features vacant and her eye dilated*) Give me your hand, Willie. Let us walk together. Your father is in Heaven, and we remain on earth to think of him and love his memory. He is dead, Willie—dead, my child—perhaps poisoned! And I yet live to tell you of it. When you are young and strong it is so difficult to die! Where are you, my little son? My pretty playmate? Where? Where? (*turns and sees open window. The fog is now thick on the water. The gauzes down*) Why, there you are! I see you stretching forth your hands to me as if inviting me to Heaven! I'll come to you! Your mother will join you there—on earth—by sea—or in the sky!

> *She steps into the boat. Takes up the chain. The chain falls into the boat, and the boat floats away. Mechanical change and effect. The flats, &c., run forward. Music forte. When the flats are drawn off, the river is discovered—at night, during a fog. Nothing seen but the water and gauzes.* MARY *standing in the boat, the stem to the audience, lighted up by the green moonlight. The boat and her figure reflected in the moonlight. (This must be done by means of looking-glass let into the sea-cloth near the boat.) All round* MARY *is dark—her figure is light and bright.* MARY'S *eyes fixed in madness. She sings the song of the first Act. A shadowy boat, supposed to contain* ISMAEL *and the child, glides by at the back, as the drop descends.*

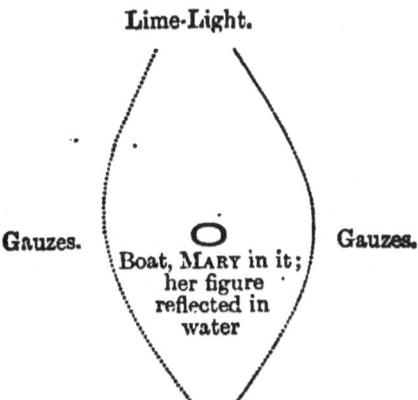

Lime-Light.

Gauzes.   Boat, MARY in it;   Gauzes.
                 her figure
                 reflected in
                 water

ACT IV.

SCENE.—*A Square in London.   Snow on the ground. Railings, lamp-posts, trees, &c.   Night.   House brilliantly lighted* L.U.E.   *An awning over the door for the arrival of guests.   The awning continued off stage.   Noise of carriages, &c., heard near awning.*

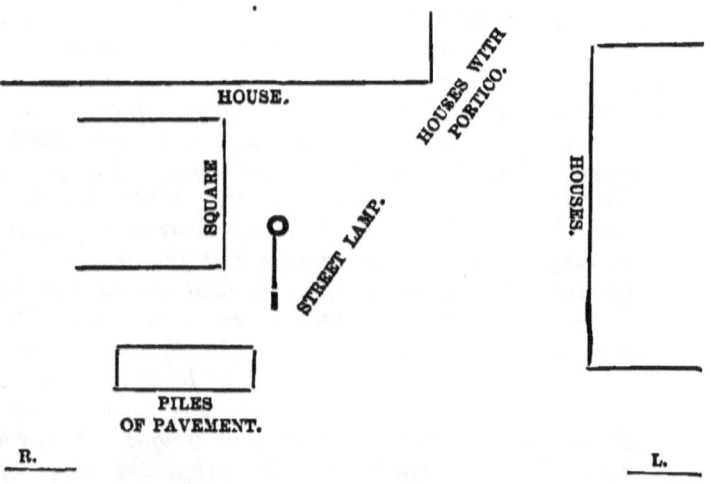

Enter KEZIAH *and* MARY, *both very poorly dressed,* L.H. 2 E.

KEZ. No, no, my dear! you mustn't think of it.

MARY. But what can we do? The rent is due to-night—we are strangers in the house—and it must be paid.

KEZ. The woman must wait.   I shall get the money for the things to-morrow, and we can pay her then.

MARY. Oh, my good Keziah! To think that I should have to live upon your earnings.

KEZ. Why not? I lived long enough on yours, and the idea of you—a lady—singing in the street for coppers from the passers-by—you, who have been a primer toner at the grand opera, to spoil your beautiful voice by straining it in the open air—not while a pennorth o' yellow soap will float in a tub, or there's my fingers left to scrub with!

MARY. But, my good Keziah——

KEZ. But, my beautiful Mary——

MARY. (*mournfully*) Not now—not now.

KEZ. Well, then, my beautiful Mary that used to be
Think of how grateful we ought to be. Think on that
dreadful night when Willie was lost—or stolen—how you
went mad, and got into that boat somehow by yourself, and
floated about in the dark, Heaven knows where, and Providence preserved you! ˙ Who could have guessed that two
boatmen should have found you, and rowed you to the
house near the beach, where the good people recognised you
from having seen you on the stage, and who tended you
through that long awful time when you did not know me
nor any one?

MARY. And kept shrieking out that my boy, Willie,
was dead!

KEZ. He's not dead! And we should have found him
long ago if you hadn't been ill so long, and we hadn't been
so poor. That bit of newspaper I picked up on the floor
of the lodgings in Portsmouth was a clue. Even the
detective said it was a clue; but "You see, missus," he
said—(*with imitation*)—"we cannot purceed in the business
unless we has money." But we shall find him, dear, we shall
find him again, as sure as soda makes the hands hard. But
I must go; becos I *might* get the money to-night by asking
for it. I shan't be more than an hour and a half—so—go
home, dear, won't you? You will—promise me! (*Mary
assents*) That's right; so, good-bye for a short time, and, if
I get the money, I'll bring in a bundle of firewood under
my arm and a quarter of a hundred of coal in my reticule.

(*shows bag. Exit* KEZIAH R.H. 1 E.)

MARY. I cannot face that woman, with her demand for
money, nor will I live entirely on the kindness of this generous
girl. No; it must come, and better to-night than to-morrow.
She little thinks how ill I am—how near—death! The snow
makes it so light that the passers-by can see my face, and I
shall be ashamed. Well, the nightingale sings by night. The
cold stones are now my stage, and the gas-lamps my footlights.
(*she gets near pillar letter-box and leans against it*) Oh! I
am faint. The hunger has passed, and left only sickness;
but I must sing—sing for bread to give me strength. I
must be strong—I will be strong—that I may find him—
—my boy—my darling. (*coughs*) It is very cold; and
I fear I am still hoarse. Oh! for one hour of the voice I
had when thousands hung on my notes, and I had but to
smile to charm. (*staggering*) Great Heavens! what is this
feeling? Surely I am not dying? No—no! Let me sing

E E

—I must sing! (*seeing house illuminated*) There is a
party there, and the good people inside the bright, warm
house are merry, and perhaps they will send out a shilling
to the poor outcast.

> *Snow begins to fall. She sings the song of the 1st Act.
> During song carriages are heard to arrive, and
> guests pass under portico of house,* L.H. 2 E.,
> *among others,* HAROLD, CHEPSTOWE, *and* POMEROY.
> *Near the end of song,* MARY *breaks down, and falls
> fainting among the paving stones, piled up,*
> R.H. 2 E. *Burst of joyous music in house. Car-
> riage heard,* R.H. 1. E. *The snow ceases.*

ISM. (*outside angrily*) The house is on the other side of
the square. You did'nt know? You should have known!
Drive me round? No! Among these repairs you'll upset
me; I prefer to walk across the square. Sorry, you idiot!
What's that to me?   (*carriage is heard to drive off*)

> *Enter* ISMAEL, R.H.1.E., *gorgeously dressed in the
> Eastern fashion, several decorations on his breast.*

ISM. Oh! the cold of this accursed country! Ah! there
is the house where I shall be received as an honoured guest.
(*dance-music heard in house*) How strange the vicissitudes
of fortune! How strange the circumstances! Circumstances
—psha! Destiny—that I should be placed in a high place
by these Feringhes. Fortune has smiled upon me lately.
Honoured by England—the land to which I have done such
—service—(*smiling*) in the distant East;—rich, powerful,
courted, flattered, caressed—(*after a pause*)—and—Mary
is dead. Strange that I, who never cared for women,
should be so infatuated. Her child thrives, and is happy
Pho-o-o, how cold! and what a fool am I to shiver here
when warmth and welcome await me within (*turns and
sees* MARY, *but does not recognise her*) Here is a poor
woman! Is she sleeping or is she dead? Ah, destiny
behold thy contrasts! The gay, brilliant young beauties
there—(*looking at house*)—and this outcast dying in the
road. (*snow begins to fall again*) I should like to place
a few pounds in that almost pulseless palm. Eh! the
snow! The divine instinct of self-preservation bids me take
shelter. Poor creature! It was her fate. .

> *Exit* ISMAEL *into house,* L.H.U.E. *A pause. Music.
> Guests leave the house. Carriages are heard to
> drive away.* .

Enter HAROLD, POMEROY, *and* CHEPSTOWE *from house.*

CHEP. Cab! Cab! (*pause*) I say, there's no cab!

POM. No cab?

CHEP. Isn't it a nuisance?

HAR. We must walk home.

CHEP. Spoils one's patent leathers. By Jove, how cold! No cab? Where are we? (*to* POMEROY) You're in the Engineers. You ought to know.

POM. I ought—but I don't.

CHEP. It's a strange thing, but I never came across a scientific man who ever did know anything—at least, when it was wanted.

HAR. Let's walk—we're sure to meet a cab. That's West.

CHEP. Is it? Then make it so—as that old master used to say. Pomeroy, I'll run you a mile for a skiv.

HAR. (*impatiently*) Come—come!

(POMEROY *and* HAROLD *cross to* R.)

CHEP. Wait till I light a cigar. (*goes to pillar box. Sees* MARY) Eh! Why here's a woman—evidently been enjoying herself too much. Oh! (*with mock solemnity*) Mrs. What's-your-name, how could you be so naughty? Don't you know that to be out and intoxicated at this late hour of—morning is conduct highly unbecoming a lady? Think of your poor family—and move on.

HAR. (*who has examined* MARY) Why, the woman's insensible—dying!

POM. }
CHEP. } What!

HAR. Call assistance! She's frozen to death!

CHEP. (*taking off his overcoat*) Wrap this round her.

HAR. She must have warmth immediately. Where can we——(*looking round*). Let us take her into the house. (*He raises* MARY, *and, under the light of the gas-lamp, recognises her*) Great Heavens!

CHEP. Eh!

HAR. Mary!

CHEP. Do you know her!

ISMAEL *appears at door of house*, L.H.U.E. *Stops and listens.*

HAR. Mary Waye!

CHEP. What?

HAR. Quick! find a cab! (CHEPSTOWE *runs off*, R.H. 1E.) To find her thus! Homeless! friendless!

Ism. (*advancing*) Not friendless. She is my ward! You know me, do you not? Ismael-al-Moolah!

Har. You here!

Ism. Yes. Heaven has restored my dear ward to me!

Har. Your ward!

Ism. By her dead husband's will, praised be Allah! I would say, Glory to the Highest, I have found her, and can again fulfil my duty to her.

     (Chepstowe *runs on* r.h. 1. e. *Noise of cab*, r.h.)

Chep. Here's the cab!   (*noise of carriage*, l.h. 2 e.)

Ism. I can take her to my house in my carriage.

Chep. (*seeing* Ismael, *who does not see him*) Bahauder Khan!

Ism. Give her to me. (*taking* Mary) Poor child! Poor child! Your troubles now are over. I am, as you know, a skilled physician. Help me to place her in the carriage.

Chep. I'd swear to him.   (*to* Pomeroy)

     Harold *reluctantly passes* Mary, *who is still insensible, to* Ismael.

Ism. At last!   (*with triumph*)

PICTURE—DROP QUICKLY.

ACT V.

SCENE.—*A country churchyard. Church porch and church,* L. II. 3 E. *Path from porch running off,* R. H. 2 E. *Grass, tombstones. A child's grave newly dug, and new tomb-stone. The back of the tombstone towards audience—about* C. *Wall* 7*ft. high, running from* R. *to* L. *No entrance to churchyard seen. Landscape cloth.*

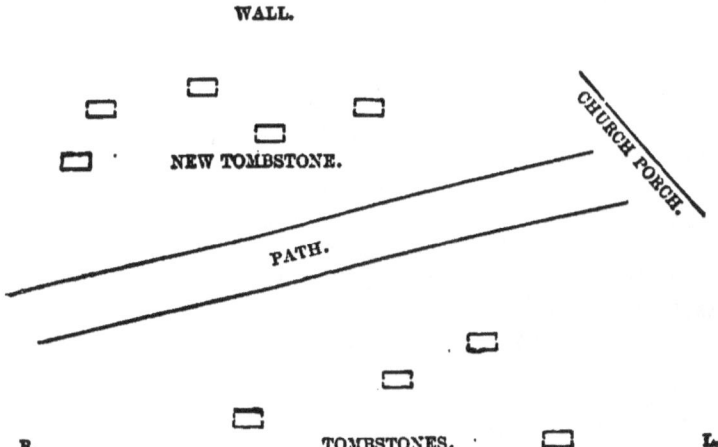

WALL.

NEW TOMBSTONE.

CHURCH PORCH.

PATH.

R.   TOMBSTONES.   L.

(HAROLD *discovered sitting near church porch.*)

Enter CHEPSTOWE, R. 2 E. *He taps* HAROLD *on the back.*

HAR. You are behind your time.

CHEP. I have been detained.

HAR. Is all ready?

CHEP. Everything! And Cassidy and Andrews are here to identify him. There are ten other men in the company who were prisoners at the same time. He struck Cassidy over the face with the hilt of a sword. He will bear the mark to his dying day.

HAR. I have received every aid from the authorities. When I told them the infamous rebel, Bahauder Khan, one of the chief leaders of the mutiny, was in England, they would not believe me, until I produced my proofs.

CHEP. I left the men a mile off, and now my friend

B.K., I think we've got you. Only to think that the rascal who fired on the rafts, who gave the orders for the massacre of prisoners, women, and children, should be so close to us! But there are several things I don't understand.

HAR. What are they?

CHEP. Why he returned to England.

HAR. Perhaps he thought himself safer here than in India.

CHEP. But so many things against him. The forgeries—Waye's murder.

HAR. Nothing can be proved—he was too cunning.

CHEP. He stole Mary's child. What was that for?

HAR. To give him power over the mother.

CHEP. Then why erect this tombstone when——

HAR. He had insured the boy's life heavily in three different offices, which are now assisting us.

CHEP. He is a singular scoundrel. The most complicated piece of rascality I ever heard of. He had Mary most carefully tended—brought her down here.

HAR. To renew his odious suit to her—so Keziah guesses.

CHEP. Keziah! What a clever woman that is! To think of her finding out the child, and telling the old lady in charge of her——

HAR. (*looking off* R.) Hush!—the enemy! Is all ready?

CHEP. Yes. Keziah and the——.

HAR. Not a word. They are here.

Exeunt CHEPSTOWE *and* HAROLD L. 3 E.

Enter MARY, *followed by* ISMAEL, *who carries a small basket of flowers.*

MARY. Why give me the pain of refusing you again, again, and again? I recognise your kindness, your attention to me in my illness, your hope that the air of the pleasant village would revive me. I am grateful to you; I can be no more.

ISM. Always cold—always proud! Is it prejudice or is it race? Is it because my skin is dark that my affection cannot touch you?

MARY. I have told you candidly—I tell you again—that I have an undefinable feeling that a union between us could not be a happy one.

ISM. Why not?

MARY. The past forbids it—and the future.

ISM. Why the past?

MARY. My dead husband.

ISM. And can that pale phantom still shut me from your heart ?—and the future ?

MARY. My boy.

ISM. Your boy ?

MARY. I wish to see him.

ISM. And does that child stand between us ? If he did not exist, could you then think of me ?

MARY. Of what use the question ? You have had my answer. For Willie, you have told me that during my illness you discovered his whereabouts, that he is now in your hands, and in safe keeping. Again I ask you, when shall I see him ? Give him to me ! Let me feast my eyes on him ! Where is he ?

ISM. (*his voice altering*) Your child is near you now.

MARY. Now ?

ISM. Yes.

MARY. (*wild with delight*) Near me—Willie, my boy ! When shall I see him ?

ISM. You will never see him more. .

MARY. Never ?

ISM. He is dead !

MARY. Dead ?

ISM. As you will wring the sad truth from me, I tell it you. I found your child. He was in weak health. I procured for him the best advice ; but the physicians gave me no hope. He died in my arms.

MARY. As his father died?

ISM. In your weak state of body, with your mind tottering between reason and madness, I dare not tell you of it. You are now stronger, and I venture to inform you of a calamity you must know some day. I had hoped that my care and watchfulness for him might have induced you to think less harshly of me. I am disappointed. Your boy was laid reverently in the earth in this churchyard. Find where he lies, Mary, and let your hand strew these flowers—which I gathered for you—over his grave.

(*he gives her basket of flowers and goes off* R.H. 2 E.

MARY. His grave!—my Willie's grave ! (*looking among the tombstones, and threading them as she speaks*) Not this —nor this. Where is his death inscribed on these stone registers of departed life ?—of beings who have lived, and loved, and died ? My child, where do you lie ? I think that I can see your little arms held out to me—can hear your little prattling voice bid me come to you. I will not stay from your side long. (*sees the newly-dug grave and new tombstone. She reads the inscription inaudibly*) 'Tis there! Yes, he lies there, and my heart is so hard that I can read his death and live—but not for long, my child—no, not for long. (*organ heard inside church. She kneels on grave, and places flowers on it, and round the stone*) My boy, my boy, who fed at my breast and slept upon my pillow, we shall soon meet again! (KEZIAH *and little* WILLIE *appear at the church porch*) I have borne much, I have struggled, I have waited, I have prayed. I can offer up but one prayer now, to join you, my love, and quickly as may be.

WIL. (*running to her*) Mother! mother!

MARY. (*starts, sees* WILLIE. *Her face expresses the idea that he is a spirit*) My boy! Willie! as he was on earth, though he has passed away to Heaven! Oh, come to me, for I think I see you, and I am not mad!

KEZ. You're not mad! It is Willie! It is you! This is me, Keziah! It's all real! It's the tombstone that's the ghost, and not the darling child. Don't you know me, Keziah? Willie, speak to dear mamma.

> MARY, *whose face has expressed alternately fear, doubt, and wonder, fixes her eyes on the child as if her senses were leaving her.*

WIL. Mother! dear mother!

> *With a wild cry,* MARY *takes the child to her arms.* KEZIAH *cries, and dances among the tombstones, then cries, then dances again. Embraces* MARY, *&c.*

> *Enter* HAROLD, R. 2 E.

KEZ. See, missus, here's Mr. Harold! Don't you know him?

MARY. Harold, you here? But can this all be real?

HAR. All true, Mary; and your sufferings are now, I trust, about to end.

MARY. They are ended. Willie is not dead. But why this false report—this lying tombstone?

HAR. There is no time for explanation now. Let it suffice that all this is the machination of——

MARY. Of Ismael-al-Moolah.

KEZ. Yes, of that toad of a Turkey. Mr. Harold found it all out, and he's going to punish him. Mr. Harold did it all, except find the child. I did that, with the help of Heaven, and that old bit of newspaper.

> (*a whistle heard without*)

HAR. That's Chepstowe. Then all is ready. (*looking off*) That scoundrel is returning. Keziah, take the child again. Only for a moment, Mary. You shall see him again.

KEZ. Of course she shall. You can trust him with Keziah. I never trust him out of my sight. I'm as careful of him as a cat is of a kitten, or a kitten of a cotton ball. (*taking child*) Once in my arms, Courts of Chancery shan't tear him from me.

Exit KEZIAH *and child into church porch.* ISMAEL *re-enters* R. 2 E.

ISMAEL, R.   MARY, C.   HAROLD, L.

ISM. Mary. (*she recoils from him, and leans on a tombstone,* L.C.) Ah! as I feared, your new grief has overcome you. I brought you to this village because I thought that it would solace you to see his grave. The poor child! He is in a better place than this.

MARY. Yes, he is free from your persecution, as I soon shall be!

ISM. Your grief misleads you. Let us go back to the inn.

MARY. No!

ISM. No!

MARY. Your power over me is past.

ISM. Past!

HAR. (*advancing*) Yes—past!

ISM. Mr. Harold——

HAR. Ismael-al-Moolah! Your time has come! False-witness—robber—forger—murderer—you quit not this churchyard a free man!

ISM. Who shall prevent me?

HAR. I will!

ISM. For what reason?

HAR. For your crimes! For the murder of her husband!

ISM. Insolence! Touch me if you dare! Arrest me? Lay a finger on me at your peril. Where is your warrant?

HAR. For the crimes of theft, forgery, and murder, I cannot touch you. (ISMAEL *smiles*) Not so fast. I am an officer in the service of her Majesty—I have fought in India, and wherever I meet him, I have a right to arrest the attainted traitor and rebel—Bahauder Khan! (ISMAEL *starts and retires, so that his back is next the church wall,* C.) Your time has come. Surrender!

ISM. (*drawing revolver*) One step nearer and you die!

(CHEPSTOWE *appearing on wall, snatches revolver from his hand, and fires one chamber*) Not so. Jackson! Cassidy!
JACKSON *and* CASSIDY, *two soldiers, appear* R. *and* L. *They seize* ISMAEL ; *at the same moment* KEZIAH *and* WILLIE *appear at church porch.* MARY *takes child.*

CASSIDY.	CHEPSTOWE.	
ISMAEL.	HAROLD.	
JACKSON.	MARY.	*Church Porch.*
	CHILD.	
	KEZIAH.	

HAR. You see, ruffian, your power is past. Traitor and rebel, you are in the hands of soldiers in the uniform of the Queen and country you would have overthrown. Infidel and renegade—your own machinations led you to the place of your capture—the shrine of the faith you would have annihilated.

Music.

PICTURE.—DROP QUICKLY.

OURS.

AN ORIGINAL COMEDY IN THREE ACTS.

BY

T. W. ROBERTSON,

AUTHOR OF

"Caste," "A Breach of Promise," "School," "M.P.," "Birth," "David Garrick," "The Ladies' Battle," "The Nightingale," "Play," "Progress," "Row in the House," "Society," "Dreams," "War," "Home," "Faust and Marguerite," "My Wife's Diary," "Noemie," "Two Gay Deceivers," "Jocrisse the Juggler," "Not at all Jealous," "Star of the North," "Birds of Prey," "Peace at any Price," "Half Caste," "Ernestine," "Chevalier de St. George," "Cantab," "Clock-maker's Hat," "Duke's Daughter," "Sea of Ice," &c., &c.

LONDON :
SAMUEL FRENCH,
PUBLISHER,
89, STRAND.

NEW YORK :
SAMUEL FRENCH & SON,
PUBLISHERS,
28, WEST 23RD STREET.

OURS.

First performed at the Prince of Wales's Theatre, in Liverpool, August 23rd, 1866, and produced in London at the Prince of Wales's Theatre, on Saturday, September 15th, 1866.

CAST OF CHARACTERS.

	Liverpool.	London.	London, 1870.
Prince Perovsky	..Mr. Hare.	..Mr. Hare.	..Mr. Hare.
Sir Alexander Shendryn, Bt.	..Mr. J. W. Ray	..Mr. J. W. Ray	..Mr. Addison.
Captain Samprey		.. Mr. Trafford.	..Mr. Herbert.
Angus MacAlister ..	..Mr. Bancroft.	..Mr. Bancroft.	..Mr. Coghlan.
Hugh Chalcot	..Mr. J. Clarke.	..Mr. J. Clarke.	..Mr. Bancroft.
Sergeant Jones	..Mr. F. Dewar.	..Mr. F. Younge.	..Mr. Collette.
Houghton	..Mr. Tindale.	..Mr. Tindale.	
Lady Shendryn	..Miss Larkin.	..Miss Larkin.	Miss Le Thiere.
Blanche Haye ..	Miss L. Moore.	{ Mis L. Moore. / Miss Lydia Foote.	Miss Fanny Josephs.
Mary Netley	..Miss Marie Wilton.	..Miss Marie Wilton.	..Miss Marie Wilton.

Period—Before, and during the Crimean War.

ACT I.—THE PARK—*Autumn.*

ACT II.—THE DRAWING-ROOM—*Spring.*

ACT III.—THE HUT—*Winter.*

TO

JOSEPH M. LEVY,

THIS COMEDY IS DEDICATED

BY

HIS SINCERE AND OBLIGED FRIEND,

THE AUTHOR.

London, October, 1870.

OURS.

ACT I.

SCENE.—*An avenue of trees in Shendryn Park ; the avenue leading off to* R.U.E. *Seat round tree in foreground,* R. *Stumps off trees,* L.C. *and* L. *The termination of the avenue out of sight.* <u>*Throughout the Act the autumn leaves fall from the trees.*</u> CHALCOT *discovered asleep on ground under tree,* L. 2 E., *a handkerchief over his face.*

STUMP OF TREE.

O

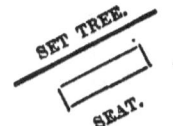

Enter SERGEANT JONES, R. 1 E., *meeting* HOUGHTON, *who enters with gun,* L. 1 E., C. *of stage.*

SER. (R.) Good morning.

HOUGH. (L.) Good morning.

SER. (*warmly*) How are you?

HOUGH. Quite well; how are you?

SER. I'm—I'm as well as can be expected.

HOUGH. What d'ye mean?

(*semi-important*)
(*with dialect*)

SER. (*with importance*) I mean that last night my missus——

(*whispers* HOUGHTON)

HOUGH. (*surprised*) Nay!

SER. Fact.

HOUGH. Two! (SERGEANT *nods*) Twins? (SERGEANT *nods*) Well, mate, it does you credit! And I hope you'll soon get over it.

SER. Eh?

HOUGH. I mean I hope your missus 'ull soon get over it. Come and ha' some beer.

SER. I must go to the Hall first. I wish they'd been born at Malta.

HOUGH. Where?

SER. At Malta.

HOUGH. Malta! Be that where they make the best beer?

SER. No; it's "furrin." When a child's born in barracks there, it gets half a pound o' meat additional rations a-day.

HOUGH. Child does?

SER. It's parents. Twins would ha' been a pound a-day —pound o' meat you know. It's worth while being a father at Malta.

HOUGH. (*looking at* SERGEANT *admiringly and shouldering his gun*) Come and ha' some beer to drink this here joyful double-barrelled event.

> *They turn up stage together, going towards* U.E.R., *meeting* BLANCHE *and* MARY *as they enter. Both fall back,* SERGEANT *to attention,* HOUGHTON *touching his cap as* BLANCHE *and* MARY *come down stage.* SERGEANT *and* HOUGHTON *exeunt.*

BLANCHE. Don't walk so fast, Mary. Lady Shendryn said she'd overtake us. Let us rest here. (*they sit on seat* R.) It's charming under the trees. I mean to look after the little boy. That's for him.

> (*puts portemonnaie into basket*)

MARY. (L.) (*taking out portmonnaie*) And I mean to look after the little girl. This is for her.

> (*puts portemonnaie into basket*)

BLANCHE. (R.) But, Mary, dear, can you afford it?

MARY. Yes; though I am poor, I must have some enjoyments. You rich people mustn't monopolise all the pleasures in the world.

BLANCHE. (*hurt*) My dear Mary, you know I didn't mean——

MARY. And *I* didn't mean; but I can't help being sensible. I know my place; and if I didn't, Lady Shendryn and the world would make me. I haven't a penny, so I'm a companion, though I don't receive wages, which the cook does. But then she's respected—she's not in a false position. I wish I hadn't been born a lady.

BLANCHE. No you don't.

MARY. Yes *I* do. I should have kept a Berlin-wool shop, and been independent and happy. And you, Blanche —you could have rolled down in your carriage, and given your orders—Miss Netley, please send me home this—or that—and so on. *(with imitation)*

BLANCHE. Mary, do talk about something else.

MARY. Well, I will, dear, to please you; but it is annoying to be a companion. Not your companion, Blanche —that's charming—to know that you're kept inthe room to save another woman from rising to ring a bell, or to hand her the scissors, or to play the piano when you're ordered. *(imitating)* Miss Netley—oh !—yes, a very nice person; so useful about the house. Useful—oh !—There, I beg your pardon, Blanche; but really Lady Shendryn's temper does upset me—one minute she's so tender and sentimental, and the next—Poor Sir Alick. Then there's that Mr. Chalcot —I detest him.

BLANCHE. Why?

MARY. Oh, for his gloomy air, and his misanthropic eye-glass. *(imitating)* Liking nothing, and dissatisfied with everything.

BLANCHE. Despite all that, he has a very good heart.

MARY. My gentleman is rich, and thinks that every girl he speaks to is dying for his ugly face, his stupid bank-notes, and his nasty brewhouse. When I look at him I feel that I could smack his face.

BLANCHE. For being rich !

MARY. Yes—perhaps. No, for being disagreeable.

BLANCHE. I'm rich; at least, they tell me so.

MARY. But you're not disagreeable.

BLANCHE. Do talk about something else.

MARY. Who—what?

BLANCHE. Anything—anybody.

MARY. Of the people staying at the Hall?

BLANCHE. Yes.

MARY. Prince Perovsky?

BLANCHE. If you like.

MARY. He means "you"; I can see it in his eye. I know Sir Alick would say yes, and so would my lady. Blanche, what would you say?

BLANCHE. *(pensively)* I don't know.

MARY. That means "yes"! A Russian prince—wealthy, urbane—quite the grand air, but dried up as a Normandy pippin. Will my Blanche be a princess?

BLANCHE. Prince Perovsky is a little old.

MARY. Not for a prince. Princes are never old.

BLANCHE. And I'm a little young.

MARY. Not too young for a princess. Princesses are never too young.

BLANCHE. Why, Mary, you're quite worldly.

MARY. Only on your account. I should like to see you a princess. You'd be charming as a princess.

BLANCHE. (*smilingly*) And if I were and had a court, what would you be?

MARY. (*rising*) Mistress of the Robes, and First High Gold Parasol in Waiting! Oh, my charming, darling Royal Highness. My Highest, Mightiest, Most Serene Transparentissima!

> *Curtseying.* CHALCOT *wakes up, and looks about him.*

BLANCHE. (*laughs*) How silly!

MARY. Who—me?

BLANCHE. Yes.

MARY. Then I renounce my allegiance—turn Radical, and dethrone you. I wish the prince would ask me.

BLANCHE. Ask you what?

MARY. (C.) To be his wife.

CHAL. (*aside*) Devil doubt you!

BLANCHE. How would you answer?

MARY. I'd answer—No!

CHAL. (*aside*) Dreadful falsehood!

MARY. Though I'd like to be a princess—a Russian princess—and have slaves.

BLANCHE. Oh! I shouldn't like to have slaves.

MARY. I should, particularly if they were men.

CHAL. (*aside*) Nice girl that!

BLANCHE. Let's leave off talking Russian.

MARY. What shall we talk then? Scotch?

BLANCHE. What a time Lady Shendryn is!

MARY. About Angus McAlister?   (*maliciously*)

BLANCHE. (*seeing* CHALCOT) Hush!

> (*rising and crossing* L.)

MARY. (R.) What?

BLANCHE. There's a man.

CHAL. (*rising*) Don't be alarmed; I've heard nothing that I oughtn't to.

MARY. (*primly*) Impossible you should.

CHAL. (C.) I fell asleep under that tree.   (*down* C.)

MARY. (R) Why did you wake up?

BLANCHE. (L.) Asleep, just after breakfast!

CHAL. Humph! There was nothing else to do.

MARY. You mean nothing else that *you* could do.

CHAL. I thought of climbing the tree; good notion, wasn't it?

MARY. Excellent—if you'd stayed up there!

CHAL. Eh?

MARY. I mean, if you hadn't come down.

(*guns fired without*)

CHAL. Sir Alick might have brought me down.

BLANCHE. Mistaken you for a rook!

MARY. (*aside*) Or a scarecrow!

CHAL. (*pointing to basket*) What have you got there?

BLANCHE. Guess.

CHAL. Can't. Never could make out conundrums—or ladies.

MARY. Beyond your comprehension?

CHAL. Quite. (*annoyed*) Confound the girl! (*aloud*) But what's in the basket?

BLANCHE. (L. *and holding up basket*) Fowls, jelly, sago, tapioca, wine!

MARY. (*repeating her words*) Wine, tapioca, sago, jelly, fowls!

CHAL. That's variety! Somebody ill?

(MARY *sits,* R.)

Enter LADY SHENDRYN, *who heard the last few words,* U.E.R.

LADY S. Ill—no! Nobody. They're all doing well.

(*down,* R.C.)

CHAL. All! Who?

LADY S. The Twins!

CHAL. (C.) Twins! What twins?

LADY S. Ours.

CHAL. Yours? Yours and Sir Al——

LADY S. (*a languishing, sentimental, frisky person*) Mine and—no, no. What a man you are! When I say Ours, I mean Sergeant Jones's.

CHAL. Sergeant Jones's!

LADY S. Of Ours — of Sir Alexander's regiment. Alexander is very fond of him; and I quite doat on Mrs. Jones. You know the barracks are not eight miles off, and the railway drops you close to (*turning* R.) Miss Netley, I'll sit down—(MARY *rises, and crosses,* L.C. *to*

BLANCHE. LADY SHENDRYN *sits*, R.) So I gave Mrs. Jones the use of the Cottage—and it's—*a* most agreeable circumstance; isn't it?

CHAL. (*thoughtfully*) Very—for poor Jones!

MARY. (*aside to* BLANCHE, L.) Make him give you something—subscription—you know.

CHAL. (R.C.) (*overhearing*) Make me! I should like to see anyone make me!

BLANCHE. (*rising, and crossing to* CHALCOT) By the way (*to* CHALCOT) I'm collecting for them. (*taking out pocket-book*) How much shall I put you down for?

CHAL. (R.C.) (*seeing* MARY's *eyes on him*) Nothing.

MARY. (L.) Nothing!

LADY S. (R.) Oh, Hugh!

BLANCHE. Oh, Mr. Chalcot!

MARY. Oh, these men!

BLANCHE. Consider poor Mrs. Jones!

LADY S. And the twins!

CHAL. Twins! I don't think those sort of women ought to be encouraged.

MARY. (*aside*) And that's a man worth thousands!

BLANCHE. (*coaxingly*) Let me put you down for something!

MARY. A shilling!

CHAL. (*to* MARY) I'm not to be put down.

LADY S. Miss Netley, pray don't interfere. (*girls go up,* L.) How charming it is here, under the trees!—so poetical and leafy!

CHAL. (*throwing insect off her mantle*) And insecty!

(LADY SHENDRYN *starts up*)

Enter PRINCE, R.U.E., *smoking a cigarette.* CHALCOT *crosses to* L. PRINCE *seeing ladies raises his hat, and throws cigarette on ground.*

PRINCE.

LADY S.   O   BLANCHE.

O   O   O MARY.

O   CHALCOT.

LADY S. Ah! here's the Prince. How charming!

MARY. He'll give something.

BLANCHE. (L.C.) Prince, I'm begging—make a subscription.

PRINCE. (R.C.) Let me trust I may be permitted to become a subscriber.

BLANCHE. For any amount you please. How much?
(*with pocket-book*)

PRINCE. I leave that to you.

LADY S. (R.) Oh, Prince, you are so kind!

MARY. (L.C.) What a difference! (*to* CHALCOT) A noble
nation the Russians! (*goes up,* R.)

BLANCHE. Will that do? (*writing, aud showing him*)

PRINCE. If you think it sufficient.

(BLANCHE *joins* MARY)

LADY S. Charmingly chivalric!

PRINCE. Shall I be indiscreet in asking the object of——

LADY S. *Objects!* There are two!

PRINCE. Two objects!

CHAL. Yes—babies.

LADY S. Twins.

CHAL. (L.) The Jones's gemini!

(*crosses up* C. *and sits under tree* R.)

PRINCE. (*to* CHALCOT) Twins! Extraordinary people
you English.

LADY S. We're going to take these things to the Cottage
for them. (*crossing* C.) Prince! will you come as far?

PRINCE. If I may be allowed to take part in so delicate
a mission.

LADY S. Blanche! the Prince will escort you.

(BLANCHE *crosses,* L.)

PRINCE. (*crossing to* BLANCHE) May I carry the basket?

BLANCHE. Can I trust you?

PRINCE. With what?

BLANCHE. The sago.

Exeunt PRINCE *and* BLANCHE, L. 1.E.

LADY S. Miss Netley will be my cavalier.

MARY. What a treat! (*coming from back* L.C. *to* L.)

LADY S. Unless you, Mr. Chalcot—

CHAL. (*eye to eye with* MARY) Thanks, no. I'll stay
where I am.

LADY S. We shall leave you all alone.

CHAL. I don't mind that.

MARY. That's just the sort of man who would pinch his
wife on his wedding day.

Exeunt LADY SHENDRYN *and* MARY, L. 1 E.

CHAL. That's a detestable girl! Whenever I meet her, she makes me thrill with dislike.

> SERGEANT *and* KEEPER *enter at end of avenue,* R.U.E., *carrying a large hamper. Meeting* SIR ALEX- ANDER, L.U.E., *in shooting dress.* KEEPER *takes gun and exits with* SERGEANT L. 1 E.

SIR A. (c.) Ah, Hugh—that you?

CHAL. Yes.   (*seated,* R.)

SIR A. What have you been doing here?

> (*sits on stump,* L.)

CHAL. Sleeping. Shot anything?

SIR A. A brace. I'm nervous. I've been annoyed this morning.

CHAL. I'm annoyed every morning—and evening, regularly.

SIR A. I'd bad news by post—and then my lady—and I'm so horribly hard up.

CHAL. A little management—

SIR A. I know; but I've other troubles, Hugh. You're an old friend, and so was your father before you. If you only knew what was on my mind. There's my lady wrangling perpetually.

CHAL. People always quarrel when they're married—or single; and you must make allowances—her ladyship is much younger than you.

SIR A. She might remember how long *we* have—— But it isn't that—it isn't that.

CHAL. What then?

SIR A. I mustn't tell—I wish I could.

CHAL. I'm open to receive a confession of early murder, or justifiable matricide.

SIR A. It isn't my secret, or I'd tell it you. Oh! my lady is very wrong. The idea of her being jealous!

CHAL. I've heard that years ago you were a great killer.

SIR A. (*not understanding*) Killer! Of what—birds?

CHAL. No. Ladies.

SIR A. Oh!—like other men.

CHAL. That's bad—that's very bad. But surely my lady knew that before marriage you were not a Joseph?

SIR A. Not she.

CHAL. But she must have guessed——

SIR A. Pooh! pooh! You're talking like a bachelor.

CHAL. A bachelor may know——

SIR A. A bachelor can know nothing. It is only after they're married that men begin to understand the purity of women—(*aside*)—or their tempers.

CHAL. But do you mean to tell me—between men, you know—that Lady Shendryn has no cause.

SIR A. Has no cause? Certainly not—

CHAL. *Had* no cause, then?

SIR A. *Had!* Um—well—the slightest possible——

CHAL. Did she find it out?

SIR A. Unfortunately she did.

CHAL. Ah! Nuisance that—being found out. Is the cause removed now?

SIR A. The what?

CHAL. The cause—the slightest possible——

SIR A. Oh yes—long ago. Gone entirely.

CHAL. Dead?

SIR A. No—married.

CHAL. Better still. Further removed than ever.

SIR A. But my lady has never forgotten it. It was an absurd scrape; for I cared nothing about her.

CHAL. About my lady?

SIR A. (*irritably*) No—the——

CHAL. Slightest possible—no, no.

SIR A. Where is my lady?

CHAL. She has gone to the Cottage to see the interesting little Joneses. The Prince went with her—and Blanche—and—that other girl.

SIR A. Mary Netley! Charming girl that!

CHAL. Very.

SIR A. She's the daughter of very dear old friends, who died without leaving her a penny.

CHAL. Very dear old friends always do.

SIR A. What?

CHAL. Die without leaving pennies.

SIR A. Poor little thing! I wish I could find her a husband!

CHAL. What a misanthropic sentiment!

SIR A. Now, there's Blanche; she's a fortune. She, like Mary, has no guardians but us—neither father nor mother.

CHAL. Splendid qualification that; but Blanche is much too nice a girl to have a mother.

SIR A. She's another anxiety.

CHAL. All girls are anxieties.

SIR A. You were wrong to let Blanche slip through your fingers.

CHAL. Me marry an heiress! Ugh! (*shudders*) There's
Prince Perovsky, he is very particular in his attentions.

SIR A. Yes; it would be a good match. He owns two-
thirds of a Russian province.

CHAL. Poor devil! Isn't it rather awkward, his staying
here? If war is to be declared—

(*rises and goes up looking off* R.)

SIR A. He's off in a couple of days; besides, after all,
Russia may not mean fighting.

CHAL. There's Angus, coming down the avenue!

SIR A. (*rising*) Between you and me, Hugh, I wish he
wouldn't come so often. He's too fond of teaching Blanche
billiards. I'm always finding them with their heads closer
together than is warranted by the rules of the game. When
children, they saw a good deal of each other. Blanche is my
ward, and an heiress; Angus, a distant cousin, poor as a rat
—the Scotch branch of the family. I shouldn't like it to be
thought that I threw them together.

CHAL. No, no.

SIR A. I'll go and meet the people at the Cottage. I
promised to join them. (*taking letters from his pocket, select-
ing one*) I daren't take this into the house with me; eh—
yes I may—this from Lady Llandudno. She's in a terrible
fright about the prospect of war. You know her boy's in
Ours. Asks me if I think the regiment will be ordered
out. I may show my lady that. (*replaces letter in pocket,
then tears another into very small pieces. Sighs deeply*)
Heigho! It's not much use. It is sure to be found out at
last. (CHALCOT *sits by stump* R., *on ground*)

> *Exit* SIR ALEXANDER, L. 1 E. ANGUS MACALISTER
> *comes down the avenue*, U.E.R. CHALCOT *smokes
> incessantly; as soon as one cigar or pipe is out, he
> lights another.*

CHAL. Well, Gus. Just got in?

ANGUS. (R.) Yes. Slept last night in barracks. Got
leave again for to-day.

> ANGUS *is grave and composed in manner; as he
> speaks, he looks about him, as if his thoughts were
> away.*

CHAL. Bring down a paper with you?

ANGUS. Yes. (*gives him newspaper, which* CHALCOT *looks
over*) Where are all the people gone? There's nobody in the
Hall.

CHAL. Gone to the Cottage to try on a pair of new twins—born on the estate. My lady, Sir Alick, Miss Netley, the Prince, and Blanche.

ANGUS. Have they been gone long?

(crosses to seat R. *and puts* R. *foot on it)*

CHAL. No. I haven't quite made up my mind whether I like that Prince Perovsky or not. Do you like him?

ANGUS. I never think about him.

CHAL. *(aside)* That's not true, Angus, my man. *(aloud)* I wonder if we shall have war with Russia?

(eyeing ANGUS*)*

ANGUS. I don't know—I don't care—I wish we had!

CHAL. Out of sorts?

ANGUS. Yes.

CHAL. Have a weed. *(handing cigar-case.* ANGUS *goes to* CHALCOT *and takes cigarette)* Why want war? For the sake of change?

ANGUS. Yes.

CHAL. Change of scene?

ANGUS. Change of anything—change for anything—silver, copper—anything out of this!

(goes to seat R. *and sits)*

CHAL. Out of what? *(puffing smoke)*

ANGUS. Out at elbows! If there's no war I shall go to India. What use in staying here—without a shilling or a friend? *(plucking leaf)* What chance is there?

CHAL. What chance! You mean what chances? Plenty. You're young—good family—marry a fortune.

ANGUS. Marry for money! That's not the way with the MacAlisters.

CHAL. Umph! Marriage is a mistake, but ready money's real enjoyment; at least, so people think who haven't got it. I suppose you've made your choice?

ANGUS. I have. Perhaps you're aware of that?

CHAL. Yes.

ANGUS. And who it is?

CHAL. Yes.

ANGUS. I'm a bad hand at concealment. I'm too proud of loving her I love to hide it. That's why I mean to go to India. *(crosses to tree,* R.*)*

CHAL. Better stop here and smoke. I feel in a confidential humour. So you're in love with Blanche?

ANGUS. YES.

CHAL. I saw that long ago. You know that I proposed to her?

ANGUS. Yes.

CHAL. But I'm proud to say she wouldn't have me. Ah! she's a sensible girl; and her spirited conduct in saying "No!" on that occasion laid me under an obligation to her for life.

ANGUS. She declined?

CHAL. She declined very much. I only did it to please Sir Alick, who thought the two properties would go well together—never mind the two humans. Marriage means to sit opposite at table, and be civil to each other before company. Blanche Haye and Hugh Chalcot. Pooh! the service should have run: "I, Brewhouses, Malt-kilns, Public-houses, and Premises, take thee, Landed Property, grass and arable, farm-houses, tenements, and Salmon Fisheries, to my wedded wife, to have and to hold for dinners and evening parties, for carriage and horse-back, for balls and presentations, to bore and to tolerate, till mutual aversion do us part"; but Land, grass and arable, farm-houses, tenements, and Salmon Fisheries said "No"; and Brewhouses is free. (*strikes match*)

ANGUS. At all events, you could offer her a fortune.

CHAL. And you're too proud to make her an offer be-cause you're poor! (ANGUS *sighs*) You're wrong. You're very wrong. I have more cause for complaint than you. I'm a great match. My father was senior partner in the brewery. When he died, he left me heaps. His brother, my uncle, died—left me more. My cousin went mad—bank-notes on the brain. His share fell to me; and, to crown my embarrassments, a grand-aunt, who lived in retirement in Cornwall on four hundred a year, with a faithful poodle and a treacherous companion, died too, leaving me the accumulated metallic refuse of misspent years. Mammas languished at me for their daughters, and daughters languished at me as their mammas told them. At last my time came. I fell in love—down, down, down, into an abyss where there was neither sense, nor patience, nor reason—nothing but love and hope. My heart flared with happiness as if it were lighted up with oxygen. She was eighteen—blue eyes—hair the colour of wheat, with a ripple on it like the corn as it bends to the breeze—fair as milk. She looked like china with a soul in it. Pa made much of me—ma made much of me; so did her brothers and sisters, and uncles and aunts, and cousins

and cousinettes, and cousiniculings. How I hated 'em!
One day I heard her speaking of me to a sister; she said—
her voice said—that voice that, as I listened to it, ran up
and down my arms, and gave me palpitation—she said, "I
don't care much about him; but then he's so very rich!"
(*his face falls*) That cured me of marriage, and mutual
affection, and the rest of the poetical lies. (*knocking ashes
out of pipe*) You've youth, health, strength, and not a
shilling—everything to hope for. Women can love *you*
for *yourself* alone. Money doesn't poison your existence.
You're not a prize pig, tethered in a golden sty. What is
left for me? Purchasable charms; every wish gratified;
every aspiration anticipated, and the sight of the
drays belonging to the firm rolling about London with
my name on them, and a fat and happy drayman sitting on
the shafts, whom I envy with all my heart. Pity the poor!
Pity the rich; for they are bankrupts in friendship, and
beggars in love.

ANGUS. (*crosses to* CHALCOT *and standing over him*) So,
because one woman was selfish, you fall in love with
poverty, and the humiliations and insults—insults you
cannot resent—heaped on you daily by inferiors. Prudent
mothers point you out as dangerous, and daughters regard
you as an epidemic. You are a waiter upon fortune—a
man on the look-out for a wife with money—a creature
whose highest aim and noblest ambition is to sell himself
and his name for good rations and luxurious quarters—a
footman out of livery, known as the husband of Miss So-
and-so, the heiress. You talk like a spoiled child! The rich
man is to be envied. He can load her he loves with proofs
of his affection—he can face her father and ask him for her
hand—he can roll her in his carriage to a palace, and say,
This is your home, and I am your servant!

(*back to seat* R.)

CHAL. You talk like a—man in love. Couldn't you face
Sir Alick?

ANGUS. No. (*sits* R.)

CHAL. His marriage hasn't made him happy. Poo' Sir
Alick! He never could have been happy with his weakness.

ANGUS. You mean Lady Shendryn?

CHAL. No; she's not a weakness—she's a power. No;
Sir Alick's great regret in life is that he isn't tall. There's
a skeleton everywhere; and his skeleton lacks a foot. He
can't reach happiness by ten inches. He's a fine soldier,
and an accomplished gentleman; his misery is that he is

short. An odd sort of unhappiness, isn't it, from the point of view of men of our height?

ANGUS. What's that to do with the subject of money *versus* none?

CHAL. Nothing whatever—that's why I mentioned it.

ANGUS. Talking of money—you lent me £50. Here it is. (*giving him note from pocket-book*) I got a note for fifty, because it was portable.   (*crosses to* CHALCOT)

CHAL. (*taking it reluctantly*) If it shouldn't be quite convenient—

ANGUS. Oh, quite.

(*goes up,* R.C., *cutting at leaves of tree with cane*)

CHAL. (*aside*) Now this would be of use to him; it's of none to me. I know he wants it—I don't; I didn't even remember that I'd lent it him. Confound it. (*putting it in his pocket*) It's enough to make a man hate his kind, and build a hospital.

ANGUS. (*at top of avenue*) Coming in?

CHAL. No; I shall stay here. (*turning, and lying on ground*) The great comfort of the country is, one can enjoy peace and quiet. (*turns to* L. *A large wooden ball is thrown from* L. 1 E. *It falls near* CHALCOT'S *head. He starts up*) "Eh!" (*four more balls are thrown, each nearly hitting him*) By Jove!   (*rises and goes* R.)

ANGUS. Here they are!

Enter PRINCE, BLANCHE, LADY SHENDRYN, MARY, SIR ALEXANDER, *and* CAPTAIN SAMPREY, L. 1 E.

ANGUS.
O

CHALCOT.   MARY.
O   O
PRINCE.   LADY S.
O   O
BLANCHE.   SIR A.
O   O

PRINCE. (*looking at bowls. To* BLANCHE) Yours—that's ten. It's your first throw. Permit me.

(*picks up the bowl.* ANGUS *comes down between them*)

ANGUS. Good morning.

BLANCHE. Oh, Cousin Angus, how you made me start!

(*as the* PRINCE *hands her the ball, she drops it with a start*)

LADY S. My dear child, my nerves!

(*leans against* SIR ALEXANDER)

SIR A. Don't be so affected.

(*aside to her.* LADY SHENDRYN *sits* L.)

ANGUS. Good morning, Lady Shendryn ; good morning, Miss Netley. (C., *and raising hat*) How are you, Samprey ?
SAMP. How d'ye do, Mac ?

> *The* PRINCE *and* BLANCHE *are a little up,* R.C. ANGUS *joins them.*

CHAL. (R.C.) Who threw that ball ?

> (*pointing to the first one thrown*)

MARY. (L.C.) I did.
CHAL. It only just missed falling on my head.
MARY. I'm very sorry.
CHAL. That it missed me ?
MARY. No ; that it fell so far off.
CHAL. My head ?
MARY. No ; that other wooden thing.

> (*pointing to ball*)

> CHALCOT, *very wild, goes up* R. MARY, *laughing to herself, goes up* L.

ANGUS. May I join in the game ?
SAMP. Take my hand, Mac. (*giving him bowl*)
LADY S. It's going to rain. We'd better get indoors.
BLANCHE. Oh no, it won't. It never rains when I wish it to be fine. Now, where shall I throw it. (*going* L.)
PRINCE. (R.C.) I would suggest this side of the hillock.
ANGUS. (L.C.) I would advise the other. We couldn't see what became of it then.
BLANCHE. The other side. There !

> (*throws ball off,* R. 1 E.)

ANGUS. (*about to throw*) Now then !
  (PRINCE *and* ANGUS *both go to throw and collide*)
LADY S. (*interposing*) It's for the Prince to throw first.
ANGUS. I beg your pardon.
PRINCE. No ; after you. (ANGUS *refuses.* PRINCE *throws*)
There! (ANGUS *throws*)

> PRINCE *goes to* BLANCHE *and then to* LADY SHENDRYN *as soon as* ANGUS *has thrown, who immediately returns to* BLANCHE. CHALCOT, *in looking after the throwing, is in* MARY'S *way when her turn arrives. She coughs and he turns suddenly.*

CHAL. (R., *to* MARY) Are you going to throw now ?
MARY. Yes ; why do you ask ?
CHAL. That I may get out of the way.

> (*crosses, up* R.)

MARY *throws, then goes up, and sits on stump,* L., *looking at paper.*

PRINCE. (R.) Now, Lady Shendryn.

LADY S. (L.C.) Oh, I am so fatigued! My dear Prince, pray throw for me.

(PRINCE *throws.* LADY SHENDRYN *goes up*)

SAMP. All thrown. Who's won?

(PRINCE *and* ANGUS *start together, then stop*)

ANGUS. I beg your pardon.

PRINCE. After you.

(*they hesitate, each unwilling to precede the other*)

BLANCHE. (*crossing* R.) Oh, do go! You can't stop to behave prettily across country.

BLANCHE *exits,* R. 1 E., *followed by* ANGUS *and the* PRINCE, *then* SAMPREY.

LADY S. (*coming down,* L.C., *trying to take* SIR ALEXANDER's *arm*) I'm so tired, Alexander.

SIR A. (*avoiding her*) Do leave me alone.

(*exit,* R. 1 E.)

LADY S. Miss Netley, I must trouble you.

MARY *is seated on stump,* L. 2 E. LADY SHENDRYN *takes her arm.* LADY SHENDRYN *and* MARY *cross and exeunt,* R. 1 E. MARY *and* CHALCOT *exchanging looks.*

CHAL (*alone*) Serves her right. Poor Angus Mac-Moth. He'll flutter round that beautiful flame till he singes his philabeg. (*the patter of rain heard upon the leaves*) Lady Shendryn was right. It's coming down. That'll break up the skittle party. (*the* SERGEANT *enters,* L. 1 E., *puts out his hand, feels the rain, and takes shelter under tree,* L. 2 E. There's the Sergeant. I must tip him something in consideration of his recent domestic—affliction. (*takes out pocket-book*) I'll give him a fiver—eh? Here's Angus's fifty, I'll give him that. (*pausing*) No; he'll go mentioning it, and it will get into the papers, and there'll be a paragraph about the singular munificence of Hugh Chalcot, Esq., the eminent brewer!—eminent!—as if a brewer could be eminent! No; I daren't give him the fifty. (*stands under tree, next to* SERGEANT, L. 1 E. SERGEANT *touches his cap*) Wet day, Sergeant. (*turning up coat collar*)

SER. Yes, sir.

CHAL. Glad to hear that Mrs. Jones is getting over her little difficulty—I should say difficulties—so well.

SER. Thank you, sir; she is as a person might say, sir, ·as well as can be expected. *(with solemnity)*

During this scene the rain comes down more heavily, and the stage darkens.

CHAL. Havé a pipe, Sergeant?

SER. Thank you, sir. (CHALCOT *gives him tobacco and fusee. They fill and light pipes)* Thank you, sir.

CHAL. Sergeant, how many are you in family now?

SER. Eight, sir. *(lighting pipe)*

CHAL. Eight!· Good gracious! *(aside, and looking at note)* If I were only sure he wouldn't mention it——

SER. Yes, sir. Six before, and two this morning—six and two are eight.

CHAL. Rather a large family. May I ask what your pay is?

SER. One-and-tenpence a day, sir.

CHAL. One-and-tenp——*(aside)* P'raps he wouldn't mention it! *(aloud)* A small income for so large a family!

SER. Yes, sir; the family is larger than the income; but then there are other things, and Sir Alick is very kind, and so is my lady, and I hope for promotion—I may be colour-sergeant some day, and my eldest boy will soon be in the band; and so you see, sir, it's not a bad look-out, take one thing with another.

CHAL. *(astonished. Aside)* Happiness and hope, with a wife and eight children on one-and-tenpence a day! Oh, Contentment! in what strange, out-of-the-way holes do you hide yourself? If he wouldn't mention it! *(looking at note. Aloud)* Twins!—both of the same sex?

SER. No, sir—one boy, one girl.

CHAL. Which is the elder?

SER. Don't know, sir. Don't think Mrs. Jones knows. Don't think they know themselves. We never had a baby-girl before, sir. It's quite a new invention on Mrs. Jones's part. We always have boys, 'cos they make the best soldiers. There's one thing as strikes me with regard to these twins as being odd.

CHAL. Odd!—you mean even. What's odd?

SER. I'm their father, and so the credit of them must be half mine; and yet everybody asks after Mrs. Jones, and nobody asks after me.

CHAL. Oh, vanity! vanity! poor human vanity! *(rain hard)* By Jove, it is coming down. The skittle party must be broken up. *(crossing up, C.)* Well, Sergeant, I wish the

twins all sorts of good luck, and their mamma and papa likewise. Please buy 'em something for me. (*giving note*)
Good morning. (*hurries up avenue, and goes off*, R.U.E.)

SER. Here's luck ! (*looking at note*) Hey ! Hullo !
Here's some mistake ! (*calling after* CHALCOT) Hi ! Sir !
Sir ! (CHALCOT *re-enters*, R.U.E.) I beg your pardon, sir,
for calling you back ; but you've made a mistake ; you
meant to give me a five-pun' note—and many thanks, sir ;
but this here's for fifty.

CHAL. (*after a pause, with suppressed rage*) Thank you,
—yes—my mistake.

> *Takes bank-note, and gives* SERGEANT *the other, and
> goes off*, R.U.E.. *biting his lips with fury.*

SER. Five pounds. He's a trump ! Who'd a thought
it ?—and him only a civilian. My twins is as good as promotion. I'll go and show Mrs. Jones.

             (*Exit* SERGEANT, L. 1 E.   *Rain and wind*)

Enter BLANCHE *and* ANGUS, R. 1 E.   BLANCHE *carries
the skirt of her dress over her head.*

BLANCHE. How unfortunate, the rain coming on !

                        (*under tree*, R.)

ANGUS. Very.

BLANCHE. Where are all the other people gone ?

ANGUS. I don't know. (*aside*) And I don't care.
Your feet will get wet through on the grass. Better stand
upon the seat. Allow me.   (*helps her to get on seat*)

BLANCHE. You're very careful of me.

ANGUS. As careful of you as if you were old——

BLANCHE. As if I were old ?

ANGUS. (R.) Old china. (*gets up on seat, and stands by
her side*) This is more comfortable, isn't it ?

BLANCHE. (L.) Infinitely.   .

Enter LADY SHENDRYN *and* SIR ALEXANDER, *at end of
avenue*, R.U.E.

LADY S. (*her skirt over her head*) I said it would rain.

SIR A. I didn't contradict you.

LADY S. No, but I understood your silence.

                 (*sitting on stump of tree*, L.C.)

SIR A. Now you're under shelter, I'll leave you.

LADY S. Leave me by myself in the Park ?

SIR A. Do you suppose you'll be attacked by free-booters? What are you afraid of?

LADY S. Of—of the deer!

SIR A. (*sitting down, back to back with* LADY SHENDRYN. *Aside*) The deer! They're more likely to be afraid of you.

LADY S. (*sentimentally*) Ah! You would have been glad to have sat with me beneath the shelter of this verdant canopy years ago!

SIR A. Years ago, I was a fool! (*rain and wind*)

ANGUS. Quite a storm! You're hair will be wet!

BLANCHE. It is already.

ANGUS. Take my hat.

> *Takes off* BLANCHE'S *hat and puts his own on her head. Then hangs* BLANCHE'S *hat by ribbon on branch of tree above his head.*

BLANCHE. How do I look in a man's hat?

ANGUS. Beautiful! Take this, too. (*takes off his coat, and wraps it round her shoulders; puts his arm round her waist, and ties coat over her bosom by its sleeves*) That's much better, isn't it?

BLANCHE. But you'll catch cold.

ANGUS. No; we're used to cold in Cantyre; besides, we're trained not to care for it. There's a special sort of drill that makes us almost mackintosh! You've seen troops marching in the wet?

BLANCHE. Often.

ANGUS. That was rain drill!

LADY S. If you walked to the Hall, you could send me an umbrella.

SIR A. I'd rather you got wet. Just now you wished me to stay for fear of highwaymen.

LADY. S. I might catch cold.

SIR A. I should be sorry for the cold that caught you.

LADY S. It might be my death.

SIR A. Lady Shendryn, the rain fertilizes the earth, nourishes the crops, and makes the fish lively; but still it does not bring with it every blessing. You have no right to hold out agreeable expectations which you know you do not intend to realize.

> *These conversations to be taken up as if they were continuous.*

ANGUS. What was that song you sang at the Sylvesters'?

BLANCHE. Oh!

ANGUS. I wish you'd hum it to me now.

BLANCHE. Without music?

ANGUS. It won't be without music.

BLANCHE. You know the story: it is supposed to be sung by a very young man who is in love with a very haughty beauty, but dare not tell her of his love.

ANGUS. Of course he was poor.

BLANCHE. N—o.

ANGUS. What else could keep him silent?

BLANCHE. Want of—courage.

ANGUS. How does it go?

BLANCHE. (sings. Air, " Le Chanson de Fortunio," in Offenbach's " Maître Fortunio")

> If my glances have betrayed me,
>   Ask me no more,
> For I dare not tell thee, lady,
>   Whom I adore.
> She is young, and tall, and slender.
>   Eyes of deep blue,
> She is sweet, and fair, and tender,
>   Like unto you.
> Unless my lady will me,
>   I'll not reveal,
> Though the treasured secret kill me,
>   The love I feel.

LADY S. Advertising our poverty to the whole county; a filthy, old rumbling thing, not fit for a washerwoman to ride in. I won't go out in it again!

SIR A. Then stay at home.

LADY S. Why not order a new carriage?

SIR A. Can't afford it.

ANGUS. The air has haunted me ever since I heard you sing it. I've written some words to it myself.

BLANCHE. Oh, give them to me, I'll sing them.

ANGUS. Will you?

> Gives her verses, which he takes from pocket-book in coat pocket.

LADY S. Oh! I feel so faint I think it must be time for lunch.

SIR A. I'm sure it is. (looking at watch) And I'm awfully hungry. Confound it!

BLANCHE. (reading verses which ANGUS has given her) They're very charming.   (sighs)

ANGUS. You're faint. They'll lunch without us.

BLANCHE. Never mind.

ANGUS. You're not hungry?

BLANCHE. No ; are you?

ANGUS. Not in the least.

BLANCHE. Cousin, do you know I rather like to see you getting wet. May I keep these?

ANGUS. If you wish it.

LADY S. Where does all your money go to then? And what is that Mr. Kelsey, the lawyer, always coming down for?

SIR A. You'd better not ask. You'd better not know.

BLANCHE. But tell me, cousin, have you ever been in love?

ANGUS. Yes.

BLANCHE. How many times?

ANGUS. Once.

BLANCHE. Only once?

ANGUS. Only once.

LADY S. I know where the money goes to.

SIR A. Do you? I wish I did. Where?

LADY S. I know.

SIR A. Where?

LADY S. I know.

BLANCHE. I shouldn't like a husband who was too good, he'd become monotonous.

ANGUS. No husband would be to good for you ; at least, I think not !

LADY S. Isolating me from my family ! Never letting me see my brother !

SIR A. Your brother——

LADY A. Poor Percy ! only twenty-two, and——

SIR A. (*in a fury*) Don't mention his name to me ! I won't hear of him ! Infernal young villain ! always in scrapes himself and dragging others into them ! Don't mention his name !

LADY S. I should not have been so treated if I'd married a man of decent height. What could I expect from a little fellow of five feet two?

SIR A. Lady Shendryn !   (*rising, out of temper*)

LADY S. Such violence ! 'Tis the same as when years ago I discovered your falsehood. I know why we live so near. You have too many establishments to provide for !

SIR A. Madam !

LADY S. I suppose that when that woman——

SIR A. Lady Shendryn !

LADY S. That Mrs.——
SIR A. Silence !   (*distant thunder and lightning*)
LADY S. (*rising and clinging to* SIR ALEXANDER) Alexander !
SIR A. Don't touch me !   *Exits quickly*
ANGUS. (*nearing her*) Blanche !
BLANCHE. Angus !

> *The* PRINCE *enters,* R.U.E., *with umbrella up, followed by* SERVANT *with another, which he takes to* LADY SHENDRYN, *holding it over her as she exits,* R.U.E. (*the umbrellas to be wet*). *The* PRINCE *goes down to* BLANCHE, *and takes her off under umbrella,* R.U.E, *leaving coat in* ANGUS's *hands; at same time,* CHALCOT *and* MARY *enter,* R. 1 E., *wrangling, she saying,* " I never saw such a man ! you want all the umbrella," *&c., snatches it away from him, and runs off,* R.U.E. ANGUS, *who is reaching* BLANCHE'S *hat from tree, drops coat over* CHALCOT'S *head,* ANGUS *puts* BLANCHE'S *hat on his head,* CHALCOT *pointing to it as drop descends.*

END OF ACT I.

ACT II.

SCENE.—*Drawing-room at* LADY SHENDRYN'S, *in the neigh-bourhood of Birdcage Walk.· Centre opening with fold-ing-doors leading into inner room, with bay window, looking on to balcony. Door* L. 2 E. *Oval tea-table* R., *with afternoon tea laid and gong-bell. Ottoman* C. *down stage. Sofa* L., *with small round table at side, with cup of tea upon it. Chandelier and lamps lighted. In inner room, door* L., *piano* R., *music-stool and chair against window. Folding-doors to be closed at rise of·curtain. Small chairs head and* L. *of table* R.

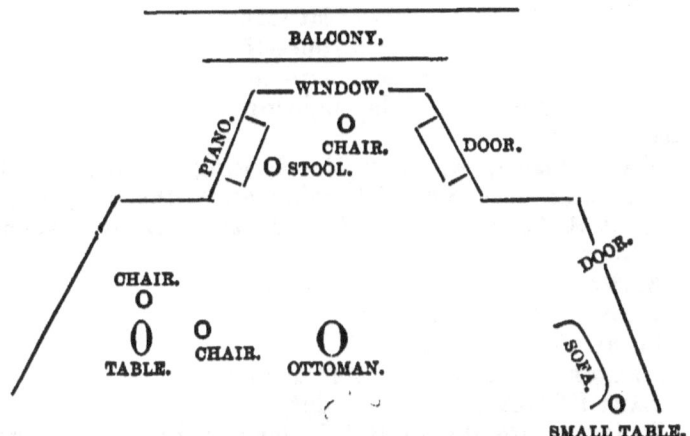

MARY *discovered presiding at tea-table,* R. BLANCHE *on ottoman,* C. LADY SHENDRYN *on sofa, reading letter,* L.

LADY S. My dear Blanche, I must request your attention to the subject of this letter again.

BLANCHE. I'm listening.

LADY S. Although I am all excitement at Sir Alexander's departure to-night, still, this affair must be settled, and at once; for not only Sir Alexander, but the Prince leaves town to-night. I'll read Lady Maria's letter again. (MARY *and* BLANCHE *exchange looks*) The last side is all that I shall trouble you with. (*reads*) "It could easily be arranged, and though a formal contract could not be entered into, a mutual agreement might be ratified, and

when the war is concluded—and I hear from the very
best authority"—"Best" underlined, my dear—"that it
cannot last long"—"Cannot" underlined, my dear—
"the Prince could return to this country and renew
his suit. This is *my* opinion"—"My" underlined,
Blanche—"and it is also the opinion of the *Duchess*,
with whom I have held counsel"—"Duchess" underlined.
—"It is *most desirable*"—"Most desirable" underlined—
"that the match should be *made*."—"Made" underlined.
—"Ever your own ADELAIDE." There, Blanche! now
you know what Lady Maria thinks! and when the Prince
comes here to-night to make his adieus, you can act in
accordance with the views she has so feelingly, so very
feelingly, expressed.

BLANCHE. But why should I be engaged to Prince
Perovsky?

LADY S. Because he's a great match.

BLANCHE. But to engage oneself to a Russian at the
very time we're going to war with them!

LADY S. But when the fighting is over, you can be
married.

MARY. (*aside*) And then the fighting can begin again!

BLANCHE. And Sir Alick going away this very night!

LADY S. (*with suppressed emotion*) It is my husband's
duty to go.

MARY. (*aside*) And his pleasure.

LADY S. And go he must.

MARY. (*aside*) And will!

BLANCHE. Poor Sir Alick! I am so sorry.

LADY S. Duty, my child! duty!

BLANCHE. (*to* MARY) But I don't want to get married
at all!

MARY. (*to her*) Duty, my pet! duty! And in this
case duty ought to be a pleasure.

BLANCHE. Duty! The same as it is Sir Alick's duty to
go and fight?

LADY S. Precisely.

BLANCHE. And a girl must put on her wedding-dress
for the same reason a soldier puts on his regimentals?

MARY. Just so. And seek the mutual conflict at the
altar.

BLANCHE. Oh, Mary—conflict!

MARY. I repeat it—conflict. And may the best man win.

LADY S. Miss Netley, I think you talk too much.

BLANCHE. Why do girls get married?

MARY. (*aside*) That's a poser!

LADY S. O——h. For the sake of society.

BLANCHE. That means for the sake of other people?

LADY S. Naturally. If people didn't marry there would be no—evening parties.

MARY. (*aside*) And what a dreadful thing that would be!

BLANCHE. But I don't want to get married.

LADY S. Then you ought to do.

BLANCHE. Ought I, Mary?

MARY. I don't know—I never was married.

LADY S. (*severely*) And never will be. With your views, Miss Netley, you don't deserve to be. Marriage is one of those—a—dear me—I want a word. Marriage is one of those——.

MARY. Evils?

LADY S. No. (*angrily*)

BLANCHE. Blessings?

LADY S. Blessings—yes—blessings, which cannot be avoided.

BLANCHE. What do you think, Mary?

MARY. It is woman's mission to marry.

BLANCHE. Why?

MARY. That she may subdue man.

LADY S. Quite so.

MARY. The first step to man's subjugation is courtship. The second matrimony. Any more tea?

(*they signify* No)

BLANCHE. (*rising and going to* MARY *sitting in chair* L. *of table* R.) Don't talk about it any more. Think of poor Sir Alick!

MARY. (*to* BLANCHE) And Angus MacAlister.

LADY S. What's that? (*sharply*)

BLANCHE. Nothing! What's what?

(*rising with* MARY *quickly*)

LADY S. Didn't I hear the name of Angus MacAlister?

BLANCHE. }
MARY. } (*together*) Oh, no.

BLANCHE. She doesn't believe us.

MARY. She knows better.

Enter SIR ALEXANDER, L.D., *in regimentals.*
BLANCHE *and* MARY *meet him,* C., *back of ottoman.*

MARY.
O
· O SIR A.
O
BLANCHE.

SIR A. Well, girls, my time is up, and I've come to bid you good bye.

BLANCHE. ⎫
MARY.   ⎬ Oh, Sir Alexander !

SIR A. You won't see me again till I come back—if ever I do come back. One word with my lady. (*the* GIRLS *sit at tea-table as before.* SIR ALEXANDER *goes down beside* LADY SHENDRYN *on sofa,* L.) Diana, you know the dispositions I have made, and how I have left you—in case any —in case anything should befall me. For ready money, there is £2,000 at Coutts's in your name.

LADY S. (*dignified*) You are very kind—indeed, you are very liberal.

SIR A. With every possible allowance for your temper, and customary misapprehension of my conduct, I cannot understand why you should meet me in this way.

LADY S. £2,000 ! Where does the rest of the money go ? I know your income. What have you done with it ?

SIR A. Is this the moment—when I am about to leave you—perhaps never to return—to quarrel about money ?

LADY S. Money ! You know that I despise it. I only speak of the disappearance of these large sums as a proof—

SIR A. Proof !—proof of what ?

LADY S. (*with tears*) Of your faithlessness — your infidelity !

SIR A. Consider the girls.

LADY S. They cannot hear me.

(SIR ALEXANDER *back to audience*)

BLANCHE. (*to* MARY) This is all very dreadful. I don't think I'll ever marry.

MARY. Yes, you will.

BLANCHE. To quarrel with my husband ?

MARY. Think how pleasant it is to own a husband to quarrel with !

LADY S. Such large sums unaccounted for !

SIR A. I know it.   (*turning*)

LADY S. Where do they go ?

SIR A. I cannot tell you. You are the last person in the world I would have know.

LADY S. Doubtless !

SIR A. Diana, you are wrong—very wrong !

LADY S. Alexander Shendryn, you know how you have treated me. You know——

SIR A. I know that at one time you had just cause of

complaint. I confessed my fault, and entreated your forgiveness. Instead of pardoning, you have never forgotten my indiscretion ; but have dinned—dinned—dinned it into my ears unceasingly.

LADY S. And, pray, sir, what divine creature is a man, that he may be faithless to his wife with impunity? What are we women, that our lot should be that we must be deceived that we may forgive; that we may be deceived again that we may forgive again, to be deceived again? Sir Alexander, these expenses from home demand my scrutiny, and I insist on knowing why they are, and wherefore? But perhaps I am detaining you, and you have adieux to make elsewhere !

SIR A. Diana, I lose all patience !

(goes down R. *corner)*

Enter a SERVANT, L.D.

SERV. The orderly is below, Sir Alexander, and wishes to speak to you.

SIR A. May he come up here?

LADY S. If you wish it.

SIR A. (*after motioning to* SERVANT, *who goes off,* L.D., *coming to* LADY SHENDRYN) Consider, £2,000 is a large sum—more than enough for your immediate requirements !

LADY S. (*with exultation*) My requirements ! All I ask is a cottage, and a loaf of bread—and all your secrets told to me !

Enter SERGEANT, L.D.

SIR A. Now, Sergeant !

SER. (*saluting*) This letter. Colonel. Mr. Kelsey, the lawyer, brought it himself.

LADY S. Mr. Kelsey?

SIR A. To the barracks?

SER. Yes, Colonel ; he said it was of the utmost consequence, and that you was to have it directly, and that he would be back in half an hour at your quarters to receive your instructions.

(SIR ALEXANDER *goes into inner room, and reads*)

SIR A.
O

SERGEANT.
O

MARY.
O

O
BLANCHE.

O LADY S.

LADY S. Mrs. Jones quite well, Sergeant?

SER. Middling, my lady, thank you.

BLANCHE. And the children?

SER. Quite well, thank you, miss; all but the twins. The twins has got the twinsey !

BLANCHE. } The what?
MARY.

SER. The twinsey, inside their throats—just here—under the stock.

MARY. You mean quinsey?

SER. Very like, miss. It's a regulation infant complaint !

BLANCHE. And what does Mrs. Jones think of your going away to Varna?

SER. Well, mum, she don't like it much. She is a little cut up about it, and has made me a outfit—six new shirts complete. (*piqued*) The twins don't seem to care much—but children never seem to know when you've done enough for 'em !

MARY. And how do you like it?

SER. Well, miss, I'm sorry to leave the missus and the children—'specially them twins, who wants more looking after than the others, being two ; but I shouldn't like to stay behind. I don't think the company could get along without me.

SIR A. (*coming down* C., *violently agitated*) Good heavens !

LADY S. What's the matter?   (*all rise*)

SIR A. Nothing !   (*pacing stage*)

LADY S. Can I——   (*offering to take letter*)

SIR A. (*crushing letter in his hand. Aside*) What's to be done? What's to be done? What's to be done? (*looks at time-piece*) Sergeant, take a cab, drive to the Garrick—the Garrick Club—as hard as you can go. Ask for Mr. Chalcot ; bring him here directly. He's dining there, I know. Lose no time, for I haven't a moment to spare .

(*Exit* SERGEANT, L.D., *after saluting*)

LADY S. More mystery !   (*sits on sofa*)

BLANCHE. } (*together*) { You quite frighten me.
MARY.   { Can I be of any——

SIR A. No, my dears—no. I must speak to your aunt again, but alone. Step into this room for a few minutes.

Signifies to them to go into inner room. MARY *and* BLANCHE *go in, exchanging glances.* SIR ALEX-ANDER *closes door after them.*

LADY S. What's coming now ?

SIR A. (*looking at letter. then advancing*) Diana, I grieve to tell you that I cannot leave you the £2,000 I spoke of.

LADY S. What ?

SIR A. (*looking at letter*) I can only leave you £500.

LADY S. This is that letter ?

SIR A. Yes.

LADY S. From Mr. Kelsey ! Whenever that fellow shows his face, there is always trouble.

SIR A. Don't wrong poor Kelsey. He is an excellent man.

LADY S. £2,000 !—£500 ! Why this sudden call for £1,500 ?

SIR A. I dare not tell you.

LADY S. Show me that letter.

SIR A. Impossible !

LADY S. Why not ?

SIR A. I cannot tell you. I must ask you to have confidence.

LADY S. Confidence !—in you ?

SIR A. I have sent for Chalcot to—to——

LADY S. To borrow money of him ?

SIR A. Yes.

LADY S. For me ?

SIR A. No.

LADY S. And I am not to know the reason of this sudden call upon your purse ?

SIR A. You must not. (*going* R.)

LADY S. (*rising*) I will ! (*advancing*)

SIR A. (*about to tell her*) Diana—no ! no ! You must not know !

LADY S. (*trying to snatch letter*) That letter !

SIR A. (*struggling*) Diana !

LADY S. I am your wife. I will have it. I will know this woman's name.

> *As she gets hold of the letter, it tears in half. She has the blank side. Enter* SERGEANT *and* CHALCOT *in evening dress,* D.L. BLANCHE *and* MARY, *hearing the noise, enter from inner room, and go down* R.

LADY S. (*showing blank*) The blank side !

SIR A. (*showing written side*) Thank heaven !

(*crosses,* R.)

CHAL. (*up stage ; aside*) There's been a row.

SER. Colonel, I met Mr. Chalcot as I was going to the cab-rank.

SIR A. (*crossing*, L.) Chalcot, a word ! — Sergeant. (*speaks to* SERGEANT, *who salutes*) In this room, Chalcot.

CHAL. An awful row !   (*aside*)

> SIR ALEXANDER *and* CHALCOT *go off through folding-doors.*

LADY S. (*after a pause, crossing and sitting*, R.) Sergeant, I shall take care of your wife while you are away.

SER. (L.) Thank you, my lady.   (*dolefully*)

BLANCHE. And the children.

MARY. And the twins.

LADY. S. ⎫
BLANCHE. ⎭ (*together*) Oh, the twins ! certainly.

SER. (*affected*) Thank you, ladies. It'll make me more comfortable to know that they will be cared for, if anything should—if anything—'cos accidents will happen with—the best regulated enemy. She's waiting below to march with me to parade, so as to see the last of me. (*a pause*) Thank you, ladies. Good evening.

> *Exit* SERGEANT, L.D.L.   *The* WOMEN *look sorrowfully and go up*, R.   *Enter* SIR ALEXANDER *and* CHALCOT, C. *door.*

SIR A. You understand ?

CHAL. Perfectly !

SIR A. And you'll see that it's explained as I——

CHAL. Certainly.

SIR A. Thanks. (*shaking hands*) You are a friend indeed.

> *Sits on sofa*, L., LADY SHENDRYN *and* BLANCHE *sitting at table*, MARY R. *of ottoman*, CHALCOT *on ottoman.*

LADY S.
O

BLANCHE.   MARY.
O   O

CHALCOT.   SIR A.
O   O

CHAL. (C.) This is a charming wind-up to a jolly evening. Parting with all my pals. I didn't know I cared at all about them ; and now they're going, I find out I like them very much. Saw Sergeant Jones's wife crying in the hall. Why don't she stop at home and cry ? Why does she come and cry where I am ?

MARY. (*half crying, coming down,* R.) What a world this is !

CHAL. Sad hole, I confess.

MARY. And what villains men are !

CHAL. They are !—they are !

MARY. To quarrel and fight, and bring grief upon poor women—and what fools women are——

CHAL. They are !—they are !

MARY. (*impatiently*) I mean, to cry about the men ! How stupid you are !

CHAL. I am !—I am ! You're quite right (*rising*) I agree with you entirely.   (*coming down,* R.)

BLANCHE. You two don't often agree.

CHAL. No ; but then we very seldom meet.

MARY. Thank goodness !

CHAL. Thank goodness !

MARY. At all events, Mr. Chalcot does not deny that women are far superior to men.

CHAL. Pardon me. He does deny it—he denies it very much.

BLANCHE. (R.) Which, then, are the better ?

CHAL. Neither !—both are worst.

BLANCHE. }
MARY.   } Oh !

CHAL. And, as a general axiom, this truth is manifest. Whatever is—is wrong !

> *Goes up* L. BLANCHE *and* MARY *go up* R. LADY SHENDRYN *comes down a little to* C.

SIR A. (*advancing to* LADY SHENDRYN) And now there is no more to say, but good-bye, and God bless you ! (*holds out his hand.* LADY SHENDRYN *remains motionless. A pause*) Won't you bid me good-bye ?

LADY S. (R.C.) The letter !

SIR A. (L.C.) Impossible ! It would make you more miserable.

LADY S. Doubtless.

SIR A. Diana !   (*holding out his hand*)

LADY S. You are waited for elsewhere. Kiss and bid good-bye to those you love.

SIR A. It may be for the last time.

LADY S. The letter ! (SIR ALEXANDER *dissents, and again holds out his hand*) Your lady-love is waiting. Waste no more time with me.

SIR A. (*aside*) Ah ! I may find peace in the campaign

—I cannot find it here.   I can control a regiment, but not
a wife. Better battle than a discontented woman. (CHALCOT
persuades him to go back.   Aloud) Good-bye, Chalcot—
(*shaking hands*)—and remember! Good-bye, Blanche—
Good-bye, Mary.   (*kissing them*)

BLANCHE. }
MARY.   } (*hanging about him*) Oh, Sir Alick!

> *They look appealingly at him, and then towards*
> LADY SHENDRYN, *who remains motionless.* SIR
> ALEXANDER *again goes to her, and offers his
> hand. She takes no notice of him. He bows and
> goes off hurriedly,* L.L.D., *followed by* BLANCHE,
> *crying.* MARY *turns at door to look at* LADY
> SHENDRYN, *and meeting* CHALCOT'S *eye, stamps at
> him, saying, "*Go away,*" and slams the door.*
> CHALCOT *looks with contempt at* LADY SHENDRYN,
> *who sinks on to ottoman.*

LADY S. Mr. Chalcot—don't leave me! Ring for Jen-
nings, my maid.   Give me some air—the heat overpowers
me.   Open those doors.

> CHALCOT *opens folding-doors and rings gong bell on
> table* R.   *Enter* LADY'S-MAID, L.D. LADY SHENDRYN
> *motions her down and takes her arm.*

LADY S. Thank you Mr. Chalcot.   I'm better now—
much better.   (*is led off by* MAID, L.D., *nearly fainting*)
CHAL. No better than you should be.   Oh temper—
temper! And that's matrimony! (BLANCHE *enters hurriedly
through door in inner room, followed by* ANGUS *in regimentals. She sits at piano and begins playing the Chanson of the
1st Act.* ANGUS *leaning over her at top of piano. Immediately*
CHALCOT *hears the music he gets over to* L.D. *noiselessly,
shaking his head*) How people with these before their eyes
can fall in love?   (*Exits on tiptoe*)

> BLANCHE *sings the song of Act I.   She breaks down
> at the last words with a sob, and lets her face and
> arms fall on piano.   Pause.*

ANGUS. Won't you sing the words I wrote?
BLANCHE. I can't sing to-night.   I can't play.
(*rising, and coming forward.   Sits on ottoman,* C.)
ANGUS. I shall often think of that air, when I am far
away.   (*standing by her side,* R.)

> *This scene to be broken by frequent pauses.*

BLANCHE. (L.C.) I—I am very sorry you are going.

ANGUS. (R.C.) I have few reasons for wishing to remain —hardly any—only one.

BLANCHE. And that one is——

ANGUS. (*nearing her*) To be near you !

         (*kneeling on ottoman*)

BLANCHE. (*averting her eyes*) Oh, cousin !

ANGUS. In the old days a soldier wore a badge, bestowed on him by the lady he—he vowed was the fairest in the world ! They were his own individual personal colours ! Some say the days of chivalry are over ! Never mind that ! Give me a token, Blanche—Cousin Blanche— a ribbon—anything that you have worn !

BLANCHE. (*trembling*) But, cousin, these exchanges are only made by those who are—engaged !

ANGUS. (*standing*) And if this war had not been declared, should you have been engaged to Prince Perovsky? Should you have exchanged tokens with him ?

BLANCHE. (*troubled*) Oh ! . How can I tell?

ANGUS. I should like to know before I go.

BLANCHE. And when must that be ?   (*rises*)

ANGUS. (*looking at timepiece*) In five minutes !

BLANCHE. (*approaching him*) So soon ! (*pauses*)

ANGUS. Have you nothing to say to me ?

BLANCHE. I—I hardly know—what would you have me say ?

ANGUS. Only one word—that you care what becomes of me !

BLANCHE. You know I do.

ANGUS. Care for me ?

    (*clasps her in his arms, she recoiling*)

BLANCHE. Yes—no—— Oh, cousin ! you make me say things——

ANGUS. That you don't mean ?

BLANCHE. No—yes ! You confuse me so—I hardly know what I'm doing !

  Bugle without, at distance. Roll on side drum, four beats on big drum, then military band play "Annie Laurie"—the whole to be as if in the distance. ANGUS starts up, and goes to window. BLANCHE springs up, and stands before door, L. ANGUS goes to door, embracing BLANCHE. They form MILLAIS' picture of the "Black Brunswicker."

BLANCHE. Oh, Angus—dear cousin Angus!

ANGUS. (*faltering*) Blanche! you are rich—an heiress. I am but a poor Scotch cadet; but Scotch cadets ere now have cut their way to fame and fortune; and I have my chance. Say, Blanche, do you love me? Say, if at some future day I prove myself not unworthy of you, will you be mine?

BLANCHE Oh, Angus!

ANGUS. Answer, love; for every moment is precious as a look from you. May I hope?

> *Handle of the door moves; they separate,* BLANCHE, L., ANGUS, R. *of door. Enter* SERVANT, L. *door.*

SERV. Prince Perovsky!

> *Enter* PRINCE, L.D. *Exit* SERVANT. *A pause.*

PRINCE. (*crossing*, R.C.) I fear that I arrive inopportunely?

BLANCHE. (*advancing*, L.C.) No, Prince; my cousin is just bidding us good-bye. He is about to sail for—he is about to leave England.

> (ANGUS *comes down*, L. *to* L.L.D.)

PRINCE. (*smiling*) On service?

ANGUS. Yes, on service. I have the honour, Prince, to take my leave.

> *They bow—a momentary pause—*PRINCE *takes in situation and abruptly turns his back to* ANGUS *and* BLANCHE, *taking a pinch of snuff as the following business proceeds, viz. :—*ANGUS *goes to* L.D., *turns to* BLANCHE, *calling her by name. She rushes to him, tearing the locket from her neck, and gives it to* ANGUS, *unperceived by* PRINCE. ANGUS *holds her in his arms, kisses her, and exits hurriedly. The music of band ceases as* BLANCHE *sits on ottoman. Pause.*

PRINCE. (*turning slowly round*) Miss Haye, I am charmed to find you alone; for what I have to say could only be said *tête-à-tête.* (BLANCHE *rises*) Pray don't rise. Both Sir Alexander and Lady Shendryn are aware of the object of my visit, and do me the honour of approving it. Have I the happiness of engaging your attention? (BLANCHE *assents.* PRINCE *sits by her side, taking chair from* L. *of table,* R.) I leave London for Paris to-night *en route* to Vienna. I mention that fact that it may excuse the

permission to go on ? (BLANCHE *assents*. *He.bows*) My
mission here was not, as many supposed, diplomatic, but
matrimonial. I may say, as the man said when he was
asked who he was, "When I am at home, I am somebody." I
came to England in search of a wife—one who would be an
ornament to her station and mine. I wished to take back
with me, to present to my province and to my Imperial
master, a princess.

BLANCHE. A princess ?

PRINCE. Unhappily, this Ottoman difficulty has arisen.
I thought that diplomacy would have smoothed it away. I
was wrong—and so my mission, which was so eminently
peaceful, must be postponed until the war is over.

BLANCHE. Until the war is over?

PRINCE. That will be in very few months.

BLANCHE. (*eagerly*) Why so?

PRINCE. Wars with Russia never last long.

BLANCHE. Why not?

PRINCE. Pardon me, if for a moment I am national and
patriotic. Against Russian power, prowess and resources
are useless. The elements have declared on our side, and
in them we have two irresistible allies.

BLANCHE. And they are——

PRINCE. Frost and fire! If cold fails, we try heat—
that is, to warm the snow, we burn our Moscows. (BLANCHE
shivers) But, pardon me, you are thinking of those among
your relatives who hold rank in the English army?

(*significantly*)

BLANCHE. (*hesitating*) Yes ; Sir Alexander.

PRINCE. Of course—Sir Alexander. As I alighted,
I saw troops mustering outside—a pretty sight. Fine
fellows ! fine fellows ! But I fear I am fatiguing you ; for
I am—*helas !* too many, many years your senior to hope to
interest you personally. (*rising with courtliness and
dignity*) Miss Haye, with the permission of your guardians,
I lay my name and fortune at your feet. Should you
deign to accept me, at the end of the war I shall return to
England for my bride.

BLANCHE. (*rising, confused*) Prince, I am sensible——

PRINCE. Should you honour me by favourable consideration of my demand, in return for the honour of your hand,
I offer you rank and power. On our own lands we hold
levées—indeed, you will be queen of the province—of
400,000 serfs—of your devoted slave—my queen !

BLANCHE. (*sits on sofa*, L.) Queen ! If I should prove a tyrant ?

PRINCE. (*standing*) I am a true Russian, and love despotism !

BLANCHE. (*smiling*) And could you submit to slavery?

PRINCE. At your hands—willingly. (*sits on her* R.H.) I assure you, slavery is not a bad thing !

BLANCHE. But freedom is a better ! And you came to England, Prince, to seek a wife?

PRINCE. Not only to seek a wife—to find a princess !

BLANCHE. You can make a princess of anybody !

PRINCE. But I cannot make anybody a princess ! Let me hope my offer is not entirely objectionable, despite the disparity of our years.

> *Music—" British Grenadiers"—drum and fife heard outside.*

CHAL. (*without*) I beg your pardon.

MARY. (*without*) Beg my pardon ? Couldn't you see ?

CHAL. (*without*) I didn't.

MARY. (*without*) I was right before your eyes.

> (*Enters*, L.D.)

CHAL. (*entering*, L.D.) Perhaps that was the reason.

MARY. Tearing one's dress to pieces !

> (*coming down*, L.)

CHAL. Really, what with the troops, and the bands and the bother, I feel I must tear something !

> (*down*, R.H.)

MARY. Poor fellows—leaving their wives !

> (*going up*)

CHAL. They consider that one of the privileges of the profession.

> (*music grows distant*)

MARY. (*up*, C. *Excitedly*) Oh, when I hear the clatter of their horses' hoofs, and see the gleam of the helmets, I —I wish I were a man !

CHAL. I wish you were !

> (*standing*, C., *his glass in his eye*)

MARY. (*opening window at back*) We can see them from the balcony.

> *Music ceases. When she opens window, the moonlight, trees, gas, &c., are seen at back. Distant bugle.*

MARY. There's Sir Alick on horseback. (*distant cheers. On balcony*) Do you hear the shouts?

CHAL. Yes. (*up at window*)

MARY. And the bands?

CHAL. (*on balcony*) And the chargers prancing.

MARY. And the bayonets gleaming.

CHAL. And the troops forming.

MARY. And the colours flying. Oh, if I were not a woman, I'd be a soldier! (*going down a little*)

CHAL. So would I. (*coming down, L.*)

MARY. Why are you not?

CHAL. What!—a woman!

MARY. No—a soldier. Better be anything than nothing. Better be a soldier than anything.

> *Goes up again. Tramp of troops marching heard in the distance. Cheers.*

CHAL. (*catching* MARY's *enthusiasm, and sitting on ottoman*) She's right! She's right! Why should a great hulking fellow like me skulk behind, lapped in comfort, ungrateful, uncomfortable, and inglorious? Fighting would be something to live for. I've served in the militia—I know my drill—I'll buy a commission—I'll go! (*rises*)

MARY. (*meeting him, as he goes up*) That's right. I like you for that.

> *Music—"The girl I left behind me." Cheers and music.*

CHAL. Do you? (*distant cheers*). Come and shout. (*to* MARY; *then to* PRINCE, *who is seated on sofa, with* BLANCHE) Come and shout. Oh, I beg pardon!

PRINCE. Not at all—not at all! (*rises, and goes up to window, and looks out*) In splendid condition. Fine fellows! Fine fellows! Poor fellows! (*taking snuff, and coming down, L.*) Won't you come and look at them, Miss Haye?

> *As* BLANCHE *rises,* LADY SHENDRYN *enters,* L.D. BLANCHE *sits again on sofa.* CHALCOT *and* MARY *at window.*

LADY S. My dear Prince, I did not know you were here!

PRINCE. I profited by your ladyship's absence to urge the suit of which you have been kind enough to approve.

LADY S. And have you received an answer?

PRINCE. Not precisely. (*music stops*)

CHAL. (*at balcony*) There's Sir Alick !   (*cheers*)

SIR A. (*outside*) Battalion ! Attention ! Form fours, right ! March off by companies in succession from the front ! Number one, by your left, quick march.

> *Music.   Repeat, " The girl I left behind me."*—LADY SHENDRYN, C., *starts.   Tramp loud.*

CHAL. They're marching right past the window.   Come here and see.   There's the sergeant. (*command outside,* " Number two, by your left, quick march.")

PRINCE. Miss Haye, may I be permitted to know if I may hope ?

MARY. (*at window*) There's Angus !

> (BLANCHE *rushes up*)

ANGUS. (*without*) Number three, by your left ! Quick march !

> *Music forte.   Band plays " God save the Queen."
> Cheers.   Tramp of soldiers.   Excitement.   Picture.*
> CHALCOT *and* MARY *waving handkerchiefs, and cheering at window.* PRINCE, L., *taking snuff.*
> LADY SHENDRYN, C. BLANCHE *totters down and falls fainting at her feet.*

END OF ACT II.

ACT III.

Scene.—*Interior of a hut, built of boulders and mud, the roof built out, showing the snow and sky outside. The walls bare and rude, pistols, swords, guns, maps, newspapers, &c., suspended on them. Door, R. 2 E. Window in flat, R.C., showing snow-covered country beyond; rude fireplace, L.; wood fire burning; over-hanging chimney and shelf; small stove, R., very rude, with chimney going through roof, which is covered with snow and icicles; straw and rags stuffed in crevices and littered about floor; a rope stretched across back of hut, with fur rugs and horse-cloths hanging up to divide the beds off; camp and rough make-shift furniture; camp cooking utensils, &c.; arm-chair, made of tub, &c. Cupboards round L., containing properties; hanging lamp, a rude piece of planking before fireplace, stool, tubs, pail, &c. Portmanteau, L. table, L.C., rough chair, broken gun-barrel near fireplace, for poker, and stack of wood. Stage half dark, music, "Chanson," distant bugle and answer, as curtain rises.*

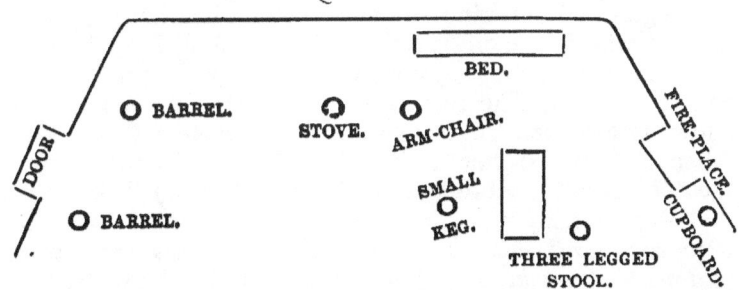

Angus *discovered, very shabby, high, muddy boots, beard, &c., seated at R. of table, reading by light of candle letters which are lying on an open travelling-desk.*

Angus. (*reading old note*) "Dear Cousin Angus,— Lady Shendryn desires me to ask you to come and dine on Thursday. The usual hour. Do come.—Yours, Blanche. P.S.—Which my lady does not see. Mary says that men ought not to be believed, for all they say is fable." (*smooths*

note, and folds it, puts it away, reads another) "DEAR
COUSIN ANGUS,—I shall not be at dinner, but I shall be in
the drawing-room, for inspection, as you call it. I don't
believe a word that you said the night before last. You
know.— BLANCHE."—*(folds it, and places it in a large
envelope, with other letters, an old glove, a flower, which he
kisses, and a ribbon, seals them up, leaving packet on top of
desk)* If the attack is ordered for the morning, Hops will
find this on the table as I told him. *(taking letter from his
pocket)* How much oftener shall I read this? It contains
the last news of her. *(reads)* "DEAR MAC,—London is
terribly slow, no parties no nothing"—um—um—um—
"All the news comes to the Rag; but of course you know.
that before we do." *(turns over)* Here it is! "I saw the
fascinating party, the thought of whom occupies your leisure
hours, yesterday; she was in a carriage with Lady Shendryn,
and Dick Fanshawe sat opposite. Dick has been often seen
at Lady Shendryn's lately. I keep you posted up on this
subject, because you told me to. Dick's uncle, the old
mining-man, died two months ago, and left him a pot of
money. Such is luck! My uncles never die, and when
they do, they leave me dressing-cases! Damn dressing-
cases! Dick's name, and that of the divine party, have
been coupled, *Apropos d'amour.* I am awfully hard up.
Little Lucy has left me. She bolted with a Frenchman in
the cigar-trade, taking all she could with her." *(rising)*
Um—that's four months ago. What a fool I am! Fanshawe's very rich, and not a bad fellow—as well he as
another. *(sighs)* The next six hours may lay me on the
snow, as has been the fate of many a better fellow. Oh!
when I think of her, I feel that I could charge into a
troop of cavalry, sabreproof with love. *(pause)* This won't
do!—I'm getting maudlin! *(looks at watch, and takes fur
great-coat and cap from arm-chair, buckles on sword,
buttons up his coat, &c.)* Mustn't be maudlin here. There's
work! *(smiling sadly, and taking up packet)* If I can't live
to marry Blanche, and make her Lady MacAlister, wife of
General Sir Angus MacAlister, I can, at least, die a decent
soldier. So there, Master Hops! *(placing packet on table,
and lighting pipe by candle, L.) Exit,* R. *door, singing—*

> "Parti-t-en guerre, pour tuer l'ennemi,
> Parti-t-en guerre, pour tuer l'ennemi;
> Revint de guerre, apres six ans et demi,
> Revint de guerre, apres six ans et demi;

Que va-t-il faire? Le Sire de Framboissey—
Que va-t-il-faire? Le Sire de Framboissey."

All exits and entrances are made from door, R. 2 E.
*Wind is heard as door opens, and snow is driven
in.*

CHAL. (*sneezes, then sings behind curtain,* L.C.)—

" In Liquorpond Street, London, a merchant did dwell,
Who had one only darter—an uncommon nice young
gal ;
Her name it was Dinah, just sixteen years old,
And she'd a very large fortin' in silvier and gold.
Ri-tiddle-um, &c."

*Drawing curtain, is discovered on a rude bed of
straw, rough wrapping, &c., his appearance
entirely altered, hair rough, long beard, face
red and jolly, his whole manner alert and
changed. He wears an old uniform coat ; one
leg is bandaged at the calf, the trouser being
cut to the knee, and tied with strings and tape ;
he sits up in bed and yawns. Rubbing his
eyes, and hitting his arms out with enjoyment.*

CHAL. What a jolly good sleep I have had, to be
sure ! (*takes flask from under pillow, and drinks*) Ah !
What a comfort it is that in the Crimea you can drink
as much as you like without its hurting you ! The
doctor says it's the rarefaction of the atmosphere. Bravo,
the rarefaction of the atmosphere !—whatever it may be.
I must turn out. (*takes pillow, and addresses it in song*)

"Kathleen Mavourneen, arouse from thy slumbers."

(*hits pillow, and gets out of bed*) Gardez vous the poor
dumb leg. It's jolly cold ! (*goes to fireplace and warms
his hands, then turns and holds them round the candle,
whilst so doing sees letters*) Oh, Gus has left his love-traps
to my keeping in case he should be potted. (*puts letters in
cupboard* L.) Now for my toilette. Where's the water?
(*goes across stage, finds bucket against barrel up stage,* R.)
Ice, as usual ! Where's the hammer? (*as he comes down
he strikes foot against old gun-barrel lying amongst the
straw on stage ; he winces from pain to leg. Breaks ice in
bucket, and taking up tin basin from side of barrel,* R.
corner, retires behind curtain. Business of pouring out

water, washing, &c.; comes out, wiping hands and face with straw) If the water's cold, the straw's warm. What luxuries those fellows in London do enjoy to be sure, soap and towels everywhere, and coffee for ringing for it. The sergeant left the coffee—good (*takes coffee-pot from stove, and pours out coffee. Drinking coffee, and shaking his head. Sings*)

"Oh! father, says Dinah, I am but a child,
 And for to get married just yet don't feel not at all
   inclined;
 If you'll let me live single for a year or two more,
 My werry large fortin' I freely will give o'er."

(*getting biscuit from canister,* L.) Oh! this poor dumb leg of mine! Just my luck! I obtain my commission all right—get into the same company as Angus—and wounded in my first engagement. If it hadn't been for the sergeant, I should have been killed. He received cut number three meant by the Russian for me. Down he went and up I got. (*sits at head of table, on barrel*) And while he was down, the brute ran his bayonet into the ca¹f of my leg. A mean advantage to take—to stick me while he was down. However, I split his skull (*cracks biscuit*), so he didn't get the best of it; and here I am — lame for another month. The first fortnight's dressing did my leg no good, for that fool of a sergeant, instead of putting on the ointment given him by the doctor, went and spread the bandages all over orange marmalade; and I should never have found it out if he hadn't served up the salve for breakfast along with the anchovies. (*eating and drinking*) Now, I superintend the cookery department— when there's anything to cook. (*knock at door,* R.) Who's there? If you're French, *Entrez*; if you're Sardinian, *Entre*; if you're Turkish, *Itcherree;* If you're Russian, *Vnutri;* and if you're English, Come in!

> *Enter* SERGEANT—*ragged great-coat, long beard, his left arm in a sling, bundle slung over his* R. *shoulder, straw bands on legs, snow on coat, boots, beard, &c. Wind heard as door opens, and snow driven in.*

CHAL. Shut the door; shut the door—it's awfully cold.

SER. (*shutting the door by placing his back against it.*

CHAL. It feels the cold, sergeant. How's your arm?

SER. Thank you, sir, it feels frosty too ; but I can move it a little. (*moves arm, and winces*)

CHAL. Gently, sergeant, gently. How about dinner?

SER. Here you are, sir. (*placing bundle on table*) Mutton, sir—for roasting.

CHAL. And vegetables !

SER. Under the meat, sir.

CHAL. (*lifting up meat*) Capital ! The muddy, but flowery potato; the dirty milky turnip; and the humble, blushing, but digestive carrot, Can you cook 'em ?
(*putting them near cupboard*)

SER. Not to-day, sir. I'm on hospital duty.

CHAL. Then I suppose I must.

SER. But I shall be able to look in, sir, now and then.

CHAL. Do ; for your legs are indispensable. Any news outside ?

SER. They say, sir, there's to be an attack shortly.

CHAL. Um !

SER. And the enemy was heard moving in the night.

CHAL. Oh !

SER. And that they're very strong in artillery.

CHAL. Oh ! (*drinking*)

SER. Talking of artillery, sir, Captain Rawbold sent his compliments to you, sir, and would you oblige him with the loan of your frying pan, a pot of anchovies, and a few rashers of bacon.

CHAL. (*annoyed*) Anything else?

SER. No sir.

CHAL. Confound Captain Rawbold !—he's always borrowing something. Last week I lent him our own private and particular gridiron, and he sent it back with one of the bars broken. (*aside*) Confound those damned gunners !—borrowing one's *batterie-de-cuisine.*
(*rising. Knock,* D.L.)

SER. I dare say that is Captain Rawbold come himself to——

CHAL. Open the door. I'll just give him a bit of my mind about that gridiron. Well (*taking frying-pan*), you don't deserve it ; but here's your frying-pan, and——
(SERGEANT *opens door.* SIR ALEXANDER *enters.* CHALCOT *sees him*) Eh !—Colonel !

SERGEANT *salutes, shutting door with his back.* CHALCOT *puts frying-pan behind him. Wind heard as door opens. Snow.*

SIR A. Good morning, Chalcot. I want to speak to
you.   (*goes to fire,* L.)

CHAL. Sergeant, my compliments—and frying-pan to
the captain—and—and— (*aside to* SERGEANT) He mustn't
do it again. (*opening door for* SERGEANT. SERGEANT, C.,
*salutes with frying-pan, and exits, holding it before his face.
Wind heard as door opens*) Did you meet MacAlister?
                                 (*crosses* L., *to fireplace*)

SIR A. (*sits on barrel at head of table*) Yes; and that's
what I came to speak to you about. He reminded me of
the documents that I intended to entrust to your care—
should anything befall me.
(*gives him packet, which* CHALCOT *places in portmanteau*)

CHAL. Is there any news, then?

SIR A. I think we shall be ordered to the front—and I
believe there is to be a combined attack, which is likely to
be decisive. Angus told me that he had made his last will
and testament, and confided it to you. I have done the
same.

CHAL. (*who is arranging a rude spit and string for
suspending mutton before fire,* L.) And while you're fighting,
I shall have to stop in here, cooking—like a squaw in a wig-
wam.

SIR A. I'm sorry you can't go with us.

CHAL. Just my luck! Where's the cookery book?
                 (*gets book from mantel-piece, and goes to table*)

SIR A. Hugh—you've been a good friend—a real friend!
At that time, when Kelsey came with that terrible news
just before we sailed——

CHAL. (*at table. Reading, and feigning not to hear*)
" Roast "—" boil "—"bake "—" fry "—" stew "——

SIR A. (*taking book from him*) Put that down and listen
to me. You know the original cause of my quarrel—with
my lady.

CHAL. The slightest possible——Oh, yes.

SIR A. You know, too, how she has wronged me since
by her suspicions. I wrote a long letter to her last night—
here it is. (*showing it*) If this general engagement should
give promotion to our senior major, send it home at once.
My lady will find—when it is too late—how far she has
been mistaken.   (*gives him letter*)

CHAL. (*endeavouring to hide his feelings, and looking at
mutton on table*) You don't know how mutton is usually
roasted, do you—I mean, which side up?
                               (*taking it in his hands*)

SIR A. I had more to say to you—but I must go.

(*rises*)

CHAL. I'd hobble with you as far as the hill, if it wasn't for the mutton. (*hangs mutton at fire*)

SIR A. (*crossing,* R.) And I could speak to you as we walked.

CHAL. (*warming himself at stove*) The sergeant will be back directly. I can leave it for a few minutes. I have it ! (*writes on a piece of paper, folds it, and sticks it on the point of a sword, then fixes sword in drawer of table, so that the point is upwards*) He can't help seeing that. (*putting on cap and cloak*) I believe I've hung it wrong side up. Now, Sir Alick ; since my wound, this will be my first walk. (*taking stick from* R.C.)

SIR A. And perhaps my last.

> *Wind and snow, as door opens. Exeunt* SIR ALEX ANDER *and* CHALCOT. *Bugle. A pause.* CAPTAIN SAMPREY, LADY SHENDRYN, BLANCHE *and* MARY, *and* SOLDIER, *pass window, from* L. *Knocking heard at* D.L. *Knocking repeated.*

SAMP. (*without*) Chalcot, MacAlister—nobody at home (*wind. Looks in, then enters*) This way, we have the field to ourselves. (*Enter* BLANCHE, LADY SHENDRYN *and* MARY, *and* SOLDIER, *with whip,* L.D.) These are their quarters.

LADY S. Oh, thank you, major—so kind of you to have escorted us from Balaklava.

SAMP. (R.) So kind of you to have accepted my escort. They are out, but I should think they're sure to be back directly. In the meantime——

LADY S. We'll stay here. I suppose we need be under no apprehension.

SAMP. My dear Lady Shendryn, let me re-assure you. Sir Alexander is quite well—so is Chalcot—and so is MacAlister. I'll now go and seek Sir Alexander—(*all this lively*)—and tell him who is here. (*crossing,* R.)

BLANCHE. (R.C.) Where are they ?

SAMP. I don't know. Pray be under no alarm—nobody will come here. There's no fighting going on—nor is there likely to be. We've no employment here but to keep ourselves warm—and to go without our dinners.

> *Exit* SAMPREY. *The* LADIES, *who are shivering with cold, run to fire.*

BLANCHE. Mary, your nose is red.

MARY. So's your's.

BLANCHE. So's my lady's.

LADY S. Blanche, how can you take such a liberty?

BLANCHE. It was the frost, not me. Let us warm our noses.

> *They go on their knees, and warm their noses at fire, rub them with handkerchiefs, &c.*

LADY S. I wonder when Mr. Chalcot will come back.

> BLANCHE *and* MARY *examine furniture, peep behind curtain, see bed, and drop curtain, exclaiming Oh!*

BLANCHE. (*at fire*) And this is a hut. And this is the Crimea which we have all heard about and read about so much. And neither Sir Alick, nor Mr. Chalcot——

MARY. Nor Captain MacAlister——

BLANCHE. Expect us, and here we are. (*seeing sword*) What's that?

LADY S. (R.C.) Looks like a sword, with a note at the top of it.

MARY. (R. *of table*) Perhaps that's the Crimean method of delivering letters.

BLANCHE. (L. *of table.* *Taking* MARY's *hand sentimentally*) Perhaps, Mary, Chalcot——

MARY. Or MacAlister——

BLANCHE. Or some comrade, has left that letter containing his last request.

MARY. Or a letter to his wife.

LADY S. More probably to his sweetheart.

BLANCHE. A few lines to his mother.

LADY S. Or his children.

MARY. Or his tailor.

BLANCHE. I wonder what *is* in it! (*crossing to sword*) I declare I feel like Blue Beard's wife at the door of the blue chamber.

MARY. So do I.

LADY S. What absurdity!

> BLANCHE, L., MARY, R., *on each side of the table.* LADY SHENDRYN *at fire.*

MARY. There's no address on it.

BLANCHE. Then it's intended for anybody.

MARY. Or nobody.

LADY S. Do you consider yourself nobody, Miss Netley?

MARY. Almost.

LADY S. Blanche I'm surprised at you. Open a letter not addressed to you ! Most un-ladylike.

MARY. (*whispering to* BLANCHE) Tell her you think it's in Sir Alick's handwriting.

BLANCHE. It's open at this end. I can read *T-h-e,* " the." I think it's Sir Alexander's handwriting.

LADY S. (*rising*) Eh ?

BLANCHE. But we mustn't open it, Mary ; so whether it is Sir Alexander's or anybody else's——

LADY S. (*down.* R.) My dear Blanche, if you insist on gratifying this childish whim——

BLANCHE. You'll let me ?

LADY S. To please you, my dear.

BLANCHE. You take it off.

MARY. No, you.

BLANCHE. No, you.

> *Pushing each other forward.* MARY *snatches letter, the sword falls to the ground.* All frightened.

ALL. Oh !

BLANCHE. It's like the taking of Sebastopol.

MARY. Yes ; only that we've got it. (*all come down stage.* LADY S., R. ; MARY, C. ; BLANCHE. L, MARY *opens letter, and reads*) " Please to look after the mutton ! "

ALL. Oh !

> (LADY S. *goes to stove.* MARY, R. ; BLANCHE, L.)

LADY S. Sir Alexander never wrote that ; it's not his style.

MARY. Such a stupid thing to say ! Now put the sword and letter back.

BLANCHE. No ; that would be mean. We'll look after the mutton ourselves. I feel so excited ; I think it must be the air. (*twirling mutton*) Isn't it fun seeing it go round ? (*standing with her back to fire*) Upon my word, Mary, I think I should make as good an officer as any of the men. I could stand with my back to the fire, as they do. (*imitating*)

MARY. (C.) But you couldn't face the fire, as they do.

BLANCHE. I don't know that. I could talk just as they do. (*imitating slow swell smoking, and taking cigars from case on mantelpiece*) Yaas, it's a very fine cigaw—but I know man—Bedfordshire man—who imports—for his own smoking, very finest cigaws evaw smoked. Now, Mary, you go on.

MARY. (*sitting*, L.C., *back. Imitating different sort of swell, with eye-glass, and hands in pockets*). Look here, old fella, if you talk of cigars—I know some cigars that are cigars—and such cigars as no other fella's got the like cigars.

BLANCHE. (*slow*) You don't say so.   (*smoking*)

MARY. (*quick*) Assure you—never saw such cigars before in all my life. (*rising*) Oh! ain't they nasty?

(they put them down)

BLANCHE. Mary, let's play at soldiers.

(snatching up sword that note was attached to)

LADY. S. Oh! you stupid girls.

(rises, and goes to fire, L.)

MARY. Oh! It's such a silly game.

BLANCHE. No, it isn't. To please me! There, take one of those guns.

(MARY takes gun hesitatingly, from L. of barrel R.)

MARY. D'ye think it'll go off?

BLANCHE. No; it is not loaded. Now, you be the soldier, and I'll be the officer.

MARY. No; I'll be the officer.

BLANCHE. No; I'll be the officer.

MARY. No; then I shan't play.

BLANCHE. We can't both be officers.

MARY. Yes we can.

BLANCHE. Then who's to give the word of command?

MARY. Both.

BLANCHE. And who's to obey it?

MARY. Neither.

BLANCHE. Nonsense.

MARY. It's going off, Blanche.

BLANCHE. (*in tone of command*) Hi! Ho! Ha! Attention! Form hollow square! Prepare to receive (*prancing over to* R.) cavalry!

BLANCHE charges upon MARY. MARY, somewhat frightened, retreats to the corner, R.   Door opens; ANGUS and CHALCOT enter. MARY gets R. corner, BLANCHE L. corner.

CHAL. (C.) Lady Shendryn!

ANGUS. (R.) Blanche!

CHAL. Miss Netley!

LADY S. (R.C.) How do you do, Hugh. (*general shaking of hands*) How are you, Angus?

BLANCHE. (L.C.) We're so glad to see you, Mr. Chalcot. (*embarrassed*) And you too, Captain MacAlister.

MARY. How do you do, Captain? How do you do, Mr. Chalcot?

> *Places stock of gun in his hand. Goes up and dis-*
> *robes.* BLANCHE, L. CHALCOT *and* ANGUS *take off*
> *overcoats, &c.* ANGUS *helps* CHALCOT *off with coat.*
> *Puts his sword against barrel* R.

CHAL. (R. *aside*) She's looking very well. But you must have dropped from the clouds.

ANGUS.   MARY.
O   O
O   O   O
CHALCOT.   LADY S.   BLANCHE.

LADY. S. It was all done in a moment. Lady Llandudno felt that she must come over here to see her boy—you know he's her only one. She sent Lord Llandudno to Southampton, where his yacht was lying, to ask the captain if the " Curlew " was big enough to make the voyage to the Crimea. The captain answered that it was, and that it could be ready in two days. During that time, Lady Llandudno called on me to bid me good-bye. I was seized with the desire to come out too. Lady Llandudno acceded to my wish. Blanche asked to accompany me : I acceded to her wish. I brought Miss Netley as a companion for Blanche ; and here we are. Major Samprey brought us from Balaklava in a cart.

CHAL. I saw female figures entering our hut from the top of the hill, and hobbled on as fast as I could. I took you for vivandieres.

(ANGUS *and* BLANCHE *never take their eyes off each other*)

LADY S. (L.C.) ⎫
BLANCHE. (L.) ⎬ Vivandieres !
MARY. (L.C.) ⎭

BLANCHE. Do vivandieres ever come here?

CHAL. (*exchanging glances with* ANGUS, R.) No; but seeing petticoats—it seems a dream. By Jove ! If this were put in a play, people would say it was improbable. (ANGUS *and* LADY S. *go up stage. Knocks his wounded leg against gun, and winces*) Oh !

MARY. ⎫
BLANCHE. ⎭ What's the matter ?

CHAL. I'm wounded.

BLANCHE. ⎫
MARY. ⎭ Wounded ?

CHAL. (R. *corner*) Yes.

MARY. But how?

CHAL. A Russian infantry man ran his bayonet in the calf of my leg.

MARY. Oh! how horrid! (*hiding her face*)

CHAL. I brought it away as a trophy.

BLANCHE. The leg?

CHAL. No—the bayonet. (*pointing to bayonet on wall*) That's the bayonet—this is the leg.

BLANCHE. What's the matter, Mary?

MARY. Nothing; but to find oneself close to the realities —to the horrors of war!

CHAL. Eh?

BLANCHE. (*laughing*) She says you're one of the horrors of war.

MARY. Oh! Blanche! How can you!

(BLANCHE *and* MARY *go to* ANGUS *at table,* L.)

MARY.
O

LADY S.
O

CHAL.
O

O ANGUS.

O BLANCHE.

LADY S. (*coming down,* L.C. *Aside to* CHALCOT) Are Sir Alexander's quarters near here?

CHAL. No. (*aside*) If he only knew who was here? At some distance.

LADY S. Is he likely to come here?

CHAL. I think so—shortly—yes. (*aside*) This is awkward. (LADY S. *returns to stove. With fashionable air. Going up*). Well, ladies, happy to see you in the heart of luxury and civilisation; welcome to this baronial hall, which, by the way, we built ourselves. Chalcot *fundavit* —Chalcot *pinxit*—Chalcot *carpetavit*. This is the boudoir. Wont't you come upon the Turkey carpet?

> *Standing upon a piece of planking, which rocks to and fro.*

ANGUS. (*bringing down rude arm-chair,* R.C.) Allow me to offer your ladyship a chair.

> ANGUS *goes to arm-chair, and then to* R. *of table, facing* BLANCHE. MARY *sits at head of table, and* BLANCHE *at end,* L.

CHAL. (R.C.) I made it myself; it's beautifully stuffed—

put your feet on the hearthrug. Dinner will be ready, when it's done. The *ménu* is substantial, but not various. *A grand gigot de mouton rôti au naturel, pas de sauce.* In the meantime, can we offer you any light refreshment—any lunch? We have an admirable tap of rum, and as for fruit, I can strongly recommend our raw onions. After dinner we can go to the Opera. (*cannonade, distant*)

LADY S. What's that?

CHAL. (*looking at* ANGUS) The overture! May I offer you some coffee?

> LADY SHENDRYN *seated at stove,* R., MARY *at head of table, and* BLANCHE *at foot,* L. ANGUS, L.C.

LADIES. Oh, yes.

> CHALCOT *hands coffee to* LADY SHENDRYN *and* MARY; ANGUS *to* BLANCHE, *fetching cups, &c., from cupboard,* R., *then a cup for himself; crossing to* BLANCHE, *stirring coffee, with his eyes fixed on her; sees she has no spoon, gives her the fork he is using, squeezing her hand.*

ANGUS. (*conscious that* LADY SHENDRYN'S *eyes are upon him. To* BLANCHE) I hope I have the pleasure of seeing you quite well!

BLANCHE. Quite well; and you?

ANGUS. Quite well.

MARY. I want a spoon.

> (CHALCOT *gives her the wooden one*)

CHAL. Our family plate. (*a pause. They sigh*)

ANGUS. Any news in London, when you left it?

BLANCHE. No; none. (*pause*)

ANGUS. No news?

BLANCHE. None; none whatever.

MARY. It's so hot.

CHAL. Have some ice in?

BLANCHE. (*pauses*) You remember Miss Featherstonhaugh?

ANGUS. No—yes. Oh—yes.

BLANCHE. The Admiral's second daughter, the one with the nice eyes; used to wear her hair in bands. Her favourite colour was pink?

> (ANGUS *puts cup to his lips, but does not drink*)

ANGUS. Yes.

BLANCHE. She always wears green now.

ANGUS. Good gracious !

CHAL. Can I offer your ladyship the spoon ?

ANGUS. (*not knowing what to say*) I heard that London
had been very dull.

BLANCHE. Oh ! very dull.

ANGUS. Seen anything of our friends, the Fanshawes ?

BLANCHE. No.

ANGUS. Not of *Mr.* Fanshawe ?

BLANCHE. Oh—Dick ! He's married !

ANGUS. Married ?

BLANCHE. Yes ; one of Sir George Trawley's girls.

ANGUS. (*with a sigh of relief*) Poor old Fanshawe ! (*He
empties cup at a draught ; sees that* LADY SHENDRYN *is not
looking, opens his coat, and taking out the locket shows it to*
BLANCHE, *and whispers*) Do you remember the night we
parted ?

BLANCHE. Yes.

LADY S. (*looking round*) Blanche, dear, are you not cold
out there ?

BLANCHE. No ; quite warm, I assure you.

CHAL. Oh, they are quite warm—that's the warmest
corner in the hut.

ANGUS. You remember it ?

BLANCHE. Yes.

> *Enter* SERGEANT *with order book, which he gives to*
> ANGUS. *He expresses surprise at seeing* LADIES.
> CHALCOT *comes* L. *of* ANGUS. ANGUS *takes sword
> and belt from barrel* R.

LADY S.   ⎫
BLANCHE.   ⎬ Sergeant Jones !
MARY.   ⎭

ANGUS. (*aside to* CHALCOT) To the front ! (*to* BLANCHE,
seeing she has observed paper) So Miss Featherstonhaugh
wears green, does she ? (*buckling on sword*) I'm afraid that
I must leave you.

BLANCHE. Must you ?

ANGUS. Yes.

BLANCHE. On duty ?

ANGUS. Yes.

BLANCHE. Shall you be back soon ?

ANGUS. I hope so. Good day, Miss Netley. Good day,
Lady Shendryn, for the present. (*pause. To* BLANCHE,
after shaking hands with CHALCOT) I hope to have the
pleasure of seeing you again.

SERGEANT *opens door.* *Exit* ANGUS, D.L. *The* " Chanson " *is played as a march by* BAND *outside ; it grows more and more distant. No snow or wind here.*

BLANCHE. What band is that playing ? (*rising*)

SER. The band of " Ours."

BLANCHE. I think I've heard that march before.

SER. (R. *corner*) We call it Captain MacAlister's march. He had it arranged by the bandmaster. They often play it.

(LADY SHENDRYN *speaks aside to* SERGEANT)

CHAL. (*at fire, observing* BLANCHE, *sings*)

" And a cup of cold pisen lay close by her side,

(BLANCHE *sits end of table*)

" And a billy-dow, which said as how for Villikins she died.'

	LADY S.	MARY.	
O	Q	Q	O Q CHALCOT.
SERGEANT.			BLANCHE.

SER. Thank you, my lady—I'm glad to hear the missus is well, and the children—and the twins—and the new one which I haven't seen.

MARY. There's a letter I promised Mrs. Jones to give you if I met you (*giving it*) I saw them all the day before we left. The twins have grown wonderfully.

SER. Have they now ? Clever little things ! Grown ! —So like 'em—just the sort of thing they would do !

BLANCHE. (*rising, sighing*) Has Captain Mac—Has the regiment to go far ?

SER. " Ours," mum ?

BLANCHE. Yes.

SER. We're going to the front, into——

CHAL. (R.C., *coming down, and crossing behind,* R. *Interrupting quickly*) To parade.

SER. (*catching his eye*) Yes ; to parade.

LADY S. (C. *advancing,* C.) Will Sir Alexander be there ?

SER. (R.) Yes, my lady. He wouldn't let the regiment go into——

CHAL. (*interrupting*) On parade.

SER. On parade—without him.

LADY S. Can we see them ? (*a pause.* CHALCOT *and* SERGEANT *look at each other embarrassed*) I mean, can we not see the regiment parading ? You can't escort us on account of your wound ; but the Sergeant could conduct us to some place where we could see them, could he not ?

BLANCHE. Oh!—I should so like that!

CHAL. Well—if you insist—Sergeant, take the three ladies to the——

LADY S. No. Miss Netley can remain here—she is such a bad walker.

MARY. No, I'm not. *(pouting)*

LADY S. We shall not be gone long.

LADY SHENDRYN *and* BLANCHE *put on wraps;* MARY *assisting* LADY SHENDRYN.

CHAL. You'll come back to dinner?

LADY S. Yes. Miss Netley will perhaps be kind enough to assist in its preparation. We shall most likely be back before Sir Alexander or the Captain.

CHAL. Most likely. *(opens door)* It's not snowing, but you'd better stay here.

LADY S. No, no.

BLANCHE. We've made up our minds.

CHAL. I understand feminine discipline too well to make another observation. *(Exeunt* LADY SHENDRYN *and* BLANCHE) Sergeant, take the ladies to Flagstaff Hill. Good-bye, for the present; and *(aside to* SERGEANT), not a word about the action! *(*SERGEANT *exits)*

CHAL. This is a singular *tête-à-tête*—shut up alone with this girl. I always hated her in England! Now I like her very much! Somehow, the air of the Crimea seems to improve everything. Everything has improved since I've had something to do—and a bayonet in the calf of my leg.

MARY. *(at fire,* L.) Now, Mr. Chalcot, what are we to do for dinner?

CHAL. (R.) Dinner?

MARY. (L. *attending to fire,* L.) Yes; of course I must obey Lady Shendryn's orders.

CHAL. Orders! *(aside)* Lady Shendryn behaves like a perfect brute to this girl. Such a charming girl, too— *(aloud)* About dinner—shall we have a set dinner?

MARY. If you like; I'm a capital cook.

CHAL. Are you?

MARY. Yes.

CHAL. What an accomplished creature it is!

MARY. In my poor father's time, I was housekeeper. He wasn't very rich; but he always said his dinners were excellent; and he ought to know, for he was a clergyman.

(goes up, L.)

CHAL. (*aside*) A housekeeper, too—ah! (*aloud*) Well, now for this dinner—this grand dinner; to begin at the beginning.

MARY. (*coming down*) Soup?

CHAL. We've got no soup.

MARY. Fish?

CHAL. We're out of fish.

MARY. (L.) Entrées?

CHAL. (R.) I don't think we'll have any entrées to-day.

MARY. The joint?

CHAL. There we are strong. (*crossing to fire, L., singing Barcarole, "Masaniello"*) See the mutton brightly—brightly burning.   (MARY *crosses to* R. *of table*)

MARY. And the vegetables?

CHAL. *Pommes-de-terre au naturel, dans leur jackets.*

(pointing to potatoes)

MARY. Game?

CHAL. No game.

MARY. Sweets—ices?

CHAL. Lots of ice outside.

MARY. Puddings?

CHAL. Unheard-of luxuries

MARY. Have you no flour?

CHAL. A barrelful.   (*pointing,* R.)

MARY. Any preserves?

CHAL. Lots—pots!

MARY. I can make a pudding.

CHAL. (*lost in astonishment*) No!

MARY. I can—a roley-poley.

CHAL. A roley-poley pudding in the Crimea! It's a fairy-tale!   (*they clear table*)

MARY. Now get the flour.

> *Turns up sleeves of her dress.* CHALCOT, *waiting on her with wonder and admiration, gets flour from barrel,* R.

MARY. I declare! here's some paste ready-made; I shall want a paste-board. (*takes up straw from floor and rubs table*) That won't do. What have you there?

CHAL. The lid of the barrel?

MARY. That'll do. Now I shall want an apron.

CHAL. An apron? (*looks round*) I know (*crosses,* L.) I've got an apron. This will do. It belonged to a pioneer of ours; he was shot at the Alma. (MARY *shrinks*) But he didn't wear it that day.

(*helps her on with pioneer's apron. She mixes pudding*)

MARY. (*mixing pudding*) Oh! I forgot.

CHAL. What?

MARY. I shall want a rolling-pin.

CHAL. Rolling pin? (*looks about—then under table, sees small barrel—takes it up and rolls it up and down table. MARY laughs but rejects it—in putting it down again CHALCOT knocks three-legged stool over—after a little difficulty succeeds in pulling one of the legs out and brings it sharply down on pudding. MARY rolls pudding, &c.*) Beauty, accomplishments, amiability, no mother, and roley-poley pudding! (*approaching her*)

MARY. My hands are all over flour! You mustn't talk to the cook. Now, the preserves!

CHAL. (*crossing, L.*) Here. (CHALCOT *gets preserves*)

MARY. What's this?

CHAL. Strawberry.

MARY. Ah! I like strawberry. That'll do. (*smells it*) Take it away. Good gracious, what's that! (*both smell it; knock heads together; business*) Why, that's varnish!

CHAL. It's that damned ointment! (*puts it in cupboard, gets another pot, breaks paper, smells it, tastes it*) I think you'll find that right.

MARY. Now the spoon—*the* wonderful spoon.

CHAL. Our piece of family plate.

> *Producing spoon from pocket.*—MARY *puts preserves in pudding.*

CHAL. With such a woman as that to sweeten one's path through life—to put—metaphorically speaking—the preserves into one's pudding—that's woman's mission.

MARY. Oh—I forgot!

CHAL. What?

MARY. A pudding-cloth. What shall we do for a pudding-cloth?

CHAL. Won't the leather apron do? (MARY *shakes her head*) Then I'm afraid our resources have broken down in the moment of victory! To think that a pudding—and such a pudding—should break down for the sake of a paltry pudding-cloth. (*after a pause*) I have it!

MARY. What?

CHAL. I received a packet of linen a month ago from England. I've never opened it. (*opens portmanteau, and takes out towel*) Eureka! I have found it! A towel!—and here have I been wiping my face with straw for the last three weeks!

MARY. Now I want a bit of string.

CHAL. (*getting string from cupboard*) Here you are.

MARY. Now get me a saucepan.

(CHALCOT *gets saucepan and puts it on table*)

MARY. Does it boil?

CHAL. (*taking lid off and throwing it on floor*) Yes, I'll take my oath it boils.

MARY. (*ties up the ends of pudding cloth, puts it in saucepan*) Now get the lid.

CHALCOT *gets lid from floor, puts it first on stool, then on table, and then on to saucepan.*

MARY. Now then stand it on the fire, just there in the right hand corner.

Pointing to fire with leg of stool, CHALCOT *puts saucepan on fire, offers it to* MARY, *who puts pudding in it, and places it in saucepan,* CHALCOT *burning his hands with lid.*

MARY. The mutton's getting on beautifully.

Pokes fire with leg of stool, and as she turns, hits CHALCOT's *leg.* CHALCOT *staggers to small barrel,* L. *of table, down stage.*

MARY. I have hurt your wound!—pray, forgive me!

CHAL. It's nothing. Do it again. I like it.

MARY. I'm very, very sorry.

CHAL. Don't mention it—hurt me again! But speak in that tone—and look in that way again!

MARY. Shall I loosen the bandages?

(*kneels,* L. *of* CHALCOT)

CHAL. If you like; but you can't fasten them up again.

MARY. I can.

CHAL. With what?

MARY. A hair-pin.

(*takes one from her hair and fastens bandages*)

CHAL. Miss Netley—Mary— (*taking her hand*)

MARY. My hands are all over flour!

CHAL. Never mind—I like them all the better. You don't dislike me—do you, Mary?

MARY. Oh, Mr. Chalcot!

CHAL. Not very much, I hope? I've always loved you —even when we used to quarrel. May I trust that some day I may not be indifferent to you ; and, if so, that I may make you my own—my wife! (*she turns away*) Don't let me frighten you. I won't tell the Colonel—I mean Lady Shendryn! I know you can't love me now—but I'll try to deserve your love : and perhaps if I try hard—and I will —I may succeed. Sebastopol isn't taken in a day ; and you'll let me try—won't you, Sebastopol?—I mean Mary?

(with great agitation)

MARY. Mr. Chalcot, you know I am a poor dependent.

CHAL. That's the very reason! I couldn't love a girl with money.

MARY. A man of your position—your property——

CHAL. For Heaven's sake don't raise up the dismal spectre of my money! Don't let cash forbid the banns! If I am rich, don't reproach me with it. I don't deserve it—it isn't my fault! I never made a penny in my life—I never had the talent. Only say you will be mine!

(bugle call without)

LADY S. Mr. Chalcot! <div align="right">(<i>outside</i>)</div>

Enter LADY SHENDRYN, quickly.

CHAL. (*kissing* MARY, *who rises quickly, going up,* L. *To* LADY SHENDRYN) All right. The mutton's doing beautifully.

LADY S. (*crosses,* L.) They're fighting!—And my husband is in the action! I—I—I—— Oh! I don't know what I'm doing! Give me your hand!

- (CHALCOT supports her)

Enter BLANCHE, hurriedly.

BLANCHE. (*to* MARY) Mary—he's fighting! He's gone to battle—with two or three thousand others! I heard the officers who galloped by say there was an engagement! He's fighting! (CHALCOT *gathers things on table*)

LADY S. (L.C.) Who?—Sir Alexander?

BLANCHE. No ; Angus.

LADY S. Angus! What, then—do you love him?

BLANCHE. (*crossing,* R.C.) Yes, I do ; and I don't care who knows it.

LADY S. Well, my child, I don't blame you. We can't help these things. (*kisses her*)

BLANCHE. Perhaps, at this very moment—even now, as I speak—a bullet may have reached his heart.

LADY S. Oh!

Both WOMEN *horrified at the picture.* LADY
SHENDRYN *and* BLANCHE *pull down* CHALCOT
to C., *and hurt his leg.* CHALCOT *has spoon in
his hand.* LADY SHENDRYN, R. ; BLANCHE, L.C. ;
CHALCOT, L. ; MARY, *up stage.*

LADY S. Do you think he will come back ?

BLANCHE. Will he return ?

CHAL. Of course he will ! no doubt of it ! How the
devil should I know ?

LADY S.   } *(together)* If he should not !
BLANCHE. }

CHAL. But he will—they will—they never do get killed
in " Ours !"

BLANCHE. (L.C.) Oh, Lady Shendryn ! I'm so sorry for
you.

> *Crossing to her, and kissing her.* MARY *has dropped
> down, to* R. *corner.*

LADY S. (L.) And I for you.   *(kissing her)*

> CHALCOT *makes an offer to kiss* MARY. MARY *puts
> apron over* CHALCOT'S *head.*

MARY. (R., *repulsing him*) I'm so glad you are not
fighting !

CHAL. (R.) Are you ! *(pointing to* LADY SHENDRYN *and*
BLANCHE) It's wrong of me to be so happy, isn't it.

> *(*CHALCOT *and* MARY *go up)*

LADY S. Think dear ; it's my husband !

BLANCHE. And the man I love !

LADY S. And we parted in anger !

> *Distant cannon and bugle calls heard throughout fol-
> lowing scene.*

BLANCHE. And he never knew how much I loved him !
Oh ! if I could see him again !

> *(knock heard at* D.L. *All start)*

BLANCHE. } *(together)* { Perhaps Angus.
LADY S. }   { If it is he !

> CHALCOT *opens door, and is met by* PRINCE PEROVSKY,
> *who wears full Russian uniform, orders, followed
> by* SAMPREY.

BLANCHE. } Prince Perovsky ?
LADY S. }

PRINCE. *(entering)* Miss Haye, Lady Shendryn.

LADY S. You here, prince ?

PRINCE. Yes—a prisoner—fortune of war.

> SAMPREY *enters.* CHALCOT *assists* PRINCE *to take off cloak.*

SAMP. (R.) Pardon me, Lady Shendryn, I have the honour to be the prince's escort. Knowing that you were acquainted, I took the liberty——

LADY S. Sir Alexander——

BLANCHE. Captain MacAlister——

SAMP. (*very gravely*) Are in the engagement. I did not see their regiment—I could not for the smoke. Excuse me, I must go. Prince, you have given me your parole. (PRINCE *bows*) I have the honour—(*presenting him with his sword.* PRINCE *bows, takes sword, and sheaths it*)

> (*Exit* SAMPREY)

> BLANCHE, *sits,* L., *with her face on table.* CHALCOT, *up* L., *with* LADY SHENDRYN *and* MARY.

PRINCE. Pray, ladies, don't be alarmed ; it is not a battle—a mere affair of outposts.

LADY S. Oh, Prince, I am beyond comfort !

> LADY SHENDRYN *goes to fire.* MARY *sits* C., *by stove.* CHALCOT *talking to her, back to audience.* PRINCE *goes to* BLANCHE, *who is sitting* R. *corner of table.*

PRINCE. (L.C. *to* BLANCHE) These are strange circumstances under which to meet. You see I am always a captive in your presence.

BLANCHE. Oh, Prince, to think that battle is raging so near us !

PRINCE. Be under no alarm ; my presence——

BLANCHE. It is not that, but——

PRINCE. You fear for those dear to you ?

BLANCHE. Yes.

PRINCE. Sir Alexander ?

BLANCHE. Yes.

PRINCE. And perhaps for some other ?

BLANCHE. Yes—my cousin Angus.

PRINCE. The young gentleman I met in London ?

> (BLANCHE *assents*)

BLANCHE. If he should be killed ?

PRINCE. *Hélas !* Fortune of war !

BLANCHE. Or taken prisoner ?

PRINCE. As I am. He would be treated with the respect and honour due to the sacred name of enemy.

Reassure yourself, my dear Miss Haye; your young soldier is sheltered by your love. (BLANCHE *goes up to* MARY, LADY SHENDRYN *drops down to seat* L. *of table,* CHALCOT *goes to fire-place*) Oh, Youth! Inestimable, priceless treasure! Lost for ever! To be a *sous-lieutenant,* and beloved as he is—psha! Am I a child, to cry for the moon? *Pat si bête!* (*goes up,* R.C., *to* BLANCHE)

CHAL. (*coming down to* LADY SHENDRYN, L.) If you see Sir Alexander again, of which I have but little doubt, I think what I am going to tell you will make you happy with him ever after. I am aware that you were jealous of him——

LADY S. Not without cause. Even years ago I had cause.

CHAL. The slightest possible. Since then he has been true and faithful. I know, for I was in his confidence. Sir Alexander's money used to go mysteriously. Do you know where it went?

LADY S. Yes; to some woman.

CHAL. No.

> BLANCHE *seated up stage,* R.C.; PRINCE *near her;* MARY *down,* R.

LADY S. To whom then?
CHAL. To your brother Percy.
LADY S. Percy!
CHAL. To save him—to save you and his family from dishonour. Five years ago Sir Alick discovered, by his banking account, that Percy had forged his name!

LADY S. What!
CHAL. You remember the night that Sir Alick left England, when Kelsey, the lawyer, sent him a letter, and he sent for me?

LADY S. And he withdrew £1,500 from my account.
CHAL. Yes; for fresh bills forged by Percy.
LADY S. (*hiding her face*) And he concealed this from me?
CHAL. Because he preferred to bear the brunt of your suspicions, rather than let you know the extent of your brother's——conduct. There is a letter, which in case of accidents, he gave to me for you; in it is contained the half of the letter you did not see, that Kelsey sent him. (MARY *goes up to back*) You need not read it now. All that I tell you is true. Sir Alick is a gallant officer, and a noble gentleman (*with emotion, then resuming his ordinary manner*), and come what may, he's sure to bring the regiment out of it creditably. So when you meet, learn to know him better.

LADY S. When we meet—oh! this suspense is terrible. Any certainty—even of the worst!

Enter SERGEANT.

SER. (R.) If you please, sir—the Colonel——

(LADY SHENDRYN *rises*)

MARY. (*running between them*) Hush! (BLANCHE *rises*)

LADY S. (L.) You need not speak—I know all!—He is dead!　　　　　(*a pause.* SERGEANT *astonished*)

BLANCHE. (C.) And Captain MacAlister?

SER. (*confounded*) Captain——　.

(BLANCHE *covers her face with one hand*)

BLANCHE. You may tell me—I can bear it.

Enter ANGUS.

ANGUS. Didn't I hear my name?

(*going to* BLANCHE *and throwing cap away*)

BLANCHE. (*rushing to him*) Oh! (*restraining herself*) I'm so glad to see you back!

CHAL. All right?

ANGUS. Quite.

BLANCHE. Unhurt?

ANGUS. Yes.

(*a pause. They look sympathetically at* LADY SHENDRYN)

CHAL. And Sir Alexander?

ANGUS. Came with me. He'll be here directly.

LADY S. (*rising*) Here! Not killed?

ANGUS. No.

LADY S. Alive?

ANGUS. Yes.　　　　　(*all look at* SERGEANT)

SER. That's just what I was going to say, only this young lady stopped me. (*all go up but* LADY SHENDRYN)

LADY S. Oh—my husband! (SIR ALEXANDER *appears at door*) If I could only see you, to kneel at your feet, and ask pardon for having so wronged your noble nature! At the very time I reproached you for ruining your fortune for another, to have borne with me for the sake of the honour of my family!

SIR A. (*advancing*) Diana! These expressions of affection——

LADY S. (C.) Alexander. (*embracing; about to kneel, he prevents her*) I know all.

SIR A. (R.) All what? (LADY SHENDRYN *shows him*

letter) Chalcot gave you this ? (LADY SHENDRYN *assents*)
Hugh ? What right had you to——
CHAL. (*coming down,* L.) None, whatever. That is
why I did it. (*goes up*)
LADY S. Forgive me!
SIR A. (R.C.) Forget it, Diana, and——
(*staggers, and nearly falls*)
LADY S. What's the matter ?
SIR A. Nothing. I——
ANGUS. (L.) Nothing. Only a slight wound.

> *All down stage but* PRINCE. LADY SHENDRYN *attends
> to* SIR ALEXANDER.

MARY. (R., *to* SERGEANT) Why didn't you say that he
was wounded ?
SER. (R.) Just what I was going to do, miss, only you
stopped me.
SIR A. It is but a scratch—the affair was but a skirmish.
The great event is postponed again. I came here to con
gratulate Angus.
CHAL. On what ?
SIR A. (*whispering, so that* PRINCE *may not hear*) He has
taken a Russian colour.
CHAL. (L.) Bravo, Angus! My luck; I am out of all
these good things. (*goes up to* PRINCE)
MARY. (*to* SERGEANT) Why didn't he mention his cap-
turing the colours ? (*all whispering*)
SER. We never do mention those sort of things in
"Ours." (*goes up, and takes off overcoat.* MARY *goes up,* R.)
PRINCE. (*coming down,* R.C.) Sir Alexander, I trust that
your hurt is but slight; wounded yourself, you will have
more compassion upon others.
SIR A. (R., *surprised*) Prince!
PRINCE. (C.) Permit me, in the hour of my adversity, to
point out to you that those two young people love each other.
Don't be surprised. Battle elevates as well as brutalises us.
I withdraw my pretensions; I am too old.
BLANCHE. (L.C., *overhearing*) Prince!
SIR A. But Angus is so poor!
PRINCE. No man is poor while he is young. Youth is
wealth—inestimable and irretrievable.
SIR A. } (*together*) { Well, but——
LADY S. } { My dear Blanche——
BLANCHE. It's no use arguing, because I won't have any

body else ; and if you don't consent, I'll wait till I'm twenty one.   You'll wait till I'm twenty-one, won't you, Angus?

SIR A. Well—well—we'll see about it.

BLANCHE. When?

SIR A. When?   When the war is over.

> SIR ALEXANDER *and* LADY SHENDRYN *go up stage·*
> *He sits.*

BLANCHE. What a horrid thing is war !

ANGUS. (L.C.) Prince, how can I express my deep sense of obligation?

PRINCE. By silence.

> *All go up.* SERGEANT *at fire, reading his letter.*
> *Tramp of* SOLDIERS *heard without.*

ANGUS. (*turns left about and runs against* CHALCOT *who has lid of barrel (flour) in his hand.* CHALCOT *takes him to* C., *and whispers*) You engaged to Mary? By what means?

CHAL. Roley-poley pudding—boiling in the pot.

> CHALCOT *and* ANGUS *go to barrel* R., CHALCOT *puts flour pan and lid down and crosses to* MARY, ANGUS *to* BLANCHE.

BLANCHE. (*aside to* MARY) You engaged to Chalcot? But he's such a little man.

MARY. You know I've no money—and I couldn't expect so big a husband as you.   (*they go up*)

ANGUS. (*crosses from* R. *to* R. *of table*) The place is not the same now you are in it, and that you are to be mine. You illuminate it—you're a chandelier !

BLANCHE. Chandelier, indeed !   A pretty compliment— all cut glass and wire !

ANGUS. Lit up by love !

CHAL. (*at fire*) The mutton's done !

> *General movement.   They place seats, &c.   All on the alert, as at a picnic.   Each person, except* LADY SHENDRYN, SIR ALEXANDER, *and* PRINCE, *has hold of either plates, or a chair, or a saucepan, &c.* CHALCOT *places mutton on table, which has been laid by* SERGEANT *and* MARY *and others.*

CHAL. *Les reines sont servies.*

> (SERGEANT *waits at table*)
> *The "Chanson" march played, piano, without.* MEN *heard marching.   Cheers.* ANGUS *opens door.*

LADY S. What's that?

SIR A. The Russian colours. (*whispering, and pointing to* ANGUS) "Ours!"

MARY. What troops are those?

CHAL. (*sitting on floor*) "Ours!"

BLANCHE. And what are we? (*to* ANGUS)

ANGUS. (*her hands in his, leaning over her*) "Ours!"

CURTAIN.

PLAY.

AN ORIGINAL COMEDY,

IN FOUR ACTS.

BY

T. W. ROBERTSON,

AUTHOR OF

"Caste," "A Breach of Promise," "School," "M.P.," "Birth,"
"David Garrick," "The Ladies' Battle," "The Nightingale,"
"Ours," "Progress," "Row in the House," "Society,"
"Dreams," "War," "Home," "Faust and Marguerite," "My
Wife's Diary," "Noemie," "Two Gay Deceivers," "Jocrisse
the Juggler," "Not at all Jealous," "Star of the North,"
"Birds of Prey," "Peace at any Price, "Half Caste,"
"Ernestine," "Chevalier de St. George," "Cantab," "Clock-
maker's Hat," "Duke's Daughter," "Sea of Ice," &c., &c.

———————

LONDON:
SAMUEL FRENCH.
PUBLISHER,
89, STRAND.

NEW YORK:
SAMUEL FRENCH & SON,
PUBLISHERS,
28, WEST 23RD STREET.

K K

PLAY.

COMEDY IN FOUR ACTS.

(Produced at Prince of Wales' Theatre, London, Feb. 15th, 1868.)

CAST OF CHARACTERS.

The Graf von Staufenberg... ...	Mr. H. W. Montgomery.
The Hon. Bruce Fanquehere ...	Mr. Hare.
Captain Stockstadt	Mr. Sydney.
Mr. Bodmin Todder	Mr. Blakeley.
The Chevalier Browne	Mr. S. Bancroft.
Frank Price	Mr. H. J. Montague.
A Croupier	M. Silveyra.
A Waiter	
Rosie	Miss Marie Wilton.
Amanda	Miss Lydia Foote.
Mrs. Kinpeck	Mrs. Leigh Murray.

Act I.—Der Brunnen (Morning).—*Garden.*

Act II.—Das Alte Schloss (Afternoon).—*Ruins of an old Castle.*

Act III.—Scene 1.—Der Vorplatz (Evening).—*Corridor.*

„ Scene 2.—Der Spiel Saal (Night).—*Gambling Saloon.*

Act IV.—Der Kursaal and Kurgarten (The Next Day) —*Garden.* Scene.—Germany.

Modern Costumes. Time of Representation, two hours and three-quarters.

PLAY.

ACT I.

SCENE—DER BRUNNEN.—*Gardens. Chestnut-trees—planted to form part of a square, open to audience, and open at back. A well with railings round it, and steps to descend, L. and R. Landscape cloth at back. Two garden chairs R. and L., second and third entrances. Two small round tables R. and L., first entrances, and stacks of chairs by them. Time, 7 a.m. Omnes in morning costume. Band plays chorale outside. People promenading under trees. Invalids, &c., some coming up steps from fountain; some seated : general movement. Curtain slow on picture.*

Enter the Chevalier BROWNE, *smoking cigarette, on last bars of music.*

BROWNE. (*sitting* L. *of table,* R.) Kellner! (*Enter* WAITER *from hotel,* R. 1 E.) Oh! you is it? A cup of coffee, and some cognac. (*Exit* WAITER R. 1 E.) So, virtuous Schwalbad turns out early and tastes the waters, and listens to the band. But the princes—the proscrits, and the punters know better. They lie in bed and meditate over martingals and a cup of coffee. (*re-enter* WAITER, *with coffee and cognac,* R. 1 E. *Exeunt* VISITORS, PEASANTS, *&c.* BROWNE *rising*) It's odd, but that little girl still runs in my head. I wish I could run in her heart! Strange for a man of five-and-thirty, past his salad and sentimental days. Five-and-thirty! Why, I'm five-and-eighty perhaps; that accounts for it. I am getting into my second childhood! Well, I'll lay long odds not to be unhappier than my first—— (*music. Enter* BRUCE FANQUEHERE, *sits* R. *of table*) Here's papa! You're early this morning. (FANQUEHERE *sits* L. *of table,* R.) How are you?

FAN. Queer!—Kellner, cognac!   *Exit* WAITER, R.

BRO. Any news?

FAN. Post isn't in. I had a letter last night, and last Saturday's "Saddle."   (*giving him a newspaper*)

BRO. Anything in it?

FAN. No! Lord Lapworth's selling his stud.

BRO. Hard up?

FAN. No! soft down. He's married—(*re-enter* WAITER *with tray, and decanter, glass, &c.;* WAITER *pours out a nip of brandy in tumbler and is going.* FANQUEHERE *calls him back*) Kellner! (*takes decanter from him, and pours a quantity into tumbler, and mixes with water. Exit* WAITER, R.I.E.)—pot o' money! and, I hear, a nice girl.

BRO. Apropos, how is mademoiselle?

(reads paper carefully)

FAN. Quite well—she only got a wetting.

BRO. How was it?

FAN. She was fishing. A carp tickled her hook, she got excited, put one foot on the gunwale of the boat, so she tells me, and over she went. (*rising*) I'm glad I wasn't there. I should have gone cranky. Poor Fred's only legacy, that dear little Rosie! All he left behind him, except debts. (*sits again*) You know the story? How father went to the bad, the same year that I did—"Diadasti's" year: the family wouldn't stand it any longer. Poor Fred went to the worse, died at Boulogne, where he was staying under a temporary cloud. (*in jerks*) Just before he went, he said, "Uncle Bruce, there's the baby—don't let those damned people"—he meant the family, he always called them the damned people—"don't let them get hold of her,—or they'll teach her family prayers, and to forget her father." Well, I went tick with the undertaker, and gave Fred a handsome funeral—took Rosie and reared her from a foal—I mean from a baby. By gad! that child, Browne (*with enthusiasm*) is the most wonderful child that ever—I dry-nursed her.

BRO. But how came young Price to fish her out?

FAN. He was on the island—saw her fall in—and dived after her like an otter. Ever been otter hunting? Splendid sport! He brought her to the shore, and carried her to the Teich haus.

BRO. Very nice, indeed of him.

FAN. What—to fish her up? Not at all—one of the Humane Society's hooks would have done that much. What annoyed me most was that she should have been saved by him.

BRO. Whom?

FAN. Hook—

BRO. Price?

FAN. I mean Price.

Bro. What is there against him ?

Fan. Don't you know who he is ?

Bro. Yes ; his name is Price—of Price, Dinbrook and Co. Young, rich, and—a fool. Grouse all over, and our game.

Fan. My dislike to him is hereditary. He's the grandson of that Price who contested the Borough with my grandfather's nominee—and won the election—which nearly ruined us. Next year, my grandfather bought up the Borough—the village I mean—and two years after the Reform Bill passed—the Borough was disfranchised—ruined us quite ! ..e ! confound Price !

Br{ .Vhy not rook him, as a return ?

Fan. So we will : so we will—Caro Cavaliero Bruno. He's a good-natured fool ! He's not an amusing scoundrel.

Bro. Hush ! here he is.

Enter FRANK PRICE, L. 3 E., *dressed in the height of Spa fashion—down* C.

Price (C.) Ah ! good. morning, Browne ! How de do ? (*sees* FANQUEHERE *confused*) How do you do this morning, Mr. Fanquehere ? (*going up*)

Bro. Going ?

Price. Yes ; you know I'm taking the waters ; and when you're taking the waters—(*his manner becomes confused*) you must walk about ; so the doctor says (*going —returns*) Miss Fanquehere quite recovered her——

Fan. Dip in the water ? Quite ! thanks.

(*lighting cigar*)

Price. (*confused*) I hope to have the pleasure of——

(*band plays German Military March*)

Enter CAPTAIN STOCKSTADT, *and the* GRAF VON STAUFENBERG, *from* L.U.E.

Bro. Good morning, Count.—Good morning, Captain

(*rises, crosses to* L.C. *They salute*)

Graf. (*down* L., *with strong German accent*) How do you do, "Illustrated London News."

Price (C.) What does he mean ?

Bro. (L.C.) It's the only English the Graf knows, and he makes use of it on every occasion. . Let me introduce you. Permit me to present to you, Graf, my friend, Mr. Frank Price. The Graf von Staufenberg. Captain Stockstadt—Mr. Frank Price.

GRAF. How do you do, " Illustrated London News."

PRICE. It's rather a limited vocabulary.

BRO. Don't you speak German ?

(GRAF VON STAUFENBERG *crosses to* FANQUEHERE, R.C.)

PRICE. No; but I can answer him in his own language "Saturday Review"; "Pall Mall Gazette"; "Times"; "Telegraph," second edition.

(GRAF VON STAUFENBERG *goes up and off* R.U.C.)

FAN. (*smiling*) Ha! Ha! He's not such a fool! He's an amusing scoundrel!

PRICE. (C.) Don't Captain—what's his name?

BRO. (L.C.) Stockstadt.

PRICE. Stockstadt—speak English ?

BRO. Not a word. He speaks French. You speak French, don't you ?

PRICE. Not a syllable. I'm an awful idiot! and· the worst is, I know it.

BRO. Here's Mrs. Kinpeck coming.

PRICE. (*moving up stage*) Then I shall go.

BRO. Are you afraid she'll borrow of you ?

PRICE. (*returning*) No; I'm afraid she'll pay me. Every time she sees me, she asks for the loan of ten florins; directly she's got 'em, she goes away. It's very cheap. I don't think ten florins could be laid out to greater advantage.

BRO. Mr. Bodmin Todder does not think so.

PRICE. No; he spends his money on himself—such an unworthy object—that is, I think so, in my idiotic way. They hate each other.

BRO. Mrs. Kinpeck and Todder ?

PRICE. Yes! You see Todder's a rich bachelor, and Mrs. K. is a poor widow. Mrs. K. spends her little income at the tables, and she'd like to have Todder's savings to speculate with. (*indicating tables*) Todder won't have her, and Mrs. K. considers that an unpardonable insult. (*advances, confused, to* FANQUEHERE) I—hope—Miss Fanquehere—that Miss Fanquehere has quite—recovered ?

FAN. From her wetting ? Quite; thank you again. We shall be happy to see you at any time that you may be passing, Mr. Hook.

BRO. Price.

FAN. I beg pardon. Price.

PRICE. (*overcome*) Oh! thank you, I—talking of water —time for my second tumbler! So good morning. (*awkwardly, aside*) Oh! if he only knew——

Sees MRS. KINPECK, *and makes a bolt down to the fountain. Band plays.* STOCKSTADT *rises and goes to well;* BROWNE *goes up stage with him. Enter* MRS. KINPECK, R. 2 E., *at the same time enter* TODDER, L. 3 E.; *they meet and shake hands, affectionately.*

TOD. How do you do, Mrs. Kinpeck?

MRS. K. (R.C.) Thank you, dear Mr. Bodmin Todder, quite well. How are you?

TOD. Thank you, Mrs. Kinpeck. (*sighing*)—Dyspep—dyspep——

MRS. K. You shouldn't eat so much.

TOD. I hardly eat anything, Mrs. Kinpeck.

MRS K. I thought not; you look half-starved.

(*with smelling bottle*)

TOD. I knew you'd say that; you are always so kind. Did you play last night?

MRS. K. I did.

TOD. And—I suppose—lost?

MRS. K. Every florin I had about me.

TOD.. That wasn't much—(*aside*) Had her there!

MRS. K. (*going round table* R., *sits* R.) The old wretch! with his thousands!

TOD. (*aside*) Pauper! pauper!

(*tumbles over* FANQUEHERE)

FAN. (*irritably*) Now then.

TOD. You were in the way, sir.

BRO. (*coming down* L.C., *with a significant motion to* FANQUEHERE) Allow me to introduce you to Mr. Bruce Fanquehere. The Honourable Bruce Fanquehere.

(BROWNE *goes up stage, reading paper*)

TOD. (*with servility*) Honourable! I beg your pardon, sir. I did not see your legs—if I might be allowed that strong expression. I hope I didn't hurt you?

MRS. K. (*aside, seated* R.) Sneak! Because the old brute's an Honourable! Hasn't a penny.

FAN. (*to whom* BROWNE *has whispered*) Don't mention it, Mr.——

TOD. (L.C.) Todder. Bodmin Todder, of Bodmin. Do you know Bodmin, sir?

FAN. No, nor Todder, until this present moment, when I have the pleasure——

TOD. (*flattered*) Oh! I was christened Bodmin because

I was born in Bodmin ; one of the most disagreeable towns
to be born in you can imagine.

MRS. K. I should think so.

TOD. I hate the place. I left it at an early age.

MRS. K. Happy Bodmin !

TOD. (*wincing*) Ugh !

FAN. Your name is familiar to me. Have you ever been
in Parliament ?

TOD. No.

MRS. K. Dear Mr. Bruce, you have seen his name in the
advertisements in the newspapers. "Use only Bodmin
Todder's Original Patent Starch." "Do you like a stiff,
clean collar ? Use Bodmin Tod—— "

TOD. (*wincing*) Um ! Yes, Mr. Bruce Fanquehere, as
my dear friend, Mrs. Kinpeck—(*aside*) curse her !—(*aloud*)
says, I have made my fortune by starch. I'm not ashamed
of it. I am proud of it.   (*goes up*)

MRS. K. Stuff !   (*smelling bottle*)

FAN. Sir ! It is a thing to be proud of. (*declaiming*)
The British merchant who founds a colossal fortune, forwards
his country's interests, and benefits his fellow man by means
of——

MRS. K. The wash-tub.

TOD. Starch !

FAN. Starch—is one of the noblest—exemplars—of a—
commerce—nationality, and national commerce—(*aside*)
Confound it ! Those are the sort of lies I don't tell well.

TOD. My dear Mr. Bruce. Yes ; I worked hard. I made
my fortune, but I lost my stomach. It's gone !

FAN. Gone ? Good heavens ! Where ?

TOD. I mean my digestion. I worked too hard. Business
is incompatible with good digestion. My doctor told me so.
I resolved to sacrifice myself on the altar of commerce. I
grew rich and dyspeptic. I am proud of it ! Proud of
both, sir ; proud of both.   (*as he passes up to* BROWNE)

> FANQUEHERE *sits* L. 2 E. MRS. KINPECK *goes up
> and converses with* FANQUEHERE. *Enter* FRANK
> PRICE *from fountain, and strolls at back.* MRS.
> KINPECK *leaves* FANQUEHERE *and joins* PRICE.
> *Enter* WAITER, *who removes tray, &c.*

BRO. (*advancing* R., *reading*) No news, but bad news.
I must hedge on the handicap. Eh ! What's this ? (*reads*)
"Death of an eccentric. Mr. Fowler Tredmayne, once so
celebrated on the turf, died at his own residence, in his

seventy-seventh year, on Thursday, the 19th inst. The deceased, who, in the earlier part of his career, lived at an almost prodigal expense, for the last forty years has been considered a miser. His accumulated savings, with the exception of some few legacies, go to the daughter of a favourite niece, Miss Rosie Fanquehere, who, we are informed, is residing abroad." Little Rosie, old Tredmayne's heiress! If I can keep this from old Fan. ! Fanquehere, have you seen this?

FAN. No! I only want to read Strawyard's weekly letter. Done with it? *(holds out hand for paper)*

BRO. *(sits)* In one moment.

(FANQUEHERE *rises, goes up* L.)

BRO. *(cuts out corner of newspaper on table)* He hasn't seen it. *(band plays)* I think the girl likes me. At all events I could make her. But then the other! Oh! what a fool I was to throw away my chances before I knew they would come. *(during this* TODDER *enters* L. 2 E., *meets* MRS. KINPECK, *who is strolling at back; he pretends not to see her, and exits,* R. *to* E.) It's the second wife that is supposed to be injured by the law, and if that engagement for America took her away for only a year—— It's worth the risk! I'll risk it! *(music off. Rises, crosses* L., *gives* FANQUEHERE *the paper)* Rosie is young and impressionable, sick of the society of this worldly, wigged, drinking old roué. The powder's there. *(touching his heart)* If I can but apply the spark. By Jove! she's here! *(OMNES *rise)*

Enter ROSIE, R.U.E. FRANK PRICE *hovers about watching her. Enter* TODDER, R. 2 E.

ROSIE. *(to* FANQUEHERE) Oh! here you are! How d'ye do, everybody? I am so tired, uncle, dear. *(music ceases)*

FAN. My dear, sit down.

(seats her in chair, L. *of* R. *table)*

BRO. *(sits* R. *of* R. *table, near* ROSIE) How are you this morning after your accident? I wish I had had the good fortune to be near the lake.

ROSIE. Why?

BRO. I should have had the happiness of saving you.

(TODDER *and* MRS. KINPECK *sit* L.)

PRICE. *(aside, at back)* There she is! I wish I could speak to her.

(FANQUEHERE *goes up* R., *reading the newspaper)*

TOD. (*to* MRS. KINPECK) Nice girl that. Charming!

MRS. K. (*surveys* ROSIE *through eye-glass*) Um! Yes.

TOD. (L. *of table* L.) You see she has the advantage of youth.

MRS. K. (R. *of* L. *table*) And of good health.

BRO. I couldn't sleep last night, for thinking of you.

ROSIE. Now that is odd! For I dreamt of *you*.

BRO. (*interested*) Indeed!

ROSIE. I dreamt I saw you in church, being married.

BRO. (*aside*) Has she heard? (*aloud*) And who was the bride?

ROSIE. I couldn't see her. She had her white satin back to me.

TOD. (*to* MRS. KINPECK) Her youthful freshness is delightful. I like to watch it. I never like to watch old women.

MRS. K. That's because young women never like to watch you.

PRICE. (*after making several false starts to get at* ROSIE, *and being intercepted by* FANQUEHERE, *who is walking at back, smoking*) Miss Fanquehere—quite recovered from her——

FAN. From her dip in the water? Quite! The child—here she is to answer for herself. (*advances with* PRICE) My dear, thank your deliverer. Here is Mr. Hook.

(*crosses and sits,* R. 1 E.)

ROSIE. (*rising,* R.C.) Mr. Price. (*shakes hands*) How do you do? I know who you are, though we were never introduced, until we met under the water.

PRICE. (C.) Charmed, I'm sure, to make your acquaintance under any water—I mean circumstances.

MRS. K. (*to* TODDER) What is that man Browne looking so disgusted at? (*uses smelling bottle*)

TOD. P'raps he's looking at you! (*aside*) Had her there, I think.

BRO. How was it?

ROSIE. I was fishing, and my float went bob. I knew I had a bite! I grew so excited, I don't know what I did; just as I was going to pull in my line, I saw Mr. Price's face opposite on the island.

PRICE. I was fishing too; and at the same moment *I* had a bite.

BRO. (*sneeringly*) That must have been sympathy.

TOD. (*literally*) No; it must have been—fish.

ROSIE. Just as I had the bite, I felt the bob, and I saw Mr. Price's face——

PRICE. And I saw yours.

ROSIE. All at once, over I went, and in I went, and down I went, didn't I? And you came in after me, didn't you?

PRICE. I did.

BRO. Lucky fellow!

FAN. Very plucky, very plucky indeed!

TOD. But very wet.

MRS. K. But then you see he's young and not a coward.

BRO. And how did you feel when you were under water?

ROSIE. Strange, but not frightened. First of all I wondered why the fish didn't swim round me, and snap at me.

BRO. A charming bait!

ROSIE. I didn't feel that I was drowning. When I touched the ground at the bottom, I didn't lose my confidence, I stayed there for a second, and I wondered when and how I should get up again: then I began to rise, and to feel a sort of pleasant dizziness, and everything grew light, and my face came above the water, and I saw the sky, but only for a second, the water closed over me again, and all was dark; my clothes grew heavy, and I went down down, down, and my thoughts flew back to you, uncle, and to my old nurse, Martha, who is gone; and I wondered if ever I should see you both again; for I forgot that Martha was dead: and I went to the earth again, and in a moment I went up, up, up, and I remembered when I was a little child, and I tried to think of a prayer—when all of a sudden something banged against me, I was seized as by a vice, and I felt a strong arm round me—it pressed me close——

PRICE. (L.C.) Close.

ROSIE. (R.C.) And we cleaved through the thick darkness with amazing swiftness. I knew it was you, I knew the face near mine was the face I had seen upon the island; and all about grew white, and light, and bright, and then —I remember nothing more till I found myself on the couch at the Teich Haus.

FAN. (rises, excited, crosses to PRICE and shakes his hand) Will you come and—(gasping, trying to hide emotion) dine with us—at—the—Bellevue—always happy to see the—the child's preserver, (breaks down) Mr. Hook—I mean Price.

(goes up, R.)

BRO. (aside, rising, R.) Damn him!

PRICE. Oh, it's nothing? You make me quite ashamed.

BRO. You deserve a medal from the Humane Society.

PRICE. I hope I shan't get one.

FAN. (*aside*) Though he's a Price, Dinbrook and Co., I can't help liking him.

                                  MRS. K.   TOD.
                                    O   O
                    FAN.
                     O   ROSIE.
BROWNE.   O   PRICE.
   O   O
R.   L.

ROSIE. (*to* PRICE) And I thank you for my life.

PRICE. (*embarrassed*) A mere trifle, I assure you——

ROSIE. Oh!   (OMNES *laugh*)

PRICE. I—no—no—I mean——

ROSIE. (*to* TODDER) Odd, isn't it? To have been nearly drowned!

TOD. (*seated* L. *of table* L.) Don't know—never was drowned.

MRS. K. (R. *of table* L.) You ought to have been.

PRICE. If you say any more, I shall run away. It's nothing. I only swam. If Mrs. Kinpeck had been upset from a boat——

TOD. That's quite another thing.

BRO. (*interrupting*) I've something to propose. We're all here together. Suppose we go for an excursion this afternoon?

MRS. K. An excursion!

BRO. Yes, to the Alte Schloss. It's only six miles!

ROSIE. Oh, that will be delightful!

BRO. I proposed it because I thought it would please you.

ROSIE. Shall we go, uncle?

FAN. If you like, my child.   (*rising*)

MRS. K. (*rising*) Mr. Price, you shall take *me*.

TOD. (*aside*) Poor young man!

PRICE. Pleasure.

MRS. K. (*aside*) He'll pay my share of the carriage.

PRICE. (*aside*) To be near her, I'd take the devil at one dose.

BRO. I'll order the traps from the hotel. We'll start at eleven, and lunch at the restaurant. Allons!

> *Band lively.* VISITORS, PEASANTS, *male and female, enter various entrances. Cross* R. *and* L., *and gradually exeunt.* WAITER *takes on table* R.C., *and lays cloth.* ROSIE *takes* BROWNE'S *arm, and they exeunt. Exit* FANQUEHERE, R. *Exit* MRS. KINPECK

and TODDER *last. He takes out a box of lozenges.* MRS. KINPECK *takes one, quite unexpected by* TODDER. *He looks amazed. They exeunt,* R. 1 E. *Enter* STOCKSTADT L., *and crosses to and sits* R. *of table* R.

PRICE. (*sits* L.H. *corner, looking at watch*) Nearly eight. Three hours till I see her again. Three long mortal hours ! What shall I do with them ? I'll go and taste the waters. (*rises, goes up, returns*) No, mine's a fever they can't allay. I *thought* it was when I first saw her. I *knew* it was when I felt her arms wound round me under the water in the lake. If I could only tell anybody, but I can't. Browne, he'd sneer. Todder, he'd jeer. Mother Kinpeck, she'd— no, she'd borrow florins—it is her nature to. Besides, they'd all tell the Honourable Bruce, who doesn't like me, because my grandfather did something that his great-uncle didn't like. If I could only find someone to confide in, someone to whom I could heave off this great load of love. (*stumbles over* STOCKSTADT'S *table, and upsets his tumbler of seltzer*) I—I beg your pardon ! (*aside*) It's the little Prussian captain ! All wrinkles and medals ! (*aloud*) Ten thousand pardons ! I am very sorry, I am sure.

STOCK. Ne vous dérangez pas, ce n'est rien.

(wiping his trousers)

PRICE. I don't understand a word you say. But it is very kind of you to take it in that light. (STOCKSTADT *indicates by action that it is of no consequence, and sits again*) He doesn't speak a word of English ! (*suddenly*) I'll confide in him. He can't betray my confidence, for he won't understand a word I say. No matter. I feel half mad, and it will relieve me. (*sits opposite* STOCKSTADT) Captain Stockstadt, I dare say my manner seems to you awfully absurd, but I know I'm an an ass, and so would you if you understood English. But I'm in love ! Madly, desperately, all over !

STOCK. (*sententiously*) So !

PRICE. A fortnight ago, I saw Miss Fanquehere on the terrace of the Kursaal. The first look—the first shock, I should say—was enough. I was struck, pierced, potted ! I was seized with a dizziness in the legs, and I felt my knees palpitate as if they were two big beating hearts.

(strikes table)

STOCK. (*amazed at his vehemence*) So !

PRICE. I could die for her ! And when I dived after

her into the lake, I wished we never could come up again. I felt that I could have taken her to the top of a high tower, and, with our arms fast locked together, leap with her into the air—(*feverishly*) into the air! (STOCKSTADT *more amazed and offended*) I could shoot the man she loves. (*with action*) Shoot him! Dead as game! Don't tell anybody—not a word! not a word! Will you? (STOCK-STADT *rises, offended.* PRICE *forces him back into chair*) Don't go! don't go!

> *Enter* MRS. KINPECK, R. 2 C., *she sees what is going on, uses her smelling bottle, and listens.*

PRICE. I'm very foolish. I feel—I feel I could cry. I can't get to speak to her—and—I—I—I—Oh! why did I ever come to Germany to fall in love like this? (*covers his face with his hands.* STOCKSTADT *rises and stalks off, highly indignant.* MRS. KINPECK *takes his chair. After a sob* PRICE *raises his head, meeting* MRS. KINPECK'S *eyes; she smiles, and indicates she has overheard*) Mrs. Kinpeck! (*aside*) Did she hear me?

MRS. K. Mr. Price, could you oblige me with the loan of a hundred florins?

> PRICE *rises hastily, feels for his pocket-book, counts out notes to* MRS. KINPECK; *at the same time enter* VISITORS, PEASANTS, R. *and* L. *Band plays.* STOCKSTADT *and the* GRAF VON STAUFEN-BERG *enter* R. *and cross to* L. WAITER *enters and wipes* R.H. *table. General action.*

QUICK ACT DROP.

ACT II.

SCENE.—*Ruins of an old Castle, on the summit of a mountain in the Black Forest. Ruined arches in set pieces, from* R. *to* L. *Centre arch to have stone seat in it. Ruined wall at back, to be higher than arches, to be backed by platform, for use of* AMANDA *and* MRS. KINPECK.

Enter FANQUEHERE *with race-glass, followed by* TODDER, R. 1 E.

FAN. Beautiful! beautiful! 'Pon my word, there's a good deal in nature. The green valley and the river running round in a half circle—just like the white posts on a race-course! Allow me to assist you, my dear Mr. Todder.

TOD. (*sits* R. 1 E. *out of breath*) Thank you, sir, thank you. It's very high up! I'm almost sorry I came.

FAN. Magnificent view.

TOD. (*shutting his eyes*) I can't look down.

FAN. Why not?

TOD. Dyspep!—dyspep!

FAN. This would make a splendid Grand Stand, eh?

TOD. You seem very fond of horses.

FAN. I adore them! They've been the ruin of me, bless 'em. I was nursed on harness oil, and weaned on curry-combs!

TOD. And is all that wood the Black Forest?

FAN. Yes; the country's splendidly timbered! Shall we go up higher?

TOD. (*rising*) Well, I'm much obliged to you, but I'd much rather not, as I feel somewhat fatigued.

(*sits in window seat*)

FAN. Here's Mrs. Kinpeck and Price.

TOD. (*rising with alacrity*) But not very——

FAN. Nonsense! (*forces him back into seat*)

Enter MRS. KINPECK *and* PRICE, R. 1 E.

MRS. K. Charming, is it not?

PRICE. Oh! delightful!

MRS. K. Mr. Todder, will you ever get down again?

TOD. I hope so.

MRS. K. (*sitting*) Shall *I* ever get down again?

PRICE. (*aside*) I hope not!

FAN. (*to* PRICE) Where is the child, and Browne?

PRICE. Coming up together.

TOD. (*blowing*) Oh!

FAN. (*aside*) I'll take care of this old medicine chest— the attentions of an Honourable may touch his liver! (*aloud*) Todder, my boy, shall we mount?

TOD. (*delighted*) My dear Mr. Fanquehere——

FAN. Bruce, call me Bruce, old fellow..

(*offering his arm*)

TOD. Oh! my dear sir; I'm afraid of——

FAN. Falling? Nonsense! you shan't fall (*aside*) until you've got my I.O.U.

TOD. (*ascending*) But why do they call it the Black Forest?

FAN. Because it's green.

> *Exeunt* TODDER *and* FANQUEHERE. PRICE *offers his arm to* MRS. KINPECK.

MRS. K. I'll sit down again, here.

(*sits in window seat*)

> *Enter* BROWNE *and* ROSIE, R. 1 E.

ROSIE. (*sits on stage*, R. 1 E.) Oh! I'm quite out of breath.

PRICE. I've got some lozenges. Shall I——

(*about to descend*, MRS. KINPECK *takes his arm*)

MRS. K. Now my young cavalier, give me your hand up this slope.

PRICE. (*aside*) If she would but drop over—I'd pay for a handsome funeral with pleasure.

(PRICE *and* MRS. KINPECK *disappear*)

ROSIE. Shall we follow?

BRO. This is a beautiful place, is it not?

ROSIE. (*rising*) Yes; I've often read about it in the book of Legends uncle bought at the library. This is the spot, and this is the very window near the chapel where it happened.

BRO. Where what happened?

ROSIE. The legend of the beautiful Lady in Grey. Did you never hear it?

BRO. No. Would you mind sitting down here, and telling it me? (*sits in window*, L.C.)

ROSIE. It is of the Count Wolff Von Brisgan, who was once lord of this castle, and who brought home a wife. She was very beautiful, and she always wore a strange, wild dress: its colour was grey. No one knew whence she came, but it was whispered that the fairies who live in the lake had endowed her with a genius for music. But the fairies had this hold upon her—that whenever she lost the love of her husband, her spirit should return to the lake— but her mortal form should still play on; and that the music that it made should remind her husband of his perjury and faithlessness. Well, three years passed, and Wolff fell in love with a novice in the neighbouring convent. He rode there every day for the chance of seeing her, and the more her husband's heart went away from her, the more and the more sweetly the Lady in Grey played. At last, Wolff tore the novice from her sacred home and brought her to this tower, and insisted on his wife receiving her as an honoured guest. When he presented her, the fairy wife was seated, playing on her harp the one sad, sweet melody she loved the best. Wolff bade her rise to welcome his fair guest. She still played on. He called to her—drew near her—laid his hand upon her shoulder, and found her —dead! But the chords of her harp still vibrated—the music still played on; and ever since upon the soft summer nights, the peasants see the figure of the fairy wife at the casement, and the music she made in life still floats upon the air. (*a wild strain of music—harp—is heard.* ROSIE *runs frightened to* BROWNE) What's that?

BRO. (*rises, and embracing her*) What's what?

ROSIE. (*whispering*) That strain in the air! that music!

BRO. Do you think it is the melody played by the beautiful Lady in Grey?

ROSIE. Oh! pray don't scoff!

BRO. (*aside*) She's romanesque! (*aloud, affectionately*) You are superstitious!

ROSIE. (*still in a whisper*) Very! are not you?

BRO. Not particularly. I don't believe——

ROSIE. I believe in everything. The flutter and the fear I am in now makes me sure that something is going to happen to me.

BRO. Not impossible. I regret to disturb a poetical illusion, but the strain of melody we heard just now—— (*music repeated; crosses* L.) There it is again: proceeds from an Æolian harp which is fixed in this niche—here! (*pointing*) Whenever the wind blows through this aperture, the chords vibrate; you can see it yourself. (*pokes stick in niche* L.) The name of the maker of the instrument is— " Jones "—" Piccadilly."

ROSIE. So it is! And the ghost's music turns out to

L L

be nothing but a few tightened wires! What a disillusion! (*after a pause*) It's a dreadful thing, isn't it?

BRO. What?

ROSIE. That romance is so unlike reality: that life is not good poetry, but such very bad prose. (*sits in window*, C.) I would have existence all like Tennyson, instead of which, it's nothing but butchers' bills!

BRO. (*aside*) I knew a horse named Tennyson, lost me two hundred! (*aloud*) Oh! there's plenty of real romance in this world, Rosie.

ROSIE. Tell me where to find it, and I'll go there. I suppose there are cheap excursions to it. To Fairy Land and back for five shillings!

BRO. Fairy Land! Fairy Land is Love, Rosie! Don't you believe in love?

ROSIE. Yes; just as I believe in a fairy! A beautiful bright thing that you never see, that you can't catch, and that you can only think about.

BRO. What would you say (*getting close to her*) now, if I told you that I was in love with you?

ROSIE. I should laugh like anything: it would be such fun!

BRO. Fun!

ROSIE. Yes.

BRO. Why fun?

ROSIE. Because you don't mean it.

BRO. Now, how do you know I don't mean it!

ROSIE. Because you are married (*a pause*), and a married man can't fall in love! it's not possible.

BRO. (*after a pause*) Who told you I was married?

ROSIE. Mrs. Kinpeck.

BRO. (*aside*) The old Jezebel! (*aloud, going* L.) It is quite true, Rosie, I have been married, but the match was not a happy one. (*Æolian harp*)

> *Enter* AMANDA *on staircase* R., *she does not see* BROWNE *or* ROSIE, *and they do not see her.*

ROSIE. Where is your wife now?

BRO. She is—dead.

> AMANDA *pauses, looks over into the valley, and descends* L.H. *She is dressed in grey silk.*

ROSIE. (*shocked*) I am sorry if I have hurt your feelings.

BRO. Not at all! Don't mention it.

ROSIE. I would not have asked such a question for the

world, if I had known. It must be so dreadful to have loved anyone, and lost them.

BRO. Yes; those pangs are dreadful!

ROSIE. To recall their looks—their words; the expression of the eyes that cannot smile again; the lips so cold and dumb; to think of the bright years they have not lived; the words they could have spoken; the love they could have felt.

BRO. (*after a pause*) Yes! Life is short, and full of changes.

ROSIE. Forgive me for being so foolish; but I always cry when I hear of death. I never lost anyone I loved, but my old nurse, Martha.

BRO. Pray do not apologise. We must bear these things with fortitude. It's our duty as men and Christians.

ROSIE. Of course you loved your wife very much?

BRO. Eh? Oh, yes! I—adored her; but that's a long time ago.

ROSIE. When did you lose her?

BRO. Eh? Oh—Pray don't let us pursue the subject. It—it affects you—you——(*aside*) Confound it!

ROSIE. (*rises—going up*) I'll go to uncle.

BRO. No—don't. Tell me—I thought you rather liked me?

ROSIE. Liked you?

BRO. I mean, liked to talk to, and flirt with me.

ROSIE. So I do! But that was only in play.

BRO. Play?

ROSIE. Yes; play—make-believe! Don't you know what make-believe is?

BRO. Haven't the slightest idea.

(*sits and lights cigar*)

ROSIE. I must go; for I know I have brought sad memories to your mind, and you wish to be alone with your grief. (*aside, in arch,* C.) Poor man! How I have made him suffer. I am so stupid, that I sometimes fear I have a bad heart! *Exit* ROSIE, *up.*

BRO. (*seated* L. 1 E.) This looks in bad form. Perhaps after all, it's only skittishness. She's just at that age when girls care for men fifteen or twenty years older than them-- selves. Besides, she's that sort of girl. I'll be even with that old mother Kinpeck for telling her I was married. How did the old witch guess it? Nobody knows of it! Surely Amanda hasn't been blabbing. (*Æolian harp*) No, she's too far off, and——(AMANDA *appears through broken arch. Seeing her, astounded*) Amanda !!!

AMAN. Oh! Charles! my dear, dear husband!

> *Kneeling by him,* L. 1 E., *and throwing her arms round him affectionately.*

BRO. (*repulsing her*) What are you about? Somebody might see us!

AMAN. Don't be angry with me. I couldn't stay away from you any longer. I felt I must see you; and this one moment repays me for my long, long absence.

BRO. (*disengages himself*) There are people in the ruins. When did you get here?

AMAN. Only this morning. I slept last night in Frankfort. When I got here I heard that you had gone to the ruins with a party; so I took a carriage and followed.

BRO. (*rises, crosses* R.) It's most inconvenient. I am here with the Hon. Bruce Fanquehere, and a party of friends.

AMAN. They need not know that I am your wife. (*rises, and follows him,* R.) I know it, and that is happiness enough for me. (*leaning on his arm*)

BRO. Where are you stopping?

AMAN. At the Hotel de Hesse.

BRO. And how long do you intend to stay?

AMAN. (*taking his hand*) Until you send me away.

BRO. (*aside*) If she wasn't so good! If she wasn't so damned good! (*sits in window*)

AMAN. (*going to him*) You're looking so handsome, and noble. Don't think me egotistic if I talk a little about myself. My engagements at Manchester and Liverpool, at Glasgow and Edinburgh, were all great successes. I paid the bills you told me to, and they mounted up, so that I have only brought with me three hundred and twenty pounds.

BRO. Three hundred and twenty pounds. Amanda, have you brought the money with you?

> (*rising, placing his arm round her*)

AMAN. Yes; I keep it here (*in her bosom*) for safety.

BRO. Because I thought if you had left it at the hotel——

AMAN. Oh! trust me. I'm too sharp for that. And I thought that, when I left Scotland, now I must go to Germany and see Charles. Nobody need know that I belong to him, for I know how much he sacrificed, from a social point of view, in marrying me, an actress. (*sits*) Ah! I know what the world thinks of actresses. My

husband w&s made to shine in the great world ; and I
thought that I should see you here, among your great,
noble, fashionable friends, and that, perhaps, you might
steal to see me now and then for half an hour, as a reward
for my patience.

BRO. (*leaning against wall*)   Three hundred and
twenty pounds ! !

AMAN. (*taking bank notes from pocket-book*) There it is,
darling ; all in tens.

BRO. (*counting notes*) 20, 30, 40, 50, 60, 70, 80, 90.
One ! I wouldn't have it known here that I was married
for the world ! 20, 30, 40, 50, 60, 70, 80, 90. *Two !* It
would ruin me. I have hopes of getting an appointment,
diplomatic, lucrative ! 20, 30, 40, 50, 60, 70—and an
actress ; the disgrace—80, 90. *Three !* 20 ! all right.

(*crosses to* R.)

AMAN. I've been very lucky, haven't I ? I think I am
the most fortunate woman in the world !

BRO. (*returns to* C.) And have you had many admirers?

AMAN. Heaps ! But none like my own Charlie ; and
then I had bouquets—oh ! lots !

BRO. (*aside*) That reminds me. I'll buy Rosie a
bouquet this evening.

AMAN. But my greatest reward was a letter from you !
But I used to think you should have written oftener ; for
I never knew whether the money reached you.

BRO. (*crosses to* R., *and warming with his wrongs*) Oh !
when I think that my wife has to appear upon the stage ;
to be exposed to the hisses or applause of those who—I——

(*looks over parapet, with foot on stone*)

AMAN. (R., *soothing him*) But they don't hiss me, dear,
and I don't think they ever mean to. Besides, (*sitting on
stone,* R.) what could I do, but act ? I had my mother to
keep, and I was not accomplished enough for a governess.
I know my having to get my living as an actress wounds
my Charlie's sensitive nature ; but, consider, if I hadn't
been on the stage, I should never have met you !

BRO. (*his back to wall, looking at watch*) That would
have been a serious misfortune for both of us. (*pause*) About
that engagement for America ?

AMAN. I only waited for your approval, dear. The
terms are one hundred and twenty pounds a week, all my
expenses, a carriage, table for myself, lady's maid and a
servant ; for one year through the States. The agent came

to see me in Edinburgh. They're a rapid, wide-awake people, the American managers. They're not half asleep as they are here!

Bro. One hundred-and-twenty! Um! We'll talk it over. (*aside*) Once on the other side of the Atlantic— (*aloud*) Did you leave your carriage below?

Aman. (*rising*) Yes.

Bro. You'd better return at once.

Aman. Yes, dear, but——

Bro. But, what?

Aman. I have given you all the money I had about me. I have only two Napoleons in——

Bro. Oh! (*gives her two bank notes*) Don't be extravagant. People like us must study economy.

Aman. (*hanging on his arm*) Yes, dear. But when we are rich, and we shall soon be, if my good luck continues, I'll quit the stage. We shall be always together, acknowledged man and wife, as you promised—shan't we?

Bro. Oh, yes.

Aman. (*her head on his shoulder*) What a happy time that will be!

Bro. Infinitely happy! Now——(*urging her departure*)

Aman. You haven't given me a kiss yet, Charles, dear!

Bro. (*kisses her*) There!

Fan. (*heard outside*) Browne! Browne!

Bro. (*kissing her again—petulantly*) There!

Exit Browne, *hastily*, c., *arch* L.

Aman. (*keeping the smile on her face till he is off. Sitting on stone near window*, R.C., *and hiding her face in her handkerchief*) He's handsomer than ever! But I wish he'd pretend to care to see me, even if he doesn't. However, he must love me some day or other. No one could go on being loved as he is, and not return it. I must conquer his heart in time. (*rises*) I'll go now, and think of him until I see him again.

Enter Fanquehere, L.C.

Fan. (*entering*) Browne! Browne! (Amanda *startled, drops the two notes*, Fanquehere *picks them up, returns them to her*. Amanda *bows and exits*, R. Fanquehere *sits on window*, L.C.) Nice looking woman! Her face seems familiar to me. Where have I seen her? Two ten-pound notes! I wish they'd been mine. I'd have lost them to-night at the tables. (*rising*) And, apropos, I believe that scheme of Browne's is correct. All we want is a thousand pounds! Five hundred each. I wonder if old Todder is good for that amount—paying interest, of course. I could pay him the interest. He seems toadyish to what he calls rank! He's an amusing scoundrel. Title dazzles him, and makes him feel like a child at its first exhibition of fireworks. My Lord—Fizz! Sir Somebody—Whiz! My Lady—Fizzle-Fozzle! (*imitating fireworks, by twisting his stick, and going towards* R. 1 E.) I'll try it on you, my dear Mr. Bodmin Todder. I'll call him Boddy, or Toddy. Stupid old Noddy. I've palmed Mother Kinpeck on him. Where can Browne be? *Exit* FANQUEHERE, R.1C.

Æolian harp plays. Enter PRICE *and* ROSIE, *arm in arm through arch from* L.

ROSIE. And did you never know them—never see them?

PRICE. Never see whom?

ROSIE. Your father and mother.

PRICE. Never! They died when I was quite young.

ROSIE. So did mine. (*pause*) It's very beautiful here, isn't it! So solitary, not even a bird!

PRICE. Not even Mrs. Kinpeck.

ROSIE. I feel quite tired. (*sits* R.C.) It's the clambering of so many steps.

PRICE. (*aside*) I wonder if I dare go and sit down beside her? I think I daren't. (*tries to muster up his courage but fails*) I'm sure I daren't. I knew I daren't.

(*looks off at arch,* L.C.)

ROSIE. Don't go away. Come and sit down here.

PRICE. Against you?

ROSIE. Yes—why not?

(PRICE *crosses, sits* L. *of* ROSIE, *then rises*)

ROSIE. What's the matter?

PRICE. I sat on something. (*feels his pockets*) Oh! It's a box of sweets I bought for a little child at the hotel. I forgot to give them to her.

ROSIE. Give me some; I'm fond of sweets.

PRICE. (*eagerly*) Are you? (*hands her the box*)

ROSIE. Yes! Ain't you?

PRICE. Very!

(*they eat of the sweets. Æolian harp plays*)

ROSIE. We have music to our banquet.

PRICE. Yes; it's a wind instrument that plays on strings.

ROSIE. That's very good! That's very clever!

PRICE. No, it's not. I'm not clever; and that's one of my troubles in life.

ROSIE. The Æolian harp?

PRICE. No: not being clever. You see I never had the chance, and I'm dreadfully conscious of my deficiencies. Being left so young, I lived with my guardian, and he was so good and stupid. He never went anywhere, and so he had a private tutor for me. Well, my private tutor was one of those wonderfully clever fellows who knew nothing, except what he had read in books; a genius ignorant of everything, except what somebody else had found out for him. Of course he was too clever to teach a mere boy, so, instead of reading to me, he read to himself, it pleased him and pleased me. So I grew up, knowing nothing. And I've remained in that blissful state ever since. (*pause*) But I'm afraid I'm boring you.

ROSIE. Not at all. I like to hear you.

PRICE. Do you?

ROSIE. Yes.

PRICE. Take some more sweets.

ROSIE. I like to hear you talk, because it seems to me that your life has been like mine. *I* never had any girl playmates. I only had my uncle, and my old nurse, who is dead. Poor Martha! and they, neither of them, good as they both were to me, seemed to understand me. I got on better with books; and so I grew up; and everybody treats me as if I were a baby; and sometimes I feel I am quite an old woman!

PRICE. Old! no, you're young and—take some more sweets.

ROSIE. We're robbing your little girl.

PRICE. I can buy her others. I've lots of money!

ROSIE. And I am very poor, so uncle says.

PRICE. (*aside*) Now I've done it! (*aloud*) Do you like chocolate!

ROSIE. What's that?

PRICE. Chocolate.

ROSIE. I like chocolate.

PRICE. Do you? Have a bit.

ROSIE. And we are both orphans.

> PRICE *offers her a stick of chocolate.* ROSIE *breaks a bit off, and eats,* PRICE *eats the other half.*

ROSIE. Nurse Martha said I never should be rich till I was married.

PRICE. Married !

ROSIE. Yes. (*laughing*) I should like to see myself married ! (*a pause*)

PRICE. (*gasping*) Yes—I—should—like—to—see—that —to—see—you—married.
(*a paper falls from his pocket*)

ROSIE. What's that ?

PRICE. Nothing. It's a song.

ROSIE. Your composition ?

PRICE. Y—e—s !

ROSIE. (*admiringly*) Never ! Then you're a poet ?

PRICE. (*eagerly*) No, no, I'm not. I'm not indeed. At all events, if I am, you mustn't let it prejudice you against me.

ROSIE. I've often wondered what a poet was like, and thought how beautiful it would be to know one ; and to think of you——

PRICE. You don't like it. Ah ! I thought you wouldn't. There seems to be a general objection to it.

ROSIE. You know what Lord Byron says of poets ?

PRICE. No.

ROSIE. "They are such liars": "And take all colours like the hands of dyers ! "

PRICE. Very rude of his lordship.

ROSIE. What is the song about ?

PRICE. Well, when I was at Nauheim, I went to a concert, and I heard a duet ; a very pretty tune ; but I couldn't understand a word the singers uttered, for it's an Austrian peasant's song ; and——

ROSIE. Oh ! I know it. (*sings*) La, la, la, la, la.

PRICE. That's it ! that's it !

ROSIE. We'll sing it together.

PRICE. Oh, if you would, I should feel so proud ! There are a few German phrases in it you know. They are good German, because I found them in the dictionary.

ROSIE. (*looking at paper*) It's for the gentleman to begin. Go on !

PRICE. Shall I ?

ROSIE. Of course.

PRICE. Then here goes.

DUET.

1st Verse.

Beneath the Linden trees,
With sun and summer breeze ;

'Mid blossoms falling, falling o'er the moss :
Or 'mid the forest firs,
Where not a linnet stirs,
Or on the rocks, where rears the rugged schloss ;
Or in the vineyards seen
Down in the valley green,
Where runs the winding, flowing, flowing Rhine.

ROSIE. In ambush everywhere,
Love lurks on earth, in air,
Whispering to mortals, maidens, youths, be mine.

BOTH. In ambush everywhere, &c., &c.

2nd Verse.

PRICE. Fritz draws to Lenchen near ;
And murmurs "Lenchen dear,"
"Oh, meine Liebe! oh! meine Herz! my life!"

ROSIE. And Lenchen's eyes, downcast,
Her heart feels flutter fast,
For Fritz she knows would press her be his wife.

PRICE. Fritz whispers, "List to me "—
"Meine braute wilt thou be?
"I'll go and ask thee of der Herr papa!
"Ah, sweet! Ich liebe dich!
"Oh! tell me Liebest du mich?

ROSIE. The blushing maiden fondly answers—Ya!"

BOTH. Oh! sweet! Ich liebe dich.
&c., &c., &c. (*a pause*)

ROSIE *walks to window.* PRICE *has left the parcel
of sweets on the stone on which they have been
sitting.*

ROSIE. (*suddenly*) Oh! I've dropped my parasol!

(*looks out of window into the space below*)

PRICE. (*getting out of window*) I'll get it.

ROSIE. (*holding him*) No ; you'll hurt yourself!

PRICE. I don't mind. (*half out of window*)

ROSIE. *I* do.

PRICE. Really, I'm a capital climber! And there are
steps all the way down. Let me fetch it.

ROSIE. Why?

PRICE. (*trembling*) Because I love you! There! it's
out! Since I saw you I can think of nothing else. I
adore you! · I love you till my head swims, and my eyes
throb. Now let me go! (*descending*)

Rosie. No; don't fetch the parasol.

Price. Why not?

Rosie. Because I love you!

Æolian harp plays. Pause. Price gets in rapidly, puts his arm round her waist. Rosie sits again, covering her eyes.

Price. Lovely prospect, isn't it?

Rosie. Oh! I feel so ashamed! (*rises, crosses* R.) I'll go to my uncle.

Price. No, don't.

Rosie. I must. Do you remember saving me in the lake?

Price. When I clasped you?

Rosie. Under the water.

Price. In water, on earth, or in air, I shall always love you.

Rosie. Come up! (*giving her hand*)

Price. All the way with you? It's a great height.

Rosie. Not if we climb together. Give me your hand, and I am sure not to fall.

Æolian harp. Exeunt Price and Rosie up L., his arm round her. Todder and Mrs. Kinpeck appear on the highest point, L.

Tod. (*looking down*) Are you coming?

Mrs. K. (*below him*) Oh, Mr. Todder! why go so fast?

Tod. If you will come, take hold of this.

Mrs. K. Good gracious! What a nasty break-neck way to come back, Mr. Todder, and in the blinding sun.

Tod. I don't dislike the heat.

Mrs. K. I do.

Tod. I don't.

Mrs. K. You like everything that is disagreeable.

Tod. (*with meaning*) No; not everything.

Mrs. K. Oh! if I were a man and you dared to say such things to me——

Tod. But if you were a man I shouldn't say 'em.

(*descending*)

Mrs. K. Mr. Todder! Mr. Todder! you're not going to leave me here to get down by myself?

Tod. Yes, I am. I can't bear ingratitude!

Mrs. K. But Mr. Todder, I can't stay up here.

Tod. I can't bear ingratitude!

Mrs. K. (*upon rock*) Mr. Todder! Please——

Tod. (*descending out of sight*) I can't bear ingratitude !

Mrs. K. The old villain ! (*with open parasol*) I can neither get up nor down.

Enter Amanda *through arch,* l.c., *a smelling bottle in her hand, and almost falling.*

Aman. I understand all now ! He loves another ! I watched him ; his looks, his manner, all confirm it ! and she seems a mere child ! Oh why did I come hither ?

(*falls fainting on a stone seat*)

Enter Price, *by arch,* l.c.l.

Price. I left the lozenges somewhere here, and Rosie wants one. (*sees* Amanda) Eh ! what's this ?

Amanda *reels backwards, and falls fainting into his arms.* Mrs. Kinpeck *sees all this from her perch, and gesticulates with her parasol to those above and below her. Enter* Fanquehere, Rosie, Browne, *and* Todder, *from different points, to form picture.*

Picture.

Mrs. Kinpeck.
O

Fanquehere.
O

Rosie.
O

Browne.
O

Todder.
O

Price.
O

Amanda.
O

R.   L.

If a call, change picture to Price *opposite* Amanda, *ashamed of being discovered.* Amanda *seated* l.h., *weeping.* Browne, *exultant, looking after* Rosie, *who, with her uncle, has disappeared.* Todder *tumbles down on stage, his hat and wig rolling off*

END OF ACT II.

ACT III.

SCENE I.—*Corridor leading to the Salon de Jeu. A line of columns running down each side of stage, with sufficient space between them and the wings for a person to pass. Tops of columns to meet chamber borders. Curtain to draw on in 1. Velvet ottoman on L. 1 E. During the action of this scene, people to lounge on and off.*

Enter BROWNE, L.U.E. *Enter* FANQUEHERE, R. 1 E. *Occasional bursts of music from Opera,* L.

BRO. (L.C.) Well, Fan. : congratulate me ! As soon as you are ready we can begin our speculation—speculation did I say ? It's a certainty. Look here. (*shows notes*)

FAN. (*counts them*) Five hundred ! who lent them ?

BRO. Price to-day—after dinner.

FAN. (*aside*) Clever ! clever !

BRO. So the sooner you begin to look for your share of the united capital——

FAN. I don't mean to look for it.

BRO. Eh ?

FAN. I've found it. (*shows a cheque*) Look here !

BRO. Where ?

FAN. Bodmin Todder ! The dear old snob. Told him I was hard up, till I received my rents. Ha ! ha ! my rents ! Should be happy to see him at my place in Somerset. Ha ! ha ! my place ! or my brother's at Beechington. My brother would be delighted, so would Lady Frances ; starch on both sides. Poor old Toddy ! He's an amusing scoundrel !

BRO. Then in a few days we start. (*music off* L.)

FAN. What's that music ?

Enter AMANDA, R.U.E., *she stands behind pillar, and listens.*

BRO. It's concert night, and you can hear the band here.

FAN. I'll fetch the child to hear it. She isn't well.

BRO. Indeed. (*eagerly*) Our conversation. (*aside*) She wants amusement. Bring her to the tables ; let her see the play.

Fan. What The child play? I wouldn't have her game for—for——

Bro. The price of a Derby favourite!

Fan. A Derby favourite! Not for all the racehorses that ever ruined gentlemen, or sent shop-boys to the hulks. The child, play! Phew! The very thought puts me into a cold perspiration. No! I've forbidden her entering the rooms. Here she is. (*Enter* Rosie, R. 1 E.) Come to the concert, my dear!

Rosie. (*crosses* C.) No, thanks, uncle. It's only a headache. I shall be better soon.

Bro. Perhaps the open air might——

(Amanda *crosses to pillar* L.)

Rosie. (*languidly*) Yes, let's go into the air.

Fan. She's an extraordinary child! What is it, my love? Too many sweets this morning. The excitement of going over the old castle?

Rosie. Yes. Excitement at the old castle.

Fan. Let's walk on the terrace. I want a few words, Browne, on business. We'll leave the child on a bench. Come, dear.

Bro. (*aside*) It's love! Which is the favourite— Price or me? I'll find that out.

> *Operatic music through this.* A Lady *enters* R. 1 E., *crosses, and exits* L.U.E. A Flauristo *enters* L.U.E., Browne *purchases a bouquet, and puts a note into it.* Amanda *watching all this business. Exeunt* Fanquehere *and* Rosie, R. Flauristo *having received instructions from* Browne, *follows* Rosie, *off* R. *Exit* Browne, R. Amanda, *who has remained at back, now advances, and sinks on ottoman* L. *Music.*

Aman. Lost to me! lost, as the gold, unlucky gamesters stake upon a colour. I was worthy of his love, and I deserved it. My dream is over. (*wiping her eyes*) I know his reason now for keeping me away from him. It was not shame for my calling! He loved another. Oh! how blind I have been; but my eyes are opened now. Let me dry them and look at my future—face to face. Poor girl! Poor girl! I fancy I can see myself in her. As she is, I was, when he wooed and won me! (*looks off* R.) She's coming back, and with his bouquet in her hand! (*goes up*) Should I not warn her? Should I not show her the pitfall he is preparing for her ? He is my husband. It is my duty to speak to her, and I will. (*retires*)

> *Enter* ROSIE, R. 1 E!., *agitated, bouquet and a letter in her hand.*

ROSIE. How dare he write to me ! To insult me with words of love ! And but a few hours since I saw him kneeling to that woman—the Lake fairy—the Lady in Grey ! To affront me with his flowers, and his protestations. Oh ! (*about to throw the bouquet away, relents and weeps*) I feel so miserable. (*sits on ottoman,* L.)

AMAN. (*advances to her*) Don't be surprised or angry that I speak to you without an introduction.

ROSIE. (*rising and recovering herself*) This woman ! (*crossing to* R.)

AMAN. But I see you are afflicted.

ROSIE. My griefs are my own.

AMAN. (L.C.) No ; your grief is mine, and mine is yours.

ROSIE. I do not understand you.

AMAN. You are in love ! I warn you against the man you love.

ROSIE. You warn me ! You——?

AMAN. Yes, for he once told me that he loved me.

ROSIE. I know it.

AMAN. You know it ?

ROSIE. Yes.

AMAN. How ?

ROSIE. Never mind ; but I know it.

AMAN. I saw you together in the ruins (ROSIE *sighs*), where I arrived unexpectedly. Oh ! my child, for you are younger than I am, younger in years, much younger in experience——

ROSIE. Madam, I do not understand this freedom.

AMAN. Don't be angry with me. I am his wife.

ROSIE. (*thunderstruck*) Wife ! ! His—wife !

AMAN. Yes ; we have been married four years.

ROSIE. Married ! (*with rage*) And he dare send this, and write words of love to me ! (*crosses* L.)

AMAN. Let me see what he has written.

ROSIE. (*gives her the letter, then snatching it back*) No, my poor crushed darling, it would only wound your heart. (*tears up the note*) Let his base words perish with his base thoughts. (*kisses* AMANDA) We'll be friends, won't we ?

AMAN. My poor child ! But you must not let my husband know that you are aware that he is married.

Rosie. Why not?

Aman. Because I promised to keep it secret. I have revealed myself to you from a sense of duty.

Rosie. But why keep it secret?

Aman. (*reluctantly, as if wrung from her*) Because—he is—ashamed of me!

Rosie. *He* ashamed of *you?* (*they sit* L.) Tell me all about it. It seems so strange to me. How can a man be ashamed of the woman he has married? And how, when he is married, can he love any one but his own wife?

Aman. He is ashamed of me because he is of good family, and—I—I am—an actress.

Rosie. An actress! Are you an actress?

Aman. Yes. Doesn't that shock you?

Rosie. Not at all. Why should it? I am curious, for I never saw an actress, close to, in all my life. But tell me, why is your husband ashamed of you?

Aman. I have told you.

Rosie. No!

Aman. Yes. I said he was ashamed of having a wife who earned her living on the stage.

Rosie. No! Why, if I were a man, I should be proud of it. To go to the theatre, and see my wife a queen—a heroine! (*with enthusiasm*) To listen to her declaim, and hear the rapping and applause tha followed each effort of her genius. But tell me——

Aman. (*rising and hiding behind pillar* R.) Hush!

Rosie. (*rising*) What?

Aman. I see my husband. (*looking off* R.)

Rosie. (*looking* R.) I don't.

Aman. I did, talking to an officer. He must not see us together.

Rosie. But I shall see you again!

Aman. Yes, my hotel is the Hotel de Hesse. I shall stay here to watch over him; to watch over you. (*going*)

Rosie. (*stops* Amanda, *and kisses her*) God bless you! (*Exit* Amanda, *hurriedly*, R.U.E.; Rosie *leaning against pillar*, L.) And now she's gone I'll have a good cry. (*sinks, weeping on ottoman* L.) The villain! the unmanly villain! to deceive so good a woman! Oh! why did I ever fall in love? And to think that my first love should be a married man! It's very wicked of me. Oh! what can I do, for—for excitement? I'll go and look at the lake, where I fell in, and he——Oh! (*rises*) I wish I could fall in again, without doing it on purpose. *Exit* Rosie, *weeping*, R.1E.

Enter Mrs. Kinpeck, r u.e., *she advances in thought,
and sits on ottoman* l., *and begins calculating with
card and pins.*

Mrs. K. I think this is certain, or at least certain three
times out of seven, 19, 20, 21, 22, 23, 24. The other numbers
11, 17, 30, 32 and 29. The basis of the calculation is that
those numbers—the sequences are all mathematical, and
therefore to be calculated, 28 repeats itself after 28, 7 on
fourth, so after 23 and 24, 6, after 11, 3, after 17, 4.

Enter Browne, *and leans on colonnade* r.

· Bro. Off in three days! So, in three days I shall have
Rosie all to myself, away from Mr. Frank Price. Was it
seeing Frank at my wife's feet that has discomposed her!
I'll send Amanda off, perhaps to America. This old scamp
knows nothing of Rosie's good fortune. Besides I really
like the girl, and with her first year's money——

Mrs. K. After 17, 4.

Bro. If my first marriage should be blown, old Fan
would shut his mouth for a share.

Mrs. K. One fourth again; always divide by four!

Bro. His influence and mine would win over the girl!

Mrs. K. The same combinations apply to colours——

Bro. As for Price, he'll soon be out of the way.

Mrs. K. Stake accordingly.

Bro. Odd that Stockstadt should come to me. I saw
the advantage at once.

Mrs. K. And stake accordingly.

(*chink of money heard*)

Bro. There's the chink of the pewter, which Frank
Price says always reminds him of the laugh of the devil.

Mrs. K. 18, 19, 30, 23, 30! Yes, at least twice
thirty—(*Enter* Todder, r. 1 e., *he pauses, and bows to* Mrs.
Kinpeck, *and goes off* r. 1. e.)—mean old beast!

Bro. (*coming down* r. c.) There they go! Pater and
Materfamilias from virtuous Clapham Rise, dissipated
Tyburnia, prim Peckham, and stuck-up Bayswater. Folks
who, in England, pay pew-rents and go in for goodness!
Angelic householders, who, when they leave their native
West an Sou'-West Postal District, spend the Sunday
morning at the racecourse, the evening at the theatre,
and finish up by a pious stroll round gaming-tables.
Different longitude, different latitude. But it's hard that a
man who lives by his wits should feel as big a humbug as a
British respectability! (*crossing, sees* Mrs. Kinpeck)

MRS. K. 15, 17, 19.

BRO. (*aside, surveying her*) And here's another of 'em ! (*aloud*) Ah ! Mrs. Kinpeck, making your calculations? (MRS. KINPECK *nods ;* BROWNE *going, bows to her*) Now to find Price !   *Exit* BROWNE, R. 2 E.

MRS. K. Bad fellow that. I dislike him more than I do old Todder ; and really the sight of that repository where old Todder keeps his eyes and mouth—for I will not call it a face—reminds me of my nightmare. This afternoon, overcome by the heat, the excursion, and the dinner, I fell asleep. (*rises with sudden excitement*) My dream ! my dream ! I recollect it now.   I thought that odd man, the Croupier, who entertained a regard for me, poor man, and died of that and a complication of other diseases, last year—old Flicateau—came to me in his shroud and said, in a ghostly but Parisian accent, put your money in the hands of a young girl who has never played, and let her stake as she pleases. Trust the luck of a virgin player. He was a wonderful man that Flicateau ! Genius in his eye, and a wart on his nose. It was hereditary—the genius, not the wart. And then a face came to me, a girl's face, and old Flicateau pointed to it, and vanished, saying, " Dix-huit, rouge, pair et manque ! " I forget the face though. (*sits* L. *Enter* ROSIE, R. 1. E. ; *seeing her, starts ; aside*) Ah !—the very face ! (*aloud*) My love, I want you to do me a favour ; will you do it ?

ROSIE. What is it ?

MRS. K. Play for me.

ROSIE. Play ?

MRS. K. Yes ; play at the roulette table. Put the money on what you like, where you like.

ROSIE. But my uncle has forbidden me to enter the Sal.

MRS. K. He always plays at trente et quarante, in the big room. He won't know.

ROSIE. But I shall.   Never mind ! If he knew the pain I feel here, he'd like me to forget it, if only for a few minutes.

MRS. K. Take this cloak and hood, dear. Nobody will know you. You don't know how to play, do you ?

ROSIE. No.

MRS. K. The very thing. (*gives her a bag*) Stake as you like, dear. Of course all you win is—mine

ROSIE. I don't want your money. I have plenty of my own. Twenty pounds !

MRS. K. Good gracious ! Where did you get it ?

ROSIE. Uncle gave it me.

MRS. K. Where did he get it?

ROSIE. He borrowed it of Mr. Todder.

MRS. K. Oh! the villain! These men! these men!

Enter PRICE, R. 1 E. ; *his gaze meets the eye of* ROSIE, *she drops the bag.*

PRICE. (*radiant*) Rosie, I've bought some bon-bons.

ROSIE. (*as he approaches her*) Don't touch me! Do not speak to me!   (*going up stage*)

PRICE. (*recoils astonished*) Eh?

MRS. K. (*picks up the bag, and going after* ROSIE) Stay dear!

ROSIE. (*excitedly*) I'll play for myself.

She strikes the box from PRICE'S *hand, as he advances to her. Exit* ROSIE, R.U.E. *During the foregoing, several* PEASANTS, *male and female, have entered, lounging about.*

MRS. K. Badly brought up! badly brought up! That old Fanquehere! (*Vesper bell heard. The* PEASANTS *take off their hats*) Nuisance! I must find somebody else; for I'm sure my calculation is correct, and my dream forbodes good luck. (*turns, see* PEASANTS *with their hats off*) Oh! Vespers! and those poor people! Ah! (*shaking her head*) Ignorance and superstition! ignorance and superstition enchain both mind and body! (*sees* PRICE) Ah! Mr. Price! (PRICE, *roused from his astonishment at* ROSIE'S *manner starts, and hastily picks up the box of bonbons, and turns to* MRS. KINPECK) These for me? (*takes the box*) Thanks; so kind of you.

Exit MRS. KINPECK, L.U.E. PRICE *stands still in mute astonishment. Enter* CROUPIER, R.U.E.

CROUP. Joseph! Louis! (*Enter* SERVANTS, L.U.E.) Il y a un courant d'air dans le salon, fermez les rideaux—(*seeing* PRICE) Permettez, Monsieur.

The curtains are drawn in 1st Groves. Lights down. Vesper bell still sounding. PRICE *is shut out alone in front of curtain.*

PRICE. Don't touch me! don't speak to me! Why not? What have I done? What has happened since dinner? Was that Rosie, and is this me? What's come to us all?

(*sits on ottoman* L., *which remains outside curtains*)

Enter BROWNE, R. 1 E. .

BRO. Oh, Price! Here you are. I'm glad I've found you, though I come on rather disagreeable business.

PRICE. Go on! Go on! Don't be shy.

BRO. Captain Stockstadt, the little officer, all over medals, with a scar here, you know!

PRICE. Oh yes, I know.

BRO. Came to me two hours ago, and told me that this morning you grossly insulted him.

PRICE. (*astonished*) What!

BRO. Nay—laid hands upon him violently.

PRICE. I did!

BRO. Yes, you were seen to do so by two of his brother officers, who were sitting a few yards off. The affair has been discussed, and it has been decided that he must call you out.

PRICE. Call me out?

BRO. Yes.

PRICE. A challenge?

BRO. Yes.

PRICE. A duel?

BRO. Yes. (*aside*) Now will he fight or will he show the feather?

PRICE. (*covering his eyes with his hands*) I think I must be off my head!

BRO. (*aside*) The feather! (*aloud*) Surely, Price, you must remember what took place between you and Captain Stockstadt this morning?

PRICE. Of course I do. I was telling him——
                                        (*stops suddenly*)

BRO. Telling him what?

PRICE. (*aside*) I cannot mention that.

BRO. He doesn't speak one word of English, and you're dumb in German. What could you have to tell him?

PRICE. (*aside*) I'll confide in Browne. (*aloud*) I was telling him——

Enter FANQUEHERE, R. 1 E.

BRO. Yes——

PRICE. (*aside*) I cannot before her uncle.

FAN. Browne, the Baron tells me that there's a little woman at the tables playing in the most remarkable way, and winning all before her. Not a bad notion to go in and back her luck.

PRICE. (*seated* L.) But duels are out of date. Such a thing is never heard of now.

BRO. I beg your pardon—in Prussia—between gentlemen——

FAN. (*eagerly*) What's that, a duel?

BRO. Yes. Captain Stockstadt complains that Mr. Price, being very excited this morning, gesticulated violently, and at last laid hands on him.

FAN. Eh?

PRICE. He was getting up from his seat, and I merely put him down on his chair again.

BRO. (*crosses* R.) Oh! A Prussian officer, in uniform——

PRICE. But why should Captain Stockstadt think I wished to insult him? Why?

BRO. He attributes your assault to the eccentricity of the English character.

PRICE. I must be going mad!

BRO. Under the circumstances, I fear that you must——

FAN. (*leaning against pillar*, L.) Go out! Certainly.

BRO. Or apologise.

FAN. Or apologise! Certainly.

PRICE. I won't apologise. I've given no offence.

BRO. (*coughs*) Our position here is peculiar. Englishmen among foreigners——

FAN. Quite so!

BRO. It must get into the papers; and rather than these fellows should crow about the affair, as your countryman, I would take the quarrel on myself.

FAN. Quite so! So would I.

PRICE. (*rises*) Gentlemen, do you mean to insult me? Pray don't misunderstand me. I trust I am not a coward; but I am quite sure that I scruple to take any man's life, or even to maim him, particularly when there is no quarrel between us. Do not be under the least misapprehension nor fear that the reputation of England, Ireland, and Scotland, or of Englishmen abroad, will suffer at my hands. (*crosses to* BROWNE) I'll fight this Captain Stockstadt when and where he pleases.

FAN. Bravo!

PRICE. (*aside*) Perhaps Rosie will be sorry to hear I am shot.

FAN. Bravo! (*shaking his hand*) My dear sir! my very dear sir!

BRO. (*aside*) Good!

PRICE. (C.) And, by the way, I shall want a second—I have always read in books that there was a second in these affairs. I suppose, Browne, I may rely on your kind offices to——

BRO. My dear Price—you see—um—it's awkward—I brought you Stockstadt's message, and——

PRICE. But there's no one else I *can* ask.

FAN. (*taking off his hat*) I shall be most happy, my dear Mr. Price, most happy. I'm used to these sort of things. When I was in the service in the West Indies in '34 the past year, we often used to go out. Anything that I can do—I am aware that our families have had some differences, but abroad here, among these foreign fellows, damn it, one is English. Avant tout! I'll see you through this, my dear sir. I shall feel a pleasure in doing so; it will be some return for your saving my little Rosie's life.

PRICE. (*aside*) To get me shot! quite so.

FAN. Hist! The enemy!

Enter STAUFENBERG *and* STOCKSTADT, R. 1 E., *all salute gravely.* STOCKSTADT *crosses to seat*, L. 1 E.

GRAF. (*bowing gravely to* BROWNE) How do you do? (*to* FANQUEHERE) Illustrated London News!

BRO. Capital! I'll see how the play is going on.

Exit BROWNE, R. 1 E.

PRICE. Don't go, Mr. Fanquehere—I—(*turns immersed in thought, and sits beside* STOCKSTADT, *who stares in astonishment, and turns his back on* PRICE, *who rises abashed. Goes to* C.)

FAN. Graf!——

Exeunt STAUFENBERG *and* FANQUEHERE, R. 1 E.

PRICE. And there sits the man whom I may kill tomorrow, or who may kill me. I feel I should like to shake hands with him—(STOCKSTADT *takes out his cigar-case, finds it empty.* PRICE *continuing*)—as they do before they fight at home, where it is honest knuckles, and not cowardly knife! (*music*) He wants a cigar. I'll offer him one.

> STOCKSTADT *rises, and is going off.* PRICE *offers his cigar-case.* STOCKSTADT *surprised for a moment, then frankly accepts the courtesy, and with a grave bow, takes a cigar from* PRICE'S *case, and striking a match offers it to* PRICE; *same*

business. When both cigars are alight, they bow and exeunt. PRICE *goes off* R. 1 E., STOCKSTADT *through curtains,* C. *Ballet music through all this " Repete a l'Empereur ! " Lights up.*

CHANGE.

SCENE II.—*The Salon de Jeu. Door piece* R.U.E. *Window at back. Garden backing. Dark. The rouge et Noir Table, with* HEAD CROUPIER *presiding. Male and female* GAMBLERS *are seated round the table, also* CROUPIERS *at different points with rakes, distributing and gathering the money. Notes piled before them.* MRS. KINPECK *and* TODDER *seated at* R. *corner of table.* ROSIE *at* L.II., *with her back to the audience, her hood drawn over her head.* AMANDA *is* R. *corner of table. Characters standing— looking on, &c.* OLD GENTLEMAN *seated high up, over- looking board.*

TABLE.

AMANDA.	Old Lady.	Croupier.	Head Croupier.	Croupier.
TODDER.			⬭	Lady.
			Gentleman.	
MRS. KINPECK.	Croupier.	Gent.	Croupier.	ROSIE. Lady.

Ottoman drawn on R. 1 E.

(*music ceases as scene is opened*)

CROUP. Vingt—noir—pair—et passe. (*marking the table. Money is chinked*) Faites votre jeu, Messieurs. (*business*) Le jeu est fait. Rien ne va plus.

MRS. K. (R.) Rosie is winning everything. She's playing for me. I am so happy. I don't mind losing a few florins at this end.

TOD. This woman is such a fidget. I wish she'd go.

CROUP. Douze—rouge—pair et manque. (*chink*) Faites votre jeu, Messieurs.

AMAN. (*advancing to* R. *corner of table*) Poor child ! The old proverb is verified in our case (*crossing* R.), unlucky in love, lucky at play—— (*shows handful of notes*)

CROUP. Vingt huit noir—pair et passe. (*chink*)

Enter BROWNE, R.U.E.

BRO. I wonder who this little woman is who's winning

everything! (*suddenly confronting* AMANDA) Amanda! Why
are you here? (*they come down*)

AMAN. (*coldly, defiant*) I came to play.

CROUP. Faites votre jeu, Messieurs. (*business*)

BRO. I told you to stay at your hotel.

AMAN. I chose to come, to disobey you, and to come here.

BRO. (*whispering*) Go back!

AMAN. I won't.

BRO. What!

AMAN. Your power over me is past.

CROUP. Le jeu est fait.

AMAN. I will not go.

CROUP. Rien ne va plus.

BRO. Amanda!

AMAN. What do you want of me—more money? I have
given you enough. The bank is closed.

(*pockets her notes, and goes down* L.H.)

CROUP. Trente, rouge, pair et passe.

BRO. (R.) What does this mean?

TOD. Those florins were mine, ma'am.

MRS. K. No, mine.

TOD. I staked on the douze dernièr.

MRS. K. So did I.

TOD. No; on the douze millieu dernièr!

MRS. K. Millieu.

TOD. Ah!

CROUP. Faites votre jeu, Messieurs.

(BROWNE *has gone to table and staked his pieces*)

AMAN. (*down* L.) I feel as if I could win all before me.
I feel inspired. (*as she passes* ROSIE) Zero!

(*they stake rapidly*)

Enter FANQUEHERE *and* PRICE, *by* D.R.U.E. PRICE
very absent in manner.

FAN. Just for a moment, to see who this is they are all
talking about.

CROUP. Le jeu est fait. Rien ne va plus.

FAN. (*to whom* ROSIE *is pointed out*) Can't see her face.

CROUP. Zero! (*general movement*)

BRO. She's won again, by Jove!

CROUP. Le banque est sauté.

*Sensation. Players get on the ottoman and shout the
word "Sauté"—the word passes from lip to lip.*
ROSIE *rises, and sees* PRICE *and* FANQUEHERE.

FAN. (R.C., *horrified*) Rosie!

ROSIE *drops the notes and rouleaux of gold she has in her lap. Tableau. Cheers. No music.*

MRS. KINPECK.
   O

        FANQUEHERE.
          O

               ROSIE.
               O

AMANDA.
   O

             PRICE.
             O

        TODDER.
          O

BROWNE.
  O

R.

                                                       L

END OF ACT III.

ACT IV.

SCENE.—*The Kursaal, and Kurgarten.*

Enter PRICE, *down steps,* R. 1 E.

PRICE. What a lovely morning! Just the sort of morning a man would choose to be shot on. Not a soul on the Kursaal, and there won't be till past eleven, when the folk come back from their morning drive. And to think that while the waiters are laying breakfast, and the horses are harnessing, I shall be fighting. (*looks at his watch*) Half-past six! They say that Stockstadt is a dead shot; so in forty minutes I may be lying—there. If anybody calls out "Frank," I shan't answer. Strange! But this morning the sky seems higher and bluer, the air fresher and more pure, the trees greener, and the flowers sweeter than ever! Have they come out so beautifully to bid me good-bye? To say, Come to to us, poor little ephemeral mortal, who has lived twenty-two years of stillness, and who dies without a friend, without a hope. Twenty-five to seven, Rosie is putting on her hat, and stepping under the pink horse-chestnuts; but not to think of me! (*closing his eyes*) I can see her now, and I can hear her voice. (*falls into a chair,* R. 1 E.) Oh! it is hard to die! I wonder how I offended her? I'm sure it only needs explanation. I suppose I said something, or didn't say something; did something, or didn't do something! Just my luck. Then she played, too, last night, and won. I've written (*produces letter*) this to her, and if Stockstadt should fight me properly, she'll know that I died loving

her, and (*emotionally*) with her name upon my lips——
(*breaks down and drops his head on arms; a pause*) This
won't do! I've come to fight, not to snivel. (*rises*) I'm
supposed to be a man, and not a schoolgirl! Captain
Stockstadt's called me out: all the worse for Captain
Stockstadt; military rank, wrinkles, medals, and all told,
he is only a foreigner. What right has he to come between
me and my young life? How dare he want to shoot at me?
I'll put a bullet into his thick hide as sure as sausages are
made of pig's skin. If I could only see Rosie to explain!
Whew? Here she is. (*Enter* ROSIE, L.U.E.; *she stops on seeing*
PRICE, *and turns as if to go away*) Don't go, Rosie—Miss
Fanquehere. I request the favour of a few words conver-
sation with you.

ROSIE. (L.C.) I didn't come here to see you.

PRICE. (R.C.) I know that.

·ROSIE. A letter came last night for uncle, and he didn't
see it. He wasn't in his room, so I thought I should find
him here.   (*crosses* R., *letter in hand*)

PRICE. Pray don't go——

ROSIE. I don't want to stay with you; I want to go
away.

PRICE. Miss Fanquehere, please tell me—how have I
offended you?

ROSIE. How? Ask your own heart!

PRICE. Ask——

ROSIE. Your bad, black heart!

PRICE. (*aside*) Oh! if this letter could answer for me.
(*aloud*) What have I done?

ROSIE. (*aside*) The accomplished hypocrite! (*aloud*)
Done!—Oh! don't speak to me.

PRICE. An hour hence, I shall leave this place. I am
going—away.

ROSIE. To Homburg?

PRICE. Further than Homburg.

ROSIE. Alone?

PRICE. Yes: quite alone (*aside*) Unless Stockstadt
accompanies me.

ROSIE. The more shame for you.

PRICE. Why?

ROSIE. How dare you question me, sir? I am a young
lady, by birth and feeling! What matters to me (*crossing*
L.) what happens to you?

PRICE. I may never see you again, to speak to you.

ROSIE. (*half crying*) I'm so glad!

PRICE. There must be some tremendous mistake between us, Miss Fanquehere. It is too late now to endeavour to unravel it. This letter will explain——

ROSIE. I won't read it.

PRICE. I ask it as a last favour.

ROSIE. And I refuse it. (*aside*) To hear him, could any-one suppose he was such a villain!

PRICE. (*looking at his watch*) Time! I'm to meet her uncle on the bridge, and then ten minutes to the Salines. Good-bye! Let me press your hand at parting. (ROSIE *hudders and refuses*) You won't? Miss Fanquehere—— (*Enter* AMANDA, *down steps* R. *and off* L.U.E., *unseen by* ROSIE. *Aside, seeing* AMANDA)——the Lady in the ruins! (*aloud, bowing to* ROSIE) Farewell! God bless you!

Drops his letter at ROSIE'S *feet and exits hurriedly,* L.U.E.

ROSIE. I spurn his letter, as I spurn him! And to think that with that open face, and that clear, loyal ringing voice, he can tell such lies—there's no other word for it. A traitor! Oh! I could stamp my eyes out with vexation. (*stamps her foot and then cries*) Thank goodness he can't make me like him; no, he fails there! To think that such a good-looking fellow isn't constant to his true love—the wife he took an oath in a church to——

Enter AMANDA, L.U.E., *and advances* R.H.

AMAN. My child! You here? Have you seen my husband?

ROSIE. He has just left me. (*embracing her*) Oh! my poor, poor injured dear!

AMAN. I didn't meet him.

ROSIE. I suppose you've been dreaming about him?

(*sitting* R. *of table,* L.)

AMAN. I haven't slept all night. I feel that something is hanging over him. (*sees letter on ground*) What's that?

ROSIE. A letter he left for me.

AMAN. His letter—on the ground! You wouldn't read it?

ROSIE. No!

AMAN. You're a dear, good girl; and some day Heaven will reward you with a good man's love?

ROSIE. I won't have it. I won't have anything to do with love any more. Love is a nasty, bad, mischievous boy; and the sooner he's put into convict clothes, and refused his ticket-of-leave, the better.

AMAN. And that's his love-letter—to you?

ROSIE. (*rises*) Shall I tear it?

AMAN. No! (*picking it up*) I'll read it.

ROSIE. (C.) Don't dear. (*snatching it from her*) His bad words shan't profane your good eyes. (*opens the letter*) See! there's his good-for-nothing name! Frank!

(*sinks in chair* R. *of table* L.)

AMAN. Frank!

ROSIE. Yes: Frank! Treacherous Frank!

AMAN. My husband's name is Charles! (*looks at letter*) That's not his writing.

ROSIE. No! Worse and worse! He's got somebody to write it for him, that his hand may not be known. He gave it to me just now.

AMAN. My husband?

ROSIE. Your husband! Frank Price.

AMAN. My husband's name is Charles Browne!

ROSIE. (*rises, startled*) Eh?

AMAN. The Chevalier Browne.

ROSIE. Oh! oh! (*hysterically*) Oh! Mrs. Browne! Oh! Mrs. Browne! Pray forgive me! I—I—I am so wretched. Your husband never made love to me.

AMAN. What?

ROSIE. It was my Frank! Mr. Frank Price! I saw him bending over you when you had fainted at the Schloss.

AMAN. I see. That gentleman merely assisted a lady he supposed was fainting. That wasn't my Charles.

ROSIE. No, it was Frank, my Frank! And to think of my being cruel and refusing his bon-bon box. Oh! oh! (*bursts out crying*) What a wicked girl I must be to think such bad things. I'll beg his pardon. What a load off my mind! I'm not in love with a married man! And I beg your pardon on my knees, Mrs. Browne, for daring to suspect your dear, good husband.

AMAN. (*aside*) Poor thing! She is too pure to think harm. I'll not undeceive her.

Enter MRS. KINPECK, *hurriedly*, L.U.E.

MRS. K. My love! Have you heard the news?

ROSIE. (C.) No.

MRS. K. Not of the duel?

ROSIE. Duel?

MRS. K. Yes; with pistols; going on at this very moment. Your uncle's in it.

ROSIE. (*alarmed*) Eh? (*crosses* L.)

Mrs. K. (c.) Only as second.

Rosie. (*relieved*) Oh ! Who is going to fight ?

Mrs. K. The combatants are—the Chevalier Browne——

Aman. What ?

Mrs. K. And young Frank Price—(Rosie *startled; motionless*)—behind the Salines. Why (*looking at the other ladies*), what's the matter with you two ?

Rosie. (*recovering*) Let us hasten——

Aman. Let us go——   (*going up stage*)

Mrs. K. But——   (*going up stage*)

Enter Todder, *breathless, from* R.U.E.

Tod. Oh—oh—la—dies——such news !——

Mrs. K. Of the duel ?

Tod. Y—e—s.

Aman. } Tell us.
Rosie. } Well—well.   } (*together eagerly*)
Mrs. K. } Pray be quick.

Tod. (*recovering his breath*) About the duel ?—Yes——

Mrs. K. I've told 'em——

Tod. But you haven't told 'em——

Mrs. K. Yes, I have.

Tod. But not about——

Mrs. K. Every word !

Tod. She hasn't given you the correct version.

Rosie. } Go on ! go on !
Aman. } Speak ! for Heaven's sake.

Mrs. K. (*taking* Amanda, R.) Well then, I'll tell you madam, as you appear to be anxious——

Tod. (*taking* Rosie *to table*, L.) My dear Miss Fanque-here, your uncle, that noble specimen of old England's aristo-cracy (*the next speeches of* Todder *and* Mrs. K. *are to be spoken simultaneously*) heard Mr. Price and the Chevalier disputing about a Madamoiselle Somebody ; she's stopping at the Bellevue. It appears that Mr. Price was in love with her ; so was the Chevalier. High words ensued, and Mr. Price told the Chevalier that he was a story-teller. Then Mr. Price threw a bottle of seltzer at him, which knocked him down, then the Chevalier got up, doubled his fist and knocked Mr. Price down ! Dreadful, wasn't it ? Then the Prussian officers, who were present, interfered : so did your uncle—the respected Honourable Bruce. A duel was arranged for this morning, with pistols ; and Mr. Price was shot through the left eye.

Mrs. K. Your dear husband, poor dear, it seems had

borrowed a large sum of money of Mr. Price, and Mr. Price asked him for it. Your husband said he hadn't got it, so Mr. Price called your husband a swindler. Your husband then took up the poker to hit at Mr. Price's head. Mr. Price ducked and avoided the blow; then Mr. Price struck your husband with his fists, and a regular fight ensued. The police came up—interfered, and they said it was only fun. A meeting was arranged to take place this morning, Mr. Fanque here acting as Mr. Price's second. Your husband chose to fight with swords—Bear up, my dear madam—Mr. Price has run him through the left lung, and he has been carried to his hotel upon a shutter.

Tod. (*turning round*) If you will interrupt me, madam, I will not continue.

Mrs. K. (*at the same time*) I can't get in a word for you.

Aman. What shall we do?

Rosie. Go to them at once.

Tod. } No—no—no; decidedly not.
Mrs. K. } You must not think of such a thing.

(Rosie *and* Amanda *are going off*)

Enter Fanquehere r., *carrying a case of pistols.*

Fan. Hey-day!—What's the matter?

Rosie. Oh! uncle! The duel?——

Fan. What, you've heard about it?

(*places pistol-case on table, crosses* c.)

Aman. (L.C.) Is he killed?

Fan. (c.) Is who killed? [Browne?

Rosie. } (R.C., *after hesitating*) Mr. — the Chevalier
Aman. } (L.C., *after hesitating*) Mr. Frank Price?

Fan. Killed! No. The duel didn't come off.

Rosie. } No!
Aman. } No!

Fan. No?

Mrs. K. } (L.) } I told you he knew nothing at all about it.
Tod. } (R.) } I told you she new nothing about it.

(*aside*) That abominable woman has such powers.

Mrs. K. (*aside*) Poor old man! Losing his faculties.

Fan. It was all a mistake arising from Price's not understanding German, and little Stockstadt knowing nothing of English. As we were walking to the ground, Price explained to me that yesterday morning he confided the fact of his unhappy attachment to some girl——

Mrs. K. Yes; *I* know that.

Tod. (*aside*) What a liar the woman is !

(Rosie *casting down her eyes, delighted*)

Fan. Confided it to Stockstadt. You know Price's manner—which manner, phlegmatic little Stockstadt took for intentional rudeness, and avers that Price once put him back into his seat forcibly. This Stockstadt misconstrued, called Price out. When informed of them, I mentioned the facts to Staufenberg, who, in turn, mentioned them to his principal, and——

Rosie. They explained mutually?

Aman. And didn't fight?

Fan. No.

Mrs. K. } Just as I said.
Tod. }

(Amanda *whispers to* Rosie)

Fan. Poor Price seems awfully cut up about this little girl. He wouldn't tell me her name. I wonder who she is?

Rosie. (r.c.) I know.

> Todder *and* Mrs. Kinpeck *draw nearer to* Rosie. Amanda *goes up and looks off,* l.u.e.

Fan. Who?

Rosie. Me!

Fan. (*thunderstruck*) You?—you, Rosie, my dear?

Rosie. Yes, uncle; he's in love with me; and—I—I am in love with him.

Fan. You—you acknowledge it?

Rosie. Why not? I'm not ashamed. I'm proud of it !

Fan. Why, love is worse than gaming.

(*goes up with* Rosie)

Mrs. K. Then she was the young lady—I didn't catch her name ! I'll go and tell everybody they are engaged.

Tod. So will I.

Mrs. K. You take the left from the terrace, and I'll go by the right, then we can't clash.

> They *shake hands. Exeunt* Todder *and* Mrs. Kinpeck *severally Enter* Price *and* Stockstadt, l.u.e., *crosses and exeunt* r.

Fan. (*sitting,* r.) Rosie in love ! and with a Price ! and not ashamed to own it. She's right. I'm so little in the habit of owning what I do, that it's a new sensation to me.

Rosie. (*whispering*) Uncle, there's a letter for you.

(*crosses* r.)

FAN. *(taking it)* Where are you going ?

ROSIE. To find my Frank, and ask his pardon.

Exit ROSIE, R.1 E. AMANDA *sits in arbour,* L.2 E. AMANDA *utters a loud sob.*

FAN. *(looking round)* Eh ! Browne's wife ! The lady who had the two ten-pound notes in the ruins ; whose face seemed so familiar to me.

(AMANDA *rises and comes down,* L.)

FAN. *(rises and takes off his hat)* Pardon me for my exclamation of surprise just now ; but I did not know that my friend Browne had the happiness of being a husband *(aside)*, such as it is !

AMAN. He conceals the fact of his marriage because his wife earns her living as a player.

FAN. Player !—Oh ! the tables ?—Well, I've rather a prejudice against lady gamblers ; and if you play at the tables——

AMAN. But I don't

FAN. You don't play ?

AMAN. Yes ; on the stage ! I am an actress !

FAN. An actress !

AMAN. You may have heard my name—Tarelton— Amanda Tarelton !

FAN. My dear Miss Tarelton, I have seen you act a dozen times. *(holds out his hand)* I thought I knew your face. (AMANDA *takes his hand*)

FAN. Your father and I were old friends. We were in the same regiment together in the West Indies. Tried to drink ourselves to death there—he succeeded—I survived. Browne deserves a horsewhip for daring to neglect——

AMAN. It is not of neglect that I complain, but of his attachment to another. My intention is to separate myself from him for ever.

FAN. Before taking that final step, my dear lady—*(aside)* —the very best thing she can do *(aloud)*—permit one of the oldest friends of Jack Tarelton to ask you to pause. It is a bad world, my dear madam, and men of the world are of the world, worldly. In fact, men are bad, as a rule ; and of all men, husbands are the worst—as a rule, of course there are honourable exceptions ! Good faithful fellows. *(aside)* Not worth their salt—as a rule. *(aloud)* You really should be indulgent. In your absence—away from his charming partner—if Browne has forgotten himself, I ask you for his pardon, forgiveness, my dear madam——

AMAN. My mind is made up. An engagement has been offered me in America, I shall accept it ; and it is now my duty to caution you. I watched my husband yesterday, at the old castle. The lady with whom he supposes himself in love is your niece !

FAN. Rosie ?

AMAN. Yes.

FAN. The villain ! The unmanly villain ! A mere child ! I'll—I'll—shoot him ! I'll—I'll—— (*falls into chair*)

AMAN. As you say—men, as a rule, are bad.

FAN. Bad ! But Rosie ! It's atrocious ? (*rises*)

AMAN. Your niece left you that letter.

FAN. Thank you ! Bob Bradshaw's hand ! It may be important, yet I can hardly think of anything ! Browne make love to Rosie ! It's—it's—(*opens letter*) Pray excuse me. (AMANDA *retires up* L. ; *reads*) "Dear old Loose "—Ah ! that's Bob's fun, instead of Bruce—all my friends call me "Loose." (*reads*) "My congratulations. I suppose you have seen the announcement of old Fowler Tredmayne's death ?" —Eh ?—Fowler Tredmayne, gone ? (*reads*) "As you are in foreign parts, and may not see the papers, I send you the enclosed slip, cut from last Saturday's 'Saddle.' (*reads slip*) 'Death of an Eccentric.—Mr. Fowler Tredmayne, once so celebrated on the turf, died at his own residence, in his 77th year, on Thursday, the 19th inst. The deceased, who, in the earlier part of his career, lived at an almost prodigal expense, for the last forty years has been considered a miser. His accumulated savings, with the exception of some few legacies, go to the daughter of a favourite niece, Miss Rosie Fanquehere, who, we are informed, is residing abroad.' " (*pauses in thought*) Last Saturday's "Saddle "? I read last Saturday's "Saddle," but I didn't see this. I've got it in my pocket now. (*produces newspaper*) Eh ? A corner cut off ! I remember ! I lent it to Browne. (*with a sudden inspiration*) Ah ! I see—he read it, made love to Rosie—gets his wife off to America——

Enter BROWNE, *from house,* R. FANQUEHERE, *gasping with passionate indignation, places the torn corner under* BROWNE'S *nose.*

BRO. Bruce ! (*aside*) Blown !

FAN. You—you—you—black-leg ! You—you—rook ! You—you—cut off the corner !

BRO. (L.C.) What corner ?

FAN. You villain ! You knew of old Tredmayne's death.

N N

I'll shoot you ! I'll call you out. I'll shoot you without calling you out. You—you've made love to the child—Rosie.

BRO. Pooh ! pooh ! Rosie was mistaken ; she didn't understand.

AMAN. (*advancing*) But *I* did.

BRO. (*aside*) I see.

FAN. Why, you're married, confound you ! As if to put a climax to your rascality, you're married, and disown your wife—the daughter of my old friend Jack Tarelton ! A lady by birth, and a genius by nature ! You pass yourself off as a man of family, forsooth ! Why, your dirty dissimulation shows your origin. If you'd been born a gentleman you'd have been proud of such a woman ; as it is, thank your stars you've obtained a prize that loves you, and brings you in money. *You* set up for a gentleman, quotha ! Many's the game of billiards I have played in your father's, old Tom Browne, rooms, and French Hazard when the doors were closed—you damned Cocktail ! (*crosses to* R. *corner*)

BRO. (*stung and losing temper*) You infernal old humbug! How dare you talk to me in this strain ? What if I were to speak ? Who hocussed Humiliation the night before the race ; and poisoned Remorse, by the riding boy ?

FAN. It's a lie, sir !

BRO. Joe Huggins said——

FAN. Joe Huggins is a blackguard, sir—and your friend——

BRO. You old sinner !. Your age protects you.

FAN. Ecod ! it shan't protect you.

> *Advances on* BROWNE. AMANDA *comes between them.*
> FANQUEHERE *raises his hat to her and retires to table,* R.

AMAN. (*to* BROWNE) I leave by the train this afternoon —for London, thence to Liverpool, thence to New York. Farewell ! Forget me, as I shall try to forget you.

BRO. Amanda !

AMAN. You have long been ashamed of me. It is a bitter pang for me to feel that now I am ashamed of *you.*

FAN. I should think so.

BRO. (*aside*) I never saw her look so handsome, or so noble in my life !

AMAN. (*to* FANQUEHERE, *shaking his hand*) Thank you, my dear sir, for your kind words, and for your acknowledgment of my claims to social recognition——

BRO. (*aside*) I won't lose her. (*aloud*) Amanda, one

word. You are about to leave me, perhaps for ever. Bear
with you to distant shores the avowal of my fondest love.
I have been wrong—I have injured you. Now that it is too
late, I see my error. (*wipes his eyes*) These tears are foolish.
The scales have fallen from my heart ! I deserve my fate,
but I cannot help repining. It is indeed a blow to lose such
a woman.

FAN. (*aside*) And such a salary !

BRO. My repentance is sincere. Indeed I meant to seek
you at your hotel, confess all, and implore your pardon. It
is now too late. I have been dazzled, but I am not bad at
heart. Amanda ! Oh, Amanda, I did not expect this of
you !

AMAN. Can I believe you ?

FAN. No ; don't.

BRO. Can you—can you leave me for ever ?

(AMANDA *seems to hesitate*)

FAN. (*rises, crosses to her*) Yes, do, for your own sake.
Consider what a scoundrel he has been to you. When a
woman has discovered her husband to be—(AMANDA *glances
angrily at* FANQUEHERE)—an impostor ! a trickster ! a sham
gentleman, and a thorough cad, what can she do ?

AMAN. (*after a pause*) She can forgive him !

(*takes* BROWNE'S *hand*)

BRO. Yes, dear, let us exchange forgiveness !

FAN. (*crossing to* R., *and sits*) Do, and go to America !
Well, women *are*——

AMAN. In a new land, with new associations and
surroundings——

BRO. I shall become a new man. (*aside*) It's a hundred
a week ! (*aloud*) And—(*crosses*, R.) Fanquehere, as I know
one or two unpleasant things, you'll hold your tongue for
your own sake.

AMAN. (*crosses*, R.) And for the sake of Jack Tarelton's
daughter.

FAN. On condition that he acknowledges you as his
wife before the world.

BRO. That, of course, is my intention.

AMAN. My love, fashion dazzled you ; but your heart
was always good.

BRO. How well you know me.

AMAN. (*to* FANQUEHERE) You said that men, as a rule,
were bad, but that there were honourable exceptions.

FAN. Not worth their salt—I said so, yes. To think

that she should forgive him ! Well, well—in the Race of Love, the woman invariably is both favourite and outsider !

Enter ROSIE, *crying, and* PRICE, R. 1 E.

ROSIE. Oh ! don't forgive me, please ; I don't deserve your forgiveness.

PRICE. We're both equal. I don't deserve your love.

ROSIE. Yes, you do.

PRICE. No, I don't. But I'll take it all the same.

ROSIE. No ; I won't have it. I'll go into a convent and take the veil.

PRICE. Don't. Stop outside, and marry me. The ceremony is quite as interesting, and the results are more agreeable.

FAN. (*seated at table*, R.) Heyday ! heyday !

ROSIE. Uncle, you are the very person we both wish to see.

FAN. You do?   (*rises*)

ROSIE. (*taking* FANQUEHERE'S *arm, and walking to and fro, to* PRICE) Don't we?

PRICE. Yes. (*aside*) No.

ROSIE. Listen, uncle—I want to marry Frank.

FAN. Is that all ?

PRICE. Oh ! if I only had her impudence.

FAN. That's all, is it ? But do you know that you're a mere child—an infant—a baby? And that Frank is hardly a man ?

ROSIE. But we don't want to be married just yet. We can wait for years. He'd like to wait for years, wouldn't you, Frank?

PRICE. (*a little back*, C.) No ! (*aside*) Yes.

FAN. Then, my Rosie, don't you know that you're a great match ?

PRICE. }
ROSIE. } Eh——?

FAN. That you have a large fortune !

ROSIE. What ! That which I won from——

FAN. From the devil ! No, this comes from your other uncle.

PRICE. (*sighing*) Just my luck !

ROSIE. But you always said that I was poor !

FAN. Yes ; but now somebody's dead, and you're rich.

ROSIE. Am I ! How it would have pleased nurse Martha !

FAN. Besides, there is a sort of feud. The politics of Mr. Price's connections——

PRICE. Ah! that's the worst of having grandfathers.

ROSIE. Oh! politics! Such nonsense when people love each other. Frank will change to whichever side you like —won't you?

PRICE. Yes. No!

FAN. (*aside*) Poor young things!

ROSIE. So, till we're married, Frank can visit us as often as he pleases.

FAN. We'll see about it.

(ROSIE *and* PRICE *go up stage*)

BRO. Permit me to introduce you to Mrs. Browne.

ROSIE. (*aside to* AMANDA) I'm so glad.

(FANQUEHERE *comes down and sits at table,* R.)

BRO. (C.) Price, you must have seen my wife act at one of our London theatres, Miss Amanda Tarelton.

PRICE. (L.C.) Oh!

BRO. (*to* FANQUEHERE) What do you think of that for repentance?

FAN. Like most repentance—Humbug!

BRO. *Your* conversion to the side of virtue is rather sudden.

FAN. Yes, it's late in life to be taken up with that sort of thing; but better late than never.

Enter MRS. KINPECK, L.U.E., *out of breath.*

MRS. K. (*down* R.) Dear Mr. Fanquehere, Mr. Todder and I have been telling everybody that dear Rosie is engaged to Mr. Price. They are coming to congratulate them.

FAN. (*enraged*) You have? It's not true. They're too young.

Rises. MRS. KINPECK, *crosses up,* L.H. *Enter* TODDER *down steps,* R.

TOD. (*advances* C.) My dear Bruce——

FAN. My dear Todder, you're a fool! (*crosses* L.) I have paid you your £500; so I don't mind telling you.

Enter OMNES, *during which* BROWNE *introduces* AMANDA *to* MRS. KINPECK *and* TODDER.

MRS. K. (*to* TODDER) She's an actress! (*music*)

TOD. Good gracious!

STOCKSTADT, STAUFENBERG, *and others congratulate* ROSIE *and* PRICE.

FAN. I'll be revenged upon these old devils. My dear
friends, permit me, in my turn, to present to you another
young couple, who are also engaged, fiancé, verlotten.
Mrs. Kinpeck and Mr. Bodmin Todder are shortly to be
led to the Hymeneal altar. My dear young friends ! (*with
hat off*) Permit me.   (*crosses to* L. *corner*)

> OMNES *congratulate* TODDER *and* MRS. KINPECK,
> TODDER *awfully annoyed.*

GRAF. (*to* MRS. KINPECK) How do you do ? (*to* TODDER)
Illustrated London News !   (*tableau*)

CURTAIN.

PROGRESS.

A COMEDY IN THREE ACTS.

(FOUNDED ON "LES GANACHES," BY VICTORIEN SARDOU.)

BY

T. W. ROBERTSON,

AUTHOR OF

"Caste," "A Breach of Promise," "School," "M.P.," "Birth,"
"David Garrick," "The Ladies' Battle," "The Nightin
gale," "Play," "Ours," "Row in the House," "Society,"
"Dreams," "War," "Home," "Faust and Marguerite," "My
Wife's Diary," "Noemie," "Two Gay Deceivers," "Jocrisse
the Juggler," "Not at all Jealous," "Star of the North,"
"Birds of Prey," "Peace at any Price," "Half Caste,"
"Ernestine," "Chevalier de St. George," "Cantab," "Clock-
maker's Hat," "Duke's Daughter," "Sea of Ice," &c., &c.

———————

LONDON:
SAMUEL FRENCH,
PUBLISHER,
89, STRAND.

NEW YORK:
SAMUEL FRENCH & SON,
PUBLISHERS,
28, WEST 23RD STREET.

PROGRESS.

(Produced at Globe Theatre, London, September 18th, 1869.)

CAST OF CHARACTERS.

Lord Mompesson	MR. COLLETTE.
Hon. Arthur Mompesson	MR. H. NEVILLE.
Dr. Brown	MR. J. CLARKE.
Mr. Bunnythorne	MR. PARSELLE.
Bob Bunnythorne	MR. E. MARSHALL.
John Ferne	MR. J. BILLINGTON.
Mr. Danby	MR. WESTLAND.
Wykeham	
Eva	MISS LYDIA FOOTE.
Miss Myrnie	MRS. STEPHENS.

ACT I.—DRAWING-ROOM IN MOMPESSON ABBEY.

ACT II.—THE TAPESTRY CHAMBER IN THE ABBEY.

ACT III.—*Scene same as Act II.*

Modern Costumes.   Time of Representation, two hours and three-quarters.

SCENE.—MOMPESSON ABBEY.

PROGRESS.

ACT I.

SCENE I.—*Drawing-room in Mompesson Abbey. Door* C. *Small door* R. *Old-fashioned large fireplace* R. *Scene enclosed. Window* L. (See diagram.) *Outside window, garden and park seen. The trees covered with snow. Large fire burning. Pictures on walls, &c. Sofas, chairs, couches, tables, all old-fashioned. An air of great antiquity, and tumble-down comfort about everything. Vestiges of feudalism ranged here and there.*

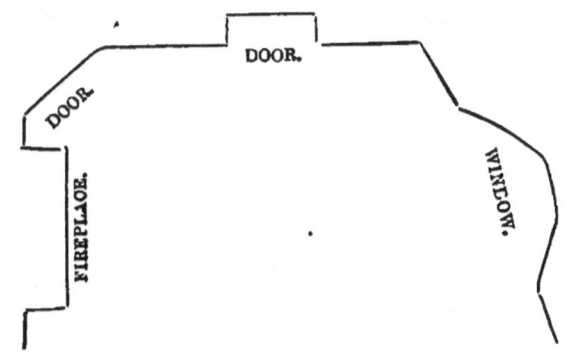

Enter DANBY *and* FERNE, *conducted by* WYKEHAM, C.D. FERNE *carries a portfolio.*

WYK. (*an old servant, of about sixty-six*) If you'll be good enough to sit down, gentlemen, Mr. Arthur will see you directly. *Exit* WYKEHAM, C.D.

FER. A fire—a lovely fire. My fingers are almost frozen.

DAN. So odd that I should find you sketching and planning as I drove past. It's more than two years since we met.

FER. I was going to call here when I'd finished my plan. I have business with Lord Mompesson.

DAN. With old Lord Mompesson? You'll find it difficult to transact business with him.

FER. Why?

DAN. He never attends to business. He's too old.

FER. Too old : A man of fifty?

DAN. Fifty ! Why, he's over eighty !

FER. What ! is not the old lord dead yet ?

DAN. No. I suppose you're thinking of his only son, the Honourable Arthur. Do you know him ?

FER. I did some years ago.

DAN. How was that ?

FER. My grandfather was a tenant.

DAN. Oh, yes ; I remember. Before '32 ?

FER. Yes. They quarrelled with my father about his vote on that occasion. My father left the farm.

DAN. And took to scientific drainage ; lucky for you, for thanks to that, here you are, at thirty years of age, a rising engineer, making a fortune and a name.

FER. Never mind that. Tell me about the Mompesson family. But, first, how is it I find you here ?

DAN. Don't you know ? Since my father-in-law retired from practice I'm the family lawyer.

FER. And the old lord is still living ?

DAN. Yes,—that is, he lives a little, preparatory to dying a great deal.

FER. He was a very old man when I was quite a boy.

DAN. Of course ! You know the story, don't you ? The old lord—always a poor man—had hopes for his son in Parliament, so in '29 he bought a rotten borough—Wapshot-cum-Chuddock.

FER. Which in '32 was disfranchised.

DAN. Just so—and the family was ruined. However, there was but one son—this Arthur—who at that time was in the Guards, a fine, handsome, young officer. Well, father and son took this misfortune so to heart that young Arthur left the army, and, with his father, settled down here in the old Abbey, on their own estate, near Stickton-le-Clay, and have given no attention to politics or public life ever since. This, they say, is a degenerate, peddling age, and they will have none of it ; they have cut the world—a slight of which the world is quite unconscious.

FER. And what sort of a man has the Honourable Arthur crusted into ?

DAN. A country gentleman of the old school. Urbane, refined, polished, and prejudiced. A great man at Quarter Sessions—and at the County Ball. A crystallised Quixote, doing battle with everything new.

FER. Is he clever ?

DAN. He has a gentlemanly intellect, somewhat narrow-minded—and large-hearted. He is a noble fellow despite his prejudices. High-minded, chivalric, brave,.and courteous. He would have made a splendid crusader, if he'd had the ill-luck to have been born six hundred years ago. Chop him into mincemeat, and every atom would be gentleman.

FER. And such a man can shut himself up in this hole of a village ?

DAN. With his father—to whom he is devoted. He has also another attached friend, who almost lives in the house. One Dr. Brown—a most amusing inconsistency—moral, political, and medical. A Radical—a Chartist—a Republican of the reddest dye ; a materialist of the old French revolutionary type ; an adorer of Cromwell, Voltaire, Robespierre, and William Cobbett ; a man who wants to root up thrones and pull down churches—behead kings and burn clergymen—in the cause of order, law, liberty, equality, and fraternity. But with all this old-world folly the Doctor is an excellent man ; high-minded and straightforward ; a most skilful physician ; indeed, it is he who keeps the old lord alive.

FER. But how does the Doctor—this acid of Radicalism, agree in the same house with the alkali of aristocracy ?

DAN. Meaning the Honourable Arthur ? Admirably. They used to hate each other, but when Arthur Mompesson fell from his horse in the hunting-field and broke his leg, the Doctor attended him, and, ever since, their personal attachment has been equal to their political antagonism. They discuss and quarrel over their wine. Let me tell you the Doctor is a teetotaller. Oh ! how they discuss. Then there are two other people here, quite characters.

FER. Who are they?

DAN. Old Bunnythorne, a retired contractor :—supplied provisions for the Navy ; his father made a fortune at Portsmouth during the war.

FER. And what is he like?

DAN. Oh ! he too grumbles at everything new, and growls a perpetual chorus of compliments to the good old times. Not that he has much cause to grumble. Oh, yes, I forgot. He has one.

FER. What's that?

DAN. His son,—his only son,—Bob, a conceited young lout, who, because his father won't give him money to go up to London to waste his time and health there, gets drunk at the " Mompesson Arms " here every night in the society of

Miss Brill the barmaid and one Jack Topham, a man much looked up to in these parts by ostlers and stable boys. Bob, too, considers himself quite a literary character.

FER. Why?

DAN. I don't know. I suppose because he can't spell properly, or because he's thoroughly impracticable, and never understands the poetry he reads.

FER. A very singular family group. And are there no women in the house?

DAN. Yes, two. One a Miss Myrnie, a detestable old maid—scandal-loving, mischief-making, snuff-taking, poodle-doggy, and generally disagreeable. She is some sixteenth cousin, and remains here out of——

FER. Charity?

DAN. No;—kinsmanship. She has, perhaps, five drops of the Mompesson blood in her, and that is quite enough for my lord and for his son.

FER. And the other lady?

DAN. Oh! a girl of eighteen,—also some distant cousin. I don't know much about her, except that her mother made some *mésalliance*, and married a man in business. The father and mother dying, the girl was received here. I have been told that at first neither my lord nor his son cared much about her presence, they were so indignant at her mother's conduct, but now they are both very much attached to her. Poor girl! she has been very ill, and is only just recovering.

FER. (*looking at his watch*) Time that I should go, and so I must leave my card (*leaves card in basket*), and call again when I am here in two months' time.

DAN. Won't you drive back with me and dine?

FER. Impossible. I must finish my plan, and sleep in London to-morrow night, to meet the Board the next morning.　　　　　　　　　　　　　　　　　　(*going*)

DAN. Well, good-bye. Stop! You're doing well, and making your fortune. Why don't you get married?

FER. (*smiling*) Married! I never have the time. You must meet a girl at least three or four times before you propose to her, and what with one thing and the other——

DAN. Have you never met anyone who——

FER. Well—yes,—(*reflecting*)—I did think: but no, it was nothing. (*looking at watch*) Matrimony doesn't go well with engineering, so I must die a bachelor. (*looks at watch*) Good-bye!

Dan. (*shaking hands*) Good-bye. (*Exit* Ferne, c.d.) How that young fellow has got on since I first knew him; but no wonder—clever, sober, industrious——(*Enter* Bob, *followed by* Wykeham, c.d. Danby, *seeing him*) Ah! this is quite another sort of thing.

Wyk. Really, sir, you must not smoke anywhere but in the smoking-room : my lord don't like it.

Bob. Old fool!

Wyk. Mr. Arthur don't like it.

Bob. Old fool!

Wyk. And your father don't like it, sir.

Bob. Another old fool! There! (*putting up his pipe in case*) That's gone out, and now you can go out! (*Exit* Wykeham) Another old fool! Everybody here's an old fool—except me. Eh! Danby, is that you? I thought it was my guv'nor.

Dan. I have not the good fortune to be your guv'nor.

Bob. You're lucky!

Dan. I think so.

> Bob *to be got up like the conventional poet; but dirty and slovenly, velvet coat, long black hair, pale face, spectacles, a sort of pot-house Manfred.*

Bob. My father's as much behind the age as I am above these wretched, stupid surroundings. I rust here—rust—regularly rust. I'm like a bright sword steeped in ditch water.

Dan. (*aside*) More like a soft spoon steeped in beer.

Bob. (*spouting*)—

"My thoughts from 'mid the vulgar herd gyrate from pole to pole ;
Patience, my heart, oh rest, my brain, oh wait, my weary soul !"

Did you ever read my poems! My "Thoughts in a Crater"?

Dan. No.

Bob. I'll lend 'em to you. They're in manuscript.

Dan. (*quickly*) Thanks. I have no time.

Bob. The guv'nor won't let me publish. He won't give me the money. Could you lend me a sovereign?

Dan. I'd rather not, if it's all the same to you.

Bob. Like the rest of 'em! O world! world!

(*spouts*)

"Patience, my heart, oh rest, my brain, oh wait, my weary soul !"

Dan. Why not thirsty soul?

Bob. Danby! To the calm and dispassionate observer it is curious to think what an infernal old fool my father is! If my poems were published in London, I should realise a fortune; then, with his capital, I could start a new magazine or a daily newspaper!

DAN. And does he refuse to indulge you to that trifling extent?

BOB. He does! Oh, these fathers! what misfortunes they are to men of genius.

BUN. (*without*) The horse is right enough—never mind the horse! Look after me! I think I've broken something somewhere!

BOB. There he is!

Enter BUNNYTHORNE, C.D., *his hat smashed; hat and coat covered with snow.*

BUN. (*as he enters*) Send for the doctor!

DAN. ⎱ What is the matter?
BOB. ⎰ What's happened, guv'nor?

BUN. I was driving back—everything was white with snow—and, I suppose, I got off the road into the ditch. Down we went—and then on one side—b-r-r-r-r-r. What weather! There never used to be any snow in the winter when I was a young man!

BOB. No snow!

BUN. At least, if there was, the snow wasn't cold, and it never filled up the ditches. Everything has degenerated, even the snow!

BOB. Guv'nor, the fact is, if you don't know how to drive, you should get somebody to drive you.

BUN. Hold your tongue! It was that beast of a horse; but there are no horses nowadays! No beasts worth their straw!

BOB. No beasts?

BUN. Except you! Why didn't you come home last night?

BOB. I slept at Jack Topham's.

BUN. Jack Topham's! A nice acquaintance for a young man of fortune!

BOB. Pretty fortune! Ten bob a week for pocket-money!

BUN. With your prospects!

BOB. Pretty prospects! Stickton-le-Clay and its neighbourhood!

BUN. Hold your tongue!

BOB. Can't I speak?

Bun. No! Not when your father's been thrown out of a gig!

Bob. I wish to console you.

Bun. Console—humbug! Hold your tongue!

Bob. I shan't!

> *Enter* Dr. Brown. *Blue coat, brass buttons, dark drab breeches and gaiters, all loose and easy, spotlessly clean; very loose large white neckerchief; red healthy face; a homely grandeur about the man; long white hair flowing over the coat collar.*

Doc. Now, what's all this fuss about?

Bob. The guv'nor's spilt himself.

Bun. I didn't—it was the gig. The gigs never used to spill in my time.

Doc. (*feeling his arms, &c.*) Stand up. Move your arms—so.

Bob. (*to* Danby) The gig spilt him,—reasonable, isn't it? Nice lot of old fools I'm condemned to waste my burning youth among.

Doc. You're all right. (*to* Bunnythorne) Perhaps a bruise or two. I'll make you up an embrocation.

Bob. You're not hurt. (*spouts*)

"For the linnet loves its egglets ere a feather deck their wings;
And the love-birds peck their mother, as their lullaby she sings."

Doc. What, ain't you dead yet? (*to* Bob)

Bob. Doctor!

Doc. At the rate you're going it, I give you eighteen months longer. You're as white as a sheet. Look at your liver, sir!—look at it! I should like you to see your own liver.

Bun. I shouldn't.

Bob. Really, if I'm treated in this way, I'll go——

Bun. Do—do—and don't come back.

Bob. Such language to your own son——

Doc. Pooh! Parentage is a mere accident.

Bun. Accident! In this case it's an offence.

Bob. Of all the ignorance——

> *Enter the* Hon. Arthur Mompesson, c.d. *Morning dress of the late Duke of Wellington, blue frock coat, buff waistcoat, black stock, grey trousers, grey hair.*

Art. Good morning, my dear Mr. Danby. I fear I've kept you waiting.

DAN. I have some leases that want renewing, and a few other papers to submit to Lord Mompesson.

ART. He will be here directly. Bunnythorne, I hear you've had a bad fall.

BUN. All falls are bad nowadays. Augh! I've no patience. When I used to fall, thirty years ago, I didn't feel it half so much.

BOB. You were younger then.

BUN. I was not. (*in a passion*) Don't talk to me.

DOC. Don't excite yourself. You'll bruise your— intellect.

BOB. He won't feel it in that quarter.   (*aside*)

> *Enter* MISS MYRNIE, C.D., *an old maid of fifty-three, rusty black silk, and mortified manner of a pew-opener. She carries in her arms a little lap-dog.*

MISS M. (*carneying*) Good morning, dear Mr. Arthur. I was not down soon enough to meet you at breakfast. (*to* DOG) Wish Mr. Arthur good morning, Pamela. Dear Mr. Bunnythorne, how do you do?

BUN. Black and blue all over.

MISS M. And dear Robert, too. (BOB *nods sulkily*) And the Doctor. (*aside*) An irreligious wretch. (*to* DOG) Never mind him, Pamela; he shall not harm us. (ARTHUR *and* DANBY *talking near fireplace* R. BOB *seated* R. BUNNYTHORNE *and* DOCTOR L.) Oh, Mr. Bunnythorne, here's your newspaper.   (*giving it*)

BUN. (*unfolding paper*) And a pretty thing a newspaper is nowadays. Why, they sell some of 'em for a penny. Nice news they must contain for a penny!

DOC. Ay, indeed; Cobbett's Weekly Register——

BUN. Bother Cobbett!

DOC. Don't abuse Cobbett.

ART. Why not? He abused everybody.

DOC. You must not touch giants. Respect the ashes of the great Cobbett, and of Cromwell, and——

ART. Cromwell—a butcher!

BUN. No; a brewer.

DAN. (*aside*) Now they've begun.

BUN. I always liked Cromwell.

DOC. Why?

BUN. Because he *was* a brewer.

ART. And rose from his malt-tubs to usurp a throne. A regicide!

Doc. That was his great merit. He taught indignant people to kill kings.

Miss M. Listen to him, Pamela, and bite him when he's not looking.   (*to* Dog)

Doc. The three great epochs of modern times were '89, '32, and '48; since then the world has ceased to move. Cromwell showed the French the way to deal with despots.

Bob. I don't think much of Cromwell.

Doc. *You* don't think much of Cromwell? You! I wonder what Cromwell would have thought of you.

Bob. His killing of Charles——

Art. Assassination!

Doc. } Righteous execution! }
Art. } Infamous assassination! }   (*together*)

Bob. His suppression of his breathing apparatus. There! Cromwell was only an imitator; Brutus killed Cæsar in the Capitol long ago.

Bun. In the good old times!

Doc. What the devil——

Art. (*pointing to* Miss Myrnie) Hush! hush!

Bun. (*who has been reading paper*) Another railway accident. Go it! go it! nineteenth century!

Art. Not a fatal accident, I hope.

Bun. One woman killed!

Doc. Only a woman!

Miss M. Only a woman!

Doc. I meant only *one* woman.

Art. Are you disappointed that a dozen were not sacrificed to this modern scientific apparatus for swift slaughter?

Doc. Woman, considered from the point of view of reason, is an inferior animal to man.

Miss M. The villain! (*to* Dog) You hear what he says of us, my dear?

Doc. Anatomy proves it.

Art. Anatomy! What has the mutilation and desecration of the dead to do with the beauty of a life? What has the grace, charm, goodness, heroism, patience, the *mind*, the soul, to do with anatomy?

Doc. Nothing whatever. I speak as a materialist. Woman——

Miss M. (*rising*) Doctor, if you are going to use bad language we will retire.

Doc. Miss Myrnie, when I said woman I meant nothing personal to you.

o o

Miss Myrnie, *appeased, sits down again; the* c. *door is opened by* Wykeham, Lord Mompesson *led by* Eva *enters.* Lord Mompesson, *an old man of eighty, in a dressing-gown and skull-cap.*

Lord M. Good morning, good folks, good morning. Mr. Danby, how do you do? Excuse me for having kept you waiting. Arthur, have you made my excuses to Mr. Danby? My good Doctor, you don't know how much I am indebted to my good nurse. She's been reading to me this morning. She is quite my *gouvernante.*

Miss M. Good morning, my lord! (*to* Eva) Good morning, dear! (*aside*) He never asks me to read to him. Ah, (*to* Dog) Pamela, we have none of the beauty of the serpent when the serpent's an egg!

Doc. Miss Eva is the best nurse in the world.

Lord M. Why—why—why did you not come here sooner, Eva? You've not been here—no, not twelve months; and we're all in love with you, aren't we, eh?

Miss M. (*aside*) I'm not in love with her. Ah, these men! They never will understand women!

Eva. Oh! Don't talk in that way. You'll make me so vain! You'll spoil me!

Bun. (*to* Bob) Go and talk to her. If you are a poet, behave as such. (Bob *gets near to* Eva, R.H.)

Art. Mr. Danby has some business—if you could see him. (*to* Lord Mompesson)

Bob. (*aside*) She is not a patch upon Miss Brill at the "Arms." (*to* Eva) Eva, you've never read my poems?

Eva. No; I've been so well lately, and the weather's been so fine.

Bob. Then you don't know my lines—— (*spouting*)

"When the white-winged wind woos winter, and the robin flees the wold,
And the lover leaves his lyre, lest his fire turn to cold."

Pretty lines, aren't they?

Eva. Very. What do they mean?

Lord M. Mr. Danby, come with me. Come into my room.

Art. Shall I——

Lord M. No, no. When we want you, we'll send for you.

Arthur *opens door.* Danby *offers his arm to* Lord Mompesson. *They both go out,* C.D.

Bob. (*pursuing* Eva)

' For the Mayflies live in summer, though their life last but a day :.
And the summer of a lover is as one eternal May."

Eva. (*turning over card-basket*) This young man always smells so dreadfully of tobacco. (*sees* Ferne's card ; starts*) Oh !

Art. What's the matter ?

Eva. Nothing. (*aside*) Has he been here ?

Bun. Pretty couple, aren't they ?

Miss M. I don't know. I never recognise couples. I consider them improper.

Doc. Why so ? There's you and Pamela.

Art. I don't consider Bob pretty.

Bun. But he will be—he will be. I was just the same at his age.

Art. That hardly reassures me. But what do you mean ?

Bun. I mean,—why not marry them ?

Art. ⎫
Miss M. ⎬ (*astounded*) What ?
Doc. ⎭

Bun. Make 'em man and wife. Bob would turn steady, and——

Miss M. I don't like marriages, unless they are contracted in a Christian spirit.

Art. (*his pride wounded*) A member of my family.

Bun. Exactly ! Family on your side, money on mine.

Art. Money.

Eva. Can he have been here ?   (*aside*)

Doc. Pooh ! pooh ! Eva can't marry.

Art. ⎫
Miss M. ⎬ Certainly not !

Bun. Why not ?

Doc. Why not ? She is hardly convalescent. She has not entirely got over her last illness. Look at her now ;— her eyes dilated ; the nostrils distended ; the short, catchy breathing,—all signs of poor, thin, weak, bad blood.

Art. Bad blood ! My cousin !

Bun. We Bunnythornes have always had good, rich blood ! Look at the spots on Bob's face.

Art. ⎫ The blood of the Mompessons ! ⎫
Bun. ⎬ The blood of the Bunnythornes ! ⎬ (*together*)

Doc. Blood ! What *is* blood ?   (*contemptuously*)

BUN.   ⎧Oh! don't begin——
ART.   ⎪For goodness' sake——
MISS M.   ⎨Never mind them, Pamela!   ⎫ (together)
BOB.   ⎩(spouting) "When the watch-   ⎭
              dog barks his welcome."

Enter WYKEHAM, C.D.

WYK. Lunch is on the table, sir.

ART. I have lunched.

BUN. I have not;—but I will.   (*rising*)

MISS M. So will I.   (*rising*)

DOC. And I.   (*rising*)

BOB. Eva!—may I——

EVA. (*thinking of card*) No, thanks, I never lunch.

BOB. Nor I. I've no appetite.

DOC. I should think not, the life you lead. Go back to the public-house.

BUN. Leave the boy alone; you're always at him.

DOC. So are you.

BUN. But I'm his father.

BOB. And I wish you weren't.   (*spouts*)

"Patience, my heart, oh rest, my brain, oh wait, my weary soul!"

MISS M. A set of brutes!   .

Exeunt all but EVA *and* ARTHUR, C.D.   EVA R., ARTHUR L.

EVA. How could that card find its way here?

ART. (*looking at her*) 19,—19 from 50; 9 from 10, 1; 2 from 53,——31; 31 years. It's a long time to look forward to, but a short time to look back on. I feel as young as ever,—younger; for I can appreciate the love of a good woman, as no lad of twenty knows how. (*mournfully*) Perhaps because I can no longer inspire it. A wasted life. A wasted life! And Arthur Mompesson, the dandy Guardsman, has sunk into an old bachelor with a talent for whist. Augh! (*sighs*) That cub, Bob! Old Bunnythorne to dare to—— Why not! Bob is her own age. Oh, youth! youth! To think that Bob should be so young and I should be so old. (*crossing to* R.) Eva! (EVA *starts*) What are you thinking of?

EVA. (*placing card in basket*) Thinking of—nothing.

ART. Why, your eyes are quite animated; and there is a flush on your cheek that gives you an expression as of a rose surprised.

EVA. Oh, cousin, you're very complimentary!

ART. Has anything happened?

EVA. No!

ART. You are looking much better these last few weeks.

EVA. Yes; I think my illness has passed. Everybody was very kind to me—you especially.

ART. And are you really happy with us?

EVA. Very happy!

ART. And have no regrets—no thoughts of those you have left?

EVA. Oh, yes! I sometimes think of them. They were very good people.

ART. Very good sort of people, no doubt, for trades-people.

EVA. But tradespeople are as good as anybody else?

ART. Humph! *(doubtfully)*

EVA. You know papa died so suddenly that he left mamma very poor; and as mamma was not noticed by her family, she was forced to work.

ART. *(aside)* A Mompesson work?

EVA. And the Dobbses took a great deal of notice of her.

ART. The Magasin des Modes people?

EVA. Yes; and were very kind to her and to me, and paid my doctor's bill, and waited on me. Oh! so tenderly!

ART. No doubt the Dobbses are very good people, and must have expended a considerable sum of money on your account. I'll write to them to thank them, and enclose them a cheque for a hundred pounds. I suppose that will be enough?

EVA. Oh, you mustn't do that!

ART. Why not?

EVA. You'd offend them! The Dobbses are very proud.

ART. Oh, the Hobbses are proud, are they? To think that pride could find a residence among the Hobbses.

EVA. Not Hobbses—Dobbses.

ART. Dobbses?

EVA. They are truly noble people!

ART. Noble?

EVA. Not by descent, but feeling.

ART. Feeling?

EVA. Heart!

ART. Heart? Then you think that the qualities of the heart level all distinctions?

EVA. I do.

ART. *All* distinctions?

EVA. Yes!

ART. Rank—birth?

EVA. Yes!

ART. Genius—talent—wealth?

EVA. Yes!

ART. Age?—youth?   (*changing his voice*)

EVA. Yes! (*a pause*) Youth and age are only accidents If one is good and kind and tender, what does it matter in what year one was born?

ART. (*quickly*) Not a bit!—not a bit! I like the liberality of your sentiments, and—and—if—if—a—a—man—or a woman—I should say girl—were to fall in love—with—with—each other—the question of age need not——

Enter WYKEHAM, C.D.

WYK. My lord wishes to see you for a few minutes.

ART. Yes. I'll come—I—— Excuse me, cousin. (*taking her hand*) I was just going to say something which—— I'll be back directly.

Exeunt ARTHUR *and* WYKEHAM, C.D.

EVA. I cannot help wondering how that card came here. He must have called; and if he called he must——(*looking into card basket.* MISS MYRNIE *opens the little door* R. *and watches* EVA) The card looks quite new. (*going to window*) It's more than a year now since I saw him. (*at window, starts*) Why, there he is, sketching! No! I'm right! it is he! (*trying to open window*) Oh, these nasty old windows. (*opens window and beckons*) He doesn't see me. I'll send to him. Now he sees me! Here—here! Go round there to the left—to the door. How d'ye do? how d'ye do? I am so glad to see you. (*coughs and places her hand on her chest, then shuts window*) Oh, the cold air. I've not recovered yet.

Enter FERNE, C.D.   MISS MYRNIE *closes door* R.

FER. Somebody certainly beckoned me in. (*seeing* EVA) Eh, Eva! you here?

EVA. Yes, me. Didn't you see me at the window?

FER. Was that you?

EVA. But why did you not come in without waiting to be asked? My uncle, Lord Mompesson, would be very glad to see you.

FER. Your uncle, Lord——

EVA. My grand-uncle.

FER. Lord Mompesson?

EVA. Yes. My mother's uncle. Since I saw you in London I've come to live with them.

FER. You surprise me! I knew that your mamma was of good family, but not——

EVA. I've been here eight months, and they're all so kind to me. How are the Dobbses?

FER. The Dobbses? I haven't seen them since I last saw you there. I've been abroad.

EVA. Where?

FER. In Russia principally.

EVA. Engineering?

FER. Engineering.

EVA. I had a letter from Mrs. Dobbs last week. I saw your card there just now. So kind of you to call and see me.

FER. To call and see you. (*aside*) She will have it I came to see her; though I did not know she lived here.

EVA. How came you to be in this neighbourhood?

FER. Eh? oh, business! (*aside*) I came to knock the house down.

EVA. However, I must present you to my uncle; then you can call when you please. Oh! I forgot! just now he's engaged with Mr. Danby.

FER. Mr. Danby?

EVA. Yes. Do you know him?

FER. I called here with him this morning.

EVA. Oh! you called with *him*?

FER. Yes. How well you're looking. Do you remember at the Dobbses when I used to call and see you, and you sat in that big old arm-chair, by the fireside, propped up by pillows?

EVA. Oh, yes!—yes! That was a nice time!

FER. But now the colour has returned to your cheeks.

EVA. Come with me, and I'll show you over the Abbey, and by that time my uncle will be disengaged.

(*crossing to* L.)

FER. But——

EVA. It's a wonderful place, the Abbey, one of the oldest in the kingdom. There are secret staircases and walls, and places I shudder as I pass, and down below—I've never been there, I'm too frightened—there are dungeons and cells, where, they say, poor people were shut up and tortured. Oh, horrible! is it not? (*lowering her voice*) Skeletons of the victims have been found within the last three years, and beneath where we are now standing is a crypt, in which are niches where living women were walled up alive, and left to die in the dark of thirst and hunger. (*frightening herself with the recital*)

I cannot understand. The rulers of those days were good men, holy abbots, and pious pastors. Why were they so cruel? Thumbscrews, racks, dungeons, and burning stakes. Why — why — why did they brick up breathing, living women?

FER. Because — because they lived in the good · old times.

    Exeunt FERNE *and* EVA, C.D. MISS MYRNIE *opens little door,* R.

MISS M. Oh, dear me!—oh, dear me! This is very bad!—this is very bad! I never see a young man and a young woman together but I suspect they care for each other. The wretches! And that Arthur! Oh, that Arthur! I know he's fond of the girl. Old fool! Why can't he seek a wife among his own connections—a woman of his own time of life—of ripe experience—mature charms, and pious feeling. A blessing on the heavenly side of forty; but, no! Mr. Arthur likes youth, and a slim waist, and a child's complexion, and baby tattle about ribbons and rubbish. But men are like that. The idiots! It is so ridiculous, the fuss they make in praise of youth. Why, everybody's had it once, and nobody can keep it long. Then it is so perishable. Youth soon fades away, but age lasts us to the latest hour.

    Enter ARTHUR, C.D., *quickly.*

ART. Now, Eva, as I was——(*sees* MISS MYRNIE—*disappointed*) Oh! it is you, is it?

MISS M. Yes; I take that liberty. Did you expect to find Eva?

ART. (L.) Yes.

MISS M. (R.) She's not here.

ART. Where is she?

MISS M. She is showing the Abbey to a young gentleman.

ART. A young gentleman! Bob?

MISS M. No, not Bob. Ah! (*sighing*) Would it were Bob!

ART. Eh, why?

MISS M. The young man is a stranger.

ART. A stranger!

MISS M. A perfect stranger. She saw him at that window. He made signs to her, and she made signs to him. Then she opened the window and beckoned him to come in, and he came in.

    ART. (*astonished*) Impossible! How came you to know all this?

MISS M. I saw them from behind that door.

ART. Then you were watching—listening.

MISS M. Heaven forbid! I hope I know my duty better. But—sometimes—one happens to open a door—by accident —when something is happening by accident, which we see by accident; or, one is behind a door by accident, and one hears something—entirely by accident and accidentally. It's happened to me often.

ART. But to speak to a stranger from a window!

MISS M. (*crossing and closing window*) Why, the sash is still open! I thought there was a draught.

ART. I can't believe it! Eva, so good—so truthful!

MISS M. So she is; that's what I always say.

ART. To accuse her——

MISS M. Accuse her! Heaven forbid; Christian charity forbids that I should accuse anyone. I'm defending her.

ART. Defending her?

MISS M. Yes; she can't help it.

ART. Can't help——

MISS M. Running after a young man—after a *young* man —no—it's in her blood.

ART. In her blood?

MISS M. Yes; do you not remember twenty-four years ago, when her mother ran away with that low plebeian fellow Summers? It was at this very window that they used to meet. (ARTHUR *sinks in chair*) Romeo and Juliet over again; and it was like that villain Shakespeare to put it in a play.

ART. (*rising*) Do me the favour to ask the Doctor and Mr. Bunnythorne to come here.

MISS M With pleasure. As to dear Eva, I'm sure she's innocence itself. So youthful, so truthful—there's the pity. Innocence and youth are so apt to betray us, ain't they? But, as I often tell my Pamela, she's a darling girl. Bless her! Bless her! Bless her!

Exit MISS MYRNIE, C.D.

ART. Eva beckon to a strange man! Impossible! She must have known him. Some intrusive shop-boy from those people she was with—the—the Nobbses. A 'prentice? I—I—I—— At this very window, too, where her mother ——it would seem as if there were a fate in it.

Enter DOCTOR *and* BUNNYTHORNE. BUNNYTHORNE *in night-cap and dressing-gown,* C.D.

DOC. Arthur, you sent for us.

Bun. The Doctor was sending me to bed, so I came as I am.

Art. I wanted your advice. I find that there is a young man here—a stranger—come after Eva.

Doc } *(together)* { Eva!
Bun.

Art. Now should his intentions be matrimonial——

Bun. Matrimonial! Then what's to become of my boy Bob?

Art. *(out of patience)* Bob! You can't think of Eva and Bob.

Bun. Why not? They're both young.

Art. Eva is too young.

Doc. And too delicate.

Bun. Well, Bob's delicate, too.

Art. But a stranger coming here without introduction, and *sans cérémonie——* .

Doc. Insolent!

Bun. Kick him out!

> Eva *and* Ferne *appear at* c. *door,* Arthur, Bunny-thorne, *and* Doctor *with their backs to the audience,* Miss Myrnie *at* c. *door. A pause, during which* Miss Myrnie *crosses at back door* r., *and goes off.*

Eva. *(somewhat surprised at their aggressive attitude)* Cousin, let me present——

Art. Not now. Your uncle wishes to see you upstairs.

Eva. But before——

Art. Don't keep him waiting. Go at once, dear.

                              Exit Eva c.d. *Pause.*

Fer. I presume that I must introduce myself, as Miss Eva——

Art. *(stiffly)* That ceremony will not be unnecessary. Whom have I the honour of receiving at Mompesson Abbey?

Fer. My name is John Ferne, civil engineer.

Art. Ferne! a relation of the Snobbses, no doubt.
                                        (aside)

Fer. May I now inquire whom I have the honour of addressing?

Art. Certainly! Dr. Brown.

Doc. W. N. Brown. No final E.

Art. Mr. Bunnythorne.

BUN. Late of Bunnythorne and Bingham, contractors, Gosport.

ART. I am Mr. Arthur Mompesson.

BUN. The Honourable Arthur Mompesson.

DOC. What the devil's the Honourable to do with it? A man's a man, isn't he?

BUN. Not invariably. Sometimes he's a gentleman. ·

ART. Not often. *(aside)*

BUN. He gave you your title of Doctor, didn't he?— why not give him his title of Honourable?

DOC. My son wouldn't be a doctor, would he?

BUN. What nonsense you talk—you haven't got a son.

DOC. There I have the advantage of you—you have.

ART. .Chut! chut! Mr. Ferne, pray take a chair.
(they all sit)

R. · FERNE. ARTHUR. L.
DR. B. BUNNYTHORNE.

Your name is not unfamiliar to me!

FER. My grandfather was a tenant on this estate, and I remember you, Mr. Arthur, as we called him, perfectly.

ART. *(aside)* A tenant! *(aloud)* If I remember rightly, your grandfather had an old-fashioned name. Let me see —Jabez—Jabez, was it not? (FERNE· *assents*)

DOC. Jabez Ferne! Any relation to the Jabez Ferne who patented the invention for drainage by means of——

FER. His son! My father!

DOC. *(rising and shaking hands with FERNE)* He was an honour to science and his country.

BUN. *(crossing and shaking hands too)* So he was, for we bought the patent, and sold it in the colonies to an enormous profit.

DOC. Profit! Think of making two blades of grass grow in place of one. Think of benefiting your fellow-man!

BUN. Think of benefiting yourself.

ART. May I inquire if you follow the same career of sewerage your father did? Do drains run in your family?

DOC. Drains don't! Brains do!

FER. But then brains are not always hereditary. I have already told you I am an engineer.

ART. Pardon me! I had forgotten.

FER. *(aside)* They're very disagreeable.

ART. ·An engineer! Well, engineers are the heroes of the hour—I should say of the minute—for the present age goes so fast that we have to count by minutes.

FER. The present age is, certainly, the age of progress.

ART. Progress! Yes! That is the word. That is the modern slang for the destruction of everything high and noble, and the substitution of everything base and degrading. Progress! progress which pushes painting aside to make room for photography. But painting is old-fashioned; and photography—which makes men uglier than they are by nature—that's progress! Citric acid—and heaven knows what other abominations—have superseded grapes;—you literally *make* wine—that is science! Horses, which in my youth were considered noble animals, are abolished for engines that smash, for trains that smash, for velocipedes that smash; and the débris of broken wheels, boilers, bones, and shattered human beings, you call progress!

BUN.
DOC. } Bravo! bravo! beautiful. (*enthusiastically*)

ART. As to manners, progress has indeed altered them. Everyone is too much occupied to think, to feel, to love, or to improve. Progress does not permit sleep, or sentiment, or accomplishment, or leisure. To misquote Shakespeare—another illusion of my youth, and, doubtless, an impostor—"Whatever is done must be done quickly." Nowadays you eat rapidly, you drink rapidly, you make love rapidly, you marry rapidly, you go through the Divorce Court still more rapidly. Luxury everywhere; comfort nowhere. Look at your young men! cynical, sarcastic—without faith in anything; without warmth of heart, without generous enthusiasm—*blasé* and brutal—they puff the smoke of their foul cigars in the faces of their mothers, or swear before their sisters. Their talk is slang; their morals those of betting-men. Their aim to dazzle for a moment—their end bankruptcy of person, fortune, mind, heart, brain, body, and soul.

BUN. { (*rising and shaking hands with* ARTHUR, }
DOC. { *then seating themselves again*) } *together*
Too true! too true! (*shaking their heads*)

DOC. The world is going to the devil.

BUN. At express speed (limited). And it used to be so good. We used to be so good! Didn't we, Doctor?

BUN. } We did!—we did! We used to be so good. Ah!
DOC. } (*they sigh*)

DOC. These modern fellows, with their modern fashions, their beards and moustaches!

BUN. Too lazy to shave themselves. Hairy beasts!

Art. So un-English—pah !

Bun. And their floppy clothes, and their eyeglasses stuck so. (*imitating*) Ah !—ah !—ah !

Doc. And their cigars.

Bun. (*imitating*) Ah !—ah !—ah !

Doc. Ah ! The good old times !

Bun. \
Doc. } (*together*) Ah ! The good old times.

Doc. The men of old !

Art. Alfred ! the Black Prince ! the Fifth Henry !

Doc. Pooh ! Jack Cade—Cromwell !

Art. Pooh ! Claverhouse—Marlborough !

Bun. Whittington, Lord Mayor of London !

Fer. Why not his cat ?

Doc. Bacon !

Bun. Milton ! Guy Fawkes ! Mrs. Fry !

Doc. Thistlewood !

Art. Pitt !

Doc. Fox—Cobbett—Horne Tooke !

Art. Junius !

Bun. Cock-eyed Wilkes !

Doc. Walter Scott !

Art. Byron !

Bun. Old Parr ! Where do you find such pills now ? I mean, where do you find such men now ?

Art. Where indeed ?

Art. \
Doc. } Ah ! (*they shake their heads mournfully over*
Bun. / *the bright past and degenerate present*)

Fer. Do I understand the meaning of this combined attack to be because I, as an engineer, represent modern progress ? If so, I accept the challenge. All that you have said is but to contrast the vices of the present with the virtues of the past. I cannot think that we are so bad as you would make us out. Vice is vice, no matter in what epoch it exists, and I readily admit that we are not as good as we should be. But, to combat your examples. We are guilty of moustaches ; that, you say, is un-English. How about Shakespeare, and Bacon, and Sir Walter Raleigh ? They wore beard and moustache, and they were somewhat of Englishmen. We smoke cigars. Johnson and Goldsmith smoked pipes. What difference ? If we smoke more, we snuff less than our grandfathers. You have recalled the names of men dead for centuries, to ask me if I could show a parallel to them in this year of grace ?

Alfred, the Black Prince, Marlborough, and Pitt. Why not Pericles, Lycurgus, Alcibiades, or Solomon, or David, or Noah? For our manners, our cynicism, and lassitude, let it be remembered that we no longer beat watchmen, or steal knockers and bell-pulls for the sake of showing our wit. If we use slang, at least we are not guilty of the brutal oaths that, in the last century, made the name of Englishman a by-word over Europe. On one point, too, I must claim superiority even for our poor, weak, little modern selves—we keep sober. · Men do not now reel into a drawing-room and bend over our mothers, wives, sisters, and daughters, to pump out compliments with a breath reeking of fiery port, with a faltering articulation, and unsteady step, and a tongue so loose and unguarded that it can scarce refrain from insult. From the usual degradation of daily drunkenness we are freer than our fathers, and——

BUN. (*rising in indigant fury*) Who the devil are you to turn up your nose at a man that gets drunk? Let me tell you, young sir, that I got drunk before you were born. Everybody got drunk before you were born. A parcel of stuck-up sober puppies! To get drunk properly and like a gentleman is a very good thing; it's—it's—it's English— thoroughly English, and old-fashioned—and—and—all right! · (*sits down, blowing the steam off*)

FER. You have sneered at this age because it is an age of progress; I prefer to call it a period of transition. We have changed from the worst to the better—we are changing still, from bad to best; and during this transition —I am proud to know that it is I—the engineer, the motive-power—who leads the way. 'Tis I who bring industry, invention, and capital together; 'tis I who introduce demand to supply. 'Tis I who give the word— 'tis I who direct the train that flies over valleys, through mountains, across rivers—that dominates the mighty Alps themselves. 'Tis I—the engineer—who exchanges the wealth of one country against the poverty of another. I am broad, breathing humanity, that whirls through the air on wings of smoke to a brighter future. I spread civilisa- tion wherever I sit a-straddle of my steed of vapour, whom I guide with reins of iron and feed with flames. As for the tumbledown old ruins I knock down in passing, what matter? Where I halt towns rise, and cities spring up into being. 'Tis the train that is the master of the hour. As it moves it shrieks out to the dull ear of prejudice, "Make room for me! I must pass and I will! and those who dare oppose my progress shall be crushed!" Its tail of smoke is like the plume of a field-marshal; and the rattle and motion of its wheels are as the throb and pulsations of the progress of the whole world.

ART. Possibly you are right, sir. (*rising*) Coal smoke is better than pure air;—the shriek of an engine is the sweetest harmony, and rapid motion is the sole secret of truth and happiness; but in my time it was not considered the act, I will not say of a gentleman, but of an honest man, to make signs to a young lady at a window, or to enter the house where she lived to speak to her clandestinely.

FER. What! (*rising*)

DOC. You have been observed, sir. (*rising*)

BUN. (*rising*) The whole morning—drawing, writing, and making signs at this window.

FER. To Eva?

ART. Eva! (*aside; to* FERNE) To Miss Mompesson, my cousin!

FER. I am compelled to contradict you most emphatically. Eva—Miss Mompesson—whom I met in London, called me in from that window. Until she did so, I was not aware that she lived here.

ART. Then why write?

FER. Write! I was not writing; I was sketching.

DOC. Sketching?

ART. In this weather?

FER. Yes, a bird's-eye view of this place and the neighbourhood, by order of the company of which I am chief engineer.

ART. Eh?

FER. Yes! (*showing portfolio*) We are going to make a branch line from Stapleton, through Broxborough and Wainthrope to Stickton-le-Clay.

DOC. ⎫
ART. ⎬ A railway here?
BUN. ⎭

FER. Yes. (*showing drawing*) Yes, here is the line; you see it cuts this park and the house in two——

DOC. ⎫
ART. ⎬ The Abbey?
BUN. ⎭

FER. Yes! The station will be built on this site. We must pull the Abbey down.

ART. Pull down the Abbey! Do I hear rightly? Pull

down the Abbey! where my family for centuries have been born, lived, and died. Where I first saw the light; where, when my time shall come, I hope my eyes shall darken to this world, to open in a brighter and a purer. Pull down the Abbey! The royal gift of a king to my ancestor for faithful services in council and in field. A home where generations of knightly gentlemen and high-bred ladies have gone forth to rule the world and live in honour! A church, beneath whose aisles saints have spoken and martyrs have been buried. A holy shrine, reverenced by every passing peasant, where hospitality and every earthly charity, as every spiritual good were sanctified in stone. Pull down the Abbey! Sooner than see it trampled to dust and scattered to the winds, its stones shall fall and crush its master. (*giving way, sinking into chair*)

Doc. (*going to him*) Arthur!

Fer. I am very sorry——

Art. We fly their cursed civilisation—their genius of smoke—their factory palaces—their spinning-jennies—printing presses, and inventions of the devil. My father and I are not left even this retreat.

Bun. Here, here, here. This can soon be settled. (*taking portfolio*) Look here; by letting the line diverge here, at the park gates, it comes round here, knocks down old Brewster's new house, and there you are for your station; and any compliment that you may consider your due, for altering your plans, we shall be most happy to pay money down.

Fer. (*taking portfolio*). It only needed such a suggestion to recall me to a sense of my duty. I shall recommend this route. (*to* Arthur) At the same time I shall be glad for your sake, Mr. Mompesson, if the company in considering the matter should modify my instructions, and the park and Abbey should remain intact.

Art. (*rising*) You are right, sir; and I beg your pardon for having for a moment doubted you. I recognise you as a perfect man of honour, in your way—your railway; but I shall go to London—I will appeal against this invasion of my rights. (*during this last speech* Eva *enters* c.d., *overhearing the last words;* Bob *appears at* c.d.; Miss Myrnie *at door* r.) I have friends, and powerful ones; I will see whether a railway company can uproot the home of a country gentleman. (*music—piano till end of Act*)

Eva. You are going away, cousin?

Art. Yes; to London.

Doc.
Bun.
Miss M. } (*together*) To London !
Bob.

> *Picture.* FERNE *bowing to take his leave.* ARTHUR *indignant.* BUNNYTHORNE *and* DOCTOR *sympathetic.* EVA *looking at* FERNE. BOB *contemptuous.* MISS MYRNIE *watching.*

Miss M.   Bob.

FERNE.   EVA.   ARTHUR.   DR. B.   BUNNYTHORNE.

END OF ACT I.

ACT II.

SCENE I.—*The Tapestry Chamber in the Abbey. Large window,* C. *Balcony and staircase seen behind it—covered with snow. Doors* R., *and* L. 2 E. *Scene enclosed. Large old-fashioned fire-place* R. 1 E. *(See diagram.) Large fire burning. The stage furnished somewhat sparely. Old-fashioned tapestry on walls. Table and invalid chair near fire-place. Sofa* L.

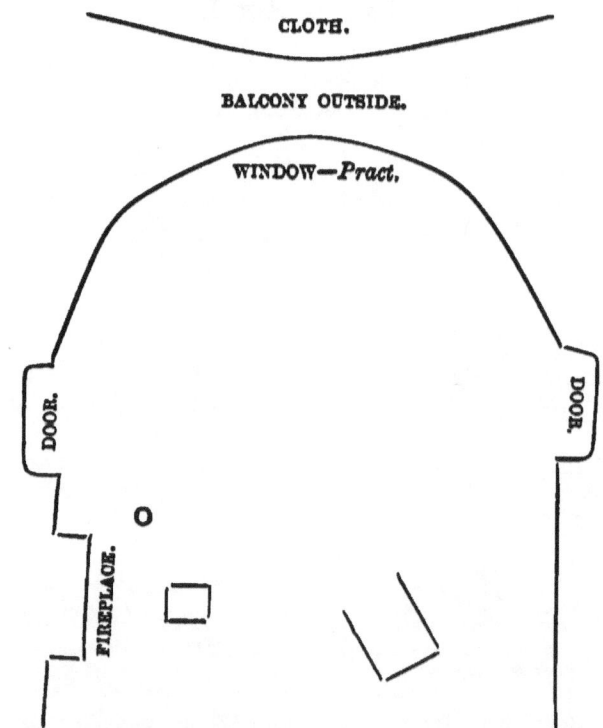

Enter DOCTOR *from door,* R (EVA'S *room*), *meeting* WYKEHAM, *on whose arm* LORD MOMPESSON, *in dressing-gown, is leaning, who enters,* L.D.

LORD M. Good morning, Doctor : good morning. How is our invalid ?

Doc. Much the same.

Lord M. Poor child! poor child! I miss her very much. She was so kind and thoughtful for me—so kind and thoughtful—so—so—Wykeham takes care of me now—don't you, Wykeham?

Wyk. Yes, my lord.

Lord M. But you're too old; ain't you, Wykeham—too old?

Wyk. Yes, my lord.

Lord M. So am I. In fact, we're both too old—ain't we, Wykeham?

Wyk. Yes, my lord.

Lord M. Do you think we shall have Arthur back to-day? *(to Doctor)*

Doc. I think so.

Lord M. Dear! dear! dear! And he thought to be only away a week, and he has been more than two months—such a long time—when one is old. Take me back to my room, Wykeham. Let me know if Arthur comes back

Doc. Of course.

Lord M. My love to Eva. Is she asleep?

Doc. Asleep? Yes.

Lord M. Ay, ay! A good thing sleep. Good morning. Now, Wykeham.

(Lord Mompesson *and* Wykeham *totter off,* l.d.)

Doc. Asleep! ah! *(sighing)* If she only could sleep.

Enter Eva, r.d. *She looks very ill, and half delirious. During the scene she excites herself so as to exhibit all the symptoms of delirious fever; she coughs at intervals.*

Doc. Have you got up, dear?

Eva. Yes; don't scold me; I was so tired of the sick room.

Doc. *(with great sympathy, all his rough manner gone, and the fine delicate nature rising to the surface)* Feel better?

Eva. *(languidly)* Just the same.

Doc. And your head?

Eva. Heavy. And my bones all ache.

Doc. Sit down by the fire.

(arranging pillows and armchair for her)

Eva. I'm always cold. My long illness began just in this way—but this time it will not last long.

Doc. Chut! chut! my dear. Come, you're more comfortable there.

Eva. I should like to be near the window.

Doc. The window is too far from the fire.

Eva. But I like to see——

Doc. There's nothing to see, my pet, but the snow that has fallen during the night.

Eva. I like to see the snow—the fantastic forms it seems to carve upon the trees—as if the whole world were made of white coral; or as if some good person were dead, and a shroud of ice had fallen upon the earth. Let me go to the window? *(rising)*

Doc. No, no; there is too much draught. It's a crazy old casement, and you mustn't catch cold. The slightest chill—an open door—or a current of air upon you in your state——

Eva. And I should die?

Doc. *(bothered)* Die! No, my love: nobody dies! it's out of date.

Eva. But it *might* kill me!

Doc. Well, it might, if it were fatal. If you must move, walk about with me—so—within range of the fire.

(she rises, takes his arm, and they walk to and fro)

Eva. Tell me, is it true that there are people in the world who believe, that when we die, all is finished—all is over—and that we do not meet those we love again in a better, higher sphere?

Doc. I—I believe that there are such people. The world is full of varieties.

Eva. *(growing delirious)* But how is it possible they can believe it? How can they believe it—at night—when the sky is full of stars? What are the stars but beacon-fires of immortality? lamps, lighting us on the Heavenly road to future and Eternal Life? Doctor, did you ever, on a bright night, see a star—fall?

Doc. Yes, often. I've seen many things fall at night.

Eva. And did you not think, as you watched it out on its bright path, through its host of shining sisters, did you not think that *you* were that star—falling, falling, falling through tremendous space—and have you not felt here, at your heart, a sense of sublime emotion—a sort of wonder and awe, but yet not fear?

Doc. No; I never felt anything of the sort. We doctors, you know, have to deal with material ailments—broken collar-bones, and not erratic nebulæ.

Eva. I saw my mother die ! When I die I shall meet her again ! I shall cleave. through the air and see the white frosty earth below me, as I aspire to a bright Heaven and her warm heart. She, above, cannot forget her poor child who, even in her earthly clay, remembers her.

(*coughs*)

D oc. My child, you're feverish, go back to your room (*seating her in armchair*) Your head is hot, and——

Eva. Yes, I feel I am very ill, but I think that when the poor body is weak the mind is clearer. (*suddenly*) Doctor, why do you never go to church ?

Doc. (*staggered*) Eh ?

Eva. Why do you never go to church ?

Doc. Me—a—a man—at my time of life.

Eva. (*slowly*) If I were to die ——

Doc. Eva !

Eva. If it were Heaven's will, and I should die, you would pray for me, would you not ?

Doc. I—I—I—you really must go to bed, my child.

Eva. God bless you for all your goodness to me.

Doc. (*awfully affected*) My love ! (*music, piano*)

Eva. (*after a pause, taking* Doctor's *hand*) They sent him away on my account ; did they not ?

Doc. Him ? Who ?

Eva. John—Ferne. You remember, I told you. They sent him away ; Miss Myrnie told me so ; because he was in love with me, and they did not think him good enough to be my husband.

Doc. Miss Myrnie told you so, did she ?

Eva. Yes.

Doc. (*aside*) The damned old ——, I'll give her some physic that will make her so ill. (*to her, soothingly*) My dear, Miss Myrnie told you a lie. So far from sending him away, your cousin Arthur likes him very much, and wishes him to marry you.

Eva. (*overjoyed*) What ?

Doc. Miss Myrnie is a mischief-making old ——. With your permission, I will think the rest in Latin. Your cousin Arthur has gone to London ——

Eva. (*eagerly*) To inquire about him ?

Doc. Yes ; yes. (*aside*) What an infernal liar I am ; but it's a pious fraud. (*to her*) And when he comes back ——

Eva. He will be my husband ?

Doc. Yes. (*she sinks into chair. A pause*)

EVA. (*after a deep sigh of relief*) Doctor, I think I'll go back to my room. I can sleep now.

DOC. Do, dear, do. (*she takes his arm*)

EVA. Will he come soon to see me?

DOC. I—I think so; but how do I know? I'm not in his secrets.

EVA. (*as they are nearing door*, R.H.) It's two months since I saw him; two months and three days.

DOC. Yes, dear, so it is. I make it out to be just two months and three days.

EVA. (*at door*) Good-night.

DOC. You mean good morning.

EVA. I shall sleep well, I'm sure I shall. (*going; returns*) If he comes while I'm asleep, you'll rouse me, will you not?

DOC. I'll come and rouse you up that instant.

EVA. Do. Oh! Doctor, why did you not tell me this good news before. I am so happy. *Exit* EVA, *door* R.

DOC. (*his handkerchief to his eyes*) Poor child! poor child!

> *Enter* BUNNYTHORNE, *all over snow*, L.D. *Skates in his hand.*

DOC. (*angrily and brusquely*) What the devil do you come in like that for? Don't you know that I've got an invalid there? (BUNNYTHORNE *is writhing in pain*) What are you doing?

BUN. I'm trying to get my back-bone straight again. I've been skating on the lake.

DOC. More fool you—at your time of life.

BUN. And I tumbled down.

DOC. Of course—and hurt yourself?

BUN. Yes.

DOC. Where?

BUN. Where I fell—on my back.

DOC. Fall on your head next time, it won't hurt you there.

BUN. Arthur Mompesson's come back from London.

DOC. No! When?

BUN. This moment. Here he is.

> *Enter* ARTHUR, L.D., *followed by* MISS MYRNIE·
> ARTHUR *is dressed in a modern morning suit,*
> *turn-down collar, modern cravat, &c. ; his whole*
> *manner changed ; he seems younger and brighter,*
> *and radiant with high spirits.*

ART. Ah, Doctor, how dy'e do? Where is my father? Where is Eva?

Doc. Not yet up.

ART. Still asleep (*looking at watch*) and past ten. The lazy creatures!

Doc. (*with his watch.* BUNNYTHORNE *and* MISS MYRNIE *take out their watches, big ones*) Past ten! Why it's not half-past nine.

ART. You're all slow here—behind time. It's past ten by the Horse Guards.

BUN. The Horse Guards at Stickton-le-Clay?

ART. No; the Horse Guards in London.

MISS M. ⎫
Doc.   ⎬ (*with contempt*) Oh, London!
BUN.   ⎭

BUN. (*dogmatically*) Our time is Stickton-le-Clay time; that's good enough for us.

ART. Well, Doctor, congratulate me, I've won.

Doc. Won!

ART. Yes; I went to the Commons—the Lords—I saw many old friends—I argued—I fought—and conquered—the line is to branch off at Broxborough. Wainthorpe is to be left to the right, and the railway line does not come here.

MISS M. (*rising and shaking hands with him*) Bless you!

Doc. ⎫
BUN. ⎬ Hurray!

ART. (*looking round with rapture*) These dear old walls; I have preserved them! They will still stand—a glorious relic of past ages—an architectural beacon to the future. Progress, with its hot oil and steam vulgarity, shall not reach us here.

Doc. ⎫
BUN. ⎬ Bravo!

ARTHUR *standing with his back to the fire,* R.H., *the others seated.*

MISS M.   DOCTOR.
ARTHUR   BUNNYTHORNE.

ART. But let us be just even to our enemies; the railway is very comfortable.

Doc. The railway?   (*astonished*)
BUN. Did you travel by railway?   (*disgusted*)
MISS M. Good gracious!   (*horrified*)

ART. As far as Stapleton. (*all aghast*) Why not? It was the nearest and the quickest.

MISS M. You travelled ——

BUN. By rail?　　　　　　　　　　　　　　(*a pause*)

ART. Yes, by rail; nice carriage—padded—tins full of hot water for your feet—very comfortable. When you stop at a station, man shouts out, Staple—ton, Staple—ton, bell, whistle, off you go—very nice indeed. (*they all sigh*) I didn't care much for the coach—the old "Perseverance" —afterwards. Not pleasant inside. Commercial man asleep on my shoulder, a good snorer; woman opposite with baby with whom travelling disagreed. Damp, bad-smelling straw, the roads awful. Had to get out and walk up the hills. Cold, wet feet—after the comfortable first-class carriage—horrible!

　　A pause. DOCTOR, BUNNYTHORNE, *and* MISS
　　　　MYRNIE *exchange glances.*

BUN. Where did you get those clothes?

ART. Oh! a tailor in Bond Street. I was so shabby. I ordered them and he sent them to Long's.

BUN. I never saw such an object in all my life. Why not wear moustaches?

DOC. And an eye-glass?

MISS M. Or smoke a cigar?

ART. Ah! You're prejudiced! I've brought presents for all of you—and as for Eva, I've ordered fresh furniture for this room.

MISS M. Fresh furniture?

ART. Yes; I mean to make it into a boudoir. Poor child! after the luxury of London, to be condemned to pass her days among these mouldy old chairs and tables. They're only fit for an outhouse.

BUN. And what are we fit for? An outhouse, too?

ART. My dear friends, my trip to London has made me twenty years younger. We'll make the old Abbey as gay as any place in the country. I mean to give a ball in honour of my victory over the railway.

MISS M.
DOC.　　} A ball!
BUN.

BUN. Do you expect me to dance?

MISS M. Or me?

ART. Why not?

MISS M. Is the ball, too, to be in honour of Eva?

ART. Yes.

Miss M. Why not marry her?

Art. Why not?

Miss M. (*rising*) Balls, Cousin Arthur, are wicked things—all sin and shoulders. If a ball is given in the Abbey I shall quit the place for ever.

Bun.⎱
Doc.⎰ (*together*) Hurray! (*congratulating each other*)

Miss M. (*hearing them, and more exasperated*) I dare say you'll be very glad.

Bun. We shall, indeed.

Miss M. I will not countenance such scandals with my presence. (*drops her spectacles*) Cousin Arthur, the place of future punishment is paved with ——

Doc. With good intentions.

Miss M. No, sir! with bare necks and shoulders, with false hair and paint, and other Babylonian abominations. Arthur, you went out from the country pure and unsullied. You have returned reeking with smoke, railways, impiety, and London. In time you will have ceased to be a single country gentleman, and sink into a married cockney!

(*she goes off,* L.D.)

Bun. (*after a pause of astonishment, seeing her spectacles on the carpet*) She's left her green spectacles. (*crushes them with his foot, then picking up the pieces*) Here, Miss Myrnie, you've dropped your spectacles.

Exit Bunnythorne, L.D.

Art. Upon my word, if Miss Myrnie were not——

Doc. Never mind the old woman—she's jealous.

Art. Jealous!

Doc. You said you'd ordered fresh furniture for Eva, and——

Art. Eva—yes—(*looking at watch*) Not up yet—lazy —I'll knock at her door.

(*going to door,* R. Doctor *stops him*)

Doc. No.

Art. Eh? Why not? (*seeing the serious expression of* Doctor's *face*) Is she ill? (Doctor *nods*) Very ill? Why did you not tell me? Why did you not write?

Doc. What use? She fell ill two days after you left, and she has got worse and worse.

Art. Is it a return of—a relapse? (Doctor *nods.* Arthur *sinks into chair*) But what cause?

Doc. What cause? (*putting both hands in his pockets and looking* Arthur *full in the face*) Love!

Art. Love! (*rising, astonished*)

Doc. Yes; for that young man—Ferne—the engineer.

Art. Impossible! He is not in love with her.

Doc. No; he is not in love with her, but she is in love with him.

Art. How do you know?

Doc. I heard her name him when she was delirious. (Arthur *resumes his seat*) I questioned her, and she confessed it. She fell in love with him more than a year ago—when they were both in London. See here—(*producing letter*), from the physician who attended her. Read.

Art. (*reading*) "If the fever returns in its full force, nothing can save her." (*rising*) But it shall not return. You are here. You can battle with the disease. You can save her!

Doc. Save her! How? Give me a body in pain, and I can try. Show me a diseased organ, and I know what I'm about. I can treat. I can reduce. I have something material to fight with. But a mind in trouble—a spirit diseased—a soul in agony—how can I treat that? I can't give her a dose of resignation or tablespoonfuls of hope. I can't cure a love-sick girl, dying of love.

Art. But no girl ever died of love. You've told me so a thousand times.

Doc. And I was right. They don't die of love, but love brings on fever, and they die of that.

Enter Bunnythorne *hastily*, l.d.

Doc. (*angrily*) How often am I to tell you to come in quietly?

Bun. (*angrily*) I shall come in as I like.

Doc. (*pointing to door*, r.) What, when ——

Bun. (*softly*) Oh, I forgot. But I'm annoyed! That young fellow—that stokineer—engineer—what is it?

Art. Ferne?

Bun. Yes, Ferne—is downstairs in the drawing-room, and wants to see you. I told Wykeham to send him away.

Doc. You did?

Bun. Yes.

Doc. You fool!

Bun. (*indignant*) Doctor Browne!

Doc. Go down again—ask him to take a glass of sherry; be attentive, polite, and bring him upstairs here in ten minutes.

Bun. Upstairs? } (*both astonished*)
Art. Here? }

Bun. But I don't understand——

Doc. Of course you don't. I don't expect that of you. *forcing him off*) Now go.

Bun. (*as he goes*) Ask that stokineer fellow——

Doc. Yes. (Bunnythorne *is forced off*, l.d.)

Art. I don't understand——

Doc. Eva must see him. Miss Myrnie told her that Ferne was ordered from the house on her account, because you and your father would not consent to the match. His presence will contradict the old serpent.

Art. But she must not believe——

Doc. Let her believe what she likes, so long as I can but save her.

Art. But it will be a lie to——

Doc. Yes, it will be a lie. Consider the lie physic, and swallow it with or without a wry face—as you please; but swallow it.

Art. But to-morrow we shall be forced to undeceive her.

Doc. Let us save her for to-day. We can think of something else to-morrow.

Art. But I will not consent——

Doc. You must!—you shall! Damn it, sir! Who commands by the sick bed-side—you or me? Give me the chance of saving her. Don't tie my hands. I'll snatch her from death if I can.

Art. Death! (*terrified*)

Doc. Yes. Send this young man away, and I'll not answer for her life eight-and-forty hours.

Art. (*despairingly*) Let him come! Let him come! Only save her, and I'll turn Radical!

(*shaking hands with* Doctor)

Doc. Hush! (*going to door*, r.) I hear her moving—place the sofa here.

> Arthur *moves sofa near fire.* Eva *opens door*, r. Arthur *offers her his arm.*

Art. My poor girl. I'm so sorry to see you ill again.

Eva. I'm so glad to see you back.

(*coughs. They place her on sofa*)

Doc. Keep yourself well wrapped up—the slightest cold—the smallest draught—and the consequences might be serious.

Eva. What a long time you've been away.

Doc. Arthur has been busy. (*motioning to* Arthur)

He has just been bothering me about a matter, which I
fear you have hardly strength enough to talk of.

Eva. (*trembling*) About——

Doc. Yes—about that—about Mr. Ferne.

(*during the Act,* Eva *coughs at frequent intervals*)

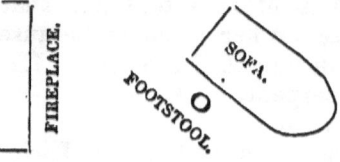

Eva. (*trembling*) Did you see him in London?

Doc. Yes. (*looking at* Arthur)   You saw him in
London?

Art. (*embarrassed*) Oh, yes.

Eva. Then you're not—you're not—angry—with him?

> Doctor *and* Arthur *are at back of sofa, so that*
> Eva *cannot see their by-play.   The red light of
> fire on* Eva's *face.*

Doc. Angry with him—ha, ha! What for?   (*Aside to*
Arthur) Say what for?

Art. (*mechanically*) What for?

Eva. For—for— Then Miss Myrnie was mistaken—and
you did not——

Doc. No, you didn't, did you? (*aside to* Arthur) Say
you didn't! I'm not going to tell all the lies—you tell your
share.

Art. Did not what?   (*to* Eva)

Eva. You did not—decline his offer.

Doc. I should think not! (*to* Arthur) Say no!

Art. (*embarrassed*) No!

Eva. Then you consent?

> *She is almost fainting.*   Doctor *applies eau-de-
> Cologne to her forehead.*

Art. (*taking* Doctor *up stage*) What are you about?
She believes that I consent to her marrying this fellow!

Doc. All the better.

Art. How can I undeceive her?

Doc. *Don't* undeceive her!

Art. You've done it, Doctor! You've done it!

Eva. (*recovering*) What are you saying?

Doc. I was saying that Ferne is such a fine young

fellow—make such a capital husband. He'll be here directly!

Eva. (*excited*) Directly!—When?—To-morrow?

Doc. When, Arthur? To-morrow; or, perhaps, sooner.

Eva. (*sitting up on sofa*) Hush! I hear his step! There are two people ascending the stairs; he is one of them. He is here. (*sinks on sofa*)

Enter Bunnythorne *and* Ferne, L.D.

Bun. (*aloud*) Here's Mr. Ferne. (*to* Doctor) Now you've got him—what do you want with him?

Art. (*going to* Ferne *and shaking hands with him with feigned cordiality*) My dear Mr. Ferne—delighted to see you —delighted.

Doc. Delighted! (*shaking hands*) Delighted!

Bun. (*to* Ferne) Eh! delighted? Why this is that fellow who was going to——

Art.) (*to* Bunnythorne) Do hold your tongue!
Doc.) Keep quiet, can't you? (Bunnythorne *bothered*)

Fer. (*surprised at the warmth of his reception*) I called partly to congratulate you on your success before the committee.

Doc. (*interrupting him*) And to inquire after Eva.

Fer. Eva!

All this takes place near L.H. *door up stage.* Eva, *who is on sofa, not hearing it.*

Bun. Eva! (*to* Doctor *and* Arthur) But I thought you didn't like the notion of——

Art.) (*together*) { Do hold your tongue. [silence.
Doc.) { Silence, you dreadful old magpie.

Bun. (*aside*) They're both gone off their heads. London has sent one mad; and living among physic has driven the other lunatic.

Art. (*aside to* Ferne) For Heaven's sake, don't contradict a word we say.

Doc. (*aside to* Ferne) We'll explain to you by-and-bye. (Ferne *astonished*)

Art. (*leading* Ferne *to sofa*) She is very ill—very ill indeed.

Fer. I am very sorry, Miss Summers, to find you suffering. So ill.

Eva. I have been ill, but I am better now.

Bun. (*following* Doctor *and* Arthur; *to them, aside*) Now perhaps you'll tell me.

Doc. { Do keep quiet. } *(together)*
Art. { By-and-bye, by-and-bye. }

Eva. And did you come down all the way here to see me?

Ferne. No. I came to see——

Doc. Yes; to see you, dear, of course—and Arthur—and all of us. (*aside to* Bunnythorne) Say as I do—make much of him.

Bun. (*mechanically crossing to* Ferne, *and shaking hands with him, quite bothered*) Yes, all of us—me particularly—always glad to see my dear friend, what's your name? Come often, and bring your steam-engine—I mean——

Eva. (*to* Ferne) When you saw my cousin in London, he didn't know I was ill?

Fer. (*mystified*) When I saw——

Art. (*interrupting*) Yes, when we met in London. They never wrote and told me. (*aside to* Ferne) For Heaven's sake don't betray us.

Doc. (*aside to* Ferne) It is life or death.

Art. We'll explain some other time.

Fer. (*to* Bunnythorne) Eh?

Bun. (*with importance*) Yes, I'll explain some other time, (*aside*) when I know what I've got to explain. (*aloud*) By-the-way, lunch is ready—so if you, my dear friend, will lunch with us, I'm sure Mr. Mompesson will be——

Art. Delighted—yes, delighted.

Eva. No, you can lunch without him. He will stay with me. You're not hungry, are you? No; he is not hungry. Besides, I want to talk to him alone.

Bun. (*astonished*) { Eh? } *(together)*
Fer. (*astonished*)

Doc. Yes. We'll go to lunch, and——

Art. (*aside to him*) Leave them together?

Doc. What is there to fear? He doesn't love her!

Art. No—but——

Doc. Do you want to murder her?

Art. No, no. There—there (*to them*)—I shan't be long.

Eva. Don't hurry on our account.

Art. (*to* Doctor) We're done, Doctor, we're decidedly done.   *Exit* Arthur, L.D.

Bun. (*to* Doctor) Now tell me why——

Doc. Don't bother now—only make much of him.
                                  Exit Doctor, L.D.

Bun. (*bothered*) All right. (*going to* Ferne *and shaking hands mechanically*) Sorry you don't lunch with us, dear Mr.—— what's your name?—but you must drop in some other time—drop in often—in a friendly way—devilish glad——

(goes off talking to himself, L.D. FERNE *astonished)*

FER. What can they mean?

EVA. *(smiling)* Well, won't you come and sit beside me?

FER. With pleasure.

(sits on sofa. EVA *near fire.* FERNE L. *of her)*

EVA. Oh! I am so glad to see you!

FER. *(embarrassed)* I, too, am delighted to have the opportunity.   *(formally)*

EVA. And they never told you how ill I was—and I might have died——

FER. Died! Oh, Eva. How can you talk in that way?

EVA. You would have mourned me—would you not? (FERNE *embarrassed*) But tell me — after you had seen Cousin Arthur in London—why did you not write to me?

FER. Write to you?

EVA. Yes; you knew the address!

FER. *(still more puzzled)* Oh, yes; I knew the address.

EVA. Well, then. Why not send me word of the good news immediately?

FER. I—I hardly felt—justified.

EVA. Why not? There was no need of any persuasion after Cousin Arthur had given his consent.

FER. Given his consent?

EVA. Yes.

FER. To—to—what?

EVA. *(blushing)* To—you know very well—why do you want to make me say it?

FER. Of course I know very well—but I should like to hear you say it, because then I might have an idea of what it was.

EVA. What a tyrant you are!

FER. Do say it, Eva. *(repeating)* Arthur Mompesson has given his consent——

EVA. To our—correspondence?

FER. Correspondence!

EVA. Had given his consent—to our loving each other. There! now are you satisfied?

FER. *(aside)* Good heavens! Does she love me?

EVA. So you could have written. Surely a man has the privilege of writing to his future wife?

FER. Wife? Then have they told you——

EVA. The Doctor told me everything; so it is no use your trying to conceal it. (*joyously—then sadly*) I know' why you and the others have tried to keep it from me.

FER. Why?

EVA. Because I was so ill, they feared the emotion—the excitement of the news might kill me.

FER. (*aside*) I understand.

EVA. But instead of increasing my malady it has improved my health. I feel stronger; I can breathe more easily. I can weep more freely. (*she weeps*) Don't be frightened, these tears do me good. They are cool, refreshing tears—not like the hot scalding drops that burnt me yesterday.

> *During this scene the sky seen through the window becomes darker as if before a storm. At the same time the glow of the fire increases in colour on the faces of* EVA *and* FERNE.

FER. But, Eva, if—if events had not turned out so happily; that is, if I had not loved you, or if I had only loved you with the affection of a brother——

EVA. Oh! I shouldn't have liked that; that would not have been enough.

FER. Or, if—mind I say if—if I had loved another.

EVA. (*shaking her head confidently*) Impossible!

FER. Impossible! Why?

EVA. I loved you so much, you could not help loving me in return. These things are fostered by fate—or, no! I should not say fate, for mutual love is the work of Heaven.

FER. Heaven! (*he rises and walks from sofa to* L. *Aside*) I can hardly believe my senses. (*returning to sofa and bending over her*) And my love makes you happy, Eva?

EVA. Happy? Oh, infinitely!

FER. (*with fervour, taking her hand*) And I, too, dearest Eva, am happy.

EVA. Now sit down here, and tell me one thing. (FERNE *sits by her side again*) Candidly, now—quite candidly.

FER. Tell you what? (*this scene to be played slowly*)

EVA. When did you first discover—that is, when did your heart first tell you that you loved me?

FER. When?

Eva. Yes. When ? (*a pause*) Ah ! you can't remember'
That's like men. Now, I'll tell you when I loved you for
the first time. (*with child-like confidence*) It was on the
twenty-eighth of September—on a Sunday. You called at
the Dobbs's, and after dinner you walked out with me in
the garden. It was the first time I had left the house
since my illness. I was still in mourning, and you talked
to me, and I fell in love with you from that moment.

Fer. (*with fervour*) Yes—yes, I remember.

Eva. You remember what you said.

Fer. No, not exactly. (*trying to remember*)

Eva. I remember every word, because, you know, I was
obliged to *guess* that you were in love with me.

Fer. Why ?

Eva. Because you never told me.

Fer. Because I was a fool—absorbed in my idiotic
business, and disregardful of the good, kind, warm, gentle
heart that beats for me. I remember now your sweet
looks, your pious resignation, your soft voice, and thousand
charms. I observed them then, though not with the
rapture I recall them now.

Eva. (*entranced*) Go on—go on. I love to hear you
talk in this way. It is the first time your heart has
declared its feeling to me.

Fer. (*his emotion mastering him*) I remember all. I
am again walking by your side in that glorious sunshine.
Again I see your pale face looking into mine—I see your
black dress—I feel your thin white hand upon my arm—I
hear your voice—that voice that death had so nearly
silenced for ever, but which returned to earth laden with
music as of another sphere. I recall all—and the sunstroke
that vivified my heart as your dear head rested there a
moment—and the tears dimmed your eyes in memory of
your mother. Eva, I loved you then, though I did not
know it. I love you now, that you can be mine—my own,
my partner through life—my wife for ever.

> *During this speech* Eva *has risen and stood by the
> side of* Ferne *as his speech reaches its climax; over-
> powered with emotion she falls unconscious on the
> sofa ; at the same moment* Arthur *enters,* L.D.

Art. (*angrily*) And I thought you were a man of
honour.

Fer. (*not seeing that* Eva *has fainted*) In what have I
forfeited that title ?

Q Q

ART. In what? (*seeing* EVA *is unconscious*) She has fainted. (*to* FERNE) Leave this house this instant.

FERNE. Leave this house! Who brought me into it, and welcomed me, and took me by the hand, and led me to hear her confession of love (*his tone rising with his words*), and to make my avowal of love to her?

ART. (*violently*) I order you to quit this house!

FER. (*placing his finger on his lip to indicate that* EVA *might hear them; scornfully*) · I obey your order; but I will return—return, despite of you, or all the world—to take away the bride I love—the wife who loves me—the woman to whom you have betrothed me! *Exit* FERNE, L.D.

ART. Curses on the time I first saw you!—and oh! my punishment for taking the advice that brought him to her side! Eva!—still unconscious!

Going to bell-rope, sees MISS MYRNIE, *who enters,* L.D.

MISS M. What is the matter?

ART. Wait here with Eva, while I fetch the Doctor.

(*crossing to* L.D.)

MISS M. (*crossing to sofa*) He's not in the dining-room!

ART. (*as he goes off,* L.D.) I'll find him.

MISS M. (*seating herself by* EVA's *side*) Poor child! What a state they've put her into!

EVA. (*recovering*) Ah! How bright my future! How happy I feel! (*seeing* MISS MYRNIE) Miss Myrnie, where is he? He was here just now!

MISS M. Do you mean Mr. Ferne?

EVA. Yes. (*the sky becomes darker outside window*)

MISS M. He's gone!

EVA. Gone!

MISS M. Yes; just this moment left the Abbey.

EVA. You are deceiving me, madam—deceiving me as you did before, when you told me that Cousin Arthur would not permit our union.

MISS M. (*enraged*) I deceive you, my child! It is they who are deceiving you; I heard them during lunch. Mr. Ferne's love for you is all a pretence.

EVA. What?

MISS M. A plan—a scheme got up between them to comfort you because you are ill, and as soon as you are better they will undeceive you. My poor child, I speak the truth, I never speak anything but truth.

Eva. His love a pretence—a plan !

Miss M. Yes, my poor child ; they're treating you as if you were a baby, and I can't bear to see it ; my sense of truth revolts at it ; so I was resolved to tell you of it, that you might assert your sex's dignity.

Eva. (*half convinced*) And yet but now he told me that—he—loved me.

Miss M. He said that, my dear—out of pity for you.

Eva. (*stricken*) Pity !

Miss M. Yes, dear ; the wretches to deceive you !—but I've unmasked them, and now you know the truth—the beautiful, the sublime, the glorious, the eternal truth !

Eva. (*after a pause*) Please leave me, I wish to be alone.

Miss M. (*rising*) Yes, dear ; thank goodness, I have done my duty. (*as she goes*) To dare to insinuate that I could tell a lie. No ! It's the men ! Men are all liars ! All ! They lie to deceive us, but they have never deceived me, and they never shall ! never ! never ! never ! never !

> *Exit* Miss Myrnie, L.D. *The snow begins to fall outside window, at first slightly, then more thickly towards end of Act.*

Eva. (*after a pause*) Pity ! His pity ! and all that he said as he sat here by my side. I remember. "If I had not loved you !" and, "If I had only loved you with the affection of a brother !" and, "If I had loved another !" (*rising from sofa*) I see it all. He does not love me, and his bright words were lies. Oh ! I am accursed ! cursed like my poor dead mother ! Why did I come here to this house from which she was banished—where I have been deceived ? (*coughs*) Oh ! air ! air ! (*approaches window*) I cannot breathe ! No ! (*returning*) I must not. The cold will kill me ! (*raising her head*) Well, why not ? Life is tasteless ! Let me die !

> *Music—piano till end of Act. She opens window and steps out into balcony amid the thick falling snow. Noise of wind heard as the casement is opened. Eva throws off the wrappings from her neck and shoulders so that she stands exposed to the snow in her petticoat body. She coughs frequently and places her hands on her chest. Ferne appears on balcony, and as she faints catches her, and brings her into the room again. At the same moment*

ARTHUR *and the* DOCTOR *enter,* L.D. MISS MYRNIE
stands in L. *doorway. The* DOCTOR *rushes to window
and closes it. Picture.*

DOCTOR at Window.
FERNE bending over her.   ARTHUR.
EVA on Floor.

Miss Myrnie at Door.

Drop, Quickly.

END OF ACT II. ·

ACT III.

SCENE I.—*The same as* ACT II. *Night. Stage dark. On
table, near fire, bottle and tumblers, and sugar. Small
copper kettle on fire.*

Enter BUNNYTHORNE, *in dressing-gown and night-
cap. He carries a lighted bed-candle in his
hand. He is slightly intoxicated. Clock strikes
five.*

BUN. Five! and that boy isn't home yet. I've been to
his room, and there's his bed as smooth as a—brickbat.
Oh, that boy! When I was a boy, what a charming boy
I was!—innocent, ingenuous, good-tempered, brave, handsome, sober. I've taken too much brandy! The Doctor
asked me to sit up in case he might want me, as Arthur is
knocked up, and Miss Myrnie is in the dumps; and so I—
brought the brandy—to rouse me—just to pass the time
pleasantly—and then I fell asleep; and I suppose that in
my sleep I—(*growing maudlin sentimental*) Poor child!
poor child! (*drinking neat brandy*) Oh, that boy! (*he puts
candle on table, near sofa. The candlestick falls, and the
light is extinguished. Stage dark*) Confound it! In my
time these sort of things never happened; but nowadays
—(*with disgust*)—Augh! (*he feels for candle; finds it;
contemplates it moodily*) Oh, that boy! (*places candle in*

stick, and then places the candlestick on table, then feeling on floor) Luckily the lucifers were in the—ah! (*finds lucifers on floor. During the following speech he strikes lucifers on box. They do not ignite. Irritably)* Clever! (*throwing lucifers away)* Clever! clever! That's modern science! Only a penny a-box! But they don't light! (*throwing lucifers away)* Go it! (*fondly)* And when I remember in my time how pleasant it used to be with the dear old flint-and-steel and tinder-box, and those nice wooden matches, with the brimstone at the top—and you used to hit the steel on the flint, like a harmonious blacksmith—and after the fifteenth or sixteenth stroke the spark would fall upon the tinder, and then the flames would spread about—"parson and clerk" we called 'em, in my innocent childhood—and then the match used to light—and ah! (*sighing)* The good old days! the good old days! (*a lucifer lights)* Ah! at last! (*he lights candle. Stage light. Crossing stage to L. door)* I wonder where the Doctor is? I'll go and see. (*as he reaches L. door, enter* BOB. *The draught from the door extinguishes the light. Stage dark again)* Oh, those boys! (*angrily)* Why did you open the door when you came in?

BOB. How could I come in without opening it?

BOB's boots and clothes give evidence that he has been walking in the snow. He is shivering with cold. He is partially intoxicated. To just the same extent as BUNNYTHORNE. *His greatcoat and general appearance should resemble* BUNNYTHORNE'S *in his dressing-gown.*

BUN. What d'ye mean by coming in at this time of night?—I mean morning!

BOB. I've been sitting up at the "Arms."

BUN. (*with disgust)* The "Arms"!—a tavern? When I was a young man there were no taverns, and those there were closed early.

BOB. We were talking litera-too.

BUN. Talking what?

BOB. Litera-*ture.*   (*with an effort)*

BUN. (*aside)* The boy's drunk—drunk as a fidd-l-l-l-er!

BOB. (*aside)* The guv'nor's tight—tight as a drum.

Both assume an air of excessive sobriety and dignity. BUNNYTHORNE *goes to sofa near fire.* BOB *follows him. As they cross, their resemblance to each other must be carried out by the actors' gestures and manners being arranged so as to be identical Whatever action is used by* BUNNYTHORNE *is also used inadvertently and unconsciously by* BOB.

BUN. Why did you not go up to your room?

BOB. I wanted to inquire after poor Cousin Eva! How is she?

BUN. I don't know—no better—just the same.

BOB. (*spouting*)

"She was doomed ere we were wedded, and I never saw her more.
Flame the lightnings, bray the thunders, bid the smoky torrents pour !
Bid the smoky torrents pour——"

Oh! smoky torrents—fine image, isn't it?

BUN. (*not heeding him*) Nothing to what it used to be in my time.

BOB Eh?

BUN. What's fine?

BOB. My poetry—my "Thoughts in a Crater"!

BUN. Thoughts in a coal-hole! I hate poetry—I consider it ungentlemanlike. There never used to be any poetry in my time.

BOB. (*spouting*) "Flame the lightnings——"

BUN. Flame the devil! Where are the lucifers? On the table somewhere—find 'em. (*he finds them as he is speaking, and hands them to* BOB) Here's the box—take it, can't you?

> As BUNNYTHORNE *holds box,* BOB *takes brandy bottle, helps himself, and drinks.*

BUN. Got it?

BOB. (*drinking*) Yes, I've got it.

BUN. You haven't—ah! (*lights lucifer.* BOB *puts down glass*) Hold the candle steady.

> As BOB *holds candle unsteadily,* BUNNYTHORNE *lights it also unsteadily. Stage light. They sit down again.*

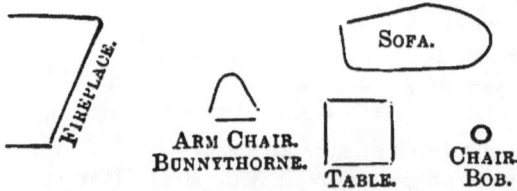

BOB. (*after looking at* BUNNYTHORNE) Tight! He's tight. (*aside*)

BUN. (*aside*) I'm sorry I didn't keep it dark.

During the scene, at intervals, they both endeavour to take the bottle at the same time, so that their hands meet, they withdraw them immediately, and endeavour to talk profoundly.

BOB. Do you know, governor, I'm getting tired of this sort of life?

BUN. I should think so.

BOB. I feel I'm wasting my abilities, and the best years of my life in—in——

BUN. In getting drunk at the "Mompesson Arms."

BOB. No, governor, *I* am not drunk; but I know who is!

BUN. (*indignant*) Who is?

BOB. Never mind.

BUN. Who do you mean, sir?

BOB. Never mind—Jack Topham.

(*evading the question*)

BUN. (*sneering*) Jack Topham—a pretty friend.

BOB. Oh! he's no friend of mine now—we've had a row.

BUN. Bravo! What about?

BOB. About Miss Brill, the barmaid; I think Jack's going to marry her. However, he cut up rough about her, and we had a row. (*taking bottle.* BUNNYTHORNE *stops him*)

BUN. No; you've had enough already. Talking of Miss Brill, Bob, I used to be afraid that you were sweet upon her.

BOB. Me! no, governor. My mind is fixed upon Cousin Eva. (*stage gets gradually lighter at* C. *window*) And if it were not for this engineer——

BUN. Those beastly railways! (*amiably*) Bob, my boy, I'd give the world to see you grow steady, and settle down with your cousin Eva.

BOB. (*affectionately*) Yes—guv—I should like to settle down. I've been stirred up enough already. (*spouting*)

"For 'tis weary, weary, wasting mind and body at the oar,
    Rest thee ——"

BUN. Yes—Yes—Bob. I like you in your good humours.

BOB. Married to Eva. She'll have money.

BUN. Yes, yes. (*aside*) He is a good affectionate boy with all his faults.

BOB. And you'd allow me something if I was married.

BUN. Of course I would, Bob.

BOB. And with that capital I could go to London, and —start a new monthly magazine.

BUN. (*horrified*) What!

BOB. There is a great want of new monthly magazines in London, and I could publish my own poetry in it, and——

BUN. (*in a passion*) You idiot—do you want to ruin me? (*rising*) You're no son of mine! I disown you. Ah! Get out!

BOB. There you go, you never will listen to reason.

Enter DOCTOR, L.D.

BUN. Not a shilling do you ever get——

DOC. (*interrupting*) Hallo! Hallo! Will you never learn to keep quiet near an invalid? Has she stirred?

BUN. No.

DOC. (*seeing* BOB) What! Not dead yet?

BOB. Doctor!

DOC. As I was looking from the window I saw your friend, Mr. Topham, and three other blackguards outside, so I went down to ask Topham what he wanted there, and he asked me to deliver this to you. (*gives* BOB *letter*) There it is. Topham, I believe, is waiting for an answer.

Exit DOCTOR, *cautiously*, R.D.

BOB. (*rises and reads letter by light of candle*) "Robert Bunnythorne, Esq. Dear sir,—Understanding from a lady" (Oh! that's Miss Brill!) "that you have spoken of me disrespectfully, I demand the satisfaction due from one gentleman to another—some mutual friends are with me who will see that all is conducted fairly—I am waiting outside for you, to punch your damned head; so come down quickly, or I'll fetch you in two two's. Dear sir, ever yours sincerely,—JOHN TOPHAM."

BUN. (*rising*) Eh! a fight with Topham! he's too much for you.

BOB. (*buttoning up his coat, and taking up his hat determinedly*) The infernal impudence! I'll thrash him till I can't stand over him.   (*goes off briskly*, L.D.)

BUN. (*agitated*) Bob! Bob! my boy, I forbid you to fight with him. He's two stun too heavy for you. Bless the boy! Just like his father. (*proudly*) My boy! my boy! Me all over! Every inch of him. Bob! (*calling*) I forbid it! I'll come and back you.

Exit BUNNYTHORNE *hastily*, L.D. *Stage lighter at window. Enter the* DOCTOR, R.D.

DOC. Phew! There's no use in prescribing anything—but the Engineer. He's got my note by this time, and will be here soon. It's the only hope. Then there's Arthur.

He's as hot-headed as a boy, and as obstinate as an old man. All the inconveniences of youth without its pliability, and the hardness of age without its obedience to the law of compromise. Here he is!

Enter ARTHUR, L.D.

ART. Well—what news?

DOC. She sleeps—for the present.

ART. Tell me, candidly—candidly—will she recover?

DOC. I don't know. (ARTHUR *sinks in chair. Aside*) Now for it. (*aloud*) I have no faith in my treatment— nor in anybody else's.

ART. Is there no hope?

DOC. Yes, one.

ART. What is it? (*rising*)

DOC. Ferne.

ART. Ferne!

DOC. Don't fly at the mention of his name.

ART. He has killed her.

DOC. No; 'tis you who will kill her by sending him away. .

ART. Me?

DOC. Yes. He, a plebeian, has dared to fall in love with the niece of a Mompesson. Off with his head—eh? Let the poor devil die of despair ; but no Mompesson must make a *mésalliance*, particularly with a rival——

ART. A rival?

DOC. Yes; a rival. I repeat it—rival. If you haven't yet confessed it to yourself, learn it from me; you've dreamt of making this dear cousin your wife—of refurnishing the Abbey, of the comforts, the joys of domesticity.

ART. (*indignant*) Doctor!

DOC. Ah! I've found the wound, then. Confess you are jealous!

ART. No! (*loudly*)

DOC. Ah! ah! On your honour—on your honour?

ART. Oh! you're the devil!

DOC. I wish I was! For if I were, I'd bribe you to do what's right, by giving you the youth (*with intention*), the appearance, and the attractions you possessed thirty years ago.

ART. But let us seek other advice—the London doctor who attended her during her last illness.

DOC. (*his hands in his pockets*) I'd give the world to consult with him.

ART. I'll write to him.

Doc. Your letter will not reach London until to-morrow evening.

ART. I'll send—I'll go myself !

Doc. There's no railway nearer than Stapleton, and that's eight hours from here.

ART. We'll telegraph !

Doc. No telegraph nearer than Stapleton.

ART. (*crossing to* R.) No rail !—no telegraph !—no anything in this damned hole ! We're in a desert, and miles away there are contrivances that annihilate time and space. (*stopping with sudden conviction*) And it was I who crushed the project that would have brought communication with the world up to this very spot. (*bitterly*) Congratulate me on my victory ! I have saved the Abbey, and I have killed Eva !

Doc. (*aside*) At last ! (*aloud*) You see, then, this young man's calling has its noble, as well as its common tradesman side. Science commands time and space. King Canute couldn't command the tide, but the engineer can build a breakwater that compels the roaring ocean to keep within its proper bounds !

ART. But of what use is all this ?

Doc. Of every use. Ferne is not, I will say, a man of good family. Well, he'll found a family, for he is a young and already distinguished man. He has that natural patent that is the commencement of distinction and nobility.

ART. And what may that be ?

Doc. Brains—that coronet worn inside the skull, that no revolution can deprive him of.

ART. But do I understand that you wish me to ——

Doc. To give her up to this young man ? Yes, I do.

ART. (*after a pause*) You are asking me to make a sacrifice—to exhibit a heroism which ——

Doc. Of course I'm asking a heroism—a self-sacrifice. What else should I ask of you ? Now take it from your own point of view, not mine. I'm a Republican—a Radical—in modern slang, a Red. I want to see some of this real nobility I hear you talk of. I want to see it, out of a picture, or a genealogical chart. I want to see it framed in flesh and blood. In this sad business I don't ask you to act like a common man ; I don't ask you to act like a gentleman —that's easy to you—you can't help it. I ask you to act like a Mompesson ! Do you remember some time ago, in the year fourteen hundred and something, how your ancestor

Raoul de Mompesson took service in Germany, and when the Archduchess Something-or-other-stein, with whom Raoul was in love, was pursued with her husband and children, by her enemies, your ancestor put on the Archduke's armour and alone met the foemen, who mistook him for his rival, and he fell pierced by their swords, and while he held the hilts of their blades to him the woman he loved gained the castle in safety ; and, don't you remember, how she and the children he had saved offered up prayers for the chivalric lover, who had died so true a knight, a gentleman, and soldier ? Well, then, Raoul de—I mean Arthur de Mompesson, remember your race, your blood, your antecedents. Cast all small selfishness aside, receive this young man. Give up Eva ! Save her life ! Honour commands ! Humanity insists. *Noblesse oblige !*

ART. (*after a pause, rising*) You are right. Send for Mr. Ferne. I'll do it.

Doc. You will ?

ART. (*extending his hand*) Upon my honour.

Doc. (*shaking hand*) Mompesson, all over. Raoul redivivus ! (*and chuckling at his success*) There's always some good in a gentleman, even when he's a nobleman ! (*knock at* L.D., *aloud*) Doubtless, that's him.

ART. Ferne ? (DOCTOR *nods*) Already ? (*mastering himself*) Come in !

> FERNE *opens* L.D., *and appears on threshold. He does not advance into room.*

FER. (*after a pause*) Pardon me. I received a note from Doctor Browne, which ——

ART. (*offering his hand*) Mr. Ferne, I have to ask your pardon for what I said yesterday. I was wrong, violent, unjust. I trust that you will accept my apology.

FER. (*hardly comprehending*) Mr. Mompesson, I ——

ART. We must talk seriously. Will you sit down ?

Doc. (*aside to* ARTHUR) Bravo !

FER. My position here is so peculiar. But I hardly know how I should act.

ART. There is, I admit, a difficulty ; but no difficulty that cannot be overcome.

> (*during* ARTHUR'S *last lines* EVA *enters*, R.D.)

EVA. (*at door*) There need be no difficulty ; or if there be, it is one in which I am concerned and have a right to speak.

ART. Eva ! (*advancing to her*)

Doc. Hush! Leave them alone.

ARTHUR *and* DOCTOR *retire to window.* EVA *advances to sofa.* FERNE *approaches her.*

EVA. Mr. Ferne, let me be candid. Yesterday you told me that you loved me.

FER. And I spoke the truth.

EVA. No. You saw me ill—as you thought dying—and you spoke from pity. I cannot accept your love as alms.

FER. Alms!

EVA. I should have been proud of your affection, I must decline your compassion.

ART. (*aside*) She rejects him. She is a Mompesson.

(*with pride*)

Doc. (*aside, at back*) Wait a bit. All the Mompessons on the female side were women, and women are fondest of their sweethearts when they quarrel with them. "It is their nature to."

EVA. You and my cousin, and the Doctor, and the rest of my kind friends, have treated me as if I were a child, and——

FER. Eva, will you hear the truth—the honest truth—the truth that a man should tell to the woman he loves—the woman he hopes to share his life with? I came here absorbed with the small cares of the outer world—unthinking of you. I saw you—and the love that I had never dreamt of—leaped up at my heart. I remembered the old days in London, when I saw you as I see you now, pale—weak—beautiful—and a new feeling came over me. The love I feel for you throngs my veins, and I speak as I think when alone, and you are not near to dazzle me, and make me forget all but the sweet intoxication of your presence. Eva, I have the consent of your cousin, I dare to believe I have the consent of your own heart; you, love me—your own sweet lips have avowed it. I love you wholly, solely, and truly. Do you believe me?

ART. (*advancing*) Yes, I believe him, and you may.

EVA. Are you sure you speak the truth?

FER. Let your heart answer for mine. My lips are silent.

EVA. (*after a pause, giving him her hand*) Yes, I believe you!

ART. It's all over, Doctor. It's all over. What shall I do?

Doc. Do! Congratulate them! (*advancing*)

EVA. But Miss Myrnie told me——

(MISS MYRNIE *appears at* L.D.)

DOC. Miss Myrnie is a deceitful old—but no—why should I libel a harmless, necessary cat, by comparing it to a spiteful unnecessary old woman? Miss Myrnie——

MISS M. (*advancing*) Miss Myrnie has heard every word, and Miss Myrnie does not think it necessary to defend either what she said to Miss Summers yesterday, or what she has said to Lord Mompesson this morning. Miss Myrnie has done her duty to her own conscience, to her religion, and to her family. (*speaking at door*) Your lordship will find every word that I have told you to be true.   .

DOC. Lord Mompesson ! }
ART. My father ! } (*together*)

DOC. The old devil.

Enter LORD MOMPESSON, L.D.

ART. (*speaking to* DOCTOR *as* LORD MOMPESSON *enters, and takes a chair,* C.) He will never consent. I know his prejudices. Now all is over !

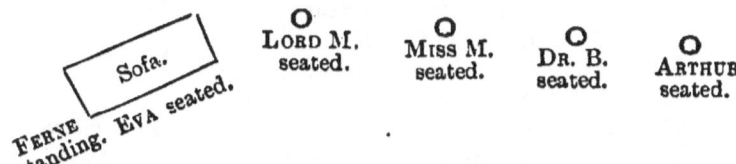

LORD M. Arthur—Eva—Miss Myrnie has been telling me of something that has been kept a secret from me.

ART. Only since yesterday.

MISS M. I have told his lordship everything.

DOC. (*aside*) And a little over. The truth made piquant with Miss Myrnie's sauce.

LORD M. Eva, my grandniece, is it true that you have received the attentions of a young gentleman?

EVA. Of Mr. Ferne,—quite true. (*rising*) Mr. Ferne, let me present you to my grand-uncle, Lord Mompesson.

(*they bow, &c.*)

DOC. (*aside*) Bravo !

LORD M. And, Doctor, is it true that in order not to contradict Eva's whims or wishes while she was so critically ill, that you and Arthur told her that Mr. Ferne might visit the Abbey as her accepted suitor ?

ART. }
DOC. } Quite true. (*together*)

MISS M. As I told your lordship, they trumped up a story——

LORD M. (*interrupting*) One moment, dear Miss Myrnie. Mr. Ferne, you told me, was not exactly a— a man of family.

MISS M. No family whatever! No blood, that is, no real blood. His veins are plebeian as potato peelings. He is connected with the railroads. I believe he is a railway guard, and his grandfather was a labourer on your lord·ship's estate.

FER. Permit me to correct you. I am an engineer. My grandfather held the Branxley Farm, close to Wood-side.

MISS M. A mere question of detail.

LORD M. Aye!—aye!—aye! Ferne. I remember.

FER. If I may be allowed to offer a remark, I would suggest that I was asked here, and that I offer marriage to your niece, Lord Mompesson; that I do so from myself, and with no doubt of my own worthiness. I court inquiry as to my character and circumstances.

MISS M. Such impudence!

LORD M. Is my niece attached to you?

EVA. Let me answer that! I am!

MISS M. Well, if ever!   (*scandalised*)

DOC. It's so many years since she felt anything of the sort she has forgotten all about it!

ART. My father will never consent. We're done, Doctor, we're done!   (*to* DOCTOR)

LORD M. Have you many relations, Mr. Ferne?

FER. None! I am alone in the world!

DOC. Oh! he's much too good a fellow to have relations!

LORD M. (*rising and going to* ARTHUR) Arthur, what is your opinion?

ART. (*the* DOCTOR'S *eyes fixed upon him*) They are worthy of each other.

LORD M. And you would have me consent?

ART. Yes!

LORD M. Mr. Ferne, Miss Myrnie has done us all a great service in facilitating our meeting, and understanding each other on this very serious subject. I must inquire into many details. We need not enter upon that now. In the meantime, and until we know more of you—which

I make a condition—visit the Abbey in the capacity of my dear grandniece's suitor. I am an old man. I shall not be here much longer. I would not see her mother after her marriage (*mournfully*), and I never set eyes on her again. Let me make those about me as happy as I can. (EVA *takes* LORD MOMPESSON'S *hand*) Dear Miss Myrnie here, I am sure, will be pleased that her kind intervention has had so happy a result. (MISS MYRNIE *astonished*)

Doc. Dear Miss Myrnie, I congratulate you.

FER. How can I find words to thank you?

(crossing to her)

EVA. (*to* MISS MYRNIE) And I was foolish enough to think that you were not my friend. Thanks!

FER. Thanks!

LORD M. Thanks!

Doc. Thanks! (*all to* MISS MYRNIE)

MISS M. (*speechless with rage, masters herself*) Don't mention it—you're quite welcome. I—I will retire to my room.

Doc. Do—do! and don't come out again!

> DOCTOR *opens door.* Enter BUNNYTHORNE *in coat and hat, followed by* BOB. BOB *has a green shade over both eyes.*

MISS M. Good gracious! (*seeing* BOB)

Doc. What's all this?

BUN. (*leading* BOB *to chair*) Bob's been having a tooth out. Topham on the eyes—but he licked him—I saw the fight—Bob licked him. (*with pride*) The very image of me when I was his age. When Eva gets better he's the husband for her.

MISS MYRNIE at window.

FERNE. EVA. LORD MOMPESSON.
        seated.   seated.

              DOCTOR.   BUNNYTHORNE.

                                  BOB.
                                  seated.

BOB.

"In the rapture of the battle, when whirls wild the foeman's glaive,
Shall thy image aye be present to the bosom of the brave."

MISS M. (*coming down to* BUNNYTHORNE) Miss Eva is engaged to Mr. Ferne by my lord's consent.

BOB. What?

BUN. Bob!

BOB. Never mind, guv'nor; the brave heart accepts its

doom. You can make me the allowance all the same. (*reseating himself moonily*)

"Though I loved her, yet she left me—it is years and years ago,
Once my eyes were dimmed with weeping, now my locks are white as snow."

(*to* Doctor) I should like to know why——

Doc. Not now—some other time.

Lord M. (*as if concluding a conversation*) Yes—yes—yes. And if all turns out satisfactory, of which I have no doubt——

Art. I will give the bride away.

Miss M. (*sneering*) With all your differences of opinion you seem quite agreed on one point, that Miss Eva must be married.

Doc. Yes, we're all agreed on that. (*pointing to* Arthur) Aristocrat.

Art. (*smiling and pointing to* Doctor) Red Republican.

Doc. (*pointing to* Bunnythorne) Man of business.

Bun. (*leaning over* Bob) And warrior!

Doc. Lords!

Bun. (*pointing to himself*) Commons!

Doc. (*pointing to himself*) The people!

Bun. (*pointing to* Bob) And the army.

Doc. Very good! Let's try again! High! (*to* Arthur. *Pointing to himself*) Low! (*indicating* Bunnythorne) Jack!

Bun. (*pointing to* Bob's *black eye, and slapping him on the shoulder*) And game! (*crosses to fireplace*)

Doc. Come, my patient, no more excitement to-day, or it will be too much for you. Let me take you to your room.

(*crosses to her. Music, piano, during* Eva's *speech*)

Eva. A few more minutes to thank you so much for all your goodness to me. I shall get better; I feel I shall! When the snow melts from the grass, I shall be stronger; and when the summer covers those black branches with green leaves I shall be able to walk down the avenue.

Fer. With me by your side?

Lord M. You, on one side—me on the other. Left to yourself your pace would be too fast, and mine would be too slow. You have youth, strength, and speed; I have age, judgment, and experience. Let Eva walk between us.

Eva. (*as they are going round door* R.) My path must lead to happiness when love and hope conduct me, and affection and experience guide me—*(smiling)*—That's Progress! *(movement of all the characters. Music ceases)*

FERNE.	EVA.	LORD MOMPESSON.	ARTHUR.	
BUNNYTHORNE.	going to door.		DOCTOR.	MISS M. at door.
seated.			congratulating	disgusted.
			each other and	
			seated.	
				BOB seated.

BUN. Now, in my time, we should have all stood in a pleasant half-circle round the stage, and thanked our friends, the public, for their kind applause; but nothing is as it should be nowadays, everything is going to the——

CURTAIN QUICKLY.

NOTE.—The last speech of Bunnythorne's was written for the late J. B. Buckstone, for whom the part was originally intended, but is never spoken.

A ROW IN THE HOUSE.

FARCE,

IN ONE ACT.

BY

T. W. ROBERTSON,

AUTHOR OF

"Caste," "A Breach of Promise," "School," "M.P.,"
"Birth," "David Garrick," "The Ladies' Battle," "The
Nightingale," "Ours," "Play," "Progress," "Society,"
"Dreams," "War," "Home," "Faust and Marguerite," "My
Wife's Diary," "Noemie," "Two Gay Deceivers," "Jocrisse
the Juggler," "Not at all Jealous," "Star of the North,"
"Birds of Prey," "Peace at any Price, "Half Caste,"
"Ernestine," "Chevalier de St. George," "Cantab," "Clock-
maker's Hat," "Duke's Daughter," "Sea of Ice," &c., &c.

LONDON :
SAMUEL FRENCH.
PUBLISHER,
89, STRAND.

NEW YORK :
SAMUEL FRENCH & SON,
PUBLISHERS,
28, WEST 23RD STREET.

A ROW IN THE HOUSE.

(Produced at Toole's Theatre, London, August 30th, 1883.)

CAST OF CHARACTERS.

Mr. Scorpion	... ...	Mr. A. CHEVALIER.
Tom	...	MR. J. H. DARNLEY.
Mr. Goodman	... ...	Mr. F. IRVING.
Jemmy	...	MR. A. D. ADAMS.
Mrs. Scorpion	... ...	MISS MAUD ROBERTSON.
Kate	...	MISS L. WALKER.
Mary...	...	MISS FLORENCE RAYBURN.

SCENE.—*A handsomely-furnished Apartment.*

Modern Costumes.   Time of Representation, thirty-five minutes.

Time—Present.

A ROW IN THE HOUSE.

SCENE.—*A handsomely furnished apartment. Enclosed doors* R. *and* L. *Door in flat,* R.C. *Window* L.H. *Tables, chairs, &c. A cabinet,* C., *the upper part painted in imitation of scarlet silk.* MARY *discovered.*

MARY. There, all's right for this morning! I wonder what will happen to-day? Really, I think that this house, which ought to be the most comfortable of the whole row, is about the most unhappy. There's master only been married six months, always miserable because he's always jealous. Then, missus is an angel if master would only let her be. Then, Miss Kate—or as she will call herself, Miss Catherine —she ought to be happy, for she's going to be married to Mr. Tom Tendon, of Guy's Hospital. She makes herself miserable because she says Mr. Tom's got no sentiment. Then, there's Mr. Goodman; he is a nice old man, always making everybody happy about him, but I think he's rather cracked about mesmerism, and galvanism, and electric telegraphism, or he wouldn't keep them queer looking things in that room. Then, there's my Jemmy, he ought to be happy, for he's my husband; but he has followed his master's example, turned as jealous as old Nick, and all because I had a sweetheart two years before I knew him. (*enter* JEMMY *with a brace of pheasants in his hand*) Well, Jemmy, what's them?

JEM. (*sulkily*) Brace of pheasants, come by rail.

MARY. Who for?

JEM. Master, (*dashing them violently on ground*) devil take 'em.

MARY. What's the matter?

JEM. What's the matter? Them pheasants is the matter. Do you know who brought them?

MARY. No, who?

JEM. (*jeeringly*) I daresay you would like to know, but you shan't.

MARY. I'm sure I don't want to know.

JEM. Then I'll tell you. (*shouting furiously*) It was Joe; Joe, the railway porter.

MARY. And who's Joe?

JEM. What! you don't know, don't you? Ha! ha! ha! You don't know Joe, him with the black whiskers that squints?

MARY. Oh! him! Well, I do know him.

JEM. You confess it?

MARY. Why, you jealous little fool, if the birds came by railway, he was forced to bring them, wasn't he?

JEM. (*with emotion*) You mean that his love for you is so strong that it carried his long corduroy legs here to see you, whether he would or not.

MARY. I mean it's his business—his duty.

JEM. Oh! he came here to do his duty, did he? (*snivelling*) I'm an undone husband, a miserable, blighted groom.

MARY. Now, Jemmy, this is too bad of you—this is. I'm sure I never gave you any cause for jealousy.

JEM. Didn't you? Hadn't you a sweetheart in the 77th Regiment of Foot sogers, two years afore I knew you?

MARY. Well! What o' that? I hadn't seen you then.

JEM. Well! What o' that?

MARY. Come, Jemmy, don't be foolish, of course the man was forced to bring the parcels.

JEM. (*relenting*) Well, perhaps he was, so I forgive you, Polly.   (*kissing her*)

MARY. That is nice. Now let us talk of something else —about that greatcoat that you think was stolen from you.

JEM. Ah! that day I drove out Mr. Goodman. It must have been stolen at the Unicorn Tap, because when I went to the police office——

MARY. Talking of that—the same day a policeman knocked at our door. I answered it, and——

JEM. You answered it—you (*muttering*)—a policeman —go on—go on.

MARY. And he said to me (*seeing the alteration in* JEMMY'S *face*)—why! Jemmy, what's the matter?

JEM. (*bursting into a passion*) So! ma'am, when I'm out with the gig, policemen come to visit you—what policeman—which policeman? I know who it was—he's after all the girls that can give away cold mutton at the area rails. It was Sergeant Crack.

MARY. Now! What! Again? Hear me out, Jemmy.

JEM. Not I. I think I've found you out. I've heard too much! Was it Sergeant Crack, or who? How many —perhaps the whole force, from A to Z.

MARY. Now, Jemmy.

JEM. Don't Jemmy me, ma'am, go to your Crack—fly to your sergeant—off to your beloved No. 19, walking to and fro in the white berlins.

MARY. Jemmy, Jemmy!

JEM. (*avoiding her*) Away, away to 19, 2, be off to buttons. Go to——

SCORP. The devil.

(SCORPION *enters suddenly with dressing-gown and paper*)

SCORP. James!

JEM. Sergeant Crack.

SCORP. I wish to speak with you. (*not seeing* MARY) Who was that you were talking to just now so loudly?

JEM. (*to* MARY) Sergeant Crack!

SCORP. Who? Oh, I see, your wife. Mary, leave the room.

JEM. (*between his teeth*) Sergeant Crack!

MARY. Oh! Jemmy, Jemmy!   *Exit* S.L.

JEM. (*calling after her*) Sergeant Crack!

SCORP. (*musing*) Yes, it must be so. She seems unhappy. She sometimes weeps in private, and when I get into a passion she seems alarmed. It's very odd; perhaps she has some secret attachment. Oh! (*looking at paper*) There are two elopements this week. Yes, she must have some secret attachment. I feel convinced of it. (*working himself into a fury*) I'll watch! I'll watch! and if I can discover—James!   (*shouting*)

JEM. (*starting from a reverie*) Sir!

SCORP. Come here, James. You have been some time in my service, and you know how cautious I am upon all points, especially those points that concern your mistress. (*mysteriously*) Has anything occurred this morning?

JEM. (*bringing down pheasants*) These, sir.

SCORP. Ha! (*snatching them, reading address*) "To Mr. Scorpion." Me! umph! to me! Stay. That may be but a blind. Any letter? Let me see. (*looking under the wings, &c., and examining them*) No.

JEM. If I was you, sir, I'd look inside 'em, sir!

SCORP. Now, who the devil could have sent me these birds? My brother John might; yet, no; somehow or other I'm convinced that these birds were intended for my wife. If old Goodman had returned from Exeter, I'd ask his opinion. Oh! agony of jealousy. (*shouting*) James!

JEM. (*starting*) James, sir!

SCORP. From you I have no disguise, and I have come to the conclusion that *she* has a *lover*.

JEM. (*shaking his head*) I'm sure she has.

SCORP. Sure! how, James? My dear, good, honest, faithful James, how—how—how are you sure?

JEM. 'Cos I am.

SCORP. Ha, ha! I'm delighted. Rapture? Torture! Excellent! Horrible! I've found them out! Ha, ha! I have found them out! Who is he, James? Who is he?

JEM. (*mournfully*) A policeman!

SCORP. (*astonished*) A policeman?

JEM. No. 19, 2, in the white berlins.

SCORP. The devil! Ha, ha, ha! Capital, a policeman. What's his name?

JEM. Sergeant Crack.   (*drops in chair*)

SCORP. Crack! Sergeant Crack! Oh, woman! Devil! Furies! Sergeant Crack, Crack, Crack. (*snapping his fingers*) My dear James, my dear, good, kind, faithful, inestimable James, I thank you. Crack! Crack! now I am happy! You have made me quite miserable; thank you, my dear James, thank you; there's a sovereign for you; thank you.

JEM. Thank you, sir.

SCORP. (*walking about*) A policeman, ha, ha! A policeman. A Crack! Crack! Crack! I'll—— When did you find this out?

JEM. To-day, sir.

SCORP. To-day! Now I think of it, a thousand circumstances confirm it. Last winter, when Hartop's house took fire, she observed what a very efficient body the police were. A very efficient body, no doubt. Crack, Crack, ha!

JEM. (*dolefully*) Then she'd a soger afore she was married.

SCORP. (*shouting*) What!

JEM. A private in the 77th Foot.

SCORP. (*amazement*) A policeman, and a private soldier. Abandoned wretch!

JEM. Then she'd a cousin she was fond on, who went to America.

SCORP. A cousin!

JEM. A plumber and glazier.

SCORP. Great Heaven! a policeman, a private soldier, and a plumber and glazier!

JEM. She had 'em all three.

SCORP What! Mrs. Scorpion?

JEM. No, Polly.

SCORP. Polly ! My wife's name is Maria !

JEM. What of that ?

SCORP. What of that ? (*seizing him*) Didn't you tell me that before she was married the lover to my wife was in the 77th Foot ?

JEM. No, sir.

SCORP. Didn't you say she loved a plumber and glazier, who went to America ?

JEM. (*astonished*) No, sir.

SCORP. And that she had a present lover in the person of a policeman—one Sergeant Crack ?

JEM. Sergeant Crack isn't.

SCORP. What is he, then ?

JEM. No. 19.

SCORP. No. 19 ?

JEM. 2.

SCORP. No. 19, 2. What the devil do you mean ? Explain yourself, or I'll murder you. (*shaking him*)

JEM. (*coolly*) I wish you would, it will save me the trouble of committing groomicide. I said that I had found out my wife's love for Sergeant Crack.

SCORP. (*letting him go*) What ! your wife's ?

JEM. Yes, sir.

SCORP. Not my wife's ?

JEM. No, sir.

SCORP. Then all this time you've been talking about your wife ?

JEM. Yes, sir.

SCORP. Not my wife ?

JEM. No, sir.

SCORP. My dear James. (*embracing him*) La ! la ! la ! (*dancing*) What an ass I am to annoy myself. Hence, suspicion. Away jealousy ! " Richard's himself again." Yet stop, is this fellow deceiving me ? No ! she dare not bribe him. La ! la ! la ! la ! James, I sympathise with you. La ! la ! la ! (*dancing*)

JEM. (*crying*) Thank you, sir.

SCORP. Jealousy is indeed misery.

JEM. It is.

SCORP. And there is no reparation but revenge.

JEM. Oh ! Thank you, sir. I'm quite happy now that I'm quite miserable. There's a sovereign for you, sir. (*giving it*)

SCORP. What for ?

JEM. Making me miserable—you gave me one, you know.

Scorp. Psha! leave the room.

Jem. Yes, sir. Oh! oh!   (*crying*)

Scorp. Don't make that noise.

Jem. No, sir. (*crying louder*) Oh! oh!

Scorp. (*angrily*) Go to the devil.

Jem. I'll go to my wife, (*with fury*) and if I catch her
with Sergeant Crack, I'll crack Crack's crown, if I'm
hanged for it.   *Exit* Jemmy.

Scorp. What a fool that fellow is to be. jealous of his
wife. Silly, groundless suspicion. I wonder if Mrs.
Scorpion ever heard of Sergeant Crack? Pooh! Nonsense.
Tho' I'm cautious, I'm above vulgar suspicion. Surely
James was not deceiving me? No, his sorrow was real.
Yet, some accidental circumstance might—ah! there's the
devil of it. Circumstance would corrupt a votaress.
(*reading*) "Their intimacy first began in January, 1848,
when the defendant visited the plaintiff at Hampstead."—
Whew! It makes me perspire, when I think of it. "Since
then many opportunities occurred when the plaintiff was
from home."—Whew! Opportunity. S'death, yes, opportunity. Here comes my wife. Now, why the devil did
she come downstairs? The window upstairs looks into the
garden, this into the street. The street, ah! all my
suspicions return. She looks adorable. (*enter* Mrs. Scorpion,
pensive and sad) My dear, why did you come downstairs?

Mrs. S. I was tired of being alone.

Scorp. Now, why should she be tired of being alone?
that's suspicious.

Mrs. S. It was so dull, besides I wished to have a glimpse
at the people passing in the street.

Scorp. She owns it! Oh! my dear, why do you wish to
see the people passing in the street?

Mrs. S. It's more lively, that's all.

Scorp. (*walks to* R. ; *turns back to audience*, L., *and
watches* Mrs. Scorpion, *who goes to window*, R.) More lively!
the devil take such lively temperaments. (*with passion*) Very
odd, ma'am, that you can't find amusement in your own house,
without gaping from the windows at every puppy that
passes!

Mrs. S. What! you're beginning again, heigho!

Scorp. Now she's unhappy. She goes to the window,
doubtless an appointment! Damnation! If I thought——
She comes away, perhaps that is a signal that I am at home,
and on the watch. I'll try her. Ha! look my dear, there's
a policeman! (*a pause*) She doesn't start, nor blush, oh!

art! art! all art! Why dear me, it's Sergeant Crack! (*another pause*) I say, ma'am, there's Sergeant Crack.

MRS. S. Who?

SCORP. Don't you know Sergeant Crack?

MRS. S. Sergeant Crack?

SCORP. No. 19, 2.

MRS. S. Not I. If, sir, you are again bent on abusing me by some absurd and unfounded accusation——

SCORP. I didn't accuse you, ma'am; you are very ready to snap at the chance of a quarrel.

MRS. S. Oh! dear me. I'll not stay to contend with you. (*going to door* L.) Mary, my bonnet and shawl.

SCORP. Where do you want to go to?

MRS. S. Only to the draper's to——

SCORP. To the draper's—the devil's. What! you want to go sniggering at that young counter-jumper with the sandy hair?

MRS. S. Oh! Mr. Scorpion. You cruel——(*sobbing*)

> MARY *enters, crosses stage, and returns with bonnet and shawl;* JEMMY *watching her.*

SCORP. She's crying, I can't bear that. But all women can cry—tears at the shortest notice, and on the most unreasonable terms. My dear, why do you wish to go out?

MRS. S. I won't go if you don't wish me——

SCORP. That's odd! Very! A wife obeying her husband, it's so damned unnatural! Thank you, my dear, for complying with my wish. Take that bonnet and shawl away—continually gadding. (MARY *exits*, JEMMY *after her*) James! my hat and coat.

MRS. S. Are you going out, then?

SCORP. Only for a few minutes.

MRS. S. Then I'll send for Kate to sit with me. Mary! (MARY *enters;* JEMMY, *with hat and coat, watching her*) Go to my sister and tell her—stay, I'll go myself.

> *Exit* MRS. SCORPION. MARY *follows her;* JEMMY *follows* MARY.

SCORP. Yes, I think she don't deceive me. James! (JEMMY *enters, looking off after* MARY) My hat and coat. (*takes off morning gown*) Now then! (JEMMY *still looks off*) What are you about? Help me! (JEMMY *still looks off, and gives him coat with the laps upward*) What the devil are you doing?

JEM. I beg your pardon, sir, it was a lapsus linguæ.

SCORP. Psha! My hat! (JEMMY *holds it from him*) Are you mad! What's the matter with you?

JEM. Sergeant Crack.

SCORP. Ha! ha! ha! Silly fool. Shut that door. (JEMMY *does so, and looks through keyhole;* SCORPION, *supposing* JEMMY *is close to him*) Now then, when I go out——(*seeing him at the door and dragging him down*) What the devil are you doing there? Who are you looking for?

JEM. Sergeant Crack.

SCORP. Pooh! psha! ridiculous! Don't be an ass. Don't be too suspicious; and hark ye, if any letters come, no matter who they are for, bring them to me.

Exit SCORPION, R.

Enter MRS. SCORPION *and* KATE, L.

MRS. S. You can leave the room, James. (JEMMY *in a reverie*) Do you hear, James, you can go.

JEM. (*starting*) I'm off in a crack, ma'am, Crack! Sergeant Crack has cracked me.   *Exit* JEMMY, L.

MRS. S. Silly fellow! heigho! My dear, you seem out of spirits this morning. What's the matter?

KATE. Nothing more than my usual depression of spirits. (*romantically*) Oh! the misfortune of a too senitive mind, and too delicate susceptibility.

MRS. S. I'm afraid, Kate, you carry this romantic humour of yours beyond all bounds. Did Mr. Tendon call yesterday?

KATE. Ah! name him not.

MRS. S. Why not?

KATE. He has an estimable heart, but he lives too much for the world, and has but little sympathy with those delicate distresses and elegant unhappinesses in the enjoyment of which I experience so much pleasure.

MRS. S. Experience pleasure in the enjoyment of distress! My dear Kate, these novels have turned your brain. Mr. Tendon is a very clever young man, expects soon to pass his examination. Then, I am sure he loves you.

KATE. I think he does. But he has no soul, no sentiment, no poetry of thought. If he were a little more like Manfred, or the Corsair, or Abder-el-Kader, or Cain, or Lucifer, or Jack Sheppard, I might be happy with him. But he is so vulgar, has such odd expressions, sings such horribly low songs.

Tom. (*heard without singing*)

> "My name it is Sam Hall,
> And I robs both great and small."

Upstairs, is she? La-ri-e-te!

Kate. There he is, and apparently in those rude spirits, and with that abominable gaiety, which are the invariable characteristics of an essentially vulgar soul.

Tom. (*entering*, L. *dressed very flashy and gentish*)

> "One day upon a donkey,
> I rode my love to see "—

Kate, my beauty, how d'ye do?

> "Kathleen Mavourneen."

Mrs. S. Good-day.

(Kate *receives him very haughtily*)

Tom. Hollo! Kate! what's the matter? What's up?

Kate. (*with disgust*) What's up? Why, Thomas, why will you persist in patronising those vulgarisms of expression indulged in by the plebeian herd?

Tom. What! Slang, eh? Can't help it, my compound packet of mixed sweets. We all do it; you think it vulgar!

> "For now tho' I'm grand, and I am rich,
> Not one of your upstarts I be;
> And I smokes a short pipe on the box,
> For there's nothing like pride about me."

Kate. Faugh! Horrible! If you repeat the offensive expressions you will compel me to retire.

Tom. Now, Kate——

Kate. Catherine——

Tom. Well, Catherine. Why do you wish to put my tongue into the stocks, and talk in the style of the troubadour, of old? Nowadays chivalry is done up.

> "It's all u-p with us, d'ye see!"

Kate. (*aside*) I must get up a delicate distress with him. I have it. Thomas! (*theatrically*) I have a question to demand of you. Will you answer it?

Tom. If I don't, damme.

Kate. With truth?

Tom. Safe as houses.

Kate. This moment perhaps may separate us for ever.

Tom. (*astonished*) What!

KATE. Were you at the Casino last night?

TOM. No.

KATE. Beware.   Thomas, beware—add not falsehood to your other villainy.

TOM. Villainy?

KATE. Did you not dance with Miss Muff, the milliner?

TOM. I wasn't there at all.

KATE. You were.

TOM. I wasn't.

KATE. You were.

TOM. Damned if I was.

KATE. (*recoiling*) Horror!   I leave you, sir, for ever.

TOM. Stay—who told you I was there?

KATE. (*aside*) Who shall I say?—Jemmy.

TOM. Jemmy!

KATE. Jemmy.   (*rushes off* R.)

TOM. I'll break his neck.   Stay Kate—D——n it, she must be cracked.   Kate! here!   *Exit after* KATE.

MRS. S. That silly sister of mine.   .

> SCORPION *enters, foaming with rage, a cane in his hand.*

SCORP. So ma'am, so——

> (*gesticulating, but speechless with passion*)

MRS. S. What's the matter now?

SCORP. I'd no sooner left the house than that rascal came to the back door.   I watched him, went to him, he wanted to impose on me with a lying tale about a coat that James lost, but his designs were not easily covered by a groom's greatcoat.   No—he came here, ma'am, to see you —you—you—you!

MRS. S. Who came?

SCORP. (*starting*) Sergeant Crack!

MRS. S. Good heaven; the man's mad.   Mary! Mary!

SCORP. (*walking about*) I see it all.   James told me the truth this morning, but fearing the consequences shifted the blame from her to his poor wife.   The scoundrel, when I catch him I'll murder him.

MRS. S. Mr. Scorpion, are you mad? Hear me——

SCORP. Away! away!

MARY. (*entering*) Did you call!

SCORP. (*dragging her down*) Speak, woman, you know who is her paramour?   Speak, speak!

JEM. (*rushing on furiously, a greatcoat on his arm*) So, ma'am, he brought the coat.   He said the carrier Jones took it by accident. He asked for the cook, too ; the cook, ma'am. He asked for the cook, but I diskivered him ! Oh !

MARY. Lor, Jemmy, I——

JEM. The back door. He asked for you.

MARY. Who ?

JEM. Sergeant Crack.

SCORP. (*to* MRS. SCORPION) Yes, ma'am, Sergeant Crack. Oh ! horror, furies, torture ! I believe it all ; the private, ma'am in the 77th.

JEM. (*to* MARY) Yes, ma'am ; the private in the 77th.

SCORP. (*to* MRS. SCORPION) The cousin who went to America.

JEM. (*to* MARY) Yes, the cousin who went to America.

SCORP. And this—this—this policeman !

JEM. Sergeant Crack !

MRS. S. }
MARY. } They're both mad.   (*sink in chair*, L.)

SCORP. Oh ! agony ! (*suddenly seizing* JEMMY) Villain, you first awoke me to my misery. Dog ! Wretch !

      (*caning* JEMMY *violently. The women scream*)

TOM. (*heard without*) Good-bye, then, ma'am, for ever.

Enter TOM *and* KATE.

MARY. (*to* TOM) Save my poor little husband.

TOM. Jemmy—the rascal. How dare you say last night I was at the Casino ?

> *They beat* JEMMY *with their sticks.* JEMMY *backs to the table, seizes the pheasants, and defends himself with them. The women try to hold their arms. As they near the door,* L.C., GOODMAN *enters.* JEMMY *puts* GOODMAN *before him, so that he receives all the blows. They advance* C. *Picture.*

GOOD. What does all this mean ? (TOM *and* SCORPION *desist.* JEMMY *falls,* C. *The ladies all embrace* GOODMAN) Are you all mad ?

JEM. O—o—o—oh.   (*crying*)

GOOD. What does this mean ?

OMNES. Why, my dear sir, the fact is—you see, &c.

            (*all talking together*)

GOOD. For heaven's sake, one at the time. Silence ! What is the cause of this disturbance ?

JEM. (*on the ground*) Sergeant Crack !

TOM. Get out you scoundrel.   (*kicks* JEMMY *off*)

GOOD. Will any of you speak ?

TOM. I'll call on you again, Kate, when you're not quite so cranky. (*to* GOODMAN) Good-bye, governor, I want to consult you. I'll be back when the coast's clear. Ta ! Ta ! Kate.   *Exit* TOM, *singing.*

> " Good-bye, my love, I'm going far from my dear Dinah,
> Down among the swamps," &c., &c.

GOOD. Dear me ! What is the cause ? (KATE *shudders, presses her hands to her head and exits, melodramatically*) Umph ! (*to* MRS. SCORPION) Ma'am ! what is the meaning ? (MRS. SCORPION *walks of with great dignity*) Ha ! Mary ! what is all this about! (MARY *exits, crying loudly and bitterly*) Now, Sigismund, perhaps you'll tell me. Stop, first let me put away these papers. I made a compromise with my antagonist's lawyer—and all is settled ; nothing like a compromise—saves so many words. (*takes out papers, unlocks cabinet, puts them in and locks door, and leaves key in door*) Now, Sigismund, what is the matter?

SCORP. The fact is I'm miserable.

GOOD. Oh ! I see—you're jealous again, why ?

SCORP. I don't know.   (*they sit*)

GOOD. Are you jealous of any particular person ?

SCORP. I don't know that I am.

GOOD. Have you any tangible ground for suspicion ?

SCORP. I don't know that I have.

GOOD. Does she exhibit any lack of affection for you ?

SCORP. I don't know that she does.

GOOD. You don't seem to know anything ! What was the cause of this noise and fighting ?

SCORP. (*jumping up*) Why, the fact is, there is a very fine-looking man in the police force, and I have watched him come here twice.

GOOD. Had he no reason for coming ?

SCORP. Why, James lost a coat or had it stolen from him, and——

GOOD. And this policeman returned it—of course it was his duty.

SCORP. Do you think it was ? Do you really think he had no other motive ?

GOOD. Of course not.

SCORP. (*sitting down*) My dear uncle. How I have ill-used her ! Stop ! There's another suspicious circumstance occurred this morning—a brace of pheasants were sent to me, and I don't know whom they came from ! (*walking about*)

Good. Is that all?

Scorp. Yes. Very odd anyone should send me——

Good. Not at all odd. I sent them.

Scorp. You did!·

Good. Yes, from Exeter.

Scorp. (*sitting down*) My dear uncle, I'm so happy—— Stop! (*jumping up*) Why did she want to go to the draper's this morning?

Good. Why, to purchase something, I should imagine.

Scorp. Good! that never struck me before—so she might —I'll be reconciled to her directly—yes (*with magnanimity*) I'll forgive her.

Good. Do—do. I'll go and make some experiments for my "GRAND PATENT ANTI-COMBUSTIBLE ELIXIR" for extinguishing fire.

Scorp. Mind it don't explode. I'll send for my wife.

Good. Do—and mind you don't explode.

Exit Goodman, R.

Scorp. (*dancing and singing*) La! la! la! la! What a brute I have been. I'll never be jealous again—never. I'll write an apology to her, see her, and sue for pardon. (*sits and writes*) " My Dearest Maria,—Forgive the ground-less suspicions that spring from a love too deeply seated to be always under the control and influence of reason. I swear to you that henceforth I will banish the absurd passions and ridiculous jealousy that——"

Enter Jemmy, *hastily.*

Jem. Sir!.

Scorp. Don't interrupt me. "The absurd passions and ridiculous jealousy that——"

Jem. She's a-looking into the street from the upstairs window.

Scorp. What! (*jumping up*) Damnation! Torture! just as I was—yes—I was right, and Goodman is an ass, who lets his own kind heart deceive him. Mrs. Scorpion was looking from the window, was she?

Jem. No, sir.

Scorp. No, didn't you say just now she was?

Jem. No, sir.

Scorp. No, sir—you infernal——

Jem. Don't begin again, sir! I'm black and blue all over.

Scorp. Didn't you say you saw my wife at the upstairs window, looking into the street?

JEM. No, sir.

SCORP. Who then?

JEM. My wife, sir.

SCORP. Your wife! Psha! you jealous little fool. La!
la! la! la! Goodman was right then, after all. I'll finish
my letter—(*sits*) "Banish the absurd passions and ridiculous jealousy that——"

JEM. And missus was a-looking over her shoulder.

SCORP. (*jumping up*) What! Mrs. Scorpion!

JEM. Yes, sir.

SCORP. My wife!

JEM. Yes, sir.

SCORP. Not your wife?

JEM. No sir.

SCORP. Death and fury—when I was writing her this—
"Banish the absurd passions and ridiculous jealousy."
(*tears letter*)   Damnation! James! Where was she looking?

JEM. Into the street, sir.

SCORP. Psha! I know that—but for whom—for whom?

JEM. Sergeant Crack!

SCORP. You infernal——(*shaking him violently, and
then embracing him*) My dear James, you're the only friend
I have in the house; a real friend. There's half a crown
for you. Tell your mistress I want to speak with her now
—now—now! (*shouting*) Oh! (*throwing himself on sofa*)
Agony! Oh!

MRS. S. (*without*) Come with me then, Mary, for I dare
not trust myself alone with him.

SCORP. (*jumping up*) Not with me, but you would with
your lover. Your——Oh! If I caught him I'd——

> *Seizes sofa pillow, kicks it about; then opens window
> and throws it out. All this in a transport of passion.
> JEMMY enters and sees him.*

JEM. That's right, sir, give it him! If I cotched my
wife's fancy man, I'd——

> *Seizes partridges, beats them, wrings their necks, and
> throws them out of window*

SCORP. She comes. I won't even speak to her.

(*crosses,* L.)

JEM. Nor I, neither.

Enter MRS. SCORPION *and* MARY.

MRS. S. Now, sir, your pleasure.

MARY. Now, James, what is it?

MRS. S. I am, here, sir, at your desire.

MARY. (*to* JEMMY) What have you got to say?

SCORP. (*to* MRS. SCORPION) Why were you looking out of window?

JEM. (*to* MARY) Why were you looking out of window?

MRS. S. What absurdity!

MARY. Oh! you soft fool.

MRS. S. Your jealousy converts everything into vice—tortures the most trivial circumstances into substantial proof. I can explain.

SCORP. I'll hear nothing.

MARY. And I can explain.

JEM. I'll hear nothing.

MRS. S. When this morning—you——

SCORP. Away—away.

MARY. The very first thing——

JEM. Be off—be off——

MRS. S. Hear me, sir.

SCORP. Not a word.

MARY. Listen, Jemmy!

JEM. Not a synnable.

MRS. S. As I am your wife.

SCORP. (*with disgust*) My wife.

MARY. As sure as my name's Polly Joggles.

JEM. Polly Joggles! Polly Bigamy!

MRS. S. Hear me.

SCORP. I'm deaf.

MARY. One word.

JEM. (*stopping his ears*) Get a speaking trumpet.

MRS. S. Sigismund!

SCORP. No.

MARY. Jemmy!

JEM. Nay.

MRS. S. An instant.

SCORP. No more words.

MARY. A second.

JEM. Shut up shop.

MRS. S. Well, sir. (*much offended*) Since you will not deign to hear me, let me tell you that from this time forth I cease to consider you my husband. I have borne with your idle suspicions, your ceaseless jealousies, too long. But I will leave you, and your house, sir, for ever.

MARY. And I'll follow my missus.

SCORP. (*relenting*) But, Maria!

Mrs. S. I'll hear nothing.

Jem. But Polly!

Mary. I'll hear nothing.

Scorp. If you'll only listen.

Mrs. S. Away, away.

Jem. I can soon show.

Mary. Be off, be off.

Scorp. Listen to me.

Mrs. S. Not a word.

Jem. Polly.

Mary. Not a synnable.

Scorp. A moment.

Mrs. S. I'm deaf.

Jem. Half a second.

Mary. (*stopping her ears*) Get a speaking trumpet.

Scorp. Maria.

Mrs. S. No.

Jem. Polly.

Mary. Nay.

Scorp. If you would but——

Mrs. S. No more words.

Jem. Just for——

Mary. Shut up shop.

Scorp. }
Jem. } (*together*) Will you leave me, then?

Mrs. S. Yes, sir, for ever.   *Exit*, L.

Mary. Yes, sir, for ever.   *Exit*, R.

    Scorpion *and* Jemmy *look at each other, then burst into tears.*

Scorp. O—o—oh!

Jem. A—a—ah!

Scorp. What a woman have I lost.

Jem. So have I.

Scorp. A perfect treasure.

Jem. A regular Koh-i-noor.

Scorp. When she tells me she will leave me.

Jem. When she says she's going to cut.

Scorp. And all for what?

Jem. Sergeant Crack.

Scorp. (*seizing him*) You villain—'tis your fault.   I'll annihilate you.   (*striking him*)

            Enter Tom.

Tom. Do—do—it'll save me the trouble—if I catch him—d——n me, I'll dissect him.

          (Jemmy *avoids him with horror*)

Scorp. My dear Tom, I've such afflicting news.

Tom. So have I.

Jem. (*coming down*) And so have I.

Scorp. My wife——

Tom. And Kate——

Jem. And little Polly——

Tom. Be off.

Scorp. Is about to leave me.

Jem. Goin' to hemmigrate.

Tom. Get out. And Kate's sent and she won't even see me.

Scorp. Oh, Maria!

Tom. Oh, Kate!

Jem. Oh, Polly!

Tom. Be off.

> *Rushing at* Jemmy, *who runs off, meets* Goodman, *and they fall together.*

Good. (*rising*) Dear me, what *is* the matter? This is a most extraordinary house, always troubling and fighting.

> (Tom *makes another rush at* Jemmy, *who exits*)

Tom. If I catch that infernal groom I'll break his collaris. He told Kate I'd been to the Casino.

Good. (*who has been conversing with* Scorpion) Never mind. I'll undertake to reconcile you.

Scorp. You will?

Good. On condition that you never again——

Scorp. Of course not—oh, Maria!

Good. There now—leave me.

Scorp. Then you'll——

Good. I'll do it. Come back here in five minutes; go. (*pushes him off*) Now, Tom, what do you want?

Tom. Why, Kate.

Good. I know. I'll reconcile you—go.

Tom. But——

Good. Now go. I left my Grand Fire Extinguisher when I heard of the quarrel. Come back here in five minutes—go. (*forces* Tom *off*) James, bring candles. (Jemmy *brings them on, sighs, and exits*) That fellow, too, I see, wants reconciling. I have it—ha! ha! ha! I have it—it'll do, it'll it'll do—ha! ha! (*Enter* Mrs. Scorpion, *weeping*) Now my dear Maria, I'm sorry to see this.

Mrs. S. If you could only——

Good. I know, I can. I'll make him never again have these silly—go into that room for a few minutes.

MRS. S. I'll take a candle.

GOOD. No, never mind a candle.

MRS. S. But it's quite dark.

GOOD. You'll hear better in the dark—go, there's a dear. (*Exit* MRS. SCORPION. *Enter* KATE, *weeping*) My dear Kate.

KATE. My dear uncle—if you knew——

GOOD. I know. I'll make it all right. There, go into that room.

KATE. It's quite dark.

GOOD. Never mind, people going to be married often take a leap in the dark—go.

KATE. I obey — quite dark — how romantic and mysterious. *Exit* KATE.

GOOD. Now she's gone. (*Enter* SCORPION *and* TOM, *smoking*) My dear Sigismund, I have a word to say to Tom, excuse me for a moment (*apart to* TOM) Tom, I want to speak to Scorpion, excuse me for a moment—just step in there. (*to* SCORPION)

SCORP. Certainly.

Exit SCORPION. GOODMAN *locks him in.*

GOOD. Just step in there. (*to* TOM)

TOM. Certainly.

GOOD. Shan't be a moment (*Exit* TOM, R.; GOODMAN *locks door. Enter* MARY, *weeping*) Where am I to put her? I see—Mary, go in here. (*pointing to cabinet,* C.)

MARY. (*astonished*) Lor, sir.

GOOD. No words—go in (*pushes her in*) Now I'll find James, and leave them till they make it up.

Exit GOODMAN.

Enter JEMMY.

JEM. I will see Mr. Goodman, and ask him to see Polly for me, oh, dear! (KATE *screams within*)

TOM. (*shaking door,* R.H., *violently*) Let me out—let me out.

JEM. Mr. Tom's voice—if he sees me he'll murder me.

TOM. Let me out. (*kicking door*)

> JEMMY *runs to* L.D.; *finds it locked; then seeing the cabinet opens it;* GOODMAN *runs on, shoves him into cabinet and locks door; violent knocking from doors and cabinet, and cries of* "Let us out."

GOOD. (*his back to the audience, laughing; the keys in his hand*) Not till you've made it up.

Violent knocking, an explosion heard, R.H. ; GOODMAN
runs to unlock door ; KATE *rushes out ;* TOM *and*
KATE'S *faces blackened on one side, a broken retort*
in TOM'S *hand ;* GOODMAN *assures himself that* TOM
is not hurt, then unlocks L.H. *door ;* SCORPION *and*
MRS. SCORPION *enter.*

SCORP. ⎱ We've made it up.
MRS. S. ⎰

TOM. So have we.   Kate and I are not going to quarrel.
any more, though we've both had a blow up.

GOOD. How did it happen ?

TOM. My cigar fell into the mortar.

GOOD. In which I had prepared the PATENT ANTI-
COMBUSTIBLE ELIXIR for extinguishing fire !

JEM. (*in cabinet*) Let us out.

MARY. (*in cabinet*) I'm being smothered.

> GOODMAN *draws down the upper portion of the*
> *cabinet, and discovers* JEMMY *and* MARY.

MARY. It's all right, sir.

JEM. We've made it up.
> (*they remain in cabinet till end*)

GOOD. From this time henceforth let your minds be
freed from jealousy.

SCORP. ⎱ Agreed.
MRS. S. ⎰

TOM. ⎱ Agreed.
KATE. ⎰

JEM. ⎱ Agreed.
MARY. ⎰

SCORP. One kiss, Maria.   (*they embrace*)

MRS. S. Take it.

TOM. Kate.   (*following suit*)

KATE. Oh, Tom !   (*resisting*)

TOM. Oh, stuff !   (*taking it*)

MARY. Go it, Jemmy.

JEM. I ain't got room enough.

SCORP. Let their hands (*to audience*) ratify our joy,
dear spouse.

MARY. Please just kick up one more Row in the House.

CURTAIN.

SCHOOL.

A COMEDY,

IN FOUR ACTS.

BY

T. W. ROBERTSON,

AUTHOR OF

"Caste," "A Breach of Promise," "Progress," "M.P.," "Birth,"
"David Garrick," "The Ladies' Battle," "The Nightin-
gale," "Play," "Ours," "Row in the House," "Society,"
"Dreams," "War," "Home," "Faust and Marguerite," "My
Wife's Diary," "Noemie," "Two Gay Deceivers," "Jocrisse
the Juggler," "Not at all Jealous," "Star of the North,"
"Birds of Prey," "Peace at any Price," "Half Caste,"
"Ernestine," "Chevalier de St. George," "Cantab," "Clock-
maker's Hat," "Duke's Daughter," "Sea of Ice," &c., &c.

LONDON:
SAMUEL FRENCH,
PUBLISHER,
89, STRAND.

NEW YORK:
SAMUEL FRENCH & SON,
PUBLISHERS,
28, WEST 23RD STREET.

SCHOOL.

(Produced for the first time on January 16th, 1869, at the Prince of Wales's Royal Theatre, London, under the management of Miss Marie Wilton.)

CAST OF CHARACTERS.

Lord Beaufoy...	MR. H. J. MONTAGUE.
Dr. Sutcliffe ...	MR. ADDISON.
Beau Farintosh	MR. HARE.
Jack Poyntz ...	MR. BANCROFT.
Mr. Krux	MR. F. GLOVER.
Vaughan	MR. HILL.
Mrs. Sutcliffe...	MRS. B. WHITE.
Bella ...	MISS CARLOTTA ADDISON.
Naomi Tighe ...	MISS MARIE WILTON.
Tilly ...	MISS AUGUSTA WILTON.
Milly ...	MISS GEORGE.
Laura ...	MISS PHILLIPS.
Clara ...	MISS UNAH.
Kitty ...	MISS HUTTON.
Hetty ...	MISS ATKINS.

Scene.—In and near Cedar Grove House.   Time.—The Present.

ACT I.—THE GLADE.—*A Glade in a Forest.*—RECREATION.

ACT II.—THE HOUSE.—*A School-room.*—EXAMINATION.

ACT III.—THE GROUNDS.—*A School-yard.*—FLIRTATION.

ACT IV.—THE GROUNDS.—*Same as* ACT III.—REALISATION.

Modern Costumes.   Time of Representation, two-hours and three-quarters.

*Between the first and second Acts eight days are supposed to elapse.
Between the second and third, two hours.
Between the third and fourth six weeks.*

[For the outline of the Plot of this Comedy the Author is indebted to a German Play by Mr. Roderich Benedix, called " Aschenbrödel."]

SCHOOL.

ACT I.

Music from " La Cenerentola " before the Curtain rises.

SCENE.—*A Glade. All the* GIRLS *discovered in various positions.* BELLA *standing. The* GIRLS *have wild flowers, ivy, &c., in their laps.*

CHILD seated on Sloping Bank.

BELLA standing, L.C., against large Tree.

KITTY seated.

MILLY seated.

HETTY seated.

NAOMI TIGHE

CLARA seated on cut-down branch of Tree.

TILLY seated, seated on Mound.

leaning against TILLY.

LAURA lying asleep, her head resting on same branch of Tree.

NAOMI TIGHE has a long string of wild flowers in her lap. which she is engaged in weaving together ; other girls have ivy, &c. BELLA has a small branch, which she uses as a wand.

BELLA. And her two haughty sisters stepped into a beautiful carriage and drove towards the palace, and when they were out of sight, Cinderella sat down in a corner and began to cry. Her godmother asked her what ailed her. "I wish—I wish—," said Cinderella, but she sobbed so she couldn't say another word. The godmother said, "You wish to go to the ball." (*imitation of godmother*) Now this godmother was a fairy.

NAOMI. I wish my godmother had been a fairy.

GIRLS. Hush ! silence !

NAOMI. Girls without fathers or mothers ought to have fairies for godmothers, to make up for the loss.

BELLA. "Be a good girl," said the fairy godmother, "and you shall go." "But," said poor Cinderella, "I can't go, for I've no things fit to go in."

GIRLS. Poor girl ! (*with deep sympathy*)

NAOMI. If I hadn't nice dresses I should die.

GIRLS. Hush !

BELLA. "Run into the garden," said the fairy god-mother, "and bring me a pumpkin." Cinderella brought a pumpkin, and her godmother scooped out the inside.

HETTY. (*eagerly*) Was it nice ?

BELLA. The godmother scooped out the inside, leaving nothing but the rind. She then touched it with her wand, and the pumpkin instantly turned into a fine coach, gilded all over with gold.

NAOMI. Bravo, pumpkin.

GIRLS. Hush ! Go on, Bella.

BELLA. Then Cinderella looked into the mousetrap, where she found six mice all alive and kicking.

NAOMI. (*with a shudder*) I hate mice.

(*all shudder slightly*)

LAURA. (*waking up*) Whenever I think of mice they make me feel quite—sleepy. (*goes to sleep*)

BELLA. Cinderella lifted the door of the trap very gently and the fairy godmother touched the mice, and they turned into beautiful horses of a fine dapple-grey mouse-colour.

GIRLS. Oh !

BELLA. Then the fairy turned two rats into postillions.

GIRLS. Oh !

BELLA. And six lizards into six footmen.

GIRLS. Six ! my !

BELLA. "There," said the godmother, "there is an equipage." "Yes," said Cinderella, crying, and pointing to her nasty ugly grey dress, "but I cannot go in these filthy rags." Then the godmother touched her with her wand, and her rags instantly became the most magnificent ball-dress that ever was seen.

GIRLS. Oh !

BELLA. Covered with the most costly jewels.

GIRLS. Oh !

NAOMI. I should like to be godmothered in that way.

BELLA. To these were added a beautiful pair of glass slippers. Then Cinderella, seated in her beautiful coach, drove off to the palace.

NAOMI. Gee up, gee oh ! (*sings " Post Horn Galop "*)

BELLA. As soon as she arrived, the King's son——

GIRLS. The King's son ?

BELLA. A most beautiful young man——

KITTY. This is interesting.

BELLA. Presented himself at the door of her carriage, and helped her to alight.

HETTY. I should like to be helped twice to King's son.

GIRLS. Silence !

BELLA. The Prince then conducted her to the place of honour, and soon after took her out to dance with him.

GIRLS. Oh !

CLARA. Think of that—a Prince.

NAOMI. Hetty would like to eat a Prince ; wouldn't you ?

TILLY. So should I.

CLARA. So should we all.

BELLA. The Prince fell in love with her.

GIRLS. Oh !

TILLY. Why shouldn't he ? I suppose princes fall in love the same as common people.

KITTY. But they don't do it in the same way.

NAOMI. (repeating) Go on, Bella. The Prince fell in love——

CLARA. What is love ?

MILLY. You silly thing !

TILLY. Such ignorance !

KITTY. That stupid Clara !

CLARA. I don't believe any of you know, not even you big girls.

TILLY. Everybody knows what love is !

CLARA. Then what is it ?

NAOMI. Who's got a dictionary ?—you're sure to find it there.

TILLY. My eldest sister says it's the only place in which you can find it.

KITTY. Then she's been jilted !

MILLY. My pa says love is moonshine.

NAOMI. Then how sweet and mellow it must be !

MILLY. Particularly when the moon is at the full !

NAOMI. And there is no eclipse !

TILLY. It seems that nobody knows what love is.

KITTY. I despise such ignorance !

CLARA. Then why don't they teach it us ? We've a music-master to teach music, why not a love-master to teach love ?

NAOMI. You don't suppose love is to be taught like geography or the use of the globes, do you ? No, love is an extra.

TILLY. Perhaps it comes naturally. Ask Laura what love is.

CLARA. (rousing LAURA, who is asleep) Laura, what is love ?

LAURA. (*waking suddenly*) J'aime, I love; tu aimes, we lovest; il aime, they love; nous aimons——

(*all laugh*)

BELLA. Hush, here's governess.

Enter MRS. SUTCLIFFE, R.H.U.E. *All rise, curtsey to* MRS. SUTCLIFFE, *who comes down to* C., *and surround her, except* LAURA.

MRS. S. Well, young ladies, what is the cause of your merriment? What is the subject under discussion?

NAOMI. Governess, we wish you to tell us something.

MRS. S. What is it, dear?

GIRLS. What is love?

LITTLE GIRL. Yes, what is love?

MRS. S. (*dumbfounded*) What is love? I—I—here is the Doctor!

Enter DR. SUTCLIFFE, R.H.U.E. *Comes down* R. *of* MRS. SUTCLIFFE. GIRLS *curtsey to the* DOCTOR.

DOCTOR. MRS. SUTCLIFFE.
O   O

BELLA.   O CHILD.
O
O
NAOMI.

MRS. SUTCLIFFE *a woman of sixty; the* DOCTOR *a man over sixty-five years of age—scholastic, genial, and a cross of the clergyman in his manner.*

MRS. S. Doctor, I have just had a most extraordinary question proposed to me.

DR. S. Indeed, dear!

MRS. S. Yes, Doctor—What is love?

NAOMI *and* GIRLS. Yes, Doctor—What is love?

LITTLE GIRL. Yes, Doctor—What is love?

DR. S. (*for a moment puzzled*) What is love? The cuneiform inscriptions on the Babylonian marbles have only been recently deciphered, so I will answer according to the comparatively modern notions of the Greeks. By them love was called Eros, but there were three separate Erotes. There was the Eros of the ancient cosmogonies. Hesiod, the earliest author who mentions him, calls him the cosmogonic Eros. In Plato's "Symposium," he is described as the eldest of the gods. Then there was the Eros of the philosophers, and, lastly, the Eros of the later degenerate Greek poets, who said, erroneously, that he was the youngest of the gods. The parentage of Eros or Cupid is doubtful. It is generally assumed that he was the son of Zeus, that is Jupiter, and of Aphrodite, that is Venus——(MRS. SUTCLIFFE *coughs*)—so that he was both the son and grandson of—(MRS. SUTCLIFFE *coughs, and arranges her dress. The* DOCTOR *takes the hint*) That is love ! I mention these facts because I am about to say no more upon the subject.

NAOMI. I know what love is.

MRS. S. (*aside*) Goodness forbid !

DR. S. How forward the child is !

NAOMI. (*fondling* BELLA) I love Bella—and Bella loves me ; don't you, Bella ?

(BELLA *afraid and constrained before* MRS. SUTCLIFFE)

DR. S. (*taking* BELLA's *hand*) We all love Bella. It is impossible to know her without loving her. Goodness and amiability must command affection and esteem.

NAOMI. He talks just like a copy-book, don't he ?

DR. S. And I suppose, Bella, my child—(MRS. SUTCLIFFE *coughs and arranges her dress*)—that you are going to aid the young ladies in their botanical researches ?

MRS. S. Yes; young ladies, if you have sufficiently reposed yourselves from your walk across the meadow, you can resume your self-imposed labours.

All the GIRLS *go off*, U.E.L., *singing.* BELLA *standing on platform until all are off except* NAOMI, *who crosses behind* MRS. SUTCLIFFE *to* LAURA *and wakes her—they follow the others*, 3 E.L.

" Through the wood, through the wood, follow and find me,
'Search every hollow, and dingle, and dell,
I leave not the print of a footstep behind me,
So they who would search for must look for me well."

(*which dies away in the distance*)

MRS. S. It is an extraordinary thing, Doctor, that, despite all my remonstrances, you will constantly show your too obvious preference for that girl Bella. It has a most injurious effect upon the other pupils.

DR. S. My dear, she is an orphan, without friends or protectors, dependent entirely on us; that sad social anomaly, a pupil-teacher, less self-reliant than a servant, and only half a lady. Then, poor Bella is so pretty, and so young.

MRS. S. Ah !—(*sits on branch of tree*, L.C., *under large tree.* DOCTOR *sits on her* R.)—there it is—so young. (*nearly weeping*) Cruel Theodore, to remind me of my lost youth.

DR. S. Amanthis, my love, that was far from my intention. You are too sensitive.

MRS. S. Your thoughts are ever fixed on the fleeting and unsubstantial charms of youth and beauty.

DR. S. No, no, ho, no!

MRS. S. Yes, yes, yes, yes! Do you not remember five-and-thirty years ago?

DR. S. Amanthis! to recall that error of my youth.

MRS. S. It is always present to my mind.

DR. S. My love, I only danced with her three times, and it is five-and-thirty years ago.

MRS. S. I remember! We had scarcely been married seven years.

DR. S. Since then you have been constantly reproaching me.

MRS. S. It seems but as yesterday.

DR. S. It seems to me much longer.

MRS. S. Ah, Theodore, unfeeling.

DR. S. No, no, Amanthis. I did not mean that. I meant that thirty-five years' conjugal serenity ought to compensate for dancing with a young lady three times at a ball; where, from the fault of hosts too hospitable, the negus had been made too strong. Come, Amanthis, don't be hard on Theodore. Think what Jason says: " Credula res amor est."

MRS. S.   Utinam temereria dicar.
Criminibus falsis insimula visse.

Enter KRUX, 1 E.R.   *He is reading a book.*

DR. S. (*correcting her*) Insimulasse virum. The contraction for the pentameter. (*they join hands.* KRUX *comes down*, R.H. DOCTOR *rises*) Ah! Mr. Krux! Enjoying this beautiful day?

KRUX. No, sir; I was enjoying this beautiful book.

MRS. S. (*rises*) What is it?

KRUX. " Hervey's Meditations among the Tombs."

DR. S. Rather a serious work.

KRUX. Not to my taste, sir. This splendid sky, the plashing brook, the verdant meadow, these rustling trees and sweetly singing birds—all turn my thoughts unto the grave.

MRS. S. Good gracious!

DR. S. (*indignant*) It turns my thoughts to nothing of the sort. On the contrary, it sends them back to years when——

MRS. S. (*aside to him*) Not thirty-five years, Theodore.

DR. S. No, Amanthis, not thirty-five; to thirty-four or thirty-six, but not to thirty-five. Come, let us join the pupils. (*taking her arm*) For the present, Mr. Krux. (*bows; aside*) Prig! I can't bear prigs, particularly young prigs.

Exeunt DOCTOR *and* MRS. SUTCLIFFE, 3 E.L.

KRUX. Upstarts! I hate those people. But then, I hate most people; I think I hate most things—(*crushing beetle with his foot*)—except Bella, and when I look at her, I feel that I could bite her. Here she is. (*Enter* BELLA, 1 E.L. *She crosses to* R., *reading a book*) Bella, where are you going?

BELLA. (R.C.) Mrs. Sutcliffe has sent me to fetch her goloshes.

KRUX. (L.C.) Stay one moment. Sit down.

Seating himself left of BELLA, *on large branch, under tree,* R.C.

BELLA. Mrs. Sutcliffe told me I was not to loiter.

KRUX. What are you reading?

BELLA. A fairy tale. What are you reading?

KRUX. "Hervey's Meditations." A different sort of literature. Do sit down. (BELLA *sits on branch of tree*)

BELLA. (*reading*) "The King's son, the handsome young Prince, was continually by her side, and said to her the most obliging things imaginable."

KRUX. What a beastly world this is, Bella, isn't it? Attend to me for a short time. I want to speak to you particularly.

BELLA. Be quick, then.

KRUX. Mr. and Mrs. Sutcliffe are getting very old.

BELLA. They are not *getting* old; they *are* old.

KRUX. And, therefore, must soon die.

BELLA. (*shocked*) Oh, Mr. Krux, what a dreadful notion.

KRUX. We are all worms; particularly Doctor and Mrs. Sutcliffe. All men must die some time, the Doctor and Mrs. Sutcliffe included.

BELLA. Mrs. Sutcliffe isn't a man.

KRUX. She ought to have been. But as I was saying, Bella, when they are dead and buried——

BELLA. Mr. Krux!

KRUX. They will be no longer able to keep on the school, will they? Then who is to keep on the school, eh?

T T

BELLA. I don't know; I don't like to think of such things.

KRUX. I do. I repeat, who is to keep on the school? I am the only resident master; I am known to all the pupils.

BELLA. Alas, yes!

KRUX. I am known and, I hope, loved.

BELLA. No; feared.

KRUX. It's the same thing in a school. Bella, you're a very good scholar.

BELLA. No, I'm not.

KRUX. Yes, you are; and you understand all about the kitchen—pies, and coals, and vegetables, and the like. You're an orphan.

BELLA. Yes. *(sighing)*

KRUX. So am I. You have no relations?

BELLA. No.

KRUX. Nor friends?

BELLA. Oh, yes; Mr. and Mrs. Sutcliffe, and the school, and the people in the village.

KRUX. I don't count them. I have no friends.

BELLA. No, not one?

KRUX. When the Sutcliffes (BELLA *looks at him*) go—why shouldn't we keep on the school?

. BELLA. *(astonished)* We?

KRUX. Yes, you and I; we are quite capable; I am clever, so are you; we could enlarge the connection. You could manage the girls, I could manage the boys. Think how pleasant to make money—take in pupils, teach them and correct them. I should like to correct them, particularly the boys. We should get on, Bella, if we got married——

BELLA. Got married!—who got married?

KRUX. You to me—me to you! Mr. and Mrs. Krux, of Cedar Grove House. I love you, Bella.

✓ BELLA. *(rises suddenly, drops her book, and hides her face in her hands)* Oh, don't; on such a nice day as this.

KRUX. Eh?

BELLA, Poor dear Mr. and Mrs. Sutcliffe, to think of their dying, it makes me cry—*(crying)*—so kind as they've been to me.

KRUX. She's a fool—*(rises)*—Bella.

✓ BELLA. Go away, you bad man, do—to think of death and marriage, and such dreadful things.

KRUX. You won't tell the Sutcliffes, Bella, will you? I

proposed it all for your good, and because I love you—
(BELLA *shudders*)—you won't tell 'em, will you, dear, and
get me into trouble? Promise me you won't tell 'em!
(*carneying*) Promise me ; do, do !

BELLA. I won't tell 'em, if you'll promise me never to
mention such subjects again.

KRUX. I won't—I'll take my oath I won't. Take your
oath you won't tell' them of me, Bella; take your oath,
dear, will you?

BELLA. No—I give you my word. To think of our
kind benefactors dying. You wicked man, I wonder that
something doesn't happen to you. I wonder—— (*two shots
heard without*, R.H.) Oh ! (KRUX *frightened*) I won't
stay any longer.

KRUX. Where are you going?

BELLA. To fetch the goloshes.

Exit BELLA, R.H. 1 E.

KRUX. A bad girl ! a bad girl ! a bad girl ! She'll come
to no good, if I can help it ; an ungrateful beast—after the
offer I made her. What is she ? A nobody, a foundling, a
pauper—(*Enter* LORD BEAUFOY *and* JACK POYNTZ, *in shooting dress, followed by two* KEEPERS, R.H. 3 E.)—brought up
on charity. Oh, if she were a man, I'd——

LORD BEAUFOY *comes down on* KRUX'S L., *and touches
him with gun, before he speaks*

LORD B. Have you seen anybody pass this way?

KRUX. A young girl, sir, (*meekly*) with a book?

LORD B. No—an old gentleman and two servants?

KRUX. No, sir.

JACK. (*aside, down* L. C.) What a mangy looking cur !

KRUX. (*aside*) Two young puppies.

LORD B. (*to* KEEPERS) Are you sure this was the place
where lunch was to meet us?

JACK. (*looking off*) Yes—for here it comes.

Enter TIGER, *carrying two small folding chairs ; two
SERVANTS, one with picnic case, with lunch plates,
knives and forks. The other has a tray-stand and
butler's tray, which he places* C. *They spread the
lunch.*

JACK. (*seeing* KRUX) Good morning.

KRUX. (*servilely*) Good morning, sir. (*aside*) Upstart
beasts !

Exit KRUX, R. 1 E.

Enter BEAU FARINTOSH, *led on by* VAUGHAN, U.E.L.,
who carries a camp stool, which he places at table C.
for the BEAU; FARINTOSH *is a thin old man of
seventy, dressed in the latest fashion, wigged, dyed,
padded, eye-glassed, a would-be young man, blind
as a bat—peering into everything.*

FARIN. (*shaking hands with* JACK) My dear boy—my
dear boy, how d'ye do ? The very image of my poor sister—
so glad to see you.

SERVANTS.

KEEPERS.   VAUGHAN.

TIGER.

JACK.   FARINTOSH.

LORD BEAUFOY.

JACK. Thank you, Mr. Farintosh, but my mamma had
not the happiness of being your sister. That is Lord
Beaufoy.

FARIN. Ten thousand pardons, but my eyes are so—so
—so—which is him, where is he ? (*going to and shaking
hands with* LORD BEAUFOY) My dear Arthur, quite well, eh?
Strong, yes—you look so—very image of my poor sister.

LORD B. I'm quite well, Beau ; you, too, I hope.

FARIN. Never better—never better—strong, active, fine
condition—fine condition. (*striking himself on chest*) Bellows
to mend, eh—bellows to mend—ha ! ha ! ha ! Sit down.

LORD B. Let me introduce my friend—Mr. Poyntz—
Mr. Percy Farintosh.

FARIN. Poyntz ! Worcestershire Poyntzes ?

JACK. Worcestershire Poyntzes !

FARIN. Knew your grandfather. I mean your father—
well—he was my second in Paris just after the battle of—
no—no—sit down.   (*they sit*)

LORD B. May I—(*helping lunch*) You may go. (*to*
SERVANTS, *who exeunt*, U.E.L.)

FARIN. Nothing before dinner, thanks.

LORD B. When we arrived at your place last night, you
had gone to bed.

FARIN. Yes, early to bed—late up, my way.

LORD B. And your man gave us your message ; told us
to shoot this morning—and that you——

FARIN. Would meet you here to lunch, if fine. Pleasant
in the open air. (*to* JACK) You appear to have a good
appetite, Mr.——

LORD B. Poyntz.

JACK. Yes—I'm quite a celebrity that way. It is my principal talent.

FARIN. Ah! a very enviable one.

JACK. It is convenient at dinner time.

LORD B. Your last letter said that you had some business?

FARIN. Yes, yes, yes!

JACK. Shall I and the lunch retire, and amuse ourselves together?

LORD B. No, no—Jack is an old friend. I presume it is on the old subject?

JACK. (*eating*) Ah, debt!

LORD B. No; marriage!

JACK. Oh, family troubles—shall I——

FARIN. No, no, no, Mr.——

LORD B. Poyntz.

FARIN. Mr. Poyntz, my nephew and I are at logger heads. You shall judge between us.

JACK. Most happy.

FARIN. I wish him to marry.

JACK. Hard, very; but some uncles are like that.

FARIN. Have you ever been married?

JACK. Never; but once I was in quarantine ten days off Malta.

FARIN. (*downcast*) I have been married.

JACK. There I have the advantage of you—I am the singlest young person possible; open to competition, and to be influenced only by money.

LORD B. (*in answer to a look from* FARINTOSH) You mustn't mind Jack, it's his humour to talk in that way.

FARIN. My poor wife died early; had she lived I should have been a different man—a different man.

JACK. (*aside*) Ah—dead most likely.

LORD B. It's a melancholy story, Jack, and I shall get over it quicker than the Beau. My uncle's wife died, leaving a son: this son married——

FARIN. Against my wishes.

LORD B. And he died——

FARIN. Without seeing me, that I might ask his pardon and forgive him.

LORD B. He, too, left a child; of this child and her mother, my uncle has been unable to find the least trace.

FARIN. I would give thousands to find them.

JACK. Try the second column of the *Times*. If you were to put in an advertisement, " Wanted, a young person to adopt, by a gentleman of fortune," you'd have lots of applicants. Indeed, why go further than this present spot? Here am I, ready to be adopted. I should like to be adopted by any gentleman or lady of means. Here you are, a strong, healthy, useful orphan, with good appetite and expensive habits all ready laid on ; no objection to travel, or to go in single or double harness.

FARIN. Your friend has a very singular humour.

LORD B. Yes, and it sometimes runs away with him.

JACK. And sometimes puts me down when I least expect it. Pray forgive me.

FARIN. But revenons a nos—fleurs d'oranges. I want Arthur to marry.

JACK. But Arthur would rather not.

LORD B. I won't marry.

FARIN. Did you ever hear such infatuation? It's tremendous. What was man invented for, but to marry?

LORD B. My tastes are so singular; I should want such a singular wife.

JACK. What sort? Give particulars—name your age, weight, and colour.

LORD B. My wife must be a woman.

JACK. Plenty about.

LORD B. Aye, but I mean a real woman.

JACK. That's difficult.

LORD B. Not a regulation doll of the same pattern as the other dolls—the same absence of thought, the same simper, same stupid dove-like look out of the eyes. (*imitating*) "I love papa, I love mamma. I go to church on Sunday; I can walk, and talk, and play. Je suis une jolie poupée et je veux bien un bon petit mari pour m'acheter des toilettes et me faire promener au bois."

FARIN. Did you ever hear? It's profane—quite profane.

JACK. (*lighting cigar*) Do you?   (*offering him*)

FARIN. I don't smoke. (*taking snuff*) Do you?

(*offering him*)

JACK. I do everything.   --   (*taking snuff*)

FARIN. How you must enjoy life.

JACK. (*smoking hard*) Sir, for sensual enjoyment I would give Caligula six, and distance him. It's a great comfort having no intellect.

FARIN. Many people find it so. Your language, Arthur, is blasphemy, perfect blasphemy, against the loveliest portion of creation.

LORD. B. What is loveliness? Something to be bought in bottles and put on with a brush?

FARIN. You don't dislike beauty?

LORD B. No; but I hate paint.

FARIN. Paint?

LORD B. Paint! Shall I promise to love and cherish a plaister cast? Shall I promise to cleave only unto a living fresco, decked out in dead hair? I want a young wife, not an old master; I want charms that won't rub off on my coat sleeve if I touch them before they're dry. Pigments and spices are for Egyptian mummies; not for breathing flesh and blood. Can I exchange words of love with one who, before she has spoken, is a built up falsehood? I choose men friends who don't tell lies; I choose women who don't look them.

JACK. Which means that when you're eighty you'll marry your cook, because she doesn't use pearl powder when on active service.

LORD B. The charms of my love must be warranted to wash.

JACK. You mean not to wash off.

FARIN. Arthur, I'm shocked; your opinions are—are—atheistic.

LORD B. It's not only cosmetics I do battle with. Some women would kill gallantry and chivalry by something called equality with men. What is equality with men? Having their clothes made by a he tailor instead of a she milliner. How pleasant for man and wife to be measured together; or, at an election, for him to walk arm-in-arm to the hustings with a wretched, half-mad, whole mannish creature, who votes for the candidate you wish to exclude.

JACK. I agree with you there; if women were admitted to electoral privileges, they'd sell them for the price of a new chignon; man, as the nobler animal, has the exclusive right to sell his vote—for beer!

LORD B. Give me simplicity. I'm one of the old school.

FARIN. (*rising*) And I'm one of the new. Give me chignons, cosmetics, perfumes—in short, civilisation. I do not see why beings endowed with immortal souls should not repair the ravages of time by the appliances of art. As you say, it all depends upon the school one has been reared in. (*sits*)

JACK. What does it matter? Indeed, in this world, what does anything matter—after dinner?

FARIN. Your sentiments are revolting, and remind me

of the works of Burke and Hare, and Tom Paine and Voltaire, and other persons out of the social pale. Knowing your singular views, I had prepared a splendid *parti* for you, an heiress.

LORD B. I don't want money.

JACK. Not want money ! you should be photographed. The man who don't want money deserves to be put into an album, and kept there.

FARIN. Miss Naomi Tighe—a West Indian heiress, without father or mother.

JACK. No father and no mother, and an heiress. It's a gorgeous thing in matrimonials. But why offer it to Arthur ? He don't want it. I do.

FARIN. She's at school close by here, with some old friends of mine. I was asked to go and see the preliminary examination of the young ladies before the holidays. I thought it would be an excellent thing to take you with me, that you might see Miss Tighe, and, as I hoped, approve of her, for her guardians are also my oldest friends.

LORD B. I'd rather not go.

Rises and beckons on SERVANTS. *Enter* KEEPERS *and* VAUGHAN, U.E.L. *They remove table, &c., off* U.E.L.

FARIN. The examination is to-day week.

LORD B. I'll go, uncle, to please you.

FARIN. Will your friend accompany us ?

JACK. Thanks, I'll go to please myself.

FARIN. Here's Vaughan to take me home. I always sleep before I dress for dinner. Till then——

JACK *sees something in the bushes. Motions* KEEPER *for a gun.* KEEPER *gives it him.*

JACK. No; the rifle.

KEEPER *gives* JACK *breech-loader, which* JACK *loads, and goes off* R.U.E.

FARIN. What's he doing ?

LORD B. He's going to kill a bird with a bullet. He's a wonderful shot.

FARIN. Now give me your arm. (*taking* VAUGHAN'S *arm*) Ah, there you are; till dinner, Arthur——

Exeunt FARINTOSH, VAUGHAN, *and* KEEPERS, U.E.L.

LORD B. Marry me to a young lady, all bread and butter and boarding-school. Time enough for marriage when I'm forty-five, and wear a waist belt. Marriage ! Tut—a pile of boxes when you travel. Female friends to tell your wife what happened or what didn't happen before she was your wife. Hysteria when she's contradicted. Tears when you're cruel—that is, when you won't let her have her own way. Mild accents of mother-in-law. " Is this the lot, sir, you have prepared for my dear child ? Come home, love, come home." By Jove, she might go home for me ; there's always something the matter—a pain here or there, a sinking, or a swimming, or a floating, or a darting, or a shooting. (*turns up stage. Shot heard without.* BELLA *runs across stage, frightened, and loses her shoe, from* R.1 E. *Exit* L.1 E. LORD BEAUFOY *does not see her*) Then the brothers ! What a horror is the brother of the girl you're spooning, particularly if he is like her ; the thought will come that she might have been him, or he might have been her. No ; love is a species of lunacy, of which marriage is the strait waist-coat. (*kicks against shoe left by* BELLA) What's this ? Shoe ! Child's shoe ? No ! Woman's shoe ? No ! Girl's shoe ? (*picks it up*) Pretty little shoe; must belong to a pretty little foot, very pretty little foot. Now, why on earth could any young girl come into this wood for the purpose of losing her shoe ? I should like to know who it belongs to ? I feel quite a curiosity to——(NAOMI *screams outside*, R.1 E.) Eh, perhaps this is the fair and shoeless owner.

NAOMI *runs on*, R.1 E., *and* BELLA *from* L.1 E. *She runs to* NAOMI, *meeting her* R.C.

		LORD B.
NAOMI.	BELLA.	up stage,
R.C.	C.	L.C.

BELLA. Oh, my darling, there you are. (*they embrace*)

NAOMI. Oh ! I thought we were both killed—that dreadful cow !

LORD B. Quite girls, both. Now to which does this belong ? It is the very tiniest shoe (*loudly*) Ahem !
(*comes down back of them*)

NAOMI. Oh, it's the gentleman who shot him. Oh, sir, so many, many, many thanks.

BELLA. Sir, you saved our lives ; pray accept our grati-tude.

LORD B. Gratitude for what ? (*aside*) Surely not for finding——

BELLA. I was walking across the meadow. ·

NAOMI. And I saw her, and ran to meet her, when a great big ugly cow——

BELLA. Ran at us, and wanted to trample us to death——.—

NAOMI. When you shot him.

LORD B. I shot him !

NAOMI. And we ran away.

BELLA. We might have lost our lives.

LORD B. Haven't you lost anything else ?

BELLA.
NAOMI. } (*feeling her chignon*) } (*together*) No !

LORD B.
BELLA. } (*together*) { Not———?
NAOMI. { No. { Nothing.

(*runs across to* BELLA, L.)

LORD B. I thought you had.   (*disappointed*)

Enter JACK POYNTZ *at back* R., *with gun.*

LORD B. Jack, was it you fired just now ?

JACK. Yes.

NAOMI, BELLA.
up stage, L.C.

JACK.   LORD B.
R.   R.C.

LORD B. What have you got there—birds ?

JACK. No ; boots.   (*producing a pair of goloshes*)

LORD B. Good gracious! does it rain boots about here?

(*producing shoe*)

JACK. Just now I was going to pot a bird, when I saw two girls running away like mad from—what the newspapers call an infuriated animal ; so I sighted him, and hit him just between the horns ; out of compliment to my shooting he fell down dead, and the two girls ran away ; I walked up to the scene of slaughter, and at first I thought that these (*showing goloshes*) belonged to the defunct, but of course that was quite impossi*bull.*

NAOMI. (R.C. *Crossing to* JACK) Then, sir, it was you who shot the cow ?

JACK. (R.) Yes ; I shot the cow. The cow was a bull ; but that is a detail.

NAOMI. It was you, and not this gentleman !

JACK. If a bull is shot, what does it matter who shot him, particularly to the bull !

LORD B. (*aside*) I wish I'd shot him. Confound that Jack, what luck he has.

JACK. May I ask if you know the owner of these (*showing goloshes*) trophies from the field of battle ?

BELLA. (L.C. *Advancing*) Oh, they're mine !

LORD B. (L. *Astounded*) Yours ?

BELLA. Yes; at least, I was carrying them to Mrs. Sutcliffe.

LORD B. Mrs. Sutcliffe !   (*relieved*)

NAOMI. Yes; our governess !

          (BELLA *takes goloshes*)

LORD B. (*to* BELLA) Then, I presume, that these belong to Mrs. Sutcliffe.

BELLA. Yes.

LORD B. Then Mrs. Sutcliffe's foot is somewhat large; and who does this belong to ?

BELLA. (*seeing her foot is unshod*) Oh, that's mine.

LORD B. (*relieved*) I'm so glad.

BELLA. I didn't know I'd lost it, I was so frightened. (*taking it*) Thank you so much, sir, for saving my—— shoe.   (*goes up*, L.C., *and puts it on*)

JACK. May I know who I have the pleasure of addressing ?

NAOMI. My name is Naomi Tighe.

JACK. (*aside*) The heiress——

JACK. LORD BEAUFOY.
O   O
NAOMI.   BELLA.
O   O

LORD B. And your name ?   (*to* BELLA)

BELLA. Bella !

LORD B. Bella ?

NAOMI. We're both pupils at Mrs. Sutcliffe's.

BELLA. That is, I'm not quite a pupil—I'm only a pupil-teacher.

JACK. (*pointing to the red portion of* NAOMI'S *dress*) It was this attracted the bull.

NAOMI. Oh, don't look at me. I can't bear to be looked at.   (*puts her handkerchief over her face*)

JACK. How singular. (*to* LORD BEAUFOY) This is the very girl your uncle spoke of.

LORD B. Yes; do you think her handsome ?

JACK. Not bad for an heiress. And the other ?

LORD B. Charming.

BELLA. If you please, gentlemen, don't mention to Mrs. Sutcliffe that we have been attacked. She is so nervous; it would make her ill.

    (GIRLS *without, singing* " *Through the Wood* ")

NAOMI. Here's governess.

LORD B. Let us go; our staying may embarrass.

JACK. No; let's stop and see them take their gallops.

The School passes across the stage from L. 3 E. *r.* 3 E., *singing, " Through the Wood," &c. ; i* DOCTOR *and* MRS. SUTCLIFFE *last.* BELLA *off* MRS. SUTCLIFFE *her goloshes.* NAOMI *is platform when* DOCTOR *appears, waving har kerchief to* JACK *and laughing. The* DOCT *touches her on the shoulder; the expression on l face alters suddenly, and she runs off, followed* DOCTOR. MRS. SUTCLIFFE *signifies to* BELLA *retain goloshes, and exits, followed by* BELLA, w *looks at* LORD BEAUFOY. *As soon as she is c* JACK *runs on to platform and waves his cap his gun,* LORD BEAUFOY *watching* BELLA *fr below.*

Song—

" When the red sun sets at eve you may hear me, .
Singing farewell to his rays as they fade;
But as soon as the step of a mortal is near me,
I take to my wings and fly off to the shade."

(dies in the distance, as curtain falls quickly)

LORD BEAUFOY
up C.   JACK.
                 L.C.

END OF ACT I.

ACT II.

SCENE.—*The Schoolroom. Shelves with books. Scene enclosed. Window* R. *and* L. *flat. Door* R.H.U.E. *Desks, desk for Master, &c. Maps. Music from "La Cenerentola" as drop rises.* BELLA *discovered, seated at small table near open window,* R.II., *shelling peas.*

Landscape Cloth at back.

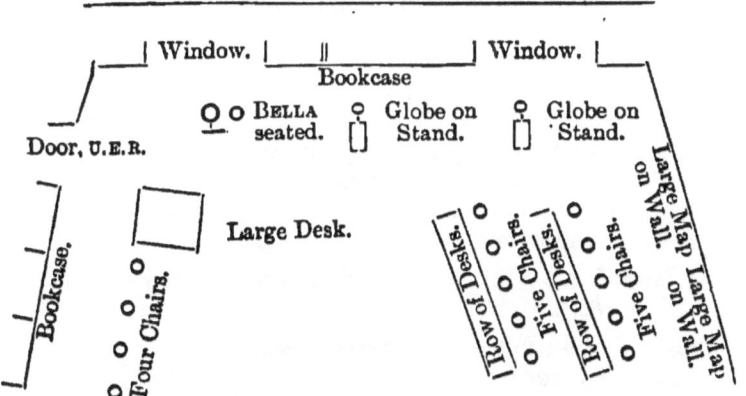

BELLA. (*humming*)

> Said the Prince unto the maiden,
>   "There is none I love but thee";
> "Let me hence, then," said the maiden,
>   "You are not of my degree."
> "Love can raise thee to a lady,
>   Say, my Princess wilt thou be?"
> Faster, faster, flew the maiden,
>   Faster, faster followed he.

NAOMI, *in a hat and shawl, appears outside window* R. *flat; she touches* BELLA *on the shoulder.*

BELLA. Nummy, is that you?
NAOMI. Yes, dear; what are you doing?
BELLA. Shelling peas, and——
NAOMI. Yes.
BELLA. And thinking——

NAOMI. (*in a whisper*) About the goloshes?

(BELLA *nods*)

BELLA. But only a little—only a little.

NAOMI. Bella, dear, I dreamt last night, and this morning I feel as if something were going to happen; that is, I feel quite hysterical, as if I should like somebody to hug or to scratch at. I dressed myself quickly, on purpose that I might come out into the garden and have a good think. It is so nice to think in the shrubbery.

BELLA. I'm afraid we are too young to have a right to think upon such subjects.

NAOMI. Not a bit: one is always old enough for a sweetheart. I'm eighteen. How old are you?

BELLA. I don't know.

NAOMI. Then, perhaps you're twenty. I knew two girls who were married before they were nineteen; but then some people have such luck! Ain't you going to dress yourself for this examination, like the other girls?

BELLA. This is my Sunday frock.

NAOMI. But you can have my pink, my darling; you can wear anything of mine.

> *Kisses* BELLA *through window, and steals peas and eats them.*

BELLA. You musn't eat the peas, dear.

NAOMI. Why not?

BELLA. They're not nice.

NAOMI. Yes, they are, if you eat them when nobody's looking.

> *Enter* MRS. SUTCLIFFE, R.H.D., *dressed for dinner.* NAOMI *starts from window.*

MRS. S. Bella, what are you doing there?

BELLA. Shelling peas, ma'am.

MRS. S. Shelling peas in the school-room!

BELLA. They are so busy, and so pushed for room in the kitchen with the dinner, that I brought them here; I can take them back.   (*rising and taking basin*)

MRS. S. (*looking at watch*) It is nearly time that Mr. Farintosh and his friend should be here. Bella, if the young ladies are dressed, you can tell them that I will inspect them in this apartment.   (R.H.D. *opens*)

BELLA. Here are the young ladies.

MRS. S. Good!

> BELLA *resumes her pea-shelling. Enter all the* GIRLS

(*dressed for the examination*) *one by one, in the following order :*—MILLY, CLARA, HETTY, KITTY, LITTLE GIRL, D.U.E.R. MRS. SUTCLIFFE *turns them round, signifying approval or the reverse ; they take their respective seats at the two desks,* L. —NAOMI *last but one. They seat themselves thus :*—

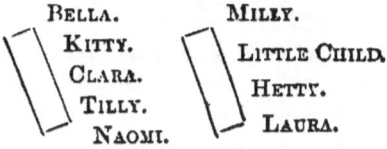

BELLA.   MILLY.
KITTY.   LITTLE CHILD.
CLARA.   HETTY.
TILLY.   LAURA.
NAOMI.

MRS. S. (*to* LITTLE GIRL) You shall be examined with the others to please you. What are you going to answer?

LITTLE GIRL. They condemned him to shoot——

MRS. S. Yes, yes, that's right. (CHILD *goes to her seat* Why Naomi, my dear, you've been crying.

NAOMI. No, I haven't.

MRS. S. Miss Tighe! Miss Tighe! you should say I was mistaken.

NAOMI. Then you are ; and if I have been crying it's only a few tears. (*goes to her seat*)

TILLY. (*to* NAOMI) What could you cry but tears ! You couldn't cry cucumbers, could you?

Enter LAURA, R.H.D. *sleepy, her dress badly put on.*

MRS. S. Now then, Laura, you're last again.

LAURA. Somebody must be last. (*goes to her place*)

BELLA *goes off at* R.H.D., *with peas, and returns immediately.*

MRS. S. The Doctor will put you through an examination on the arrival of our friends. It will be an excellent bit of practice for the grand examination at the end of the half-year. The musical examination will take place in the drawing-room after dinner. Mr. Farintosh brings a friend with him, Lord Beaufoy (*excitement of* GIRLS), the owner of half a county.

TILLY. Half a county? Which half?

CLARA. And which county?

NAOMI. Is he a real lord?

MRS. S. Real? Yes.

NAOMI. But I mean a real, real, lord. When I get near him I'll pinch him, and see if he is flesh and blood, like other people.

TILLY. Oh, I daresay lords are very flesh.

NAOMI. And very blood—very good blood. I mean.

(gate bell, R.II.)

MRS. S. Hush ! (awful silence) They are here.

NAOMI. Oh, I feel so nervous. I should like to scream.

MRS. S. Young ladies, I have only time to say that I rely on you with every confidence.

> GIRLS rise, curtsey, and seat themselves. Enter DR. SUTCLIFFE, followed by BEAU FARINTOSH, LORD BEAUFOY, and JACK POYNTZ, dressed for dinner (not evening dress), R. door. The GIRLS all rise. BEAU FARINTOSH and LORD BEAUFOY speak to DR. and MRS. SUTCLIFFE. JACK POYNTZ wanders down row of desks until he comes to NAOMI.

NAOMI. (recognising JACK) It's the cow.

> Sinks on chair, blushing and giggling ; then rises again, trying to restrain herself.

JACK. (seeing her) It's the little thing in red, who had the attack of bullock—the heiress.

(to LORD BEAUFOY, R.C.)

MRS. S. Young ladies, let me have the honour—Lord Beaufoy.

DR. SUTCLIFFE.

BEAU FARINTOSH.   O

         O   MRS. SUTCLIFFE.

LORD BEAUFOY.   O

         O

JACK POYNTZ.

         O

BELLA. (at back) He Lord Beaufoy !

(MRS. SUTCLIFFE presenting them. GIRLS curtsey)

MRS. S. Mr. Percy Farintosh, Mr. ——

> NAOMI giggles again, and is silenced by a look from MRS. SUTCLIFFE.

LORD B. Poyntz.

MRS. S. Mr. Poyntz.

NAOMI. (whispering to herself, and writing it on slate) Poyntz, Poyntz, Poyntz, Poyntz !

FARIN. A friend who was staying with me, and whom I have taken the liberty——

MRS. S. { Charmed. } (shaking hands with JACK)
DR. S. { Delighted. }

FARIN. (going towards desks) My dear young ladies, permit me to say how highly I feel honoured by being permitted, by the kindness of my friends, Mrs. Sutcliffe and—and Theodore—and the Doctor, to be present at this charming a—a——.

LORD B. { Inspection ! }
JACK. { Review ! } *(together)*

FARIN. Inspection—review—whatever it may be.

DR. S. Examination.

FARIN. Examination. Indeed, this is one of the proudest privileges of my life.

MRS. S. My dear Mr. Farintosh !

DR. S. Percy, my old friend.

FARIN. (*fumbling for his eye-glass*) To see so much grace and beauty, 'tis like gazing on a parterre of beautiful flowers, whose colours are audible and whose perfume is melody.

DR. S. Bravo ! Very elegant.

MRS. S. Flowing.

LORD B. Like Tom Moore.

JACK. Broken-winded.

MRS. S. The old school.

FARIN. Vielle école ! Bonne école !

JACK. Good show of girls.

FARIN. That is new school—short, pithy, ungraceful——

JACK. And meaning what it says.

> *They talk in group.* BELLA, *who during this has been unobserved, crosses to door.* LORD BEAUFOY *turns and recognises her.*

LORD B. My fairy in the wood.

NAOMI. (*aside*) It's the shoe-horn.

DR. S. Bella, my dear, you are not going?

BELLA I—I——

> (*faltering ; comes down back of chairs to* R.C.)

DR. SUTCLIFFE.
LORD BEAUFOY.   O

JACK POYNTZ.   O
        O   BEAU FARINTOSH.

O   O   O
BELLA.   MRS. SUTCLIFFE.

MRS. S. Miss Tighe, let me introduce you to Mr. Percy Farintosh.

FARIN. (*crossing to* R. *Mistaking* BELLA *for* NAOMI) Miss Tighe, I knew your guardians intimately. I have——

MRS. S. That is not Miss Tighe ; that is Bella. (BELLA *and* BEAU FARINTOSH *scrutinise each other. During this*

U U

GIRLS *whisper*) A little thing I took in out of charity. Makes herself very useful about the house.

DR. S. (*coming down to* BELLA) The best scholar we can boast of; the pupil of whom I am most proud. Take your accustomed place, Bella, at the head of the class.

> BELLA *goes to her place, followed by* DR. SUT-CLIFFE.

NAOMI. Bravo!

MRS. S. (*looks at* NAOMI) Pray be seated.

> *To* GENTLEMEN, *who sit* R.H., *thus,* BEAU FARINTOSH *placing* MRS. SUTCLIFFE'S *chair for her :—*
>
> MRS. SUTCLIFFE.
> BEAU FARINTOSH.
> LORD BEAUFOY.
> JACK POYNTZ.
> R.   L.

NAOMI. (*looking at* JACK) I can't answer a single question if he looks at me.

LORD B. Handsome girls!

FARIN. Delightful! Can't see a single feature.

> *Fumbles for his eye-glass, which is at his back.* BEAUFOY *finds it for him. All seated.* NAOMI *makes eyes at* JACK, *who has been gazing at her steadfastly, and then laughs.*

MRS. S. Hush, hush! Miss Tighe.

DR. S. (*standing* C., *at desk*) The ancient Romans——

MRS. S. (*coughs*) Doctor, as we are rather late and dinner will be punctual, if you would kindly make the preliminaries to the examination as short as possible.

DR. S. I will so, my dear. We will begin with Roman history.. (*as he asks the question, he indicates with a rule the* GIRL *he means, who rises as she answers*) There were different forms of government in Rome. Please to inform me in what order those forms of government ruled the Roman people.

TILLY. First the regal power, that is the kings; next the consuls, until the first dictator was chosen; then the power of the decemviri; consular government again; imperial dictatorship; then the emperors.

FARIN. My dear Mrs. Sutcliffe, let me congratulate you on your fair charges.

JACK. How the propria quæ maribus they can remember it I can't make out.

LORD B. I suppose it's cram.

DR. S. After Romulus had appointed the lictors, what other royal or civic guard did he appoint?

MILLY. The Celeres.

DR. S. Who were they?

MILLY. A guard of young men, numbering three hundred, who accompanied Romulus for the purpose of defending him.

LORD B. Sort of Life Guards!

JACK. Yes, without boots or breeches.

LORD B. Cool to fight in.

JACK. And convenient for fording rivers.

DR. S. Name the reign and date rendered illustrious by Belisarius?

NAOMI. The reign of Justinian, in the year 561.

DR. S. Who was Belisarius?

TILLY. Belisarius was a Roman general, who rendered the highest services to his country.

DR. S. How was he rewarded?

CLARA. They deprived him of his dignities, and put his eyes out.

JACK. That must have been done by a Committee of the Period! (MRS. S. *coughs*)

DR. S. Now for English history. With regard, now, to the ancient Druids. In what garments were the ancient Druids clothed when they offered——(MRS. SUTCLIFFE *coughs; all the* GIRLS *hide their heads behind their slates or on the desks.* FARINTOSH, BEAUFOY, *and* JACK *laugh among themselves, and the* DOCTOR *mops his forehead. General discomfiture*)—I should say—ahem—In what reign was the ceremony of marriage first solemnized in churches?

ALL THE GIRLS. (*all rising*) In the reign of Henry III.

JACK. They all know that.

FARIN. Wonderful, wonderful; and all single girls, too.

DR. S. What is the difference between the political parties, Whig and Tory?

TILLY. None whatever.

DR. S. By whom were the Britons first conquered?

NAOMI. (*with fire*) They never were conquered—they'd sooner die.

JACK. Girl of spirit, by Jove!

DR. S. In what reign was the famous Gunpowder Plot discovered?

CLARA. In the reign of November the 5th.

FARIN. Wonderful! My dear Mrs. Sutcliffe——

BELLA. In the reign of James the First.

DR. S. Who was the chief instigator, criminal, and author of that atrocious plot?

CLARA. Oliver Cromwell.

TILLY. Guy Fawkes.

DR. S. How was Guy Fawkes punished?

LITTLE CHILD. They condemned him to shoot an apple off the head of his own son.

DR. S. Hum! Astronomy. How far distant is the moon from the earth?

NAOMI. (*after a pause*) It depends on the weather. I knew I couldn't do it.

DR. S. Bella, dear.

BELLA. The mean distance of the moon from the earth is 236,847 miles.

JACK. Good gracious!

FARIN. Wonderful!

DR. S. I told you Bella was our best pupil. And the diameter of the moon?

BELLA. Its apparent diameter is variable according to her distance from the earth. Her real diameter is 2,144 miles.

NAOMI. (*whispering*) What do they call the moon "her" for?

TILLY. Because the moon's a lady.

NAOMI. The more shame for her to be out so late at night. What would they say if we did it?

TILLY. Consider her age.

DR. S. And the magnitude of the moon?

BELLA. About one-fiftieth of the magnitude of the earth.

FARIN. Tremendous! In astronomical knowledge that young lady is a perfect Sir Isaac——Davy.

Enter KRUX, *dressed for dinner*, R.H.D.

KRUX. (*to* MRS. SUTCLIFFE, *on her* L.) Pardon my interruption, but the servant didn't like to mention that dinner was ready, and——

MRS. S. Oh, thank you. (*rising*) I fear we cannot proceed with the examination further. (*all rise except* GIRLS) Mr. Krux, as Mr. Farintosh has brought two friends, one more than expected, I fear there will not be room for you at table; so—if you wouldn't mind excusing——

KRUX. (*mortified*) Oh, never mind me, Mrs. Sutcliffe; I'm of no consequence.

MRS. S. Oh, thank you ; so kind of you.

FARIN. (*mistaking* KRUX *for* DR. SUTCLIFFE) My dear Doctor, so many thanks. I shall be able to tell you all my admiration during dinner.

>DOCTOR *taps* FARINTOSH, *on shoulder who acknowledges mistake.*

MRS. S. Ladies (GIRLS *rise*), then, until after dinner, when we will resume our studies.

>GIRLS *curtsey,* KRUX *goes up and leans against desk at back,* FARINTOSH *offers* MRS. SUTCLIFFE *his arm, and they go off.* JACK *goes towards* NAOMI, *nodding and laughing and backing towards door at same time, finally knocking up against* KRUX, *who is annoyed.* BEAUFOY'S *attention is rivetted on* BELLA. DOCTOR *at door* R. *coughs.* BEAUFOY *bows, goes to door, looks back and exits ; followed by* DOCTOR. *All exeunt* R.H.D. *As soon as they are off,* GIRLS *sit down, chatter, talk, and laugh loudly, taking no notice of* KRUX'S *authority.*

KRUX. And they dine without me, and I'd kept such a good appetite, because I knew the dinner was nice. Silence, ladies ! Oh, those upstarts—and the guests are as bad as the hosts. Ladies ! That old fool and those two young idiots, I don't suppose they could conjugate a verb between them. (KRUX *has a white mark on his left shoulder, as if he had rubbed against a whitewashed wall*) Ladies ! Ladies ! ! Ladies ! ! ! (*rapping desk*) I must request your attention. Miss Hetty, take your arms off the desk. Miss Laura, heads up ! (*the* GIRLS *eat apples, write on slips of paper, draw on slates, &c. They see, as he turns, the white mark on his back, and laugh*) Silence, if you please.

NAOMI. He's been powdering himself for dinner.

(*laugh*)

TILLY. It's not powder, it's flour—he's been kissing the cook.

NAOMI. Oh ! how I pity the cook. (*laugh*)

KRUX. Silence, ladies ; we will resume our studies in geography. Miss Laura, will you tell me in what country we left off yesterday ?

LAURA. (*half asleep*) In bed.

KRUX. Nowhere near it—we left off in South America. Miss Amelia ?

MILLY. We left off in the mountains ?

KRUX. What mountains.

MILLY. The Alps.

KRUX. Wrong.

KITTY. The Appennines.

KRUX. Wrong.

TILLY. The Pyrenees.

KRUX. Wrong.

CLARA. The Tiber,

KRUX. No—the Chimborazo. Where are the Chimborazo mountains, miss?

LITTLE CHILD. Wherever you please, sir.

KRUX. That's a nice child—she's respectful, though she's stupid. What is the height of the Chimborazo, Miss Naomi?

NAOMI. I don't know.

KRUX. Answer me, miss.

NAOMI. I can't.

KRUX. Why not?

NAOMI. Because I can't. I feel as if I could cry my eyes out.

KRUX. You're hysterical, and should go outside and have your head pumped on; but to resume—(*turns up stage and shows white on coat again—laugh*)—what are you laughing at? There is nothing to laugh at in me, I should think.

TILLY. You've got your coat all over white. (*laugh*)

KRUX. Oh, Bella, fetch me a brush. (BELLA *pauses.* GIRLS *look indignant, and* NAOMI *slaps book on desk.* KRUX *looking triumphant*) Didn't you hear me?—fetch me a brush. (BELLA *goes off door,* U.E.R.) What is the height of the Chimborazo mountains?

CLARA. Four hundred miles—(*laugh*)—no, I mean four hundred yards. I made a mistake.

KRUX. Wrong again—mountains of that height do not exist. The height of the Chimborazo is about one mile.

> BELLA *returns with brush, which she offers to* KRUX.

KRUX. Oh, brush me! (*a pause—*BELLA *stands motionless on* KRUX'S R.H.) Did you hear me? Brush me!

> BELLA *crosses up stage, and places the brush on desk.*

BELLA. (*facing him*) I can't do that.

GIRLS. (*murmur*) What a shame.

KRUX. (*savagely*) Silence in the class. (*to* BELLA) Do you know who I am?

BELLA. I'm not a servant.

KRUX. (*with a sneer*) Not a servant. If you shell peas you can brush coats. Then, pray, what am I?

NAOMI. (*who has endeavoured to restrain herself but failed*) You're a beast! Bella is here to teach ladies, not to brush blackguards. Insulting our Bella! Girls, don't stand it. (*throws book at him ; all the other girls rise and are about to throw books, &c., at* KRUX, *as enter* DR. SUTCLIFFE, *holding up his hands,* MRS. SUTCLIFFE, LORD BEAUFOY *and* JACK POYNTZ. FARINTOSH *at door with napkin round his neck.* GIRLS *resume their seats as if studying.* NAOMI *hides her head behind slate which has a comic drawing in chalk of* KRUX *upon it, and* BELLA *kneels at feet of* DR. SUTCLIFFE.

Picture.

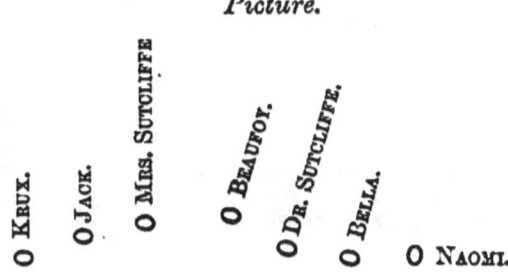

END OF ACT II.

ACT III.

SCENE.—*The Grounds of Cedar-Grove House.   Evening. Stage half dark.*   LORD BEAUFOY *discovered, seated on garden chair,* R.C.   *Piano heard playing in house,* R.H., *and a joyful shout of laughter from the* GIRLS *as curtain rises.*

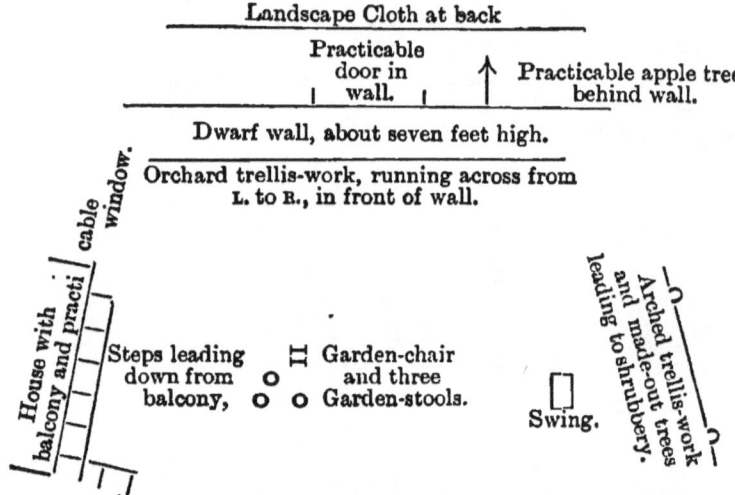

LORD B. 'Pon my word, this is a very pretty place ; so secluded, rustic, and all that.   People seem to pass their lives so innocently, so different from Paris, or Vienna, or any big city.   After all, big cities are only agglomerations of brick and mortar, while the country is made up of trees, and fields, and flowers, and birds, and mushrooms, and truffles, and the rest of it.   There's better shooting in the country, too.   The dinner was very good, and (*meditating, looking up*) it's eighty something miles from here to the moon—eighty——something, I forget the odd thousands and hundreds.   (*rises and wanders towards* R.H.)   Singular little girl, that—fresh as nature and artless as moss. (*plucking a piece of moss from wall of steps,* R.H.   *Dreamily*) I wonder who she is, in her nice quiet grey dress, so different from those young persons in Paris, and the tremendous tame tiger lilies one meets in town.   (*leans against swing*)   Ah ! simplicity—beautiful simplicity ! how·

you are neglected in this nineteenth century! She doesn't seem to be a boarder like the other girls. I don't care for that Miss Tighe. Poor Uncle Beau, he'll be disappointed in that match again. Jack's got my cigar-case. (*feeling in his pocket*) I must find him. (*Enter* BELLA, 1 E.R., *a large jug in her hand*) I beg your pardon.

(*nearly running over her*)

BELLA. Oh! my lord, you nearly made me drop the jug.

LORD B. I'm very sorry.

BELLA. It's of no consequence. (*crosses to* L., *up stage*)

LORD B. May I ask where you are going?

(*following her*)

BELLA. I'm going for some milk, my lord.

LORD B. Alone?

BELLA. Yes.

LORD B. But do you feel equal to the task of going for milk without an escort?

BELLA. Oh, yes! Cook has used more milk than they expected; and so——

LORD B. The deficiency has to be supplied. (*leaning on back of chair facing* BELLA) But it seems so odd that you should have to go for milk. I thought that in the country they always carried about milk in cows. I mean that they had it on the premises, and drew it up in a bucket from a well.

BELLA. Drew milk from a well!

LORD B. No, no; of course—not milk, that's water; though sometimes the two things do get mixed up in one another. But couldn't they send a servant?

BELLA. They're all busy, and I'd nothing else to do.

LORD B. Very amiable of you; but perhaps you find it amusing.

BELLA. No, my lord; but I'm not a boarder here.

LORD B. No?

BELLA. No! Mrs. Sutcliffe took me into the house out of charity.

LORD B. (*aside*) God bless Mrs. Sutcliffe.

BELLA. And to please the Doctor.

LORD B. Ah! I meant God bless the Doctor.

BELLA. So, of course, I try to make myself as useful as I can, my lord, in return for their kindness.

LORD B. And your father and mother, do they approve?

(*the piano is again heard playing in the house*, R.H.)

BELLA. I have neither father nor mother.

LORD B. An orphan ?

BELLA. Yes.

LORD B. What an interesting girl !

BELLA. I never knew my parents. My mother died in the village close by, when I was quite a baby, and then the poor woman where I was left, Mrs. Marks, brought me up till I was nine years old.

The moon shines brightly from this time from behind the house up stage, R.II.

LORD B. Is that Mrs. Marks still living ?

BELLA. No, my lord ; she died two years ago.

LORD B. (*aside*) Confound these good folks, they always die ; but I suppose it is to make room for the bad ones.

BELLA. It was my first sorrow. Then I came here and——

LORD B. You are an excellent scholar——

BELLA. I have tried to improve myself in order that when I am older I may no longer be a burden.

LORD B. And who in the school is your most particular friend ?

BELLA. Nummy.

LORD B. Nummy !—what a singular name.

BELLA. I mean Naomi—Miss Tighe—we're the best friends in the school.

LORD B. She's very rich—is she not ?

BELLA. Very ; indeed she's as rich as she's good, so you may fancy what a lot of money she has. She, too, is an orphan like me ; perhaps that's the reason we're so fond of one another ; though we're very different in some respects —for she is wealthy and I am—not.

LORD B. Not wealthy (*aside*) How these great natures misunderstand themselves.

BELLA. But I'm forgetting my errand.

(*runs up and opens door in wall*)

LORD B. Oh, never mind the milk ; let it bring itself. (BELLA *comes down stage again on* LORD B.'s L.) I mean —is it far to the moon ?

BELLA. Eh ?

LORD B. I mean is it far to the milk ?

BELLA. Only across the field.

LORD B. That's a pity. (*after a pause*) May I be allowed to accompany you ?

BELLA. Oh, my lord, so much trouble.

Lord B. No trouble. The milk here is so pure it's a pleasure to walk with it. What a lovely night, so bright and —— How far did you say it was from this grass plat to the moon?

Bella. Two hundred and thirty-six thousand eight hundred and forty-seven miles.

Lord B. It's a long way.

Bella. It's very kind of the moon to shine down here such a distance.

Lord B. Not at all—the grass plat is so soft and pleasant the moon can't help it. May I carry the jug?

Bella. Oh! my lord——

Lord B. I should like it above all things. (*takes jug*) Thanks. Will you take my arm?

(*church clock strikes eight very distinctly*)

Bella. My lord! I don't like to——

Lord B. You shouldn't take dislikes so suddenly,

Bella. (*taking his arm*) Oh, it isn't that.

(*the piano stops playing*)

Lord B. (*up stage, c.*) What long shadows the moonlight flings. See—there I am.

Bella. But so tall—so high.

Lord B. And there you are.

Bella. But not so tall as you are.

Lord B. And yet you're nearer the skies—see! (*moving*) Now we're far apart.

(*the moonlight throws long shadows from R. to L.*)

Bella. And now—(*moving*)—we're joined together. Wonderful things, shadows, are they not?

Lord B. Yes, when they lie before us.

Bella. I often wonder what they're for—what they mean?

Lord B. No one can tell, except poets, and painters, and lovers; and they know all things, and what they don't know they feel. See, we are divided again.

Bella. No. (*placing her hand on jug*) The jug unites us.

Lord B. Only for the moment—(*piano music again; the plaintive character of which is changed at their exit to a lively tune, to bring on* Jack) Only for the moment.

Exeunt, through door in wall. Enter Jack, *smoking,* 1 e.r.; *goes to swing, and sits in it.*

Jack. (*after swinging*) Very nice girls these, particularly that Miss Tighe. Girl of spirit; pitched into that infernal teacher ; quite right. (*stop the music*) She's rather pretty, too ; I wonder if she's clever ; the two things don't often go together. When Nature makes a pretty woman, she puts all the goods into the shop-window. I wonder where she is. They were all walking about just now. My short day in these female infantry barracks has quite impressed me. Seeing a lot of pretty girls accidentally makes one feel like—going to church when you're not used to it. Let me see, what's the quotation?—oh—"Those who went to cough remained to pray." (*Enter* NAOMI *from* R.H.U.E., *her dress, lined with white, over her head, so that she looks like the traditional ghost. She stands motionless*) Here's a ghost ; now really this is pleasant. I'm fond of ghosts, particularly ghosts in petticoats. If you are the departed spirit of any late friend, come back to earth to tell me that you've left me money, please mention it at once.

NAOMI. (*lowering her dress from her face*) Weren't you frightened ?

JACK. Awful ! I'm a very timid man.

NAOMI. I've been in the Shrubbery, frightening the girls, but it's very slow work ; I'd rather talk to you.

JACK. I feel flattered in the highest degree.

NAOMI. Now don't go on like that ; if you do, I shall run away. (*she goes out at door in wall,* L.C., *and shuts it ; then opens it a little way, peeping in*) You musn't come after me.

JACK. Not for worlds.

NAOMI. (*going, then returning*) I can't understand you at all.

JACK. Why not !

NAOMI. You talk so oddly. You seem to tell truths as if they were not true, and fibs as if they were truths ; but I like to hear you.

JACK. To hear me tell fibs or the truth ?

NAOMI. Both. Go on ; tell me something.

JACK. What about ?

NAOMI. About yourself.

JACK. Really, the subject is so barren.

NAOMI. What are you ?

JACK. Nothing ; it's the occupation I'm most fitted for.

NAOMI. But you must be something.

JACK. No ; I'm only myself.

NAOMI. Were you ever anything before you were what you are now ?

JACK. Eh?

NAOMI. I mean—what used you to be?

JACK. I used to be—a little boy, but I got nothing for it—not even the birch.

NAOMI. Lord Beaufoy said you'd been in the army. (*looking at him admiringly*) Were you a horse soldier or a foot soldier?

JACK. Foot—a very foot soldier.

NAOMI. And he said you were in the Crimea.

JACK. Yes; I was there.

NAOMI. Were you at the Battle of Inkerman?

JACK. Yes.

NAOMI. Then, why didn't you mention it?

JACK. Hardly worth while; so many other fellows were there?

NAOMI. Did you fight?

JACK. I was forced to.

NAOMI. Did you like it?

JACK. No; detested it.

NAOMI. Then why did you do it?

JACK. I was hired for the purpose; besides, I hadn't pluck enough to run away.

NAOMI. Did they give you much money for fighting?

JACK. Not much; but if they gave me very little money, I did very little fighting, so I was quite even with them in that respect.

NAOMI. I wish I was a man!

JACK. I don't.

NAOMI. Why not?

JACK. You're so much nicer as you are.

NAOMI. If you say that, I'll run away.

JACK. Then I won't say it. I'll keep on not saying it. (*aside*) Jolly girl for an heiress! (*takes stage a little to* L.)

NAOMI. (*aside*) He's beautiful; he's lovely, perfectly lovely. (*aloud*) Are you fond of reading?

JACK. Um—yes—middling.

NAOMI. I am. Did you ever read "Othello"?

JACK. Yes; I don't consider it nice reading for young ladies.

NAOMI. Othello used to tell Desdemona of all the dangers he had passed, and the battles he had won.

JACK. Othello was a nigger, and didn't mind bragging.

NAOMI. Still it must have been very pleasant for Desdemona.

JACK. A black man!

NAOMI. Yes; it must have been like looking at your husband through a piece of smoked glass.

JACK. As if he were a planet.

NAOMI. A heavenly body !

JACK. More like an eclipse. Shall we walk ? May I be allowed ?   (*offering his arm*)

NAOMI. I don't like to.

JACK. You'll find it go very easy. (*music of piano in house*, R.H.) Am I too tall ?   (*as she takes his arm*)

NAOMI. No; I like to look up (*going* L.H.) And you've never been anything at all ?

JACK. Never !

NAOMI. Not even married ?

JACK. Not even married. Melancholy waste of time, isn't it ?

NAOMI. (*looking up*) I know what could be made of you.

JACK. What ?

NAOMI. You'd make a capital belfry.

JACK. Am I so deserving of a rope ? Then you should be the belle.

NAOMI. Yes; I'd be the belle, and my tongue should go ding dong.

JACK. Yes; you should be a ding dong; a *dindon*, a *dindon truffé*.

> *Exeunt into Shrubbery*, L.H.1 E. *The door in the wall*
> L.C. *opens, and* LORD BEAUFOY *and* BELLA *appear.*
> LORD BEAUFOY *with the iug.*

BELLA. We're soon back.

LORD B. I'm sorry to say we are.

BELLA. So, if your lordship will give me the jug——

LORD B. Must you leave me ?

BELLA. I must take the milk to the kitchen.

Enter KRUX *from behind house* U.E.R.   *The music stops.*

LORD B. Just as she was beginning to be so charming. (*sees* KRUX, *who comes down*, R.H.) Oh, here, you'll do. (*offering* KRUX *jug*) Take this to the kitchen, will you ?

BELLA. Oh, no !

KRUX. (*indignant*) Me—me—milk—me ?

BELLA. I'll take it, my lord. (*takes jug.* LORD BEAUFOY *turns*) I shall be back directly.

LORD B. (*aside to her*) I shall wait here.

> *Exit* BELLA, R. 1 E. KRUX *following her down to* R.
> BEAUFOY *goes to swing.* KRUX *then crosses to*
> BEAUFOY *with mock deference.*

KRUX. My lord! such invidious distinctions——

LORD B. Pardon me, Mr.——

KRUX. Krux, my lord.

LORD B. Krux, I mistook you in the dark for——

KRUX. One of the female servants—very natural, my lord. Beautiful evening!

LORD B. Beautiful! Good-night!

KRUX. Good-night, my lord! (*aside*) Ahum!—aha!

> *Retires up* R.H., *and pretends to go off behind house. Enter* BELLA, R. 1 E., *running; she stops short on seeing* LORD BEAUFOY—*she is out of breath.*

LORD B. I'm so glad you've come back.

BELLA. I made all the haste I could.

LORD B. The Shrubbery runs nearly round the whole garden, does it not?

BELLA. Yes, my lord.

LORD B. (*offers his arm, which she takes. Pause*) You're sure that when I go away to-night you won't quite forget me.

BELLA. Oh, yes! On a first acquaintance, and in so short a time, I never——

LORD B. Never——

BELLA. Liked to hear anybody talk so much. You're the first lord I ever saw.

LORD B. And you're the first little lady I ever took a liking to. (*walking towards* L.) And I shall be so sad at leaving you.

BELLA. Sad, my lord!

LORD B. Really.

BELLA. Why?

> *They talk off into the Shrubbery,* 1 E.L.H. *Enter* KRUX, R.U.E., *from behind house,* L.C.

KRUX. Where's Mrs. Sutcliffe? Where's Mrs. Sutcliffe? (*going to* L. *and peering into the darkness*) So you wouldn't brush me, Miss Bella, wouldn't you, and my lord takes me for a female servant! Very good—we'll see—we'll see.

> *Exit* KRUX, 1 E.L. *Enter* SCHOOLGIRLS *from different entrances,* LAURA *and* KITTY *from* R.H., MILLY *and* LITTLE GIRL, U.E.L., HETTY *and* CLARA *from* 2 E.L., *all down,* L.C.

MILLY. Where is that Naomi?

CLARA. And Mr. Poyntz? The little flirt!

KITTY. To keep him to herself!

MILLY. I hate such selfishness!

HETTY. So do I.   When one gets hold of a lord, one ought to divide him fairly, like a cake!

Enter TILLY *from Shrubbery,* L.U.E.

TILLY. Girls! Girls!

GIRLS. What?

> TILLY *points, and* GIRLS *retire into shadow, down* L. LORD BEAUFOY *and* BELLA *cross—his arm round her waist.   They walk   slowly, and are quite silent.   Clock strikes nine very distant.*

TILLY. (*after a pause*) Well!

MILLY. There!

KITTY. I never!

CLARA. Nor I; but I should like to——

LAURA. So should I.

MILLY. What?

LAURA. To go to sleep.

TILLY. That artful Bella!

MILLY. Hush!

> KRUX *appears at the entrance of the Shrubbery,* L.U.E., JACK *appears from the same entrance with* NAOMI, *and pushes* KRUX *on one side.*

JACK. Take care—thank you.

> (JACK *crosses with* NAOMI, *and off* U.E.R.)

TILLY. Ah!

MILLY. Oh!

ALL THE GIRLS. Well!

MILLY. Oh, those two!

CLARA. You mean those four.

LAURA. (*sleepy*) Twice two are four.

> *Enter* FARINTOSH *agitated—a letter in his hand.* DR. *and* MRS. SUTCLIFFE, R.1 E.

MRS. S. Only another hour!

DR. S. A glass of sherry or a sandwich } (*together*)

FARIN. My dear friends excuse me——

This letter, which my man has just brought me, is most important. If I drive home immediately, he can put my things together, and we can catch the next night train to town.

MRS. S. But——

FARIN. Forgive me, I entreat, and let me thank you for a most charming and instructive day—instructive day; but this is imperative—imperative; the—the—search of a life, of my whole life, indeed; the news has so agitated me that —I—I feel quite—quite agitated. Where is Arthur?

During this JACK *and* NAOMI *have entered, and also* LORD BEAUFOY *and* BELLA—KRUX *following.*

VAUGHAN. KRUX.

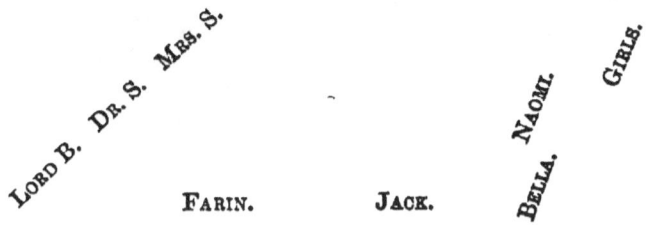

LORD B. DR. S. MRS. S. GIRLS. NAOMI. BELLA.

FARIN. JACK.

FARIN. (*mistaking* JACK *for* ARTHUR) Oh, Arthur, here you are; important business takes me to town to-night, so I shall take the carriage; you and your friend can walk home—the night's very fine, very fine; and apropos of your friend, Mr. Poyntz, the girls tell me that he's been seen paying too strong attentions to Miss Tighe, whom I had hoped you would have shown some, some—and I consider your friend's conduct very reprehensible, very reprehensible. (*shakes his hand*) God bless you!

JACK. So many thanks—a charming day!

NAOMI. And a most charming evening!

MRS. S. Delighted to see you at any time, Mr. Poyntz.

FARIN. Poyntz. (*crossing to* LORD BEAUFOY *and mistaking him for* JACK) Of course, Mr. Poyntz, I need not say that my box is at your disposal so long as you choose to remain to shoot here—to shoot here. One word—these school-girls have wonderful eyes; they see everything, like me; and they tell me that Arthur has paid not the slightest attention to any one of them, except a Miss Bella something; now he shouldn't have done that, should he? Very wrong of him, very wrong. (*goes up*) So, once more, (*to* DOCTOR *and* MRS. SUTCLIFFE) my dear friends, adieu! and wish me good luck in my search. (*brings* DR. SUTCLIFFE *down, mistaking him for* MRS. SUTCLIFFE) My dear Mrs. Sutcliffe, I must tell you one thing—but not a word to Theodore, not a word to Theodore—poor Theodore, I think he is looking very ill—very ill indeed. I noticed at dinner, too, that he drank too much, much too much; digestion going —poor Theodore, digestion going; take great care of him

X X

or you'll lose him, you'll lose him. Young ladies, good-night, and—and—and bless you all, very much. Receive the thanks of a man old enough to be—to be the father of anyone here, my dear friends, the Dr. and Mrs. Sutcliffe excepted ; and I feel as if I were their child, I do indeed. (MRS. SUTCLIFFE *indigant*) Now—(*taking* KRUX'S *arm, mistaking him for* VAUGHAN)—to the carriage, and home quickly. I beg your pardon. (VAUGHAN *offers his arm*) Oh, thank you—thank you—Good-night !—good-night !

> *They go off,* C. *door.* DOCTOR *and* MRS. SUTCLIFFE *and* KRUX *exeunt* R. 1 E. JACK *and* LORD BEAUFOY *take their leave of* BELLA *and* NAOMI, *and go up stage* C., *and the other* GIRLS *cross over to* R.H. *and converse together.*

JACK. Arthur, you've been paying too much attention to that little girl—I'm surprised at you !

LORD B. Not more than you've been paying to the little heiress !

JACK. But heiresses are heiresses ; and, of course, to heiresses one's attentions are always the correctest thing possible.

LORD B. Give me a cigar and a light. (*they light cigars from each other's cigars*) Do you think I've behaved badly ?

JACK. Very : walking her about and spooning her ; I shall keep my eye upon you ; you belong to the old Satanic school. .

LORD B. And you to the modern cynical.

JACK. Poor little thing, like Faust and Marguerite.

LORD B. And you're the Mephistopheles.

JACK. Mephistopheles be——

LORD B. Unnecessary ; he is already. (*to* GIRLS) Once more ladies, good-night ! (*looking to* BELLA) I trust I may say, *au revoir.*

> JACK *and* NAOMI *exchange glances.* *Exeunt* JACK *and* LORD BEAUFOY, *at gate,* C. NAOMI *and* BELLA *watch them out.*

ALL THE GIRLS. (*cross to and attack* NAOMI *and* BELLA) Well I'm sure, I——

> *Enter* MRS. SUTCLIFFE, DR. SUTCLIFFE, *and* KRUX, R. 1 E. GIRLS *stop suddenly.*

MRS. S. Oh, Mr. Krux—(*agitated*)—if it should be true—(*sinks on garden seat,* C., *almost fainting*—BELLA *takes her hand ; she repulses her*)—Don't touch me—how dare you ? You, whom I have reared out of charity, how have you behaved this night? Your conduct towards Lord Beaufoy is known to me—touch me with your hand—or, rather, yes—give it me. (*takes* BELLA's *hand*) Where did you get that ring?

BELLA. (L.C., *trembling*) Lord Beaufoy gave it me.

GIRLS. Lord Beaufoy!

KRUX. (R.) I told you—I told you!

MRS. S. (C.) You have been watched, you wicked creature!

KRUX. (*aside*) Yes, I did that. (*proudly*)

MRS. S. Walking alone, and talking to Lord Beaufoy.

NAOMI. But there's no harm in that—I was walking and talking with Jack.

GIRLS. Oh!

NAOMI. Mr. Poyntz! Mr. Poyntz, and I'm sure——

MRS. S. Silence, Miss Tighe. Little did I think when I took you into my house I was nourishing a serpent in my bosom.

DR. S. (R.C.) My dear!

MRS. S. Silence, Theodore! Young ladies, to your dormitories.

GIRLS *cross silently.* NAOMI, *trying to get a word with* BELLA, *is prevented by* MRS. SUTCLIFFE.

BELLA. (*to* GIRLS) Good-night! Wish me good-night!

MRS. S. Don't stir! You abandoned girl, do not dare to address any of the young ladies.

(*motions to* GIRLS *to go. Exeunt* GIRLS, R. 1 E.)

NAOMI. I will!

Kisses BELLA, *and as she goes off* R. 1 E. *turns and makes a grimace at* KRUX.

KRUX. (R.) Hussey! too proud to brush her betters.

MRS. S. (R.C.) You leave this house to-morrow morning. The man will drive you to the station, and, in London, you can go, for one month only, to my friend Mrs. Stanton. By that time you may find some situation. You to dare, under my very eyes, to cast out lures to my guests. You——

DR. S. (R.C.) My love!

MRS. S. (*violently*) Theodore, silence!

DR. S. (*in a subdued passion*) Amanthis, hold your tongue! (MRS. SUTCLIFFE *dumbfounded*) The pupils are not here now, and I will speak. (*crosses to* BELLA) Tell me, Bella did Lord Beaufoy give you that ring?

BELLA. (L.C.) Yes.

DR. S. And why did he give it you?

BELLA. I must not tell you that.

KRUX. There!

DR. S. (*turning and raising his stick*) Out of my sight, or I shall strike you. (*Exit* KRUX, *hastily*, R. 1 E.) Did Lord Beaufoy tell you that he loved you?

BELLA. Yes.

MRS. S. I said so.

✓ DR. S. Good heavens! what harm is there in that?—perhaps he spoke the truth. 'Tis easy to love Bella—I love her!

BELLA. (*gratefully*) Oh, Doctor!

MRS. S. Take me into the house, or I shall faint.

DR. S. You are harsh and cruel.

MRS. S. (*weeping*) Oh, Theodore, you no longer love me.

DR. S. No dear—I mean—yes—I——

MRS. S. Go, go, leave me—the same as thirty-five years ago!   *Exit*, 1 E.R.

DR. S. (*following her*) My love—Amanthis!

Exit, 1 E.R.

19 BELLA. (L.) Was I so wrong to listen to him? Is it so wicked to wear the ring he gave me? If I thought so, I'd—(*about to throw it off, retains it*)—No, it seems to comfort me. And to-morrow I must go. Must I leave you, my dear home?—the only home I ever knew—and my companions, and the old servants who have been so kind to me? What will become of me—how can I face the world alone? (*sobbing, sinking on her knees*) I am thrust forth—alone—alone—alone!

> *During the last few words* NAOMI *has opened the window and appeared on balcony.*

NAOMI. Not alone, dear—I'm here, and I'll go with you. Here's my jewels—(*throws down small parcel on stage*)—and my purse. There's more than fourteen pounds in it—(*descends staircase*)—and we'll go together; and never, never will we be separated in this world, until death do us part.

> *The two* GIRLS *embrace each other, and sob as they kneel upon the ground.*

BELLA. No, no, Naomi.

NAOMI. I will—I will—I will!   (*fondling*)

> LORD BEAUFOY *appears on wall, near tree*, L.H.U.E.—JACK *watching him at wall*, R.U.E. *Tableau.*

END OF ACT III.

ACT IV.

SCENE.—*Same as Act III. Morning. Discovered*—GIRLS *at play: Skipping rope, battledore, hoops, &c.* NAOMI TIGHE *sitting apart, c., pale and melancholy.*

MILLY. Naomi, will you play ?

NAOMI. I've got a headache.

TILLY. Thinking of Bella ?

NAOMI. Yes; thinking of Bella.

CLARA. Poor Bella !

NAOMI. I wonder where he is !

GIRLS. *He* is ?

NAOMI. I mean *she* is—how could Bella be a *he ?*

MILLY. You've never been well since she went away.

TILLY. And that's just six weeks ago.

NAOMI. Six weeks to-day. (*sighs. All the* GIRLS *mimic and laugh*) You're an unfeeling set of brutes ; and, if you tease me, I'll slap your faces.

TILLY. (*crosses from* R.C. *to* NAOMI, R.H.) Really, Miss Tighe, you should remember that you are with white young ladies, and not among your blackamoor negroes, now. I should like to see you slap my face.

NAOMI. You shall feel me do it in a minute ! Oh, I wish Bella was here.

TILLY. Bella was a servant.

NAOMI. She was not.

TILLY. She was.

NAOMI. She wasn't.

TILLY. She was.

NAOMI. She wasn't.

TILLY. Sighing about a little kitchen girl, because she was useful to you. Girls, did you like Bella ?

GIRLS. U—m. N—o !

MILLY. She hadn't spirit enough for me.

KITTY. She was so stupid.

CLARA. She was too clever for me.

LAURA. I didn't care much for her, because she was so terribly wide awake.

HETTY. (*in swing*) I liked her.

GIRLS. Why ?

HETTY. Because she used to give me her bread and butter. (*laugh—school-bell rings*)

HETTY. O, there's breakfast.   (GIRLS *going*, R.)

NAOMI. I shan't go in to breakfast. Mrs. Sutcliffe said that when I had my headaches I might stop out here for the fresh air.   (*laugh*)

TILLY. Fresh air! Fresh——(*pretending to see her*) Oh, here's Bella!

NAOMI. (*turning*) Eh!

        (GIRLS *laugh, and exeunt*, R. 1 E.)

TILLY. (*going. Returns and gives* NAOMI *a sweet*) Never mind the sneerers. There's an acid drop.

            (*gives her one, and goes*, R.)

NAOMI. I wish I'd been a boy! I don't see what use girls are—boys are so much more manly. (*rises, looks round to see if she is unobserved—sits on garden seat*, C., *then draws letter from her bosom, and reads*) " My dear, dear Naomi!" (*laughs, blushes, and hides her face in her hands*) —" My dear, dear Naomi!"—(*business repeated*) " My dear, dear Naomi!"—I read that so often that I hardly ever get to the rest of the letter—" Though I have no business to write to you,"—such nonsense—" I cannot refrain from sending you these few lines, to tell you what I have been about since my last. You see, my love"—(*laughs again*)— " You see, my love"—how well he does express himself, to be sure. He's quite an author—" You see, my love, I thought it necessary to see your guardian before I renewed my correspondence with you, because you are so young."—I hate that; Jack's always flinging that in my face. People can't be born grown up, can they? No! I wish I was as old as Mrs. Sutcliffe; then people couldn't say I was too young—"However, Mr. Farintosh was so ill that he couldn't see anybody. The poor old fellow had a sudden attack, and for three days his life was despaired of. However, he is now better. I saw him yesterday; he could hardly speak, but, as good fortune would have it, one of your guardians was with him, so I was introduced; and I am to dine with him to-morrow."—I wish I was my guardian, to have my Jack to dine with him; but I daresay he won't appreciate him; it requires great intellect and good taste to understand Jack—" I have not heard a word of your friend, Bella, beyond what I have told you; she arrived safely at Mrs. Stanton's, where Mrs. Sutcliffe sent her, and three days after she disappeared. Mrs. Stanton is of opinion that she has not gone to any situation. I have again tried to find Lord Beaufoy, but without success. So, dearest,"

—oh, that's beautiful—" So, dearest, wish me luck to-morrow at dinner, where I will feign all the interest in the money market, and the tallow ditto, and in hides, cochineal, indigo, and grey shirtings, which these interesting topics are calcu- lated to inspire"—he spells cochineal with two e's, but affection is superior to orthography, and I love him all the better for his bad spelling—" And now, dearest Naomi, to talk about ourselves. When I first saw you I looked at you with curiosity, because I had heard that you were very rich; but when I left you that evening I felt that I was in love,"—ah (*sighs*)—" and since I left you I am as unhappy as a sailor without a ship. You know that I am poor;" now he's going to talk rubbish again, what has that to do with it? £10,000 couldn't look, and walk, and talk as he does. £10,000 couldn't have been fighting in the Crimea. £10,000 couldn't put his arm round your waist and squeeze you, could it? (*fiercely, then subsiding into gentleness*) No!—"but I love you, fondly, truly, and devotedly (*beginning to cry*); and if I am happy enough, through old Farintosh's intercession, to please your guardians, the conduct of my life shall prove the truth of your affectionate and faithful Jack."—(*crying*) —that's real poetry—" Your affectionate and faithful Jack."

> *Cries in her pocket-handkerchief.* JACK *looks over wall.*

JACK. (*whispering*) Naomi.   (NAOMI *starts*)

NAOMI. Is it you? (*hiding letter.* NAOMI *opens gate. Enter* JACK, *with muddy boots, &c.; they come down stage and look at each other. A long pause*) Well, what have you to tell me?

JACK. Loads; but now I see you I forget it.

NAOMI. When did you come?

JACK. By the night train. I walked from the station here, over the fields.

NAOMI. Then you haven't been in bed all night?

JACK. No.

NAOMI. (*aside*) What devotion. (*sits. Another pause*) Why did you come so suddenly, without letting me know?"

JACK. (*fetching chair and sitting* L. *of* NAOMI) I called yesterday at old Farintosh's, and the servant told me that he had started for his box here; so I came on by the night train, because I knew, Naomi, that he would bring me with him, and that I should see you; so I wandered about, waiting for him, for I know he'll be here shortly; but I couldn't resist looking over the wall, and——

NAOMI. Here I was. (*another pause*) Are you quite well?

JACK. Quite; are you?

NAOMI. Yes, thank you. (*another pause*) When sweethearts meet after a long absence their conversation is so interesting, isn't it? Then you've had no breakfast?

JACK. No.

NAOMI. Neither have I. What sympathy! But what can old Farintosh want so particularly with the Sutcliffes?

JACK. I don't know; but tell me what has happened here since——

NAOMI. Since Bella left? Oh, Mrs. Sutcliffe was very ill, and the Doctor has been very cross. (*whispering*) The other day I overheard him talking about Mr. Krux, and he said, D—a—m. Dam!

JACK. Tremendous!

NAOMI. But my guardians—what did they seem to think of you?

JACK. They're both City men, and they can't think. By-the-way, do you know how old you are?

NAOMI. Yes. Eighteen.

JACK. No; you're nearly twenty-one. Your guardians told me that you were so forward, and they didn't know where to send you, so they deceived you on the point of age intentionally.

NAOMI. What a shame, swindling a girl out of three years in that way. And Bella——

JACK. Poor girl!

NAOMI. I loved her so much, and she's never written a word to me. I think it pays best to put all your love upon a man—girls are so deceitful, and men are quite the contrary.

JACK. Some men. There are men, and—individuals.

NAOMI. Will you always be good to me?

JACK. I'll try.

NAOMI. I should like you to be bad, though, sometimes.

JACK. Why?

NAOMI. Because then I should have the pleasure of forgiving you.

JACK. (*rising and putting chair back to L.*) I think I shall be able to accommodate you, as far as that goes.

NAOMI. Jack, when a girl is in love, why do they call her spoons?

JACK. Because she's so often carried to the lips.

> JACK *is about to kiss* NAOMI *as* KRUX *enters* R. 1 E.
> NAOMI *crosses to* L.

KRUX. (R.) Miss Tighe. How do you do—I hope I have the pleasure of seeing you in health?

JACK. (C.) Quite.

KRUX. I'm quite well, thank you.

JACK. I didn't ask the question.

KRUX. I did not know that you were here.

NAOMI. (L.) That's not the only thing he don't know.

JACK. I came to tell the Doctor that Mr. Farintosh is expected at the lodge, and seeing the gate open——

KRUX. The gate open! tut, tut, tut. Now who could have opened the gate?

NAOMI. The cat.

KRUX. The cat—what cat?

NAOMI. (*crossing to* KRUX) A cat I keep to scratch spies' eyes out. (*to* JACK) You've been in the army—tell me, would it be wrong to kill Mr. Krux?

JACK. (L.) By no means.

KRUX. (R.) Mrs. Sutcliffe sent me to tell you that Mr. Farintosh had arrived.

JACK.
NAOMI. (C.) } Arrived!

KRUX. Yes, and here he is.

JACK. (*to* NAOMI) You'll hardly know the beau again. Since his recovery, he no longer dresses himself in the lastest mode, but goes about like any other old gentleman, and looks much the better for it.

> *Enter* DR. SUTCLIFFE *and* MRS. SUTCLIFFE, *both very grave*, R. 1 E.

JACK. My dear Doctor and Mrs. Sutcliffe, so glad to see you. I got here before Mr. Farintosh, and was just going——

MRS. S. (*saluting* JACK—*seeing* NAOMI *about to go*) You may remain, Miss Tighe; Mr. Farintosh wishes to see you.

> NAOMI *delighted.* *Enter* FARINTOSH, *his appearance entirely altered—silver hair, whiskers, and his dress appropriate to his age.*

FARIN. My dear Miss Tighe, your guardians send you their love. Eh, Poyntz, you here!—How's that? how's that?

JACK. I came down by the train, because I heard you had come on here.

FARIN. Very kind, very kind.

JACK. And while I was waiting about——

FARINTOSH.

JACK.

NAOMI.

DOCTOR MRS. S.

KRUX.

KRUX. The garden gate was opened by the cat!

DR. S. Eh ?
MRS. S. What ? } (*together*)

JACK. I—I—I saw the cat outside waiting to come in, so I opened the gate for him or her !

KRUX. From the outside ?

JACK. No ; I was lifting the animal over the wall, when seeing Miss Tighe in the garden——

NAOMI. I opened the gate ; Mr. Krux, you can shut it.

(KRUX *shuts gate, and then comes down* L.H.)

MRS. S. Mr. Poyntz, let us thank you for the efforts you have made to find that poor girl.

FARIN. Yes, yes ; a sad affair—a sad affair.

DR. S. A child I was so much attached to !

KRUX. So was I !

> DOCTOR *gives* MRS. SUTCLIFFE *chair*, R.C. DOCTOR *sits between her and* FARINTOSH, *who sits on chair which* JACK *takes from* KRUX, *who was about to sit on it close by swing.* JACK *and* NAOMI *down* L.

DR. S. We have only just broken the news to our old friend.

FARIN. (*to* JACK, *slily*) It appears that the young lady went off with somebody who was not a young lady. These things happen—girls are but girls ; we must not expect them to be angels.

KRUX. (*shaking his head*) If you do you'll be disappointed —continually disappointed.

FARIN. However, my dear friends, the news I bring will, I am sure, give you pleasure even in the midst of

MRS. S. DR. S. FARIN.   JACK. NAOMI. KRUX.
seated on Garden Seats, R.C.   standing L.C.

your grief. You know, Theodore, that my poor son (*with emotion*) died without my forgiveness—my boy died leaving a wife and child. For years I have been in search of them, but owing to the frequent names assumed by poor Fred for the sake of avoiding creditors, and to his having been some time abroad, I could find no traces either of my daughter-in-law or my grandchild. At last they are found.

DR. S. My dear old friend, receive my congratulations.

MRS. S. And mine.

NAOMI. (*crossing to* FARINTOSH) Oh, I am so glad, it, must be so beautiful to have a father !

FARIN. (*taking* NAOMI'S *hand*) My dear child, you shall soon see our meeting. As I said, my lawyer has traced them out ; my daughter-in-law, poor Fred's wife, is dead.

KRUX. I congrat——   (JACK *stops* KRUX)

FARIN. But her child lives—lives—lives !—my dear friends, lives to be a central object of my affections—lives to be a solace and a comfort to the few years yet remaining to me ; for I have been a foolish, vain old fellow, and tried to pass for a young fop, when I was really an old fool. I thought of all this, night and day, as I lay in bed, when they told me I was dying, and the hardest pang of all was that I should not live long enough to see my grandchild—but I recovered ; I was never better—never so thankful—or so well.

DR. S. We are so pleased.

MRS. S. Your happiness compensates us for our grief.

FARIN. My dear friends, if you had children, or if you ever have—but I suppose that is almost past hope now— you could imagine my joy. You shall witness it. I invited you on purpose, for my granddaughter is here.

JACK. Here !

FARIN. Yes.

NAOMI. Here ! Is it Milly, or Tilly, or Laura, or Clara, or Hetty, or Kitty ?

MRS. S. Did you bring her with you ?

FARIN. What ! Didn't I tell you ? What a stupid old man I am. Now comes the tremendous and delightful surprise. My poor boy's last alias was Mountain—his wife's

maiden name. Pursued everywhere by creditors, she retained
the name after his death. Mrs. Mountain, as she called
herself, died in the village here, close by. Her child was left
to an old woman named Marks, who brought her up, till
you—you adopted her—you best of men and women. You,
my old college chum—(*shaking* Dr. Sutcliffe's *hand*)—and
you my old sweetheart. (*kissing her hand*) She is known
here by the name of Bella Marks. I suppose I saw her
when I was here a month ago, but I did not remember her
among so many. Perhaps—ah, me!—I did not notice her.
Now, where is she? This is the supreme moment of my life.
Give her to me! I can contain myself no longer! My heart
is hungry for her! Call Bella—my grandchild—call her—
give her to me! (*all aghast. A pause*) What is the matter
with you? Isn't she at home? Is she out on a visit? If
so, never mind, send for her! (Naomi *bursts out sobbing*)
My child! (*a pause*) She's not—dead! (Naomi *gives him her
hand*) No! no! Thank heaven! Well, then—what—what
—what—what- (*getting alarmed*) Tell me—tell me——

(a pause)

Krux. (*with concealed triumph*) Sir, if no one else will
tell you, I will.   (*crosses to* c.)
  Farin. Go on.
  Krux. Your granddaughter left here six weeks ago. It
seems that, in mentioning to you the fact of a pupil who
was missing in London, Mrs. Sutcliffe has not mentioned
her name. (Mrs. Sutcliffe *indicates that she has not*)
The girl whom she has told you of, who eloped clandestinely,
was Bella Marks—I should say, is Bella Farintosh, your
granddaughter.
  Farin. (*seizing him by the collar*) You lie! I'll throttle
you! I'll kill you! (Jack *releases* Krux *from* Farintosh,
twisting Krux *into* l.h. *corner*) It's not true! Theodore,
my friend, say it's not true! Jack! my child! Speak!
speak!

Doctor and Mrs. Sutcliffe take his hands. He
sinks into a chair. They surround him.

  Krux. (*frightened*) It is quite true—upon my honour
as a gentleman.
  Dr. S. My dear friend!
  Farin. To find her, but to find her—lost!
  Dr. S. It may not be as we suppose.
  Mrs. S. My husband went to London to seek out——

FARIN. And the name of—of the man—she was supposed to accompany. (*another pause*) His name? You may tell me—I can bear it now. His name, I say?

KRUX. Lord Beaufoy.

FARIN. (*his hands hiding his face*) My nephew!

(*a ring heard at the gate.* KRUX *opens it*)

KRUX. Lord Beaufoy!

Enter LORD BEAUFOY. KRUX *shuts gate.*

KRUX. Lord Beaufoy.

LORD B. (*radiant*) My dear uncle, Doctor, Mrs. Sutcliffe, Jack. (*smiling and affable. Pause*) Why, what's the matter?

DR. S. (*rising*) My Lord Beaufoy, we believe that you, and you only, can tell us the hiding-place of Bella Marks.

NAOMI. (*crying*) My dear Bella!

KRUX. A most improper young person.

LORD B. The hiding-place of Bella Marks! Yes, I admit I know it—what then?

DR. S. What then! (*calming himself*) But I forgot, Lord Beaufoy—you are ignorant that——

FARIN. (*rising*) Let me tell him, Theodore. You are ignorant that Bella is my granddaughter and your cousin.

LORD B. No; two days ago my lawyer, who, as you know, is also yours, informed me of the fact.

FARIN. And fearing that I should alter the disposition of my property, you accomplished this ruin for revenge.

LORD B. Not so; when Miss Farintosh left Mrs. Stanton's, I believed her to be only Bella Marks.

FARIN. (*advancing*) Then all may be repaired. Arthur —my nephew—you—you know I'm very rich; my granddaughter shall inherit all I have—I can't last long. Let me implore you, marry her.

LORD B. Marry her? Impossible!

FARIN. Impossible?

LORD B. Yes; I cannot.

FARIN. Why not?

LORD B. I am already married.

JACK. } Married?
FARIN. }

FARIN. Secretly?

LORD B. Yes, secretly.

(FARINTOSH *sinks again into chair*)

FARIN. My punishment! My punishment!

LORD B. And apropos, Jack——

(*all in consternation.* LORD BEAUFOY *turns to* JACK)

MRS. S.   DR. S.   FARIN.   LORD B.   JACK.   NAOMI.   KRUX.

JACK. Lord Beaufoy, understand that from this time we are strangers. My contempt for you is too deep for utterance.

LORD B. You shall apologise to me for those words.

JACK. Apologise?

LORD B. And be sorry that you used them. Your (*to* JACK) indignant virtue amuses me; and so does yours (*to* DR. SUTCLIFFE) and (*to* FARINTOSH) yours. (*to* JACK) I thought you were a cynic; you used to profess that no occurrence on this earth could be of the slightest consequence. Was your cynicism only a sham? If so, how do you defend it? If mock virtue be a bad sort of hypocrisy, what is mock vice? For you—(*turning* R)—how can you reproach me? Bella is contented and happy. (*to* MRS. SUTCLIFFE) She does not fetch or carry like a servant. She rings bells —she does not answer them. (*to* FARINTOSH) Your paternal interest is a somewhat sudden spasm of affection. You lived the last eighteen years happily without her—whence this new-born feeling? Am I to suppose it is compensation, or too late remorse? or a desire to be attended by a nurse who takes no wages? Why has this neglected child become so suddenly an object of such tenderness? Not because she has been poor, unloved, and unprotected, but because she is the grandchild of a rich, proud gentleman, who has forgotten his duty to her for twenty years, to remember it during his seventy-first.

DR. S. (*crossing to him,. and speaking in a whisper*) Lord Beaufoy, ladies are present; I am an old man; if you do not instantly quit this place, by heaven! I'll conduct you by the collar.

> *Enter all the* YOUNG LADIES, R. 1 E. *Hats on, as from their morning walk.*

MILLY. Oh, Mrs. Sutcliffe, we saw such a lovely carriage and footmen, coming towards the school.

(GIRLS *indicate they see* LORD BEAUFOY *and* JACK)

LORD B. (*to* DOCTOR) I will go without assistance—but before I go, Mrs. Sutcliffe, let me present you to—Lady Beaufoy! (*opening gate, and discovering* BELLA, *dressed*

as a bride; two footmen attending her. LORD BEAUFOY
brings her down L.C.) My wife and your grandchild.

.   (*picture*)

FARIN. My child—my dear—dear grandchild !
                                                               (*embraces her*)
MRS. S. (BELLA *goes to* MRS. SUTCLIFFE) My favourite
pupil !   (*kissing* BELLA)
NAOMI. (*hysterical*) Please pass her round ! I want to
kiss her, too ! (BELLA *crosses to* NAOMI L., *embracing her*)
Oh, my darling—my darling, my true, real lady !

> FARINTOSH, *in his excitement, kisses* MRS. SUTCLIFFE.
> *Everybody astonished.*

DR. S. My dear, for thirty-five years——
FARIN. But, my dear Arthur, how could you be so
cruel ?
LORD B. My dear uncle, how could you be so suspicious?
Knowing that you wished me to marry, in what conventional
cant calls my own rank, I prevailed on Bella, who
reluctantly consented to become my wife ; knowing that
once married not even an archbishop could unmarry us,
imagine my delight when, on our return to town, my lawyer
informed me that, unknowingly, I had married my own
cousin.
NAOMI. Of course, you're cousins—it isn't unlawful for
—no—cousins can marry. That's a real comfort, isn't it ?
LORD B. We went to your house ; were told that you
had flown here ; came after you. I wished to present my
lady to her friends in proper form, and really your
reception was such that I resolved to punish you.

> (*music, "La Cenerentola." Piano*)

BELLA. (*to* FARINTOSH, *who has resumed seat*, C.) You
will not be ashamed of your grandchild, because she has not
been brought up amid the luxury to which she will try to
grow accustomed ?
FARIN. Ashamed ! My—my happiness is only too
great.
BELLA. (*to* DR. *and* MRS. SUTCLIFFE) And you, my
dear, kind friends, to whom I owe everything, will forgive
me for the suspense I have caused you? I would have
written, but my lord——
LORD B. (*correcting her*) Arthur.
BELLA. Arthur wished me to keep silent, and——
DR. S. The end crowns the work !

Mrs. S. My sweet darling, I had no apprehensions ; I always knew that your destiny would be a high one.

Bella. (*to* Naomi) And you'll come and pass your holidays with me?

Naomi. Yes, dear ; and you shall show me all your new things.

Dr. S. (*surrounding* Lord Beaufoy) I have to ask your lordship's pardon.

Jack. (*ditto*) I could bite my tongue off, Arthur, for what I said just now.

Lord B. Not another word ; you were all quite right. I told you, Jack, you would be sorry. (*music ceases*)

	FOOTMAN. O		FOOTMAN. O		
GIRLS. O		LORD BEAUFOY. O		JACK POYNTZ. O	
DR. SUTCLIFFE. O		BEAU. FARINTOSH. O		NAOMI TIGHE. O	
MRS. SUTCLIFFE. O				BELLA. O	MR. KRUX. O

Bella, Mr. Krux, I am sure you wish me every happiness.

Krux. Every happiness, Miss Bella.

Naomi. (*angrily*) Lady Beaufoy. Do you know who you are talking to? Lady Beaufoy.

Dr. S. Mr. Krux (*crosses* R.C. *to* Dr. Sutcliffe), if you would like to take your usual walk don't let regard for us prevent you.

Krux. Thank you, Dr. Sutcliffe, I——

Bows to characters R. *and* L., *then going up bows to the two* FOOTMEN, *who are standing on either side of gate, and goes off by gate.*

Naomi. (*quickly*) Jack, do you love me?

Jack. Naomi!

Naomi. Then run after Mr. Krux, and give him a good thrashing. You won't mind, will you?

Jack. It will be a pleasure.

Exit JACK *after* KRUX. *Immediately after,* KRUX's *hat comes flying over wall.*

Tilly. (*who has been reading book*) " Cinderella was then conducted to the Prince, who asked her to accept his hand. The marriage ceremony took place in a few days ;

and Cinderella gave her sisters magnificent apartments in the palace."

MILLY. "And a short time after married them to two great Lords of the Court."

ALL THE GIRLS. (*cross to* L.S., *surrounding* BELLA, *who is sitting on stage by swing*) Oh, my lady !

NAOMI. It's just like the story—(*looking off*)—Prince, carriages, footmen, and all. (*taking up pumpkin*) And to think that this (*the pumpkin*) should ever grow into that.

> *Pointing to* FOOTMEN, *and placing pumpkin at the feet of* FOOTMAN.

FARIN. And. in this fairy story, what am I ?

NAOMI. You ?—you're the godmother.

LORD B. (*taking parcel from* FOOTMAN) Knowing my wife's talent for narrative, I have here something I could only offer to her on the spot.

BELLA. Another present !

LORD. B. (*opening case*) A pair of glass slippers.

GIRLS. Oh !

> *They surround him. Re-enter* JACK *through gate in wall,* L.C., NAOMI *meeting him.*

NAOMI. Did you do it ?

JACK. Yes.

NAOMI. Did you hurt him much ?

JACK. He said I did ; and I believe he spoke the truth.

FARIN. (*taking the. hands of* DOCTOR *and* MRS. SUTCLIFFE) See, my friends, how a good deed germinates into a great one. Your past kindness to a friendless orphan girl is the cause of our all present happiness.

DR. S. No, no, not so ; your nephew's nature is an exceptionally fine one. He is in the highest sense of the word a gentleman ; and there is no sight under the sun finer than a true gentleman.

FARIN. Except one.

DR. S. Eh ?

FARIN. A true lady !

DR. S. So many things are required for the composition of the real thing. One wants nobility of feeling.

FARIN. A kind heart.

DR. S. A noble mind.

FARIN. Modesty.

DR. S. Gentleness.

FARIN. Courage.

Y Y

DR. S. Truthfulness.

FARIN. Birth.

DR. S. Breeding.

MRS. S. And, above all,—School !

As LORD BEAUFOY *stoops to fit on slipper,* NAOMI *having taken off* BELLA'S *satin shoe, the Curtain falls. Music.*

CLARA.   KITTY.

HETTY.

JACK. NAOMI. BELLA. LORD BEAUFOY.

CHILD.

MRS. SUTCLIFFE.   MILLY.   LAURA.

DR. SUTCLIFFE.   FARINTOSH.   TILLY.

R.H.   L.H.

CURTAIN.

Faithfully Yours
Marie E. Zakrzewska

SOCIETY.

A COMEDY,

IN THREE ACTS.

BY

T. W. ROBERTSON,

AUTHOR OF

"Caste," "A Breach of Promise," "School," "M.P.," "Birth,"
"David Garrick," "The Ladies' Battle," "The Nightingale,"
"Ours," "Play," "Progress," "A Row in the House,"
"Dreams," "War," "Home," "Faust and Marguerite," "My
Wife's Diary," "Noemie," "Two Gay Deceivers," "Jocrisse
the Juggler," "Not at all Jealous," "Star of the North,"
"Birds of Prey," "Peace at any Price," "Half Caste,"
"Ernestine," "Chevalier de St. George," "Cantab," "Clock-
maker's Hat," "Duke's Daughter," "Sea of Ice," &c., &c.

LONDON :	NEW YORK :
SAMUEL FRENCH.	SAMUEL FRENCH & SON,
PUBLISHER,	PUBLISHERS,
89, STRAND.	28, WEST 23RD STREET.

SOCIETY.

Produced at the Prince of Wales's Theatre, Liverpool (under the management of Mr. A. Henderson), on May 8th, 1865 ; afterwards performed at the Prince of Wales's Theatre, London (under the management of Miss Marie Wilton), on November 11th, 1865.

CAST OF CHARACTERS.

	Liverpool.	London.
Lord Ptarmigant	Mr. Blakeley	Mr. Hare.
Lord Cloudwrays, M.P.	Mr. F. Cameron	Mr. Trafford.
Sidney Daryl (*a Barrister*)	Mr. Edward Price	Mr. Bancroft.
Mr. John Chodd, Sen.	Mr. G. P. Grainger.	Mr. Ray.
Mr. John Chodd, Jun.	Mr. L. Brough	Mr. J. Clarke.
Tom Stylus	Mr. E. Saker	Mr. F. Dowar.
O'Sullivan	Mr. C. Swan	Mr. H. W. Montgomery
MacUsquebaugh	Mr. Chater	Mr. Hill.
Doctor Makvicz	Mr. Smith	Mr. Bennett.
Bradley	Mr. W. Grainger.	Mr Parker.
Scargil	Mr. Waller	Mr. Lawson.
Sam Stunner, P.R. (*alias the Smiffel Lamb*)	Mr. Hill	Mr. J. Tindale.
Shamheart		Mr. G. Odell.
Doddles		Mr. Burnett.
Moses Aaron (*a Bailiff*)	Mr. Davidge	Mr. G. Atkins.
Sheridan Trodnon	Mr. Bracewell	Mr. Macart.
Lady Ptarmigant	Miss Larkins	Miss Larkins.
Maud Hetherington	Miss T. Furtado	Miss Marie Wilton.
Little Maud	Miss F. Smithers	Miss George.
Mrs. Churton	Miss Procter	Miss Merton.
Servant		Miss Thompson.

ACT I.—SCENE 1.—SIDNEY DARYL'S *Chambers.* SCENE 2.—*A West End Square.*

ACT II.—SCENE 1.—*A Parlour at the " Owl's Roost."* SCENE 2. —*Retiring Room at* SIR FARINTOSH FADILEAF'S.

ACT III.—SCENE 1.—*Same as 1st Scene, Act II.* SCENE 2.— *Apartment at* LORD PTARMIGANT'S. SCENE 3.— *Exterior at Springmead-le-Beau.*

Modern Costumes. Time of Representation, three hours.

TO

MY DEAR FRIEND.

TOM HOOD,

THIS PLAY

IS DEDICATED.

SOCIETY.

ACT I.

SCENE I.—SIDNEY DARYL'S *Chambers, in Lincoln's Inn ; set doorpiece* R. *and set doorpiece* L. (*to double up and draw off*); *the room to present the appearance of belonging to a sporting literary barrister ; books, pictures, whips ; the mirror stuck full of cards (painted on cloth) : a table on* R., *chairs, &c. As the curtain rises a knock heard, and* DODDLES *discovered opening door,* L.

TOM. (*without*) Mr. Daryl in ?

DODD. Not up yet.

Enter TOM STYLUS, CHODD, JUN., *and* CHODD, SEN.

CHODD, JUN. (L., *looking at watch*) Ten minutes to twelve, eh, guv ?

TOM. (R.C.) Late into bed ; up after he oughter ; out for brandy and sobering water.

SIDNEY. (*within*) Doddles.

DODD. (R., *an old clerk*) Yes, sir !

SIDNEY. Brandy and soda.

DODD. Yes, sir!

TOM. I said so ! Tell Mr. Daryl two gentlemen wish to see him on particular business.

CHODD, JUN. (*a supercilious, bad swell; glass in eye; hooked stick ; vulgar and uneasy*) So this is an author's crib—is it ? Don't think much of it, eh, guv ?

(crossing behind to L.C.)

CHODD, SEN. (*a common old man, with a dialect*) Seems comfortable enough to me, Johnny.

CHODD, JUN. Don't call me Johnny ? I hope he won't be long. (*looking at watch*) Don't seem to me the right sort of thing, for two gentlemen to be kept waiting for a man they are going to employ.

CHODD, SEN. Gently, Johnny. (CHODD, JUN., *looks annoyed*) I mean gently without the Johnny—Mister——

TOM. Daryl—Sidney Daryl !

CHODD, SEN. Daryl didn't know as we was coming !

CHODD, JUN. (*rudely to* TOM)   Why didn't you let him know?

TOM. (*fiercely*) How the devil could I? I didn't see you till last night. (CHODD, JUN., *retires into himself*) You'll find Sidney Daryl just the man for you; young— full of talent—what I was thirty years ago; I'm old now, and not full of talent, if ever I was; I've emptied myself; I've missed my tip.   You see I wasn't a swell—he is!

CHODD JUN.   A swell—what a man who writes for his living?

DODDLES *enters door*, R.

DODD. Mr. Daryl will be with you directly; will you please to sit down?

CHODD, SEN., *sits* L.C. ; TOM *takes a chair* L. *of table ;*
CHODD, JUN., *waiting to have one given to him, is annoyed that no one does so, and sits on table.*
DODDLES *goes round to* L.

CHODD, JUN. Where is Mr. Daryl?
DODD. In his bath!
CHODD, JUN. (*jumping off table*) What! You don't mean to say he keeps us here while he's washing himself?

Enter SIDNEY, *in morning jacket, door* R.

SIDNEY. Sorry to have detained you; how are you, Tom?

TOM *and* CHODD, SEN., *rise;* CHODD, JUN., *sits again on table and sucks cane.*

CHODD, SEN. Not at all!
CHODD, JUN. (*with watch*) Fifteen minutes.
SIDNEY. (*crossing,* C., *handing chair to* CHODD, JUN.) Take a chair!
CHODD, JUN. This'll do.
SIDNEY. But you're sitting on the steel pens.
TOM. Dangerous things! pens.

(CHODD, JUN., *takes a chair,* L.)

SIDNEY. Yes! loaded with ink, percussion powder's nothing to 'em.
CHODD, JUN. We came here to talk business. (*to* DODDLES) Here, you get out!
SIDNEY. (*surprised*) Doddles—I expect a lot of people this morning, be kind enough to take them into the library.
DODD. (L.) Yes, sir! (*aside, looking at* CHODD, JUN.) Young rhinoceros!   *Exit door,* L.

SIDNEY. Now, gentlemen, I am——

(*crossing behind table to* R.)

TOM. (L. *of table*) Then I'll begin. First let me introduce Mr. Sidney Daryl to Mr. John Chodd, of Snoggerston, also to Mr. John Chodd, Jun., of the same place; Mr. John Chodd, of Snoggerston, is very rich—he made a fortune by——

CHODD, SEN. No !—my brother Joe made the fortune in Australey, by gold digging and then spec'lating; which he then died, and left all to me.

CHODD, JUN. (*aside*) Guv ! cut it !

CHODD, SEN. I shan't,—I ain't ashamed of what I was, nor what I am; it never was my way. Well, sir, I have lots of brass !

SIDNEY. Brass ?

CHODD, SEN. Money ?

CHODD, JUN. Heaps !

CHODD, SEN. (L.C.) Heaps; but having begun by being a poor man, without edication, and not being a gentleman——

CHODD, JUN. (*aside*) Guv !—cut it.

CHODD, SEN. I shan't—I know I'm not, and I'm proud of it, that is, proud of knowing I'm not, and I won't pretend to be. Johnny don't put me out—I say I'm not a gentleman, but my son is.

SIDNEY. (*looking at him*) Evidently.

CHODD, SEN. And I wish him to cut a figure in the world—to get into Parliament.

SIDNEY. Very difficult.

CHODD, SEN. To get a wife ?

SIDNEY. Very easy.

CHODD, SEN. And in short, to be a—a real gentleman.

SIDNEY. Very difficult.

CHODD, SEN. }
CHODD, JUN. } Eh ?

SIDNEY. I mean very easy.

CHODD, SEN. Now, as I'm anxious he should be an M. P. as soon as——

SIDNEY. As he can.

CHODD, SEN. Just so, and as I have lots of capital unemployed, I mean to invest it in——

TOM. (*slapping* SIDNEY *on knees*) A new daily paper !

SIDNEY. By Jove !

CHODD, SEN. A cheap daily paper, that could—that will —What will a cheap daily paper do ?

SIDNEY. Bring the "Court Circular" within the knowledge of the humblest.

TOM. Educate the masses—raise them morally, socially, politically, scientifically, geologically, and horizontally.

CHODD, SEN. (*delighted*) That's it—that's it, only it looks better in print.

TOM. (*spouting*) Bring the glad and solemn tidings of the day to the labourer at his plough—the spinner at his wheel—the swart forger at his furnace—the sailor on the giddy mast—the lighthouse keeper as he trims his beacon lamp—the housewife at her pasteboard—the mother at her needle—the lowly lucifer seller, as he splashes his wet and weary way through the damp, steaming, stony streets, eh ? —you know.

(*slapping* SIDNEY *on the knee—they both laugh*)

CHODD, SEN. (*to* CHODD, JUN.) What are they a laughing at ?

TOM. So my old friend, Johnny Prothero, who lives hard by Mr. Chodd, knowing that I have started lots of papers, sent the two Mr. Chodds, or the Messrs. Chodd—which is it ?—you're a great grammarian—to me. I can find them an efficient staff, and you are the first man we've called upon.

SIDNEY. Thanks, old fellow. When do you propose to start it ?

CHODD, SEN. At once.

SIDNEY. What is it to be called ?

CHODD, SEN. We don't know.

CHODD, JUN. We leave that to the fellows we pay for their time and trouble.

SIDNEY. You want something——

CHODD, SEN. Strong.

TOM. And sensational.

SIDNEY. I have it. (*rising*)

TOM.
CHODD, SENR. } What ?
CHODD, JUN.

SIDNEY. The "Morning Earthquake"!

TOM. Capital !

CHODD, SEN. (*rising*) First-rate !

CHODD, JUN. (*still seated*) Not so bad.

(*goes up during next speech*)

SIDNEY. Don't you see ? In place of the clock, a mass of houses, factories, and palaces tumbling one over the other ; and then the prospectus ! "At a time when thrones are tottering, dynasties dissolving—while the old world is displacing to make room for the new——"

TOM. Bravo!

CHODD, SEN. (*enthusiastically*) Hurray!

TOM. A second edition at 4 o'clock, p.m. The "Evening Earthquake," eh? Placard the walls. "The Earthquake," one note of admiration; "The Earthquake," two notes" of admiration; "The Earthquake," three notes of admiration. Posters: "'The Earthquake' delivered every morning with your hot rolls." "With coffee, toast, and eggs, enjoy your 'Earthquake'"!

CHODD, SEN. (*with pocket-book*) I've got your name and address.

CHODD, JUN. (*who has been looking at cards stuck in glass,* C.) Guv.

(*takes old* CHODD *up and whispers to him*)

TOM. (*to* SIDNEY) Don't like this young man!

SIDNEY. No.

TOM. Cub.

SIDNEY. Cad.

TOM. Never mind. The old un's not a bad 'un. We're off to a printer's.

SIDNEY. Good-bye, Tom, and thank ye.

TOM. How's the little girl?

SIDNEY. Quite well. I expect her here this morning.

CHODD, SEN. Good morning.

(*Exeunt* CHODD, SEN., *and* TOM, *door,* L.)

SIDNEY. (*filling pipe, &c.*) Have a pipe?

CHODD, JUN. (*taking out a magnificent case*) I always smoke cigars.

SIDNEY. Gracious creature! Have some bitter beer?

(*getting it from locker*)

CHODD, JUN. I never drink anything in the morning.

SIDNEY. Oh!

CHODD, JUN. But champagne.

SIDNEY. I haven't got any.

CHODD, JUN. (L.) Then I'll take beer. (*they sit*) Business is business—so I'd best begin at once. The present age is, as you are aware—a practical age. I come to the point—it's my way. Capital commands the world. The capitalist commands capital, therefore the capitalist commands the world.

SIDNEY. (R.) But you don't quite command the world, do you?

CHODD, JUN. Practically, I do. I wish for the highest honours—I bring out my cheque-book. I want to go into the House of Commons—cheque-book. I want the best legal opinion in the House of Lords—cheque-book. The best house—cheque-book. The best turn out—cheque-book. The best friends, the best wife, the best trained children—cheque-book, cheque-book, and cheque-book.

SIDNEY. You mean to say with money you can purchase anything.

CHODD, JUN. Exactly. This life is a matter of bargain.

SIDNEY. But "honour, love, obedience, troops of friends"?

CHODD, JUN. Can buy 'em all, sir, in lots, as at an auction.

SIDNEY. Love, too?

CHODD, JUN. Marriage means a union mutually advantageous. It is a civil contract, like a partnership.

SIDNEY. And the old-fashioned virtues of honour and chivalry?

CHODD, JUN. Honour means not being a bankrupt. I know nothing at all about chivalry, and I don't want to.

SIDNEY. Well, yours is quite a new creed to me, and I confess I don't like it.

CHODD, JUN. The currency, sir, converts the most hardened sceptic. I see by the cards on your glass that you go out a great deal.

SIDNEY. Go out?

CHODD, JUN. Yes, to parties. (*looking at cards on table*) There's my Lady this, and the Countess t'other, and Mrs. somebody else. Now that's what I want to do.

SIDNEY. Go into society?

CHODD, JUN. Just so. You had money once, hadn't you.

SIDNEY. Yes.

CHODD, JUN. What did you do with it?

SIDNEY. Spent it.

CHODD, JUN. And you've been in the army?

SIDNEY. Yes.

CHODD, JUN. Infantry?

SIDNEY. Cavalry.

CHODD, JUN. Dragoons?

SIDNEY. Lancers.

CHODD, JUN. How did you get out?

SIDNEY. Sold out.

CHODD, JUN. Then you were a first-rate fellow, till you tumbled down?

SIDNEY. Tumbled down?

CHODD, JUN. Yes, to what you are.

> SIDNEY *about to speak, is interrupted by* MOSES AARON, *without*, L.

MOSES. Tell you I mush't shee him.

> *Enter* MOSES AARON *with* DODDLES, *door* L.

MOSES. (*not seeing* CHODD, JUN., *going round behind table*) Sorry, Mister Daryl, but at the shoot of Brackersby and Co. (*arrests him*)

CHODD, JUN. Je-hosophat! (*rising*)

SIDNEY. Confound Mr. Brackersby! It hasn't been owing fifteen months!—How much?

MOSES. With exes, fifty four pun' two.

SIDNEY. I've got it in the next room. Have some beer?

MOSES. Thank ye, shir. (SIDNEY *pours it out*)

SIDNEY. Back directly. *Exit door*, L.

CHODD, JUN. (L.) This chap's in debt. Here you!

MOSES. (R.) Shir.

CHODD, JUN. Mr. Daryl—does he owe much?

MOSES. Spheck he does, shir, or I shouldn't know him.

CHODD, JUN. Here's half a sov. Give me your address?

MOSES. (*gives card*) " Orders executed with punctuality and despatch."

CHODD, JUN. If I don't get into society now, I'm a Dutchman.

> *Enter* SIDNEY, R.

SIDNEY. Here you are—ten fives—two two's—and a half-a-crown for yourself.

MOSES. Thank ye, shir. Good mornin', shir

SIDNEY. Good morning.

MOSES. (*to* CHODD, JUN.) Good mornin', shir.

CHODD, JUN. Such familiarity from the lower orders. (*Exit* MOSES AARON, *door* L.) You take it coolly.

(*sitting* L. *of table*)

SIDNEY. (*sitting*) I generally do.

CHODD, JUN. (*looking round*) You've got lots of guns?

SIDNEY. I'm fond of shooting.

CHODD, JUN. And rods?

SIDNEY. I'm fond of fishing.

CHODD, JUN. And books?

SIDNEY. I like reading.

CHODD, JUN. And whips?

SIDNEY. And riding.

CHODD, JUN. Why you seem fond of everything?

SIDNEY. (*looking at him*) No; not everything.

DODDLES *enters, at door* L., *with card.*

SIDNEY. (*reading*) "Mr. Sam. Stunner, P.R."

CHODD, JUN. "P.R." What's P.R. mean? After-noon's P.M.?

SIDNEY. Ask him in.   *Exit* DODDLES.

CHODD, JUN. Is he an author? or does P.R. mean Pre-Raphaelite?

SIDNEY. No; he's a a prize-fighter—the Smiffel Lamb. (*Enter the* SMIFFEL LAMB, L. *door*) How are you, Lamb?

LAMB. Bleating, sir, bleating—thankee kindly.

CHODD, JUN. (*aside to* SIDNEY) Do prize-fighters usually carry cards?

SIDNEY. The march of intellect. Education of the masses—the Jemmy Masseys. Have a glass of sherry?

LAMB. Not a drain, thankee, sir.

CHODD, JUN. (*aside*) Offers that brute sherry, and makes me drink beer.

LAMB. I've jist bin drinkin' with Lankey Joe, and the Dulwich Duffer, at Sam Shoulderblows. I'm a going into trainin' next week to fight Australian Harry, the Boundin' Kangaroo. I shall lick him, sir. I know I shall.

SIDNEY. I shall back you, Lamb.

LAMB. Thankee, Mr. Daryl. I knew you would. I always does my best for my backers, and to keep up the honour of the science; the Fancy, sir, should keep square. (*looks at* CHODD, JUN.,*hesitates, then walks to door, closes it, and walks sharply up to* SIDNEY DARYL—CHODD, JUN.,*leaping up in alarm, and retiring to back—leaning on table and speaking close to* SIDNEY DARYL'S *ear*) I jist called in to give you the office, sir, as has always bin so kind to me, not to *put* any tin on the mill between the Choking Chummy and Slang's Novice. It's a cross, sir, a reg'lar barney!

SIDNEY. Is it? Thank ye.

LAMB. That's wot I called for, sir; and now I'm hoff. (*goes to door—turning*) Don't *putt* a mag on it, sir; Choking Chummy's a cove as would sell his own mother; he once sold *me*, which is *wuss*. Good-day, sir.

(*Exit* LAMB, *door*, L. CHODD, JUN., *reseats himself*)

CHODD, JUN. As I was saying, you know lots of people at clubs, and in society.

SIDNEY. Yes.

CHODD, JUN. Titles, and Honourables, and Captains, and that.

SIDNEY. Yes.

CHODD, JUN. Tip-toppers. (*after a pause*) You're not well off?

SIDNEY. (*getting serious*) No.

CHODD, JUN. I am. I've heaps of brass. Now I have what you haven't, and I haven't what you have. You've got what I want, and I've got what you want. That's logic, isn't it?

SIDNEY. (*gravely*) What of it?

CHODD, JUN. This; suppose we exchange or barter. You help me to get into the company of men with titles, and women with titles; swells, you know, real 'uns, and all that.

SIDNEY. Yes.

CHODD, JUN. And I'll write you a cheque for any reasonable sum you like to name.

SIDNEY *rises indignantly, at the same moment* LITTLE MAUD *and* MRS. CHURTON *enter door,* L.

L. MAUD. (*running to* SIDNEY) Here I am, uncle; Mrs. Churton says I've been such a good girl.

SIDNEY. (*kissing her*) My darling. How d'ye do, Mrs. Churton. (*to* LITTLE MAUD) I've got a waggon, and a baa-lamb that squeaks, for you. (*then to* CHODD, JUN.) Mr. Chodd, I cannot entertain your very commercial proposition. My friends are my friends; they are not marketable commodities. I regret that I can be of no assistance to you. With your appearance, manners, and cheque-book, you are sure to make a circle of your own.

CHODD, JUN. You refuse, then——

SIDNEY. Absolutely. Good morning.

CHODD, JUN. Good morning (*aside*) And if I don't have my knife into you, my name's not John Chodd, Jun.

Exeunt SIDNEY, LITTLE MAUD, *and* MRS. CHURTON, *door* R. CHODD, JUN., *door* L.

SCENE II.—*The Interior of a Square at the West End. Weeping ash over a rustic chair,* C., *trees, shrubs, walks, rails, gates, &c.; houses at back. Time evening—effect of setting sun in windows of houses; lights in some of the windows, &c.; street lamps.* MAUD *discovered in rustic chair reading; street band heard playing in the distance.*

MAUD. I can't see to read any more. Heigho! how lonely it is! and that band makes me so melancholy—sometimes music makes me feel—(*rising*) Heigho! I suppose I shall see nobody to-night; I must go home. (*starts*) Oh! (SIDNEY *appears at* L. *gate*) I think I can see to read a few more lines. (*sits again, and takes book*)

SIDNEY. (*feeling pockets*) Confound it! I've left the key at home. (*tries gate*) How shall I get in! (*looking over rails*) I'll try the other. (*goes round at back to opposite gate*)

MAUD. Why, he's going! He doesn't know I'm here. (*rises, calling*) Sid——No I won't, the idea of his—(*sees* SIDNEY *at gate,* R.) Ah!

(*gives a sigh of relief, reseats herself and reads*)

SIDNEY. (*at gate,* R.) Shut too! (*trying gate*) Provoking! What shall I——(*sees* NURSEMAID *approaching with* CHILD *from* L. 1 E.—*drops his hat into square*) Will you kindly open this? I've forgotten my key. (GIRL *opens gate*) Thanks! (SIDNEY *enters square ;* GIRL *and* CHILD *go out at gate ;* LIFE GUARDSMAN *enters,* R.U.E., *speaks to* GIRL ; *they exeunt,* L.U.E. SIDNEY *sighs on seeing* MAUD) There she is! (*seats himself by* MAUD) Maud!

MAUD. (L., *starting*) Oh! is that you? Who would have thought of seeing you here?

SIDNEY. (R.) Oh, come—don't I know that you walk here after dinner? and all day long I've been wishing it was half-past eight.

MAUD. (*coquetting*) I wonder, now, how often you've said that, this last week.

SIDNEY. Don't pretend to doubt me, that's unworthy of you. (*a pause*) Maud!

MAUD. Yes.

SIDNEY. Are you not going to speak?

MAUD. (*dreamily*) I don't know what to say.

SIDNEY. That's just my case. When I'm away from you, I feel I could talk to you for hours ; but when I'm with you, somehow or other, it seems all to go away. (*getting closer to her, and taking her hand*) It is such happiness to be with you, that it makes me forget everything else. (*takes off his gloves and puts them on seat*) Ever since I was that high, in the jolly old days down at Springmead, my greatest pleasure has been to be near you. (*looks at watch*) Twenty to nine. When must you return?

MAUD. At nine.

SIDNEY. Twenty minutes. How's your aunt?

MAUD. As cross as ever.

SIDNEY. And Lord Ptarmigant?

MAUD. As usual—asleep

SIDNEY. Dear old man ! how he does doze his time away. (*another pause*) Anything else to tell me ?

MAUD. We had such a stupid dinner; such odd people.

SIDNEY. Who?

MAUD. Two men by the name of Chodd.

SIDNEY. (*uneasily*) Chodd !

MAUD. Isn't it a funny name ?—Chodd.

SIDNEY. Yes, it's a Chodd name—I mean an odd name. Where were they picked up ?

MAUD. I don't know. Aunty says they are both very rich.

SIDNEY. (*uneasily*) She thinks of nothing but money. (*looks at watch*) Fifteen to nine. (*stage has grown gradually dark*) Maud?

MAUD. (*in a whisper*) Yes.

SIDNEY. If I were rich—if you were rich—if we were rich.

MAUD. Sidney !   (*drawing closer to him*)

SIDNEY. As it is, I almost feel it's a crime to love you.

MAUD. Oh, Sidney !

SIDNEY. You who might make such a splendid marriage.

MAUD. If you had—money—I couldn't care for you any more than I do now.

SIDNEY. My darling ! (*looks at watch*) Ten minutes. I know you wouldn't. Sometimes I feel mad about you—mad when I know you are out a smiling upon others—and —and waltzing.

MAUD. I can't help waltzing when I'm asked.

SIDNEY. No, dear, no ; but when I fancy you are spinning round with another's arm about your waist. (*his arm round her waist*) Oh !—I feel——

MAUD. Why, Sidney (*smiling*) You are jealous !

SIDNEY. Yes, I am.

MAUD. Can't you trust me ?

SIDNEY. Implicitly. But I like to be with you all the same.

MAUD. (*whispering*) So do I with you.

SIDNEY. My love ! (*kisses her, and looks at watch*) Five minutes.

MAUD. Time to go ?

SIDNEY. No! (MAUD, *in taking out her handkerchief, takes out a knot of ribbon*) What's that?

MAUD. Some trimmings I'm making for our fancy fair.

SIDNEY. What colour is it. Scarlet ?

z z

MAUD. Magenta.

SIDNEY. Give it to me?

MAUD. What nonsense.

SIDNEY. Won't you?

MAUD. I've brought something else.

SIDNEY. For me?

MAUD. Yes.

SIDNEY. What?

MAUD. These

> (*producing small case, which* SIDNEY *opens*)

SIDNEY. Sleeve links!

MAUD. Now, which will you have, the links or the ribbon?

SIDNEY. (*after reflection*) Both.

MAUD. You avaricious creature!

SIDNEY. (*putting the ribbons near his heart*) It's not in the power of words to tell you how I love you. Do you care for me enough to trust your future with me? Will you be mine?

MAUD. Sidney?

SIDNEY. Mine, and none other's; no matter how brilliant the offer—how dazzling the position?

MAUD. (*in a whisper—leaning towards him*) Yours and yours only!   (*clock strikes nine*)

SIDNEY (*with watch*) Nine! Why doesn't time stop, and big Ben refuse to toll the hour?

> LADY *and* LORD PTARMIGANT *appear and open gate,* R.

MAUD. (*frightened*) My aunt!

> SIDNEY *gets to back, round* L. *of square.* LORD *and* LADY PTARMIGANT *advance.*

LADY P. (*a very grand acid old lady*) Maud!

MAUD. Aunty, I was just coming away.

LADY. P. No one in the square? Quite improper to be here alone. Ferdinand!

LORD P. (*a little old gentleman*) My love!

LADY P. What is the time?

LORD P. Don't know—watch stopped—tired of going, I suppose, like me.

LADY P. (*sitting on chair—throws down the gloves left by* SIDNEY *with her dress*) What's that? (*picking them up*) Gloves?

MAUD. (*frightened*) Mine, aunty!

LADY P. Yours? You've got yours on ! (*looking at them*) These are Sidney Daryl's. I know his size—seven-and-a-half. I see why you are so fond of walking in the square ; for shame! (*turning to* SIDNEY, *who has just got the* R. *gate open, and is going out*) Sidney ! (*fiercely*) I see you ! There 's no occasion to try and sneak away. Come here. (SIDNEY *advances. With ironical politeness*) You have left your gloves.

> *All are standing except* LORD PTARMIGANT, *who lies at full length on chair and goes to sleep.*

SIDNEY (*confused*) Thank you, Lady Ptarm——
LADY P. You two fools have been making love. I've long suspected it. I'm shocked with both of you ; a penniless scribbler, and a dependent orphan, without a shilling or an expectation. Do you (*to* SIDNEY) wish to drag my niece, born and bred a lady, to a back parlour, and bread and cheese ? Or do you (*to* MAUD) wish to marry a shabby writer, who can neither feed himself nor you ? I can leave you nothing, for I am as well bred a pauper as yourselves. (*to* MAUD) To keep appointments in a public square ! your conduct is disgraceful—worse—it is unladylike ; and yours (*to* SIDNEY), is dishonourable, and unworthy, to fill the head of a foolish girl with sentiment and rubbish. (*loudly*) Ferdinand !
LORD P. (*waking up*) Yes, dear.
LADY P. Do keep awake ; the Chodds will be here directly ; they are to walk home with us, and I request you to make yourself agreeable to them.
LORD P. Such canaille.
LADY P. Such cash !
LORD P. Such cads.
LADY P. Such cash ! Pray, Ferdinand, don't argue
>   (*authoritatively*)
LORD P. I never do.   (*goes to sleep again*)
LADY P. I wish for no *esclandre*. Let us have no discussion in the square. Mr. Daryl, I shall be sorry if you compel me to forbid you my house. I have other views for Miss Hetherington.   (SIDNEY *bows*)

> *The two* CHODDS, *in evening dress, appear at gate,* R. ; *they enter.*

LADY P. My dear Mr. Chodd, Maud has been so impatient. (*the* CHODDS *do not see* SIDNEY—*to* CHODD

SEN.) I shall take your arm, Mr. Chodd. (*very sweetly*)
Maud, dear, Mr. John will escort you.

> *Street band heard playing "Fra Poco" in distance ;*
> MAUD *takes* CHODD, JUN.'s *arm ; the two couples*
> *go off* R. *gate ; as* MAUD *turns, she looks an adieu*
> *at* SIDNEY, *who waves the bunch of ribbon, and sits*
> *down on chair in a reverie, not perceiving* LORD
> PTARMIGANT'S *legs ;* LORD PTARMIGANT *jumps up*
> *with pain ;* SIDNEY *apologises. Curtain quick.*

END OF ACT I.

ACT II.

SCENE I.—*Parlour at the "Owl's Roost" Public-house.
Cushioned seats all round the apartment ; gas lighted* R.
and L. *over tables ; splint boxes, pipes, newspapers, &c.,
on table ; writing materials on* R. *table (near door);
gong bell on* L. *table; door of entrance* C.; *clock above door
(hands set to half-past nine); hat pegs and hats on walls.
In the chair at* L. *table head is discovered* O'SULLIVAN ;
also, in the following order, MACUSQUEBAUGH, AUTHOR,
and DR. MAKVICZ ; *also at* R. *table,* TRODNON (*at head*),
SHAMHEART, BRADLEY, SCARGIL ; *the* REPORTER *of "Belgravian Banner" is sitting outside the* R. *table, near the
head, and with his back turned to it, smoking a cigar.
The* CHARACTERS *are all discovered drinking and smoking,
some reading, some with their hats on.*

OMNES. Bravo ! Hear, hear ! Bravo !

O'SULL. (*on his legs, a glass in one hand, and terminating
a speech, in Irish accent*) It is, therefore, gintlemen, with
the most superlative felicitee, the most fraternal convivialitee,
the warmest congenialitee, the most burning friendship, and
ardent admiration, that I propose his health !

OMNES. Hear, hear ! &c.

O'SULL. He is a man, in the words of the divine
bard——

TROD. (*in sepulchral voice*) Hear ! hear !

O'SULL. Who, in "suffering everything, has suffered
nothing."

TROD. Hear, hear !

O'SULL. I have known him when, in the days of his prosperitee, he rowled down to the House of Commons in his carriage.

MacU. 'Twasn't his own—'twas a job!

OMNES. Silence! Chair! Order!

O'SULL. I have known him when his last copper, and his last glass of punch, has been shared with the frind of his heart!

OMNES. Hear, hear!

O'SULL. And it is with feelings of no small pride that I inform ye that that frind of his heart was the humble individual who has now the honour to address ye!

OMNES. Hear, hear! &c.

O'SULL. But, prizeman at Trinity, mimber of the bar, sinator, classical scholar, or frind, Desmond MacUsquebaugh has always been the same—a gintleman and a scholar; and that highest type of that glorious union—an Irish gintleman and scholar. Gintlemen, I drink his health —Desmond, my long loved frind, bless ye! (*all rise solemnly and drink*—"Mr. MacUsquebaugh.") Gintlemen, my frind, Mr. MacUsquebaugh will respond.

OMNES. Hear, hear!

> *Enter* WAITER, *with glasses, tobacco, &c., and receives orders*—*changes* O'SULLIVAN'S *glass and exits,* C.
> *Enter* TOM STYLUS *and* CHODD, JUN., C. TOM *has a greatcoat on, over an evening dress.*

CHODD, JUN. Thank you; no, not anything.

TOM. Just a wet—an outrider—or advanced guard, to prepare the way for the champagne.

CHODD, JUN. No.

> *As soon as the sitters see* TOM STYLUS *they give him a friendly nod, looking inquiringly at* CHODD, *and whisper each other.*

TOM. (R.) You'd better. They are men worth knowing. (*pointing them out*) That is the celebrated Olinthus O'Sullivan, Doctor of Civil Laws.

> O'SULLIVAN *is at this moment reaching to the gaslight to light his pipe.*

CHODD, JUN. (L.) The gent with the long pipe?

TOM. Yes; one of the finest classical scholars in the world; might have sat upon the woolsack if he'd chosen, but he didn't. (O'SULLIVAN *is now tossing with* MACUSQUEbaugh) That is the famous Desmond MacUsquebaugh, late M.P. for Killcrackskullcoddy, county Galway, a great patriot and orator ; might have been Chancellor of the Exchequer if he'd chosen, but he didn't. (SCARGIL *reaches to the gaslight to light his pipe*) That's Bill Bradley (*pointing to* BRADLEY, *who is reading paper with double eye-glass*), author of the famous romance of " Time and Opportunity " ; ran through ten editions. He got two thousand pounds for it, which was his ruin.

CHODD, JUN. How was he ruined by getting two thousand pounds?

TOM. He's never done anything since. We call him "One book Bradley." That gentleman fast asleep— (*looking towards* AUTHOR *at table,* L.) has made the fortune of three publishers, and the buttoned-up one with the shirt front of beard is Herr Makvicz, the great .United German. Dr. Scargil, there, discovered the mensuration of the motive power of the cerebral organs.

> SCARGIL *takes a pinch of snuff from a box on the table.*

CHODD, JUN. What's that?

TOM. How many million miles per minute thought can travel. He might have made his fortune if he'd chosen.

CHUDD, JUN. But he didn't. Who is that mild-looking party, with the pink complexion, and the white hair !

> (*looking towards* SHAMHEART)

TOM. Sam Shamheart, the professional philanthropist. He makes it his business and profit to love the whole human race. (SHAMHEART *puffs a huge cloud of smoke from his pipe*) Smoke, sir; all smoke. A superficial observer would consider him only a pleasant oily humbug, but I, having known him two and twenty years, feel qualified to pronounce him one of the biggest villains untransported.

CHODD, JUN. And that man asleep at the end of the table.

TOM. Trodnon, the eminent tragedian.

> TRODNON *raises himself from the table, yawns, stretches himself, and again drops head on table.*

CHODD, JUN. I never heard of him.

TOM. Nor anybody else. But he's a confirmed tippler, and here we consider drunkenness an infallible sign of genius—we make that a rule.

CHODD, JUN. But if they are all such great men, why didn't they make money by their talents?

TOM. (R.) Make money! They'd scorn it! they wouldn't do it—that's another rule. That gentleman there (*looking towards a very seedy man with eye-glass in his eye*) does the evening parties on the " Belgravian Banner."

CHODD, JUN. (*with interest*) Does he? Will he put my name among the fashionables to-night?

TOM. Yes.

CHODD, JUN. And that we may know who's there and everything about it—you're going with me?

TOM. Yes, _I'm going into society_; thanks to your getting me the invitation. I can dress up an account, not a mere list of names, but a picturesque report of the soirée, and show under what brilliant auspices you entered the beau-monde.

CHODD, JUN. Beau-monde. What's that?

TOM. (*chaffing him*) Every man is called a cockney who is born within the sound of the beau-monde.

CHODD, JUN. (*not seeing it*) Oh! Order me two hundred copies of the " Belgravian "——What's its name?

TOM. " Banner."

CHODD, JUN. The day my name's in it—and put me down as a regular subscriber. I like to encourage high-class literature. By the way, shall I ask the man what he'll take to drink?

TOM. No, no.

CHODD, JUN. I'll pay for it. I'll stand, you know.

(*going to him,* TOM *stops him*)

TOM. No, no—he don't know you, and he'd be offended.

CHODD, JUN. But, I suppose all these chaps are plaguy poor?

TOM. Yes, they're poor; but they are *gentlemen.*

CHODD, JUN. (*grinning*) I like that notion—a *poor* gentleman—it tickles me.   .(*going up* R.)

TOM. (*crossing into* L. *corner*) Metallic snob!

CHODD, JUN. I'm off now (*going up,* R.) You'll come to my rooms and we'll go together in the brougham. I want to introduce you to my friends, Lady Ptarmigant and Lord Ptarmigant?

TOM. I must wait here for a proof I expect from the office.

CHODD, JUN. How long shall you be?

TOM. (*looking at clock*) An hour.

CHODD, JUN. Don't be later.

> *Exit* CHODD, JUN., C.—*the* REPORTER *rises, gets paper from* L. *table, and shows it to* SHAMHEART, *sitting next him on his* L. *hand.*

O'SULL. Sit down, Tommy, my dear boy. Gintlemen, Mr. Desmond MacUsquebaugh will respond.

> *Tapping with hammer. Enter* WAITER, C., *and gives* BRADLEY *a glass of grog.*

MacU. (*rising*) Gintlemen.

> (TOM *taking his coat off, shows evening dress*)

TOM. A go of whisky.

WAITER. Scotch or Irish ?

TOM. Irish.

> *Exit* WAITER, C. *All are astonished at* TOM'S *costume—they cry* "By Jove ! there's a swell," &c.

O'SULL. Why, Tom, my dear friend—are ye going to be married to-night, that ye're got up so gorgeously ?

MacU. Tom, you're handsome as an angel.

O'SULL. Or a duke's footman. Gintlemen, rise and salute our illustrious brother.

> (*all rise and make* TOM *mock bows*)

BRAD. The gods preserve you, noble sir.

SHAM. May the bill of your sublime highness's washer-woman be never the less.

MacU. And may it be paid. (*a general laugh*)

O'SULL. Have you come into a fortune ?

DR. M. Or married a widow ?

SHAM. Or buried a relation ? (*a general laugh*) By my soul, Tom, you look an honour to humanity !

O'SULL. And your laundress. (*a general laugh*)

BRAD. Gentlemen, Mr. Stylus's health and shirt front.

> (*a general laugh—all drink and sit*)

TOM. (C.) Bless ye, my people, bless ye !

> (*sits, and takes out short pipe and smokes*)

O'SULL. Gintlemen (*rising*) My friend, Mr. Usquebaugh, will respond.

OMNES. Hear, hear !

MacU. (*rising*) Gintlemen——

> *Enter* SIDNEY, *in evening dress and wrapper. Enter* WAITER *with* TOM'S *grog.*

OMNES. Hallo, Daryl !

SIDNEY. How are ye, boys? Doctor, how goes it? (*shaking hands*) Mac. How d'ye do, O'Sullivan? Tom, I want to speak to you.

O'SULL. Ah, Tom, this is the rale metal—the genuine thing; compared to him you are a sort of Whitechapel would-if-I-could-be (*to* SIDNEY) Sit down, my gorgeous one, and drink with me.

SIDNEY. No, thanks.

(SIDNEY *and* TOM *sit at* R. *table head*)

O'SULL. Waiter, take Mr. Daryl's orders.

SIDNEY. Brandy cold. *Exit* WAITER, C.

MACU. Take off your wrap, rascal, and show your fine feathers.

SIDNEY. No; I'm going out, and I shall smoke my coat.

> TOM *extinguishing his pipe, and puts it in his dress-coat pocket, then puts on his greatcoat with great solemnity.*

O'SULL. Going?

TOM. No.

O'SULL. Got the rheumatism?

TOM. No; but I shall smoke my coat. (*general laugh*)

> *Enter* WAITER, C. *He gives glass of brandy and water to* SIDNEY, *and glass of grog to* SHAMHEART.

O'SULL. What news, Daryl?

SIDNEY. None, except that the Ministry is to be defeated._ (O'SULLIVAN *pays* WAITER)

ALL. No!

SIDNEY. I say, yes. They're whipping up everything to vote against Thunder's motion. Thunder is sure of a majority, and out they go. Capital brandy. (*coming forward*) Tom! (TOM *rises; they come down stage*) I am off to a soirée.

TOM. (R., *aside*) So am I; but I won't tell him.

SIDNEY. (L.) I find I've nothing in my portmonnaie but notes. I want a trifle for a cab. Lend me five shillings.

TOM. I haven't got it, but I can get it for you.

SIDNEY. There's a good fellow, do. (*returns to seat*)

TOM. (*to* MACUSQUEBAUGH, *after looking round*) Mac, (*whispering*) lend me five bob.

MACU. My dear boy, I haven't got so much.

TOM. Then don't lend it.

MACU. But I'll get it for you. (*crosses to* BRADLEY—*whispers*) Bradley lend me five shillings.

BRAD. I haven't it about me, but I'll get it for you. (*crosses to* O'SULLIVAN—*whispers*) O'Sullivan, lend me five shillings.

O'SULL. I haven't got it, but I'll get it for you. (*crossing to* SCARGIL—*whispers*) Scargil, lend me five shillings.

SCARG. I haven't got it, but I'll get it for you. (*crossing to* MAKVICZ—*whispers*) Doctor, lend me five shillings.

DR. M. I am waiting for chaange vor a zoveren; I'll give it you when de waiter brings to me.

SCARG. All right! (*to* O'SULLIVAN) All right!

O'SULL. All right! (*to* BRADLEY) All right!

BRAD. All right! (*to* MACUSQUEBAUGH) All right!

MACU. All right! (*to* TOM) All right!

TOM. (*to* SIDNEY) All right!

O'SULL. (*tapping*) Gintlemen, my friend, Mr. MacUsque-baugh will respond to the toast that——

MACU. (*rising*) Gintlemen——

SIDNEY. Oh, cut the speechifying, I hate it! you ancients are so fond of spouting; let's be jolly, I've only a few minutes more.

BRAD. Daryl, sing us "Cock-a-doodle-doo."

SIDNEY. I only know the first two verses.

TOM. I know the rest.

Enter WAITER, *gives glass of grog to* MAKVICZ.

SIDNEY. Then here goes. Waiter, shut the door, and don't open it till I've done. Now then, ready.

Exit WAITER. O'SULLIVAN *taps.*

SIDNEY. (*giving out*) Political :—

(*sings*) When Ministers in fear and doubt,
  That they should be from placc kicked out,
  Get up 'gainst time and sense to spout
   A long dull evening through,
  What mean they then by party clique,
  Mob orators and factions weak?
  'Tis only would they truth then speak
   But cock-a-doodle-doo!
  Cock-a-doodle, cock-a-doodle, cock-a-doodle-doo.

CHORUS. (*gravely and solemnly shaking their heads*) Cock-a-doodle, &c.

SIDNEY. (*speaking*) Commercil' :—

(sings) When companies, whose stock of cash
    Directors spend to cut a dash,
  Are formed to advertise and smash,
    And bankruptcy go through.
When tradesfolks live in regal state,
The goods they sell adulterate,
And puff in print, why what's their prate
    But cock-a-doodle-doo ?
Cock-a-doodle, cock-a-doodle, &c.

CHORUS. *(as before)* Cock-a-doodle, &c.

Enter WAITER, C.

O'SULL. How dare you come in and interrupt the harmony !

WAITER. Beg pardon, sir, but there's somebody says as he must see Mr. Stylus.

TOM. Is he a devil ?

WAITER. No, sir, he's a juvenile. *(a general laugh)*

TOM. Send in some whisky—Irish—and the devil.

WAITER. Hot, sir ?   *(a general laugh)*

        TOM *nods to* WAITER, *who exits,* C. door.

SIDNEY. Why can't you see your proofs at the office ?

TOM. I'm in full fig, and can't stew in that atmosphère of steam and copperas.

     Enter PRINTER'S BOY, C. ; *he goes up to* TOM *at head of* R. *table. Enter* WAITER, *with tray, hot-water jug, &c. ; he gives change in silver to* MAKVICZ, *who crosses to* SCARGIL. WAITER *puts hot-water jug and whisky before* TOM, *and exits,* C. *door.*

DR. M. Here ! *(giving two half-crowns to* SCARGIL*)* Scargil !

SCARG. *(crossing in same manner to* O'SULLIVAN*)* Here, O'Sullivan. .

O'SULL. *(crossing to* BRADLEY*)* Here, Bradley.

BRAD. *(crossing to* MACUSQUEBAUGH*)* Here, Mac.

MACU. *(crossing to* TOM*)* Here, Tom.

PRINTER'S BOY. *(to* TOM*)* Please, sir, Mr. Duval said would you add this to it ? *(giving* TOM *a proof slip)*

TOM. All right—wait outside—I'll bring it to you.

                     Exit BOY, C.

TOM. *(draws writing pad towards him, takes his grog, and is about to pour hot water from pewter jug into it, when he burns his fingers, starts up and dances)* Confound it !

ALL. What's the matter?

TOM. I've scalded my fingers with the hot water.

SIDNEY. (*taking up pen*) Here, I'll correct it for you.

TOM. Thank you.

O'SULL. Gintlemen, proceed with the harmony. Mr. Stylus——

TOM. One minute. (*to* SIDNEY) Just add this to it. (SIDNEY *sits down to write,* TOM *standing over him, reading slip*) "Fashionable Intelligence.—We hear a marriage is on the tapis between Mr. John Chodd, Junior, son of the celebrated millionaire, and Miss Maud Hetherington, daughter of the late Colonel Hetherington."

(SIDNEY *starts*)

TOM. What's the matter?

SIDNEY. Nothing!

(*he goes on writing*—O'SULLIVAN *taps hammer*)

TOM. (*speaking*) Amatory :——

(*sings*) When woman, lovely woman sighs,
You praise her form, her hair, her eyes;
Would link your heart by tend'rest ties,
   And vow your vows are true.
She answers tenderly and low,
Though from her lips the words that flow,
So softly sweet, are nought we know
   But cock-a-doodle-doo!

&c., &c., &c.

TOM *throws the five shillings to* SIDNEY, *which rattle on the table.* SIDNEY *gives him back the proof; his face is deadly pale; as his head falls on the table the Chorus is singing,* "Cock-a-doodle-doo," &c.— *closed in.*

SCENE II. — *A Retiring Room at* SIR FARINTOSH FADILEAF'S (*2nd grooves*); *large archway or alcove,* L., *with curtain drawn or doors leading to ballroom; small arch or alcove,* R., *leading to supper-room, with drawn curtain; centre opening curtains drawn; the room is decorated for a ball; candelabra, flowers. &c.**

"LADY P. (*without*) Very pretty—very pretty indeed, "Sir Farintosh; all very nice."

* The lines between inverted commas can be omitted.

LADY PTARMIGANT *enters from* R., *with* "SIR
FARINTOSH," LORD PTARMIGANT, *and* MAUD, *all in
evening dress.*

"SIR F. (*an old beau*) So kind of you, Cousin
"Ptarmigant, to take pity on a poor old widower, who has
" no womankind to receive for him, and all that.

" LADY P. Not at all—not at all ; I am only too glad
" to be useful."

LORD P. (*speaking off*, R 1 E,) Bring chairs.

LADY P. Ferdinand, you can't want to go to sleep
again !

LORD P. I know I can't, but I do.

(SERVANT *brings two chairs and a small table*, R.)

LADY P. Besides I don't want chairs here, young men
get lolling about, and then they don't dance. (LORD
PTARMIGANT *sits*, R., *and closes his eyes*) "Farintosh,
" (*knocks heard*) the arrivals are beginning.

"SIR F. But, Lady Ptarmigant, if——

" LADY P. Remember that the old Dowager Countess
"of McSwillumore has plenty of whisky toddy in a green
"glass, to make believe hock.

" SIR F. But if——

LADY P. "Now go. Oh dear me ! (*almost forces* SIR
FARINTOSH *off*, L.") Now, Maud, one word with you ; you
have been in disgrace all this last week about that writing
fellow.

MAUD. (L., *indignant*) What writing fellow ?

LADY P. Don't echo me if you please. You know who
I mean—Daryl !

MAUD. Mr. Daryl is a relation of your ladyship's—the
son of the late Sir Percy Daryl, and brother of the present
Baronet.

LADY P. (R.) And when the present Baronet, that
precious Percy, squandered everything at the gaming table,
dipped the estates, and ruined himself, Sidney gave up the
money left him by his mother, to reinstate a dissolute
beggared brother ! I don't forget that.

MAUD. (*with exultation*) I do not forget it, I never
shall. To give up all his fortune, to ruin his bright
prospects to preserve his brother, and his brother's wife and
children, to keep unsullied the honour of his name, was an
act——

LADY P. Of a noodle, and now he hasn't a penny save
what he gets by scribbling—a pretty pass for a man of
family to come to. You are my niece, and it is my solemn

duty to get you married if I can. Don't thwart me, and I
will. Leave sentiment to servant wenches who sweetheart
the policemen ; it's unworthy of a lady. I've a man in my
eye—a rich one—young Chodd.

MAUD. (*with repugnance*) Such a commonplace person.

LADY B. With a very uncommonplace purse. He will
have eighteen thousand a year. I have desired him to pay
you court, and I desire you to receive it.

MAUD. He is so vulgar.

LADY P. He is so rich. When he is your husband put
him in a back study, and don't show him.

MAUD. But I detest him.

LADY P. What on earth has that to do with it ? You
wouldn't love a man before you were married to him, would
you ? Where are your principles ? Ask my lord how I
treated him before our marriage. (*hitting* LORD PTARMIGANT
with her fan) Ferdinand !

LORD P. (*awaking*) My love !

LADY P. Do keep awake.

LORD P. 'Pon my word you were making such a noise
I thought I was in the House of Commons. (*with fond
regret*) I used to be allowed to sleep so comfortably there.

LADY P. Are you not of opinion that a match between
Mr. Chodd and Maud would be most desirable.

LORD P. (*looking at* LADY PTARMIGANT) Am I not of
opinion—my opinion—what is my opinion ?

LADY P. (*hitting him with fan*) Yes, of course.

LORD P. Yes—of course—my opinion is yes, of course.
(*aside, crossing c. with chair*) Just as it used to be in the
House. I always roused in time to vote as I was told to.

MAUD. But, uncle, one can't purchase happiness at shops
in packets, like bon-bons. A thousand yards of lace cost so
much, they can be got at the milliner's ; but an hour of
home or repose can only be had for love. Mere wealth——

LORD P. My dear, wealth, if it does not bring happiness,
brings the best imitation of it procurable for money.
There are two things—wealth and poverty. The former
makes the world a place to live in ; the latter a place to
—go to sleep in—as I do. (*leans back in chair and dozes*)

" *Enter* SIR FARINTOSH, COLONEL BROWSER, *and* LORD
            CLOUDWRAYS, L.C.

" SIR F. Have you heard the news ? The division is to
" come off to-night. Many men won't be able to come.
" I must be off to vote. If the Ministry go out——

"Col. B. They won't go out—there'll be a dissolution !

"Sir F. And I shall have to go down to be re-elected.
"Cloudwrays, will you come and vote?

"Lord C. (languidly) No.

"Sir F. Why not?

"Lord C. I'm dying for a weed.

"Sir F. You can smoke in the smoking-room !

"Lord C. So I can—that didn't occur to me !

"Sir F. Ptarmigant, cousin, you do the honours for me.
"My country calls, you know, and all that. Come on,
"Cloudwrays ; how slow you are. Hi, tobacco !

> "Cloudwrays *rouses himself. Exeunt* Sir Farin-
> "tosh *and* Lord Cloudwrays. Lord Ptarmigant
> "*dozes.*

> "Col. B. (*who has been talking to* Lady Ptarmigant,
> "*turns to* Lord Ptarmigant) As I was saying to her
> "ladyship——

"Lady P. Ferdinand, do wake up !

"Lord P. Hear, hear ! (*waking*) My dear ! "

> *Enter* Servant, r. 1 e.

Page. Mr. Chodd, Mr. John Chodd, and Mr. Stylus.

Enter Chodd, Jun., Chodd, Sen. *and* Tom, r. 1 e. *Exit*
Servant, r. 1 e.

Lady P. (l.c.) My dear Mr. Chodd, how late you are !
Maud dear, here is Mr. Chodd. Do you know we were
going to scold you, you naughty men !

Chodd, Sen. (r.c., *astonished, aside*) Naughty men !
Johnny, her ladyship says we're naughty men; we've
done something wrong !

Chodd, Jun. (r.) No, no—it's only her ladyship's
patrician fun. Don't call me Johnny. I'm sure I hurried
here on the wings of—(*crossing* l.c., *falls over* Lord
Ptarmigant's *feet, who rises and turns his chair the
reverse way ;* Chodd *seeing* Maud, *repellant*)—a brougham
and pair. Lady Ptarmigant, let me introduce a friend
of mine. Lady Ptarmigant—Mr. Stylus, whom I took
the liberty of——

Lady P. (r.c.) Charmed to see any friend of yours !

> Tom *advances from back,* r., *abashed ; as he is back-
> ing and bowing he falls over* Lord Ptarmigant's
> *legs ;* Lord Ptarmigant *rises with a look of annoy-
> ance ; they bow ;* Lord Ptarmigant *again turns
> chair and sits.*

"Lady P. Mr. Chodd, take me to the ballroom. (Chodd

SEN., *offers his arm*) You will look after Maud, I'm sure.
(*to* CHODD, JUN., *who smilingly offers his arm to* MAUD,
who, with a suppressed look of disgust, takes it) Mr. Si-len-us.

"TOM. Stylus—ma'am—my lady.

"LADY P. Stylus — pardon me — will you be kind
"enough to keep my lord awake? (*significantly*) Maud!
"Now, dear Mr. Chodd.

"CHODD, JUN. Guv!

> "*Exeunt* LADY PTARMIGANT, MAUD, *and the*
> CHODDS, L.

"TOM. (*aside*) These are two funny old swells!

"COL. B. Odd looking fellow. (*to* TOM) Nice place this!

"TOM. Very.

"COL. B. And charming man, Fadileaf.

"TOM. Very. I don't know him, but I should say he
"must be very jolly.

"COL. B. (*laughing*) Bravo! Why you're a wit!

"TOM. Yes! (*aside*) What does he mean?

"COL. B. (*offering box*) Snuff? Who's to win the Leger?
"Diadeste?

"TOM. I don't know—not in my department.

"COL. B. (*laughing*) Very good.

"TOM. What is? (*innocently*)

"COL. B. You are. Do you play whist?

"TOM. Yes; cribbage, and all fours, likewise.

"COL B. We'll find another man, and make up a rubber.

"TOM. (*pointing to* LORD PTARMIGANT *asleep*) He'll do
"for dummy.

"COL. B. (*laughing*) Capital!

"TOM. What a queer fellow this is—he laughs at
"everything I say. (*dance music*)

"COL. B. They've begun.

"TOM. (*waking up* LORD PTARMIGANT) My lady said
"I was to keep you awake.

"LORD P. Thank you.

"COL. B. Come and have a rubber! Let's go and look
"up Chedbury.

"LORD P. Yes.

"COL. B. (*to* TOM) You'll find us in the card-room.

> "*Exeunt* LORD PTARMIGANT *and* COLONEL
> BROWSER, L."

[NOTE.—*If preceding lines be omitted, the following sentence and
business,*]

LADY P. Ferdinand! (*going up* C. *to* LORD PTARMIGANT,

who awakes) Do rouse yourself, and follow me to the ball-room.

> *Exeunt all but* Tom, L. 2 E. Lord Ptarmigant
> *returns, and drags chair off after him.*

Tom. Here I am in society, and I think society is rather slow; it's much jollier at the "Owl," and there's more to drink. If it were not wicked to say it, how I should enjoy a glass of gin and water!

> *Enter* Lady Ptarmigant, L.

Lady P. (L.) Mr. Si-len-us!

Tom. (L., *abashed*) Stylus, ma'am—my lady!

Lady P. Stylus! I beg pardon. You're all alone.

Tom. With the exception of your ladyship!

Lady P. All the members have gone down to the House to vote, and we are dreadfully in want of men—I mean dancers! You dance, of course?

Tom. Oh! of course—I—— (*abashed*)

Lady P. As it is Leap-year, I may claim the privilege of asking you to see me through a quadrille!

Tom. (R., *frightened*) My lady! I——

Lady P. (L., *aside*) He's a friend of the Chodds, and it will please them. Come then. (*she takes his arm; sniffing*) Dear me! What a dreadful smell of tobacco! (*sniffing*)

Tom. (*awfully self-conscious—sniffing*) Is there?

Lady P. (*sniffing*) Some fellow must have been smoking.

Tom. (*sniffing*) I think some fellow must, or some fellow must have been where some other fellows have been smoking. (*aside*) It's that beastly parlour at the "Owl." (*in taking out his pocket-handkerchief his pipe falls on floor*)

Lady P. What's that?*

Tom. (*in torture*) What's what?

(*turning about and looking through eye-glass at the air*)

Lady B. (*pointing*) That!

Tom. (*as if in doubt*) I rather think—it—is—a pipe!

Lady P. I'm sure of it. You'll join me in the ball-room. (*going up* C. *to* L.)

Tom. Instantly, your ladyship. (*Exit* Lady Ptarmigant, L. *Looking at pipe, he picks it up*) If ever I bring you into society again——(*drops it*) Waiter! (*Enter* Page, R. 1. E.) Somebody's dropped something. Remove the Whatsoname.

---

* This incident is taken from M. Emile Augier's admirable comedy of "Les Effrontés."—T. W. R.

(quadrille music in ballroom; PAGE *goes off,* R. 1. E., *and returns with tray and sugar tongs, with which he picks up pipe with an air of ineffable disgust and goes off,* R. 1. E.) Now to spin round the old woman in the mazy waltz. (*splits kid gloves in drawing them on*) There goes one-and-nine.

> *Exit* TOM, L.   *Enter* SIDNEY, L.   *He is pale and excited; one of the gold links of his wrist-band is unfastened.*

SIDNEY. I have seen her—she was smiling—dancing, but not with him. She looked so bright and happy. I won't think of her. How quiet it is here: so different to that hot room, with the crowd of fools and coquettes whirling round each other. I like to be alone—alone! I am now thoroughly—and to think it was but a week ago—one little week—I'll forget her—forget, and ᐟhate her. Hate her—Oh, Maud, Maud, till now, I never knew how much I loved you; loved you—loved you—gone; shattered; shivered; and for whom? For one of my own birth? For one of my own rank? No! for a common clown, who—confound this link—but he is rich—and—it won't hold (*trying to fasten it—his fingers trembling*) I've heard it all—always with her, at the Opera and the Park, attentive and obedient—and she accepts him. My head aches. (*louder*) I'll try a glass of champagne.

TOM. (*without,* R.) Champagne—here you are! (*draws curtain. Enter* TOM, R. 2 E., *with champagne glass from supper-room; portion of supper table seen in alcove; seeing* SIDNEY) Sidney!

SIDNEY. Tom! you here!

TOM. Very much here. (*drinking*) I was brought by Mr. Chodd.

SIDNEY. (L.) Chodd?

TOM. (R.) Don't startle a fella. You look pale—aren't you well?

SIDNEY. (*rallying*) Jolly, never better.

TOM. Have some salmon.

SIDNEY. I'm not hungry.

TOM. Then try some jelly, it's no trouble to masticate and is emollient and agreeable to the throat and palate.

SIDNEY. No, Tom, champagne.

TOM. There you are.   (*fetching bottle from table*)

SIDNEY. I'll meet her eye to ev⸮ (*drinks*) Another, Tom—and be as smiling and indifferent. As for that heavy-metalled dog—thanks, Tom. (*drinks*) Another.

Tom. I've been dancing with old Lady Ptarmigant.

Sidney. Confound her.

Tom. I did. As I was twirling her round I sent my foot through her dress and tore her skirt out of the gathers.

Sidney. (*laughing hysterically*) Good! good! Bravo! Tom! Did she row you?

Tom. Not a bit. She said it was of no consequence; but her looks were awful.

Sidney. Ha! ha! ha! Tom, you're a splendid fellow, not like these damned swells, all waistcoat and shirt front.

Tom. But I like the swells. I played a rubber with them and won three pounds, then I showed them some conjuring tricks—you know I'm a famous conjuror (*taking a pack of cards out of his pocket*) By Jupiter! look here, I've brought the pack away with me; I didn't know I had. I'll go and take it back.

Sidney. (*taking cards from him absently*) No, never mind, stay with me, I don't want you to go.

Tom. I find high life most agreeable, everybody is so amiable, so thoughtful, so full of feeling.

Sidney. Feeling! Why man, this is a flesh market where the match-making mammas and chattering old chaperons have no more sense of feeling than drovers—the girls no more sentiment than sheep, and the best man is the highest bidder; that is, the biggest fool with the longest purse.

Tom. Sidney, you're ill.

Sidney. You lie, Tom—never better—excellent high spirits—confound this link!

Enter Lord Cloudwrays *and* "Sir Farintosh," L.

Lord C. "Sir F." } By Jove! Ha, Sidney, heard the news?

Sidney. (c.) News—there is no news! The times are bankrupt, and the assignees have sold off the events.

Lord C. "Sir F." } The Ministry is defeated.

Tom. (R.) No.

Lord C. "Sir F." } Yes; by a majority of forty-six.

Sidney. Serve them right.

Lord C. "Sir F." } Why?

Sidney. I don't know! Why, what a fellow you are to want reasons.

LORD C. Sidney!

SIDNEY. Hullo, Cloudwrays! my bright young British senator—my undeveloped Chatham, and mature Raleigh.

TOM. Will they resign?

SIDNEY. Of course they will : resignation is the duty of every man, or Minister, who can't do anything else.

TOM. Who will be sent for to form a Government?

SIDNEY. Cloudwrays.

LORD C. How you do chaff a man!

SIDNEY. Why not? Inaugurate a new policy — the policy of smoke—free-trade in tobacco! Go in, not for principles, but for Principes—our hearths—our homes, and 'bacca boxes!

TOM. If there's a general election?

SIDNEY. Hurrah, for a general election! eh, Cloudwrays? —"eh, Farintosh?" What speeches you'll make—what lies you'll tell, and how your constituents *won't* believe you!

LORD C. } How odd you are.
"SIR F."

LORD C. Arn't you well?

SIDNEY. Glorious! only one thing annoys me.

LORD C. } What's that?
"SIR F."

SIDNEY. They won't give me any more champagne.

"*Enter* COLONEL BROWSER, L."

LORD C. } Lady Ptarmigant sent me here to say——
"COL. B. } Farintosh," the ladies want partners.

("COLONEL *and* SIR FARINTOSH *go off*, L.")

SIDNEY. Partners! Here are partners for them—long, tall, stout, fat, thin, poor, rich. (*crossing*, C.) Cloudwrays, you're the man! (*Enter* CHODD, JUN., L. SIDNEY *sees and points to him*) No; this is the man!

CHODD, JUN (L.) Confound this fellow! (*aside*)

SIDNEY. (L.C.) This, sir, is the "Young Lady's Best Companion," well bound, Bramah-locked, and gilt at the edges—mind, gilt only at the edges. This link will *not* hold. (*sees the pack of cards in his hand*) Here, Chodd, take these—no, cut for a ten-pound note.

(*puts cards on small table*, R.)

CHODD, JUN. (L.C., *quickly*) With pleasure. (*aside*) I'll punish this audacious pauper in the pocket.

(*crossing to table*)

LORD C. You mustn't gamble here.

SIDNEY. Only for a frolic!

CHODD, JUN. I'm always lucky at cards!

SIDNEY. Yes, I know an old proverb about that.

CHODD, JUN. Eh?

SIDNEY. (R.) Lucky at play, unlucky in—— This link will not hold.

CHODD, JUN. (L.C., *maliciously*) Shall we put the stakes down first?

SIDNEY. (*producing portmonnaie*) with pleasure!

LORD C. But I don't think it right——

(*advancing*—CHODD, JUN., *stays him with his arm*)

TOM. Sidney!

SIDNEY. Nonsense! hold your tongue, Cloudwrays, and I'll give you a regalia. Let's make it for five-and-twenty?

CHODD, JUN. Done!

SIDNEY. Lowest wins—that's in your favour.

CHODD, JUN. Eh?

SIDNEY. Ace is lowest. (*they cut*) Mine! Double the stakes?

CHODD, JUN. Done! (*they cut*)

SIDNEY. Mine again! Double again?

CHODD, JUN. Done! (*they cut*)

SIDNEY. You're done again! I'm in splendid play to-night. One hundred, I think?

CHODD, JUN. I'd play again (*handing notes*) but I've no more with me.

SIDNEY. Your word's sufficient—you can send to my chambers—besides, you've got your cheque-book. A hundred again?

CHODD, JUN. Yes. (*they cut*)

SIDNEY. Huzzah! Fortune's a lady! Again? (CHODD, JUN., *nods—they cut*) Bravo! Again? (CHODD, JUN., *nods—they cut*) Mine again! Again? (CHODD; JUN., *nods—they cut*) Mine again! Again? (CHODD, JUN., *nods—they cut*) Same result! That makes five! Let's go in for a thousand?

CHODD, JUN. Done!

LORD C. (*advancing*) No!

CHODD, JUN. (*savagely*) Get out of the way! (LORD CLOUDWRAYS *looks at him through eye-glass in astonishment*)

SIDNEY. Pooh! (*they cut*) Mine! Double again?

CHODD, JUN. Yes.

LORD C. (*going round to back of table and seizing the pack*) No; I can't suffer this to go on—Lady Ptarmigant would be awful angry. (*going off*, L.)

SIDNEY. Here, Cloudwrays! What a fellow you are. (*Exit* LORD CLOUDWRAYS, L.C. *Turning to* CHODD, JUN.) You owe me a thousand !

CHODD, JUN. I shall not forget it.

SIDNEY. I don't suppose you will. Confound —— (*trying to button sleeve link, crossing* C.) Oh, to jog your memory, take this.

> *Gives him sleeve link, which he has been trying to button, and goes off after* LORD CLOUDWRAYS, L.C.

CHODD, JUN. And after I have paid you, I'll remember and clear off the old score.

TOM. (R., *taking his arm as he is going*) Going into the ballroom ?

CHODD, JUN. (L., *aghast at his intrusion*) Yes !

TOM. (R.) I'll go with you.

CHODD, JUN. (L., *disengaging his arm*) I'm engaged !

> *Exit* CHODD, JUN., R. *Music till end.*

TOM. You've an engaging manner ! I'm like a donkey between two bundles of hay. On one side woman—lovely woman! on the other, wine and wittles. (*taking out a sovereign*) Heads, supper—tails, the ladies. (*tosses at table*) Supper! sweet goddess Fortune, accept my thanks !

> *Exit into supper-room,* R. *Enter* MAUD *and* CHODD, JUN., L.

MAUD. (L.) This dreadful man follows me about everywhere.

CHODD, JUN. (R.) My dear Miss Hetherington !

MAUD. I danced the last with you.

CHODD, JUN. That was a quadrille. (*Enter* SIDNEY, L.) This is for a polka.

SIDNEY. (*advancing between them*) The lady is engaged to me.

CHODD, JUN. (*aside*) This fellow's turned up again. (*to him*) I beg your pardon.

SIDNEY. I beg yours ! I have a prior claim. (*bitterly*) Ask the lady—or perhaps I had better give her up to you

MAUD. The next dance with you, Mr. Chodd; this. one——

CHODD, JUN. Miss, your commands are Acts of Parliament. (*looking spitefully at* SIDNEY *as he crosses,* L.) I'll go and see what Lady Ptarmigant has to say to this.

> *Exit* CHODD, JUN. *Music changes to a slow waltz.*

SIDNEY. Listen to me for the last time. My life and

being were centred in you. You have abandoned me for money! You accepted me ; you now throw me off, for money! You gave your hand, you now retract, for money! You are about to wed—a knave, a brute, a fool, whom in your own heart you despise, for money!

MAUD. How dare you?

SIDNEY. Where falsehood is, shame cannot be. The last time we met (*producing ribbon*) you gave me this. See, 'tis the colour of a man's heart's blood. (*curtains or doors at back draw apart*) I give it back to you. (*casting the bunch of ribbon at her feet.* LORD CLOUDWRAYS, "SIR FARINTOSH, COLONEL BROWSER," TOM, LORD PTARMIGANT, *and* LADY PTARMIGANT, CHODD, JUN., *and* CHODD, SEN., *appear at back.* GUESTS *seen in ballroom*) And tell you, shameless girl, much as I once loved, and adored, I now despise and hate you.

LADY P. (*advancing, c., in a whisper to* SIDNEY) Leave the house, sir! How dare you—go!

SIDNEY. Yes ; anywhere.

> *Crash of music.* MAUD *is nearly falling when* CHODD, JUN., *appears near her ; she is about to lean on his arm, but recognising him, retreats and staggers.* SIDNEY *is seen to reel through ballroom full of dancers. Drop.*

GUESTS.

SIDNEY.

CLOUDWRAYS.   " SIR F."

TOM.   " COL. B."

LORD PTARMIGANT.   CHODD SEN

LADY PTARMIGANT.   CHODD, JUN.   MAUD.

END OF ACT II.

ACT III.

SCENE I.—*The "Owl's Roost." (same as Scene 1, Act II.) Daylight ; the room in order.* TOM *discovered writing at table,* R. BOY *sitting on table,* L., *and holding the placard on which is printed*—" *Read the 'Morning Earthquake'—a first-class daily paper,"* &c. *On the other,* " *The 'Evening Earthquake'—a first-class daily paper—Latest Intelligence,"* &c.

TOM. Um ! It'll look well on the walls, and at the railway stations. Take these back to the office (BOY *jumps down*)—to Mr. Piker, and tell him he must wait for the last leader—till it's written. (*Exit* BOY, C.) TOM *walks to and fro, smoking long clay pipe*) The M.E.—that is, the " Morning Earthquake," shakes the world for the first time to-morrow morning, and everything seems to have gone wrong with it. It is a crude, unmanageable, ill-disciplined, ill-regulated earthquake. Heave the first—Old Chodd behaves badly to me. After organising him a first-rate earthquake, engaging him a brilliant staff, and stunning reporters, he doesn't even offer me the post of sub-editor—ungrateful old humbug ! Heave the second—No sooner is he engaged than our editor is laid up with the gout ; and then Old Chodd asks me to be a literary warming-pan, and keep his place hot, till colchicum and cold water have done their work. I'll be even with Old Chodd, though ! I'll teach him what it is to insult a man who has started eighteen daily and weekly papers—all of them failures. Heave the third—Sidney Daryl won't write the social leaders.. (*sits* L., *at end of table*) Poor Sidney ! (*takes out the magenta ribbon which he picked up at the ball*) I shan't dare to give him this—I picked it up at the ball, at which I was one of the distinguished and illustrious guests. Love is an awful swindler—always drawing upon Hope, who never honours his drafts—a sort of whining beggar, continually moved on by the maternal police. But 'tis a weakness to which the wisest of us are subject—a kind of manly measles which this flesh is heir to, particularly when the flesh is heir to nothing ·else—even I have felt the divine damnation—I mean emanation. But the lady united herself to another, which was a very good thing for me, and anything but misfortune for her. Ah! happy days of youth!—Oh! flowing fields of Runnington-cum-Wapshot—where the yellow corn waved, our young loves ripened, and the new gaol now stands. Oh! Sally, when I think of you and the past, I feel that (*looking into his pot*) the pot's empty, and I could drink another pint. (*putting the ribbon in his pocket*) Poor Sidney—I'm afraid he's going to the bad. (*Enter* SIDNEY, C.; *he strikes bell on* L. *table and sits at the head, his appearance altered*). Ha! Sid, is that you? Talk of the——how d'e do?

SIDNEY. Quite well—how are you?

TOM. I'm suffering from an earthquake in my head, and a general printing office in my stomach. Have some beer?

Enter WAITER, C.

SIDNEY. No thanks—brandy——

TOM. So early?

SIDNEY. And soda. I didn't sleep last night.

TOM. Brandy and soda, and beer again.

Exit WAITER, *with pint pot off* R. *table.*

SIDNEY. I never do sleep now—I can't sleep.

TOM. Work hard.

Enter WAITER, C.

SIDNEY. I do—it is my only comfort—my old pen goes driving along, at the rate of——(WAITER *after placing pint of porter before* TOM, *places tray with brandy and soda before* SIDNEY) That's right! (WAITER *uncorks and exits*, C.) What a splendid discovery was brandy. (*drinks*)

TOM. Yes, the man who invented it deserves a statue.

SIDNEY. That's the reason that he doesn't get one.

TOM. (*reading paper*) "Election intelligence." There's the general election—why not go in for that.

SIDNEY. Election—pooh! what do I care for that!

TOM. Nothing, of course, but it's occupation.

SIDNEY. (*musing*) I wonder who'll put up for Springmead!

TOM. Your brother's seat, wasn't it?

SIDNEY. Yes, our family's for years. By-the-way, I'd a letter from Percy last mail; he's in trouble, poor fellow—his little boy is dead, and he himself is in such ill-health that they have given him sick leave. We are an unlucky race, we Daryls. Sometimes, Tom, I wish that I were dead.

TOM. Sidney!

SIDNEY. It's a bad wish, I know; but what to me is there worth living for?

TOM. What! oh, lots of things. Why, there's the police reports—mining intelligence—hop districts—the tallow market—ambition—Society!

SIDNEY. (*heartily*) Damn Society!

TOM. And you know, Sid, there are more women in the world than one.

SIDNEY. But only one a man can love.

TOM. I don't know about that; temperaments differ.

SIDNEY. (*pacing about and reciting*) " As the husband, so the wife is."

" Thou art mated to a clown :
    And the grossness of his nature
Shall have power to drag thee down ;
    He will hold thee when his passion
Shall have spent its novel force,
    Something better than his dog, and
Little dearer than his horse."

I'm ashamed of such a want of spirit—ashamed to be such a baby ! And you, Tom, are the only man in the world I'd show it to; but I—I can think of nothing else but her —and—and of the fate in store for her.

(*sobs and leans on table with his face in his hands*)

TOM. Don't give way, Sid; there are plenty of things in this life to care for.

SIDNEY. Not for me—not for me.

TOM. Oh, yes! there's friendship; and—and—the little girl, you know !

SIDNEY. That reminds me, I wrote a week ago to Mrs. Churton, asking her to meet me with Mau——with the little darling in the square. I always asked them to come from Hampstead to the square, that I might look up at her window as I passed. What a fool I've been—I can't meet them this morning ! Will you go for me?

TOM. With pleasure.

SIDNEY. Give Mrs. Churton this. (*wrapping up money in paper from* TOM's *case*) It's the last month's money. Tell her I'm engaged, and can't come—and—(*putting down money*) buy the baby a toy, bless her ! What a pity to think she'll grow to be a woman !

Enter MacUSQUEBAUGH, O'SULLIVAN, *and* MAKVICZ.

MacU. (*entering*) A three of whisky, hot !

O'Sull. The same for me—neat.

Dr. M. A pint of stoot. (*all sit,* R.)

O'Sull. Tom, mee boy, what news of the "Earthquake"?

Enter Waiter *with orders, and gives* Tom *a note.*

Tom. Heaving, sir—heaving. (Tom *opens note;* Sidney *sits abstracted*) Who's going electioneering?

Dr. M. I am.

O'Sull. And I.

MacU. And so am I.

Tom. Where?

Mac.U. I don't know.

O'Sull. Somewhere—anywhere.

Tom. (*reading note*) From Chodd, Senior—the old villain! (*reads*) "Dear Sir,—Please meet me at Lady Ptarmigant's at eleven p.m." (*suddenly*) Sidney!

Sidney. (*moodily*) What?

Tom. (*reading note*) "I am off to Springmead-le-Beau by the train at two-fifty. My son, Mr. John Chodd, Junior, is the candidate for the seat for the borough."

Sidney. (*rising*) What!—that hound!—that cur!— that digesting cheque-book—represent the town that my family have held their own for centuries. I'd sooner put up for it myself. (*rising*)

Tom. (*rising*) Why not? Daryl for Springmead— here's occupation—here's revenge!

Sidney. By heaven, I will!

(*crosses to* R., *and returns*)

Tom. (c.) Gentlemen, the health of Mr. Daryl, M.P. for Springmead. (Sidney *crosses to* L.)

Omnes. (*rising and drinking*) Hurrah!

Tom. We'll canvass for you. (*aside*) And now, Mr. Chodd, Senior, I see the subject for the last leader. I'll fetter you with your own type. (*down,* L.)

Sidney. (*crosses,* c.) I'll do it! I'll do it! When does the next train start?

MacU. (*taking "Bradshaw" from table,* R.) At two-fifty—the next at five.

Sidney. (*crossing to* L.) Huzza! (*with excitement*) I'll rouse up the tenants—call on the tradesmen!

(*crossing to* c.)

O'Sull. But the money?

Sidney. (c.) I'll fight him with the very thousand that

I won of him.   Besides, what need has a Daryl of money at Springmead ?

TOM. We can write for you.

O'SULL. (R.C.) And fight for you.

SIDNEY. I feel so happy—Call cabs.

MACU. How many ?

SIDNEY. The whole rank !   (*goes up*, C.)

TOM. But, Sidney, what colours shall we fight under ?

SIDNEY. What colours? (*feels in his breast and appears dejected;* TOM *hands him the ribbons; he clutches them eagerly*) What colours ?   Magenta !

OMNES. Huzzah !   (*closed in as they go up*)

O'SULLIVAN.   SIDNEY.

MACUSQUEBAUGH.

MAKVICZ.

R.   L.

SCENE II. — *An Apartment at* LORD PTARMIGANT'S.   (*1st grooves*)

LADY P. (*without,* L. 1 E.) Good-bye, dear Mr. Chodd. A pleasant ride, and all sorts of success. (*Enter* LADY PTARMIGANT, L. 1 E.) Phew ! there's the old man gone. Now to speak to that stupid Maud. (*looking off,* R.) There she sits in the sulks—a fool ! Ah, what wise folks the French were before the Revolution, when there was a Bastille or a convent in which to pop dangerous young men and obstinate young women. (*sweetly*) Maud dear ! I'll marry her to young Chodd, I'm determined.

Enter MAUD, R. 1 E., *very pensive.*

LADY P. Maud, I wish to speak to you.

MAUD. Upon what subject, aunt ?

LADY P. (L.) One that should be very agreeable to a girl of your age—marriage.

MAUD. (R.) Mr. Chodd again ?

LADY P. Yes, Mr. Chodd again.

MAUD. I hate him !

LADY P. You wicked thing ! How dare you use such expressions in speaking of a young gentleman so rich ?

MAUD. Gentleman !

LADY P. Yes, gentleman !—at least he will be.

MAUD. Nothing can make Mr. Chodd—what a name !— anything but what he is.

LADY P. Money can do everything.

MAUD. Can it make me love a man I hate?

LADY P. Yes; at least, if it don't, it ought   I suppose you mean to marry somebody?

MAUD. No.

LADY P. You audacious girl! How can you talk so wickedly? Where do you expect to go to?

MAUD. To needlework! Anything from this house; and from this persecution.

LADY P. Miss Hetherington!

MAUD. Thank you, Lady Ptarmigant, for calling me by my name; it reminds me who I am, and of my dead father, "Indian Hetherington," as he was called. It reminds me that the protection you have offered to his orphan daughter has been hourly embittered by the dreadfu temper, which is an equal affliction to you as to those within your reach. It reminds me that the daughter of such a father should not stoop to a mésalliance. *(crossing to* L.)

LADY P. Mésalliance! How dare you call Mr. Chodd a mésalliance? And you hankering after that paltry, poverty-stricken, penny-a-liner?

MAUD. Lady Ptarmigant, you forget yourself; and you are untruthful. Mr. Daryl is a gentleman by birth and breeding! I loved him—I acknowledge it—I love him still!

LADY P. You shameless girl! and he without a penny! After the scene he made!

MAUD. He has dared to doubt me, and I have done with him for ever. For the moment he presumed to think that I could break my plighted word—that I could be false to the love I had acknowledged—the love that was my happiness and pride—all between us is over.

LADY P. *(aside)* That's some comfort. *(aloud* Then what do you intend to do?

MAUD. I intend to leave the house.

LADY P. To go where?

MAUD. Anywhere from you!

LADY P. Upon my word! *(aside)* She has more spirit than I gave her credit for. *(aloud)* And do you mean to tell me that that letter is not intended for that fellow Daryl?

MAUD. *(giving letter)* Read it.

LADY P. *(opens it and reads)* "To the Editor of the 'Times.' Please insert the enclosed advertisement, for which I send stamps. Wanted a situation as governess by" ——*(embracing* MAUD) Oh, my dear—dear girl! you couldn't think of such a thing—and you a lady, and my niece.

MAUD. (*disengaging herself*) Lady Ptarmigant, please don't!

LADY P. (*thoroughly subdued*) But, my love, how could I think——

MAUD. What Lady Ptarmigant thinks is a matter of the most profound indifference to me.

LADY P. (*aside*) Bless her! Exactly what I was at her age. (*aloud*) But, my dear Maud, what is to become of you?

MAUD. No matter what: welcome poverty—humiliation —insult—the contempt of fools—welcome all but dependence! I will neither dress myself at the expense of a man I despise, control his household, owe him duty, or lead a life that is a daily lie; neither will I marry one I love, who has dared to doubt me, to drag him into deeper poverty.

(*crossing to* R.)

Enter SERVANT, L.1 E.

SERVANT. My Lady, there is a gentleman inquiring for Mr. Chodd.

LADY P. Perhaps some electioneering friend. Show him here. (*Exit* SERVANT) Don't leave the room, Maud, dear.

MAUD. I was not going—why should I?

SERVANT *shows in* TOM *with* LITTLE MAUD, L.1 E.

LADY P. It's the tobacco man!

TOM. (*to* CHILD) Do I smell of smoke? I beg your lady-ship's pardon, but Mr. Chodd, the old gentleman, wished me to meet him here.

LADY P. He has just driven off to the station.

TOM. I know I'm a few minutes behind time—there's the young lady. Good morning, Miss—Miss—I don't know the rest of her—I—I—have been detained by the—this little girl——

LADY P. (C.) A sweet little creature, Mr. Silenus.

TOM. (L.) Stylus.

LADY P. Stylus, pardon me.

TOM. (*aside*) This old lady will insist on calling me Silenus! She'd think me very rude if I called her Ariadne.

LADY P. Sweet little thing! Come here, my dear! (LITTLE MAUD *crosses to her*) Your child, Mr.—Stylus?

TOM. No, my lady, this is Mr. Sidney Daryl's protégé.

LADY P. (*moving from* LITTLE MAUD) Whose?

TOM. Sidney Daryl's   (MAUD *advances*)

LADY P. Nasty little wretch! How do you mean? Speak, quickly!

TOM. I mean that Sidney pays for her education, board, and all that. Oh, he's a splendid fellow—a heart of gold! (*aside*) I'll put in a good word for him, as his young woman's here. I'll make her repent!

MAUD. (R.) Come to me, child. (LITTLE MAUD *crosses to her*) Who are you?

L. MAUD. I'm Mrs. Churton's little darling, and Mr. Daryl's little girl.

Crosses to TOM, *as* MAUD *moves away.*

LADY P. (C.) His very image.   (*goes to* MAUD)

TOM. (L.) Bless her little tongue! I took her from the woman who takes care of her. She's going down with me to Springmead. I've bought her a new frock, all one colour, magenta. (*aside*) That was strong.

LADY P. Did I tell you Mr. Chodd had gone?

TOM. I'm one too many here. I'll vamose! Good morning, my lady.

LADY P. Good morning, Mr.—Bacchus.

TOM. Stylus—Stylus! I shall have to call her Ariadne. Um! they might have asked the child to have a bit of currant cake, or a glass of currant wine. Shabby devils!

Exeunt TOM *and* LITTLE MAUD, L. 1 E. *A pause.*

LADY P. (*aside*) Could anything have happened more delightfully?

MAUD. (*throwing herself into* LADY PTARMIGANT'S *arms*) Oh, aunty! forgive me—I was wrong—I was ungrateful—forgive me! Kiss me, and forgive me! I'll marry Mr. Chodd—anybody—do with me as you please.

LADY P. My dear niece! (*affected*) I—I—feel for you. I'm—I'm not so heartless as I seem. I know I'm a harsh, severe old woman, but I am a woman, and I can feel for you.   (*embracing her*)

MAUD. And to think that with the same breath he could swear that he loved me, while another—this child, too! (*bursts into a flood of tears*) There, aunt, I won't cry. I'll dry my eyes—I'll do your bidding. You mean me well, while he—oh! (*shudders*) Tell Mr. Chodd I'll bear his name, and bear it worthily!   (*sternly*)

LADY P. (*embracing—kissing her at each stop*) Men are a set of brutes. I was jilted myself when I was twenty-three—and, oh, how I loved the fellow! But I asserted my dignity, and married Lord Ptarmigant, and *he*, and *he* only, can tell you how I have avenged my sex! Cheer up,

my darling ! love, sentiment, and romance are humbug !—
but wealth, position, jewels, balls, presentations, a country
house, town mansion, society, power—that's true, solid
happiness, and if it isn't, <u>I don't know what is</u>?

Exeunt, R. 1 E.

SCENE III.—*The Wells at Springmead-le-Beau.   An avenue
of elms, sloping off to* R.U.E., *on* L. *House with windows,
&c., on to lawn; railings at back of stage.   Garden
seats, chairs, lounges, small tables, &c., discovered near
house,* L.   LORD PTARMIGANT *discovered asleep in garden
chair against house,* L., *his feet resting on another.
Enter* CHODD, SEN., *down avenue,* R.

CHODD, SEN. Oh, dear ! oh, dear ! What a day this is !
There's Johnny to be elected, and I'm expecting the first
copy of the "Morning Earthquake"—my paper ! my own
paper !—by the next train.   Then here's Lady Ptarmigant
says that positively her niece will have Johnny for her
wedded husband, and in one day my Johnny is to be a husband, an M.P., and part proprietor of a daily paper ! Whew !
how hot it is ! It's lucky that the wells are so near the
hustings—one can run under the shade and get a cooler.
Here's my lord ! (*waking him*) My lord !

LORD P. (*waking*) Oh ! eh ! Mr. Chodd—good morning !—how d'e do ?

CHODD, SEN. (*sitting on stool,* L.) Oh, flurried, and
flustered, and worritted. You know to-day's the election.

LORD P. Yes, I believe there is an election going
on somewhere. (*calling*) A tumbler of the waters No. 2.

Enter WAITRESS *from house,* L., *places tumbler of
water on table, and exits.*

CHODD, SEN. Oh, what a blessing there is no opposition !
If my boy is returned——   (*rising*)

Enter CHODD, JUN., *agitated, a placard in his hand,*
R. 2 E.

CHODD, JUN. Look here, guv ! look here !

CHODD, SEN. What is it, my Johnny !

CHODD, JUN. Don't call me Johnny ! Look here ! (*shows
electioneering placard,* "Vote for Daryl !")

CHODD, SEN. What ?

CHODD, JUN. That vagabond has put up as candidate ?
His brother used to represent the borough.

CHODD, SEN. Then the election will be contested ?
CHODD, JUN. Yes.

(CHODD, SEN., *sinks on garden chair*)

LORD P. (*rising, and taking tumbler from table*) Don't annoy yourself, my dear Mr. Chodd ; these accidents will happen in the best regulated constituencies.

CHODD, JUN Guv, don't be a fool !

LORD P. Try a glass of the waters.

> CHODD, SEN., *takes tumbler and drinks, and the next moment ejects the water with a grimace, stamping about.*

CHODD, SEN. Oh, what filth ! O-o-o-o-oh !

LORD P. It is an acquired taste. (*to* WAITER) Another tumbler of No. 2.

CHODD, SEN. So, Johnny, there's to be a contest, and you won't be M.P. for Springmead after all.

CHODD, JUN I don't know that.

CHODD, SEN. What d'ye mean ?

CHODD, JUN. Mr. Sidney Daryl may lose, and, perhaps, Mr. Sidney Daryl mayn't show. After that ball——

CHODD, SEN. Where you lost that thousand pounds ?

CHODD, JUN. Don't keep bringing that up, guv'nor. After that I bought up all Mr. Daryl's bills—entered up judgment, and left them with Aaron. I've telegraphed to London, and if Aaron don't nab him in town he'll catch him here.

CHODD, SEN. But, Johnny, isn't that rather mean ?

CHODD, JUN. All's fair in love and Parliament.

Enter COUNTRY BOY *with newspaper*, R. 1 E.

BOY. Mr. Chodd ?

CHODD, SEN. }
CHODD, JUN. } Here !

BOY. Just arrived.

CHODD, JUN. The " Morning Earthquake."

> *They both clutch at it eagerly ; each secures a paper, and sit under tree*, R.

CHODD, SEN. (R., *reading*) Look at the leader. " In the present aspect of European politics——"

CHODD, JUN. (L.) " Some minds seem singularly obtuse to the perception of an idea."

CHODD, SEN. Johnny !

CHODD, JUN. Guv !

3 B

CHODD, SEN. Do you see the last leader?

CHODD, JUN. Yes.

CHODD, SEN. (*reading*) " The borough of Springmead-le-Beau has for centuries been represented by the house of Daryl."

CHODD, JUN. (*reading*) "A worthy scion of that ancient race intends to offer himself as candidate at the forthcoming election, and, indeed, who will dare to oppose him?"

CHODD, SEN. " Surely not a Mister——"

CHODD, JUN. " Chodd."   (*they rise and come down*)

CHODD, SEN. " Whoever he may be."

CHODD, JUN. " What are the Choddian antecedents?"

CHODD, SEN. " Whoever heard of Chodd?"

CHODD, JUN. " To be sure, a.young man of that name has recently been the cause of considerable laughter at the clubs on account of his absurd attempts to become a man of fashion."   (*both crossing* L. *and* R.)

CHODD, SEN. (R.) " And to wriggle himself into Society."   (*crossing again*)

CHODD, JUN. (R.) Why, it's all in his favour.

(*in a rage*)

CHODD, SEN. In your own paper, too! Oh, that villain Stylus!   (*crossing* R.)

CHODD, JUN. (*crossing* R.) There are no more of these in the town, are there?

BOY. Yes, sir. A man came down with two thousand; he's giving them away everywhere.

CHODD, JUN. Confound you!

(*pushes him off,* R. 1 E.—*follows*)

CHODD, SEN. Oh, dear! oh, dear! oh, dear! Now, my lord, isn't that too bad. (*sees him asleep*) He's off again! (*waking him*) My lord, here's the " Earthquake"!

(*half throwing him off his seat*)

LORD P. Earthquake! Good gracious! I didn't feel anything.   (*rising*)

CHODD, SEN. No, no, the paper.

LORD P. Ah, most interesting. (*drops paper, and leisurely reseats himself*) My dear Mr. Chodd, I congratulate you.

CHODD, SEN. Congratulate me? (*looks at watch*) I must be off to the committee.   *Exit* CHODD, SEN., L. 2 E.

LORD P. Waiter! am I to have that tumbler of No. 2?

*Band heard playing "Conquering Hero," and loud
cheers as* LORD PTARMIGANT *goes into house,* L., *and
enter* SIDNEY, O'SULLIVAN, MACUSQUEBAUGH, *and*
DR. MAKVICZ, R.U.E. SIDNEY *bowing off as he
enters. Cheers.*

SIDNEY. So far so good. I've seen lots of faces that I
knew. I'll run this Dutch-metalled brute hard, and be in
an honourable minority anyhow.

Enter TOM, *hastily,* R. 1 E.

TOM. Daryl.
SIDNEY. Yes.
TOM. Look out.
SIDNEY. What's the matter?
TOM. I met our friend Moses Aaron on the platform.
He didn't see you, but what does he want here?
SIDNEY. Me, if anybody. (*musing*) This is a shaft from
the bow of Mr. John Chodd, Junior. I see his aim.
TOM. What's to be done? The voters are warm, but,
despite the prestige of the family name, if you were not
present——
SIDNEY. Besides, I couldn't be returned from Cursitor
Street, M.P. for the Queen's Bench (*thinking*) Did the
Lamb come down with us?
TOM. Yes—second class.
SIDNEY. Let him stop the bailiffs—Aaron is as timid as
a girl. I'll go through here, and out by the grand entrance.
Let in the Lamb, and——
TOM. I see.
SIDNEY. Quick! *Exit* TOM, R. 1 E.
O'SULL. Daryl, is there any fighting to be done?
MACU. Or any drinking?
DR. M. If so, we shall be most happy.
SIDNEY. No, no, thanks. Come with me—I've a treat
for you.
OMNES. What?
SIDNEY. (*laughing*) The chalybeate waters.

Exeunt OMNES *into house,* L. *Enter* CHODD, JUN.,
and AARON, R. 1 E.

CHODD, JUN. You saw him go in — arrest him. The
chaise is ready—take him to the next station, and all's
right. I'll stay and see him captured.

(CHODD *in great triumph*)

AARON. Very good, shur—do it at vunsh.

> *Is going into the house, when the* LAMB *springs out;*
> AARON *staggers back; the* LAMB *stands in boxing*
> *attitude before the door;* TOM *and* SIX *or* EIGHT
> ROUGHS *enter by avenue,* R.

LAMB. (*with back half turned to audience*) Now, then,
where are *you* a shovin' to ?

AARON. I want to passh by.

LAMB. Then you can't.

AARON. Why not ?

LAMB. (*doggedly*) 'Cos I'm doorkeeper, and you haven't
got a check.

AARON. Now, Lamb, dooty'sh dooty, and——

LAMB. (*turning with face to audience, and bringing up
the muscle of his right arm*) Feel that !

AARON. (*alarmed*) Yesh, shur.   (*feels it slightly*)

LAMB. You can't come in.

CHODD, JUN. (*crossing to* LAMB *fussily*) Why not ?

LAMB. (*looks at him, half contemptuously, half comically*)
'Cos that sez I musn't let you.   Feel it ! (*taps muscle*)

CHODD, JUN. Thank you, some other time.

> *Crossing,* R.   *The* ROUGHS *surround him, jeer, and*
> *prepare to hustle him.* TOM *mounts seat,* R.

TOM. Vote for Daryl !

LAMB. (*making up to* AARON *in sparring attitude, who
retreats in terror*) Are yer movin' ?

CHODD, JUN. Do your duty.   (ROUGHS *laugh*)

AARON. I can't—they are many, I am few.

                                (*cheers without,* R.)

CHODD, JUN. (*losin' his presence of mind*) Particular
business requires me at the hustings.

> (*goes off,* R., *midst jeers and laughter of* ROUGHS)

LAMB. (*at same time advancing upon* AARON) Are yer
movin' ?

AARON. Yesh, Mr. Lamb.

> *By this time he has backed close to* TOM, *perched
> upon the seat, who bonnets him.*

TOM. Vote for Daryl !

> AARON *is hustled off,* R. 1 E., *by* MOB, *followed
> leisurely by* LAMB.

TOM. (*on chair*) Remember, gentlemen, the officers of
the law—the officers of the sheriff—arc only in the

execution of their duty. (*shouts and uproar without*) Don't offer any violence. (*shouts*) Don't tear them limb from limb!

> *Shouts, followed by a loud shriek.* TOM *leaps from chair, dances down stage, and exits,* R.U.E. *Enter* LADY PTARMIGANT *and* CHODD, SEN., R. 2 E. LADY PTARMIGANT *is dressed in mauve.* CHODD, SEN. *escorts her to house,* L.

CHODD, SEN. But if he is absent from his post?

LADY P. His post must get on without him. Really, my dear Mr. Chodd, you must allow me to direct absolutely. If you wish your son to marry Miss Hetherington, now is the time—now or never.

> *Exit into house,* L. CHODD, SEN., *exits,* R. 1 E. *Enter* CHODD, JUN., *and* MAUD, *dressed in mauve,* R.U.E.

CHODD, JUN. Miss Hetherington, allow me to offer you a seat. (*she sits under tree,* R.; *aside*) Devilish awkward! Lady Ptarmigant says, "Strike while the iron's hot"; but I want to be at the hustings. I've made my speech to the electors, and now I must do my courting. She looks awfully proud. I wish I could pay some fellow to do this for me. Miss Hetherington a—a—a—— I got the speech I spoke just now off by heart. I wish I'd got this written for me, too. Miss Hetherington, I—I am emboldened by the—by what I have just been told by our esteemed correspondent, Lady Ptar—I mean by your amiable aunt. I—I——(*boldly*) I have a large fortune, and my prospects are bright and brilliant—bright and brilliant. I—I am of a respectable family, which has always paid its way. I have entered on a political career, which always pays its way; and I mean some day to make my name famous. My lady has doubtless prepared you for the hon—I offer you my— ·my humble hand, and large—I may say colossal fortune.

MAUD. (L.) Mr. Chodd I will be plain with you.

CHODD, JUN. (R.) Impossible for Miss Hetherington to be plain.

MAUD. You offer me your hand; I will accept it. ·

CHODD, JUN. Oh, joy! Oh——

> (*endeavouring to take her hand*)

MAUD. Please hear me out. On these conditions,

CHODD, JUN. Pin money no object. Settle as much on you as you like.

MAUD. I will be your true and faithful wife—I will bear your name worthily; but you must understand our union is a union of convenience.

CHODD, JUN, Convenience !

MAUD. Yes ; that love has no part in it.

CHODD, JUN. Miss Hetherington—may I say Maud?—I love you—I adore you with my whole heart and fortune. (*aside*) I wonder how they are getting on at the hustings.

MAUD. I was saying, Mr. Chodd——

CHODD, JUN. Call me John—your own John !

(*seizing her hand; she shudders, and withdraws it*)

MAUD. (*struggling with herself*) I was saying that the affection which a wife should bring the man she has elected as—— (*cheers without*)

SIDNEY. (*speaking without*) Electors of Springmead.

MAUD. We hardly know sufficient of each other to warrant——

SIDNEY. (*without*) I need not tell you who I am.

(*cheers.* MAUD *trembles*)

MAUD. We are almost strangers.

SIDNEY. Nor what principles I have been reared in.

CHODD, JUN. The name of Chodd, if humble, is at least wealthy.

SIDNEY. I am a Daryl ; and my politics those of the Daryls. (*cheers*)

CHODD, JUN. (*aside*) This is awkward. (*to* MAUD) As to our being strangers——

SIDNEY. I am no stranger. (*cheers*) I have grown up to be a man among you. There are faces I see in the crowd I am addressing, men of my own age, whom I remember children. (*cheers*) There are faces among you who remember me when I was a boy. (*cheers*) In the political union between my family and Springmead, there is more than respect and sympathy, there is sentiment. (*cheers*)

CHODD, JUN. Confound the fellow ! Dearest Miss Hetherington—Dearest Maud—you have deigned to say you will be mine.

SIDNEY. Why, if we continue to deserve your trust, plight your political faith to another ?

MAUD. (*overcome*) Mr. Chodd, I——

CHODD, JUN. My own bright, particular Maud !

SIDNEY. Who is my opponent ?

TOM. (*without*, R.) Nobody. (*a loud laugh*)

SIDNEY. What is he ?

TOM. Not much. (*a roar of laughter*)

SIDNEY. I have no doubt he is honest and trustworthy, but why turn away an old servant to hire one you don't know ? (*cheers*) Why turn off an old love that you have

tried and proved for a new one ? (*cheers*) I don't know what
the gentleman's politics may be. (*laugh*) Or those of his
family. (*roar of laughter*) I've tried to find out, but I can't.
To paraphrase the ballad :—

> I've searched through Hansard, journals,
> Books, De Brett, and Burke, and Dodd,
> And my head—my head is aching,
> To find out the name of Chodd.

(*loud laughter and three cheers.* MAUD *near fainting*)

CHODD, JUN. I can't stand this ; I must be off to the
hustings, Miss Heth——! Oh! she's fainting. What shall
I do? Lady Ptarmigant! Oh, here she comes! Waiter,
a tumbler of No. 2. (*runs off,* 2. R E.)

SIDNEY. (*without*) And I confidently await the result
which will place me at the head of the poll. (*cheers*)

Enter LORD *and* LADY PTARMIGANT, *from house,* L.
LADY PTARMIGANT *attends to* MAUD.

MAUD. 'Twas nothing—a slight faintness—an attack
of——

LORD P. An attack of Chodd, I think! What a
dreadful person my lady is, to be sure. (*aside, sits,* L.)

LADY P. (*to* MAUD) Have you done it?

MAUD. Yes.

LADY P. And you are to be his wife?

MAUD. Yes. (*cheers*)

Enter SIDNEY, O'SULLIVAN, MACUSQUEBAUGH, *and*
DOCTOR MAKVICZ, R. 2 E.

SIDNEY. (*coming down,* L.) Tom, I feel so excited—so
delighted—so happy—so——(*sees* MAUD *stops ; takes his hat
off ;* MAUD *bows coldly*) In my adversary's colours!

LADY P. (R.) That fellow, Sidney!

MAUD. (C., *aside*) It seems hard to see him there, and
not to speak to him for the last time.

Is about to advance when TOM *brings on* LITTLE
MAUD, R.U.E., *dressed in magenta.* MAUD *recedes.*
LORD PTARMIGANT *goes to sleep in garden seat,* L.

LADY P. The tobacco man !

TOM. (*down,* L.) Ariadne !

SIDNEY *kisses* LITTLE MAUD.   *Enter* CHODD, JUN.,
R.U.E., and down, R.

LADY P. (*with a withering glance at* SIDNEY) Maud, my
child, here's Mr. Chodd.

CHODD, JUN., *crossing* R.C., *gives his arm to* MAUD.
SIDNEY *stands with* LITTLE MAUD, L.C.   *All go off*,
R.U.E., *except* LADY PTARMIGANT, SIDNEY, LITTLE
MAUD, TOM, *and* LORD PTARMIGANT.

SIDNEY. (L.) On his arm! Well, I deserve it! I am
poor !

LADY P. (R.) Mr. Daryl.   (SIDNEY *bows*)

TOM. (L.) Ariadne is about to express her feelings; I
shall go !   *Exit*, R.U.E.

LADY P. I cannot but express my opinion of your conduct. For a long time I have known you to be the
associate of prize-fighters, betting men, racehorses, authors,
and other such low persons; but despite that, I thought
you had some claims to be a gentleman.

SIDNEY. In what may have I forfeited Lady Ptarmigant's good opinion ?

LADY P. In what, sir ? In daring to bring me, your
kinswoman, and a lady—in daring to bring into the
presence of the foolish girl you professed to love—that child
—your illegitimate offspring !

(LORD PTARMIGANT *awakes*)

SIDNEY. (*stung*) Lady Ptarmigant, do you know who
that child is ?

LADY P. Perfectly !   (*with a sneer*)

SIDNEY. I think not. She is the lawful daughter of
your dead and only son, Charles !

LADY P. What ?

SIDNEY. Two days before he sailed for the Crimea, he
called at my chambers, and told me that he felt convinced he
should never return.   He told me, too, of his connection
with a poor and humble girl, who would shortly become the
mother of his child.   I saw from his face that the bullet
was cast that would destroy him, and I begged him to
legitimatise one who, though of his blood, might not bear his
name.   Like a brave fellow, a true gentleman, on the next
day he married.

LADY P. How disgraceful !

SIDNEY. Joined his regiment, and, as you know, fell at
Balaclava.

LADY P. My poor—poor boy.

SIDNEY. His death broke his wife's heart—she, too, died.

LADY P. What a comfort!—

SIDNEY. I placed the child with a good motherly woman, and I had intended, for the sake of my old friend, Charley, to educate her, and to bring her to you, and say. Take her, she is your lawful grandchild, and a lady *pur sang ;* love her, and be proud of her, for the sake of the gallant son, who galloped to death in the service of his country.

LADY P. (*affected*) Sidney !

SIDNEY. I did not intend that you should know this for some time. I had some romantic notion of making it a reason for your consent to my marriage with—(LADY PTARMIGANT *takes* LITTLE MAUD)— with Miss Hetherington —that is all over now. The ill opinion with which you have lately pursued me has forced this avowal from me.

LADY P. (*to child*) My darling ! Ah ! my poor Charley's very image ! My poor boy ! My poor boy !

LORD P. (*who has been listening, advancing,* L.) Sidney, let my son Charley's father thank you. You have acted like a kinsman and a Daryl ! (*affected*)

LADY P. Sidney, forgive me !

SIDNEY (C.) Pray forget it, Lady Ptarm——

LADY P. I will take care that Miss Hetherington shall know——

SIDNEY. (*hotly*) What ! did she, too, suspect ! Lady Ptarmigant, it is my request—nay, if I have done anything to deserve your good opinion, my injunction—that Miss Hetherington is not informed of what has just passed. If she has thought that I could love another—she is free to her opinion !

> (*goes up, and comes down,* R., *with the child*)

LORD P. But *I* shall tell her.

LADY P. (*astonished*) You ! (*aside*) Don't you think, under the circumstances, it would be better——

LORD P. I shall act as I think best.

LADY P. Ferdinand ! (*authoritatively*)

LORD P. Lady Ptarmigant, it is not often I speak, goodness knows ! but on a question that concerns my honour and yours, I shall *not* be silent.

LADY P. (C.) Ferdinand ! (*imploringly*)

LORD P. Lady Ptarmigant, I am *awake,* and you will please to follow my instructions. (*crossing,* C.) What is my granddaughter's name ?

L. MAUD. Maud.

LORD P. Maud, Maud—is it Maud? *(playfully)*

> LORD PTARMIGANT *lifts her in his arms, and is carry-*
> *ing her off.*

LADY P. My lord! consider—people are looking!

LORD P. Let 'em look—they'll know I'm a *grandfather !*

> *Exit* LORD PTARMIGANT, *with* LITTLE MAUD, *and*
> LADY PTARMIGANT, R.U.E. *avenue.* TOM *runs on,*
> R.U.E.

TOM. (L.) It's all right, Sid! Three of Chodd's committee have come over to us. They said that so long as a
Daryl was not put up, they felt at liberty to support him,
but now——*(seeing that* SIDNEY *is affected)* What's the
matter?

SIDNEY. (R.) Nothing.

TOM. Ah, that means love! I hope to be able to
persuade the majority of Chodd's committee to resign; and,
if they resign, he must too, and we shall walk over the
course. (SIDNEY *goes up and sits,* L. TOM, *aside)* Cupid's
carriage stops the way again. Confound that nasty,
naughty, naked little boy! I wonder if he'd do less mischief if they put him into knickerbockers. *Exit,* R. 1 E.

SIDNEY. Mr. Chodd shall not have Springmead.

> *Enter* MAUD, *leading* LITTLE MAUD *by the hand,*
> R.U.E. SIDNEY'S *face is buried in his hands on the*
> *table.*

MAUD. *(kissing the child, then advancing slowly to*
SIDNEY) Sidney!

SIDNEY. *(rising)* Maud—Miss Hetherington!

L. MAUD. Uncle, this is my new aunt. She's my aunt
and you're my uncle. You don't seemed pleased to see
each other, though—ain't you? Aunt, why don't you kiss
uncle?

MAUD. (R., *after a pause)* Sidney, I have to beg your
forgiveness for the—the—mistake which——

SIDNEY. (L.) Pray don't mention it, Maud—Miss
Hetherington. It is not of the——

MAUD. (R.) It is so hard to think ill of those we have
known. (CHILD *goes up,* R.)

SIDNEY. I think that it must be very easy! Let me
take this opportunity of apologising personally, as I have
already done by letter, for my misconduct at the ball. I
had heard that you were about to—to——

MAUD. Marry! Then you were in error. Since then I have accepted Mr. Chodd. (*pause*)

SIDNEY. I congratulate you. (*turns his face aside*)

MAUD. You believed me to be false—believed it without inquiry!

SIDNEY. As you believed of me!

MAUD. Our mutual poverty prevented.

SIDNEY. (*bursting out*) Oh, yes, we are poor! We are poor! We loved each other—but we were poor! We loved each other—but we couldn't take a house in a square! We loved each other—but we couldn't keep a carriage! We loved each other—but we had neither gold, purple, plate, nor mansion in the country! You were right to leave me, and to marry a *gentleman*—rich in all these assurances of happiness!

MAUD. Sidney, you are cruel.

SIDNEY. I loved you, Maud; loved you with my whole heart and soul since we played together as children, and you grew till I saw you a lovely blushing girl, and now—pshaw! this is folly, sentiment, raving madness! Let me wish you joy—let me hope you will be happy.

L. MAUD. (*coming down*, C.) Uncle, you mustn't make my new aunt cry. Go and make it up with her, and kiss her.

' LADY PTARMIGANT, LORD PTARMIGANT, *and* LORD CLOUDWRAYS *have entered during the last speech*, R.U.E.

MAUD. Farewell, Sidney! (*holding out her hand*)

SIDNEY. Farewell!

LADY P. (*advancing*, C.) Farewell! What [nonsense; two young people so fond of each other. Sidney—Maud, dear, you have my consent.

SIDNEY. (L.C., *astonished*) Lady Ptarmigant!

LADY P. (R.C.) I always liked you, Sidney, though, I confess, I didn't always show it.

LORD P. (L.) I can explain my lady's sudden conversion—at least, Cloudwrays can.

LORD C. (R.) Well, Sid, I'm sorry to be the bearer of good news—I mean of ill news; but your brother—poor Percy—he—a——

SIDNEY. Dead!

LORD C. The news came by the mail to the club, so as I'd nothing to do, I thought I'd come down to congratulate—I mean condole with you.

LORD P. Bear up, Sidney, your brother's health was bad before he left us.

SIDNEY. First the son, and then the father.

MAUD. (L.C.) Sidney!

SIDNEY. (*catching her hand*) Maud!

MAUD. No, no—not now—you are rich, and I am promised.

LADY P. Why, you wicked girl; you wouldn't marry a man you didn't love, would you? Where are your principles?

> LORD PTARMIGANT *sits on garden seat*, L., *with* LITTLE MAUD.

MAUD. But—but—Mr. Chodd?

LADY P. What on earth consequence is Mr. Chodd?

> *Enter* CHODD, SEN., *and* CHODD, JUN., *avenue* R.

CHODD, SEN. My lady, it's all right, Johnny has been accepted!

> MAUD *goes up and sits*, L.C. SIDNEY *and* LORD CLOUDWRAYS *also go up with her.*

LADY P. (L.) By whom?

CHODD, SEN. (R.) By Miss Hetherington—by Maud!

LADY P. Why, you must be dreaming, the election has turned your brain—my niece marry a Chodd!

CHODD, SEN. ⎱
CHODD, JUN. ⎰ My lady!

LADY P. Nothing of the sort; I was only joking, and thought you were, too. (*aside*) The impertinence of the lower classes in trying to ally themselves with us!

> (*going up*, L.)

CHODD, JUN. Guv.

CHODD, SEN. Johnny!

CHODD, JUN. We're done.   (*crosses*, L.)

> *Loud cheering. Enter* TOM, R.U.E., *who whispers and congratulates* SIDNEY. *Enter a* GENTLEMAN, R. 1 E., *who whispers to* CHODD, SEN., *condolingly, and exits*, R. 1 E.

CHODD, SEN. (R., *shouting*) Johnny!

CHODD, JUN. (L.) Guv.

CHODD, SEN. They say there's no hope, and advise us to withdraw from the contest.

> (ALL *congratulate* SIDNEY, *up stage*)

LADY P. Sir Sidney Daryl, M.P., looks like old times.
(*to* LORD PTARMIGANT) My lord, congratulate him.

LORD P. (*waking and shaking* CHODD, JUN., *by the hand*) Receive my congratulations.

LADY P. Oh ! it's the wrong man !

CHODD, SEN. (R.) Mr. Stylus, I may thank you for this.

TOM. (R.C.) And yourself, you may. I brought out your journal, engaged your staff, and you tried to throw me over. You've got your reward. Morning paper !

(*throws papers in the air*)

Enter AARON, *with hat broken and head bound up,* R.U.E.

AARON. (C., *to* SIDNEY) Arresht you at the shoot of——

(*the* CHODDS *rub their hands in triumph*)

TOM. (R.C.) Too late ! too late ! He's a member of Parliament.

CHODD, JUN., *and* CHODD, SEN., *turn into* R. *and* L. *corners.*

SIDNEY. (L.C., *to* TOM) I haven't taken the seat or the oaths yet.

TOM. (R.C.) They don't know that.

SIDNEY. We can settle it another way. (*taking out pocket-book and looking at* CHODD, JUN.) Some time ago I was fortunate enough to win a large sum of money ; this way if you please.

(*goes up with* AARON, *and gives money, notes, &c.*)

CHODD, JUN. Pays his own bills, which I'd bought up, with my money.

CHODD, SEN. (*crossing,* L.) Then, Johnny, you won't get into Society.

LADY P. (*coming down,* R.) Never mind, Mr. Chodd, your son shall marry a lady.

CHODD, JUN. }
CHODD, SEN. } Eh !

LADY P. I promise to introduce you to one of blue blood.

CHODD, JUN. Blue bl—— I'd rather have it the natural colour.

Cheers. *Enter* O'SULLIVAN *and* COMMITTEE, R.U.E.
Stage full. *Church bells heard.*

O'SULL. (R.) Sir Sidney Daryl, we have heard the news.

In our turn we have to inform you that your adversaries have retired from the contest, and you are member for Springmead. (*cheers*) We, your committee, come to weep with you for the loss of a brother, to joy with you on your accession to a title and your hereditary honours. Your committee most respectfully beg to be introduced to Lady Daryl.   (*with intention and Irish gallantry*)

> SIDNEY *shows* MAUD *the magenta ribbon ; she places her hand in his.*

SIDNEY. (C.) Gentlemen, I thank you ; I cannot introduce you to Lady Daryl, for Lady Daryl does not yet exist. In the meantime I have permission to present you to Miss Hetherington.

TOM. (*leaping on chair,* R., *and waving handkerchief*) Three cheers for my lady !

> *All cheer. Church bells ; band plays "Conquering Hero."* GIRL *at window of house waves handkerchief, and* CHILD *a stick with magenta streamer attached.* COUNTRYMEN, *&c., wave hats ; band plays, &c.*

ROUGHS.	COUNTRYFOLKS.	GIRL *and* CHILD.
	SIDNEY *and* MAUD.	
MAKVICZ, TOM.	LORD P., L. MAUD.	
MacUSQUEBAUGH.	LADY P., LORD C.	
O'SULLIVAN,	CHODD, SEN.	
	CHODD., JUN.	

CURTAIN.

WAR.

A DRAMA, IN THREE ACTS.

BY

T. W. ROBERTSON,

AUTHOR OF

"Caste," "A Breach of Promise," "Progress," "M.P.," "Birth,"
"David Garrick," "The Ladies' Battle," "The Nightingale,"
"Dreams," "Play," "Ours," "Row in the House," "Society,"
"School," "Home," "Faust and Marguerite," "My
Wife's Diary," "Noemie," "Two Gay Deceivers," "Jocrisse
the Juggler," "Not at all Jealous," "Star of the North,"
"Birds of Prey," "Peace at any Price," "Half Caste,"
"Ernestine," "Chevalier de St. George," "Cantab," "Clock-
maker's Hat," "Duke's Daughter," "Sea of Ice," &c., &c.

————   ————

LONDON:
SAMUEL FRENCH,
PUBLISHER,
89, STRAND.

NEW YORK:
SAMUEL FRENCH & SON,
PUBLISHERS,
28, WEST 23RD STREET.

WAR.

(*Produced at the St. James's Theatre, London, January 16th, 1871.*

CAST OF CHARACTERS.

Colonel de Rochevannes	Mr. HENRI NERTANN.
Oscar de Rochevannes	Mr. FRED MERVIN.
Herr Karl Hartmann	Mr. A. W. YOUNG.
Captain Sound, R.N.	Mr. L. BROUGH.
Lotte	Miss FANNY BROUGH.
Blanche	Miss ALICE BARRIE.
Jessie	Miss JENNY MORI.
Agnes	Miss MARIAN INCH.
Katie	Miss LILIAN ADAIR.

ACT I.—BEFORE THE WEDDING.—*Villa and Garden.*

ACT II.—AFTER THE BATTLE.—*Exterior of Church.*

ACT III.—THE LIST.—*Same as Act I.*

Modern Costumes.   *Time of Representation, two and a-half hours.*

WAR.

ACT I.

SCENE.—*Villa and garden near Sevenoaks. Villa running
from* 3 E.R. *to* L.C. *Door* R.C. *French window, opening
on to lawn near it. Return piece from villa to back. At
back, in the extreme* L., *a door. Arched foliage, leading
from door to villa. A shrubbery, the entrance to which is*
R.U.E. *Grass plat, parterres, &c. All green leafy, &c.
Creepers over window and villa. See diagram.*

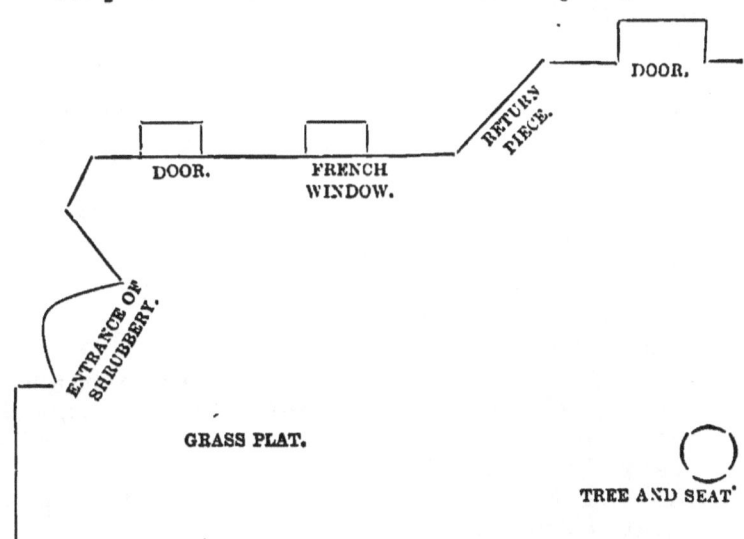

BLANCHE. (*heard without*) Never mind; I'll find her in
the garden.

JESSIE. (*heard outside*) Don't trouble yourself; I'll find
them.

> *Enter* BLANCHE *from* D. *in flat, and* JESSIE *from* D.
> *at back. They look about the stage, as if searching
> for someone. Suddenly they meet each other face
> to face, and start.*

BLANCHE. Oh!

JESSIE. Oh !

BLANCHE. Jessie !

JESSIE. Blanche !

BLANCHE. } (*together*) Is that you ?
JESSIE.

BLANCHE. You took away my breath.

JESSIE. And you've made my heart beat.

BLANCHE. Did you think I was a young man ?

JESSIE. No, but——

BLANCHE. But what ?

JESSIE. I—I don't know.

> (*each has a parcel in her hand*)

BLANCHE. (*pointing to* JESSIE's *parcel*) What's that ?

JESSIE. Nothing. (*hiding her parcel behind her*) What's
that ?   (*pointing to* BLANCHE's *parcel*)

BLANCHE. (*hiding her parcel behind her*) Nothing.

JESSIE. Then why not show it ?

BLANCHE. I can't show nothing.

JESSIE. If one can't show nothing, one can't hide nothing.

BLANCHE. Yes, one can.

JESSIE. How ?

BLANCHE. It's so pleasant to hide anything, even when
it's nothing. (*leading* JESSIE *forward*) You show me, and
I'll show you.

JESSIE. You won't tell ?

BLANCHE. No.

JESSIE. Upon your honour ?

BLANCHE. Upon my honour.

JESSIE. Will you swear it ?

BLANCHE. I will—on an ivory-backed hairbrush.

JESSIE. Then——

> AGNES *runs on from door at back. She also carries
> a parcel in her hand.*

AGNES. (*out of breath*) Oh, Blanche ! Oh, Jessie ! You
here ?

BLANCHE. } (*together*) Yes.
JESSIE.

BLANCHE. (*to* JESSIE. *Aside*) She's got a parcel, too, and
she's trying to hide it.   Let's find out what it is.

JESSIE. We will.

> JESSIE *and* BLANCHE *advance, and try to take* AGNES
> *by both hands ; she shifting the parcel from one
> hand to the other.*

BLANCHE. Agnes, dear, how well you are looking !

JESSIE. (*manœuvring so as to get sight of the parcel*) How well your frock fits behind! Does it not?

> *The girls kiss each other, then separate, each having felt the parcel. A pause.* BLANCHE *and* JESSIE *burst out laughing.*

AGNES. (*whose manner is somewhat prim and pedantic*) I know what you are laughing at!

BLANCHE.　}
JESSIE.　 } No, you don't.

AGNES. I do. You have got something behind you—I can see.

BLANCHE.　}
JESSIE.　 } (*together*) So have you.

AGNES. I know I have. What is in your parcel?

BLANCHE.　}
JESSIE.　 } (*together*) Tell us what is in yours?

AGNES. I will; but, mind, it is a secret.

BLANCHE.　}
JESSIE.　 } (*together*) Of course, it's a secret.

AGNES. Not to be mentioned to anybody.

BLANCHE.　}
JESSIE.　 } (*together*) Not to anybody.

> (*all three bring their parcels forward*)

BLANCHE. Now, let each tell at the same time, so that one has no advantage over the other.

JESSIE.　}
AGNES.　 } (*together*) Very well.

BLANCHE. When I hold up my finger, and say "Begin!" we begin. Mind, no false starts. Now, are you booted?·

JESSIE.　}
AGNES.　 } (*together*) Yes.

BLANCHE. Are you spurred?

JESSIE.　}
AGNES.　 } (*together*) Yes.

BLANCHE. Well, then—one, two, three, off!

> *Gate-bell is heard. Each of the girls starts. They separate, and put their parcels behind them.* KATIE *heard outside.*

KATIE. (*outside*) Nobody answer the door? Never mind.

BLANCHE.　)
JESSIE.　 } (*together*) It's Katie. Not a syllable.
AGNES.　) (*they separate, and walk about indifferently*)

Enter KATIE, *from door at back. She is the smallest and youngest of the four girls.*

KATIE. (*seeing them*) Ah, Blanche, dear! Jessie and Agnes! How do you do—how do you do?

BLANCHE.
JESSIE. } (*together*) How do you do, dear? (*to each other*) She hasn't got a parcel.
AGNES.

JESSIE. No, she has nothing to conceal.

AGNES. What a singular girl!

JESSIE. (*to* AGNES) Yes, Katie was always eccentric.

BLANCHE. Well, Katie, dear, are you to be one of the bridesmaids?

KATIE. You know I am.

BLANCHE. So am I.

AGNES. So am I.

JESSIE. Let us sit down and have a talk.

KATIE. I know all about it. The fact is, that because Lotte's papa is a German——

BLANCHE. Now, don't tell us that, because we know that as well as you.

JESSIE. Yes, we all know as well as each other.

BLANCHE. Girls, I have an idea. As we all know, and all want to tell, let's all tell each other.

THE GIRLS. Yes, yes, yes, yes!

BLANCHE. Well, you know, in Germany it is the custom to call a young lady a bride——

JESSIE. As soon as she is engaged.

AGNES. Just so; and everybody congratulates them—I mean the bride and bridegroom, just the same as if they were married.

JESSIE. How nice! I should like to be a bride.

BLANCHE. And I should like to be a bridegroom.

KATIE. And I should like to be both bride and bridegroom, too.

JESSIE. Oh, how selfish!

AGNES. Katie wants everything.

BLANCHE. And what a bridegroom!

JESSIE. An officer.

AGNES. A soldier.

KATIE. More—a horse soldier.

BLANCHE. And more—a French horse soldier.

JESSIE. I should like to see him in his uniform.

THE GIRLS. (*all*) Scarlet trousers.

AGNES. And a gold stripe down the seams.

KATIE. No ; a black stripe down the seams.

BLANCHE.
JESSIE. } No ; gold !

KATIE. No ; black, black, black !

AGNES. Gold, gold, gold !

BLANCHE. Well, never mind about the stripe. I see you have got your presents, and are dying to show them.

AGNES. I mean to show mine to Lotte first.

KATIE. Let us have a private view.

BLANCHE. (*with great ceremony*) Now, girls, keep your eyes on me. Attention !

> *She opens her parcel with great ceremony, and brings out a beautifully-worked sachet. The* GIRLS *admire it.*

THE GIRLS. La ! how beautiful !

JESSIE. (*reading the words upon it*) "May you be happy."

AGNES. Why, she must be happy with a sachet like that !

JESSIE. She couldn't help it.

BLANCHE.
AGNES. } Now, Jessie.
KATIE.

JESSIE. (*rises*) Attention !.

> *Opens her parcel, and pulls out a rich lace pocket-handkerchief.*

THE GIRLS. (*in ecstacies*) Beautiful !

BLANCHE. What a love !

KATIE. With such a handkerchief, it is almost a pity not to cry.

AGNES. One can always make-believe.

KATIE. It is indeed beautiful.

BLANCHE.
JESSIE. } Now, Agnes, yours—show yours.
KATIE.

AGNES. I know you will think mine pretty, because it cost a great deal of money, and we had to get Mr. Hartmann's permission before we had it made.

THE GIRLS. Show it, show it !

AGNES. (*opens a paper, which discloses a box, out of which she takes a magnificent bridal wreath*) Look

THE GIRLS. (*lost in admiration*) Oh !

AGNES. Is it not beautiful ?

KATIE. (*beginning to cry*) Oh ! it is *so* beautiful !

AGNES. What are you crying for?

KATIE. Because, because, because——

BLANCHE. Now, Katie, show us your present.

KATIE. (*running away*) No, I won't! I won't!

> *She runs towards the shrubbery, starts, and gives a little scream.*

BLANCHE. What is it—caterpillars?

> (KATIE *shakes her head*)

AGNES. Snails?   (KATIE *shakes her head*)

JESSIE. A big bumble-bee?

KATIE. (*shakes her head emphatically*) No.

BLANCHE.
JESSIE.   } What then?
AGNES.

KATIE. (*her finger on her lips, turning to the* GIRLS) Sweethearts!

JESSIE. (*approaching* AGNES) Pretty things : don't disturb them, they might run away.

KATIE. 'Tis Lotte and the Captain.

BLANCHE. His arm is round her waist.

AGNES. Oh, how wrong!

BLANCHE. Oh, how right!

KATIE. Right about waist. (*as if giving word of command*) They mustn't see us.

BLANCHE. No ; we should interrupt them, and anyone who would interrupt a girl when she is with her sweetheart ought to be sent to boarding-school for life.

JESSIE. Let's go into the house.

BLANCHE. Yes, we can listen through the windows.

KATIE. No ; it's wrong to listen.

BLANCHE. Not if we only listen a little.

AGNES. Or if we listen unintentionally.

JESSIE. If the words come to our ears, we can't help it.

KATIE. Then we won't listen ; or, if we do, we'll listen with our eyes shut.

> *The* GIRLS *run into the house through French windows and door.* OSCAR *and* LOTTE *appear at the entrance of the shrubbery. They remain there in picture.* OSCAR *is dressed in private clothes, the ribbon at his button-hole.* OSCAR *is holding up a wedding-ring.*

LOTTE. And that is the wedding-ring.

OSCAR. Our wedding-ring.

LOTTE. Gold?

OSCAR. Gold.

LOTTE. Solid gold?

OSCAR. Solid gold.

LOTTE. The most precious of all the metals, fashioned into a circle.

OSCAR. Fashioned into a circle.

LOTTE. The form suggests a snake

OSCAR. The emblem of eternity.

LOTTE. But not of eternal love.

OSCAR (*laughing*) Shall we say, then, that the folded snake signifies matrimony?

LOTTE. Don't laugh.

OSCAR. Why not? What was life made for but to laugh? I'd like my life divided into three compartments— life, laughter, and Lotte.

LOTTE. Why put Lotte last?

OSCAR. Because she is the most precious. I like life, I admire laughter, and I love Lotte.

(they advance on to the stage)

LOTTE. And in a week we are to be married.

OSCAR. In one week—seven days — one hundred and sixty-eight hours. It is a long time, and the days in Sevenoaks pass so slowly.

LOTTE. With me by your side, Oscar?

OSCAR. My love.

LOTTE. Are you sure the ring will fit my finger?

OSCAR. You know it will—I've tried it on.

LOTTE. Then try it on again. Keep trying it on.

As OSCAR takes the ring and puts it on her wedding-finger, the GIRLS tap at the window. LOTTE drops ring.

OSCAR. }
LOTTE. } *(turning round, alarmed)* Eh?

OSCAR. What's that?

LOTTE. I don't know. I thought I heard a tap.

OSCAR. Can anybody see us?

LOTTE. *(looking round)* No.

OSCAR. If they could?

LOTTE. I should die of shame.

OSCAR. Why?

LOTTE. Because it is not usual to try on wedding-rings— out-of-doors.

OSCAR. Let us go into the house. I will try the ring

on anywhere until we reach the church.   It is so pleasant to rehearse our happiness.   Here are the trees, the flowers beneath us, your home around us ; above, the sky and air ; what better altar could love have ?

> *As he approaches her, the* GIRLS *tap at window again.*   LOTTE *and* OSCAR *start.*

OSCAR. Again !

LOTTE. Someone——

OSCAR. Who ?   The gardener ?   (*a pause*)   It didn't sound like a gardener.

LOTTE. No ; the gardener has a holiday, and is gone to see his wife.

OSCAR. That's rather a strange way of spending a holiday !

LOTTE. (*reproachfully*) Oscar !

OSCAR. Ah ! you must not mind my fun, Lotte.   I am a Frenchman, and say things not to wound, but to be gay. I meant to be spiritual. One cannot be always sentimental. You are German, and sentimental by nationality ; I am gay through the same influence.   Is it not a happy union ? We are to have luncheon on the lawn, are we not ?

LOTTE. Yes, and Captain Sound is coming from Dover.

OSCAR. Fine old fellow, Captain Sound.

LOTTE. My godfather.

OSCAR. True, your godfather—(*thoughtfully*)—and we are to be married in a week—seven days—one hundred and sixty-eight hours.

LOTTE. In a week. (*a pause*) And when I am your wife, Oscar, shall you be proud of me ?

OSCAR. Proud as of my cross.

LOTTE. Really ?

OSCAR. Really.

LOTTE. But you won your cross in battle.

OSCAR. And I won you by love ; conquests both.   You can imagine which I think the greater victory.

LOTTE. You won your cross by fighting.

OSCAR. Yes—and you by courting.

LOTTE. In Algeria ?

OSCAR. No, in Sevenoaks.

LOTTE. But, Oscar, if ever you should have to go to fight again ?

OSCAR. Parbleu ! I should go.

LOTTE. But would you leave me ?

OSCAR. I should be compelled.

LOTTE. Even after we were married ?

OSCAR. Even after we were married   An order from a superior——

LOTTE. What bad people superiors must be !

OSCAR. The world is like that.

LOTTE. And you would not only leave me, but go into battle yourself.

OSCAR. Never think of that ; think only of our approaching happiness—of my love for you, of yours for me. Let me take one kiss.   (*she rises*)

LOTTE. No.

OSCAR. Why not ? We are to be married in a week.

LOTTE. Someone might see us.

OSCAR. (*looking about*) Where ?

LOTTE. If anyone were walking on the church tower.

                                   (*looking up*)

OSCAR. What the church sees no one can disapprove of. One kiss, now——

LOTTE. Only one for the present.

OSCAR. One for the present.

LOTTE. One for the present.   After we are married you may take thousands.

> As he kisses . her, the GIRLS tap at the window violently, and laugh.

LOTTE. (*seeing the* GIRLS *as they come out*) Blanche ! Jessie ! Agnes !

OSCAR. Katie !

BLANCHE. We were in the room.

JESSIE. Looking out.

AGNES. But we saw nothing.

THE GIRLS. Nothing, we assure you.

OSCAR. Upon your honours ?

KATIE. Upon our honours.

BLANCHE. We came here to present Lotte with this.

                                   (*showing sachet*)

LOTTE. How beautiful !

JESSIE. And this.   (*showing pocket-handkerchief*)

AGNES. And this. ˙   (*showing wreath*)

LOTTE. How lovely ? (*to* KATIE, *who is beginning to cry, in* R.H. *corner*) Why, Katie, what are you crying about ? Have you nothing for me ?

KATIE. Yes ; but it isn't worth having.   Ever since the bank broke papa has been so poor that I could only bring you——

LOTTE. What ?

KATIE. This.   (*producing a bunch of violets*)

OSCAR. Most beautiful present !

LOTTE. And one that I prize as dearly as the others.

OSCAR. For they are but the produce of art.

LOTTE. And this of nature. Thank you, my dear friends, very, very much.

BLANCHE. And now, Lotte, we want to ask you a favour.

LOTTE. What favour ?

BLANCHE. We want you to show us——

JESSIE. Yes, to show us——

AGNES. Yes, to show us——

LOTTE. What ?

THE GIRLS. Your wedding-ring.

LOTTE. With pleasure. (*to* OSCAR) Oscar :

OSCAR. I placed it on your finger.

LOTTE. (*after looking for it*) Then I have dropped it !

BLANCHE. What a misfortune !

(*the* GIRLS *horrified*)

AGNES. Where can it be ?

Looking on the grass. The four GIRLS *all look for the ring on the grass.*

LOTTE. A bad omen.   (*sorrowfully*)

OSCAR. Why so ? I can get another.

LOTTE. That's like you men. If I were to die, you would say you could get another. I so grieve that the ring is lost.

BLANCHE. Lost ! It is not lost.

JESSIE. We'll find it.

KATIE. Yes, if it were at the bottom of a river.

AGNES. We are not the first four girls who have gone hunting for a wedding-ring.

OSCAR. Never mind—it's a pleasure for me to buy wedding-rings. I should like to go on buying wedding rings for ever,

LOTTE. What would you do with them ?

OSCAR. Use them all to marry you with.

KATIE. (*shouting*) Tally ho ! Tally ho !

LOTTE. Have you found it ?

KATIE. Yes.

THE GIRLS. Where ?

KATIE. Here.   (*shows wedding-ring*)

BLANCHE What a remarkably fine specimen.

(*looking at it*)

JESSIE. So thick !

AGNES. And so heavy !

BLANCHE. So bright !

JESSIE. So yellow !

AGNES. So solid.

KATIE. Of all patterns for rings, that is the pattern for me. (*giving it to* OSCAR.)

> *Enter* COLONEL DE ROCHEVANNES,* D., *at back, carrying a bouquet. The* COLONEL *is in private clothes; the ribbon at his button-hole.*

COL. Good morning, mademoiselle. Good morning, my sweet daughter. My visit, which, out of doubt, you have expected, is to you. Permit that your proud father-in-law present you with this. (*offering bouquet*) I have made to you so many gallant speeches that I am at a loss what I should say now. (LOTTE *takes the bouquet*) These flowers shall bloom with flesh colours, and expand in new perfumes when that they shall be near to you.

THE GIRLS. (*admiring bouquet*) Beautiful !

COL. And the bridesmaids—how goes it with them ?— the beautiful Blanche, the pretty Jessie, the lamblike Agnes, and the timid and retiring Katie ? How they all are ?

BLANCHE. (*looking at bouquet*) Beautiful !

COL. Ah !

BLANCHE. I mean——

COL. You mean what ? You mean what you think and say, the more I think so as it is true. (*to* LOTTE) Tell me, my daughter Lotte, or, as your papa call, my dear Lottchen, tell me—where is that papa, eh ? I have not seen him since the day before yesterday, when we talked of news which was of a grave character—but it is past, it is past, diplomacy shall arrange that affair.

BLANCHE. (*to* AGNES) Wouldn't you like him for a father-in-law ?

AGNES. All father-in-laws are nice, if they have sons to marry.

---

* The Author requests this part may be played with a *slight* French accent. He is not to pronounce his words absurdly, or shrug his shoulders, or duck his head towards his stomach, like the conventional stage Frenchman. COLONEL DE ROCHEVANNES is to be played with the old pre-Revolutionary politeness—knightly courtesy, with a mixture of ceremony and *bonhommie.*

Col. Where is that papa, eh?

Enter HERR KARL HARTMANN,* *from door in house, carrying a basketful of fruit—pineapples, peaches, &c., &c., &c. He is followed by two* FEMALE SERVANTS, *who bring on a table laden with pastry, fruits, cakes, wedding presents, jewellery, wine, &c. Two tables are brought and joined together.*

HART. Papa is here. He will be here. He was and shall be here always to de side of his child, his daughter for de few days dat she remain to him. (*approaching* LOTTE) Kiss me, meine Lottchen. As de hours pass away, and I dink dat you are to leave me, I get more sad—more to remember dat I am old, and dat I shall be lonely. Ah! yaye! yaye! yaye! Dis shall not be. (*gives the basket to* LOTTE, *who goes up with it.* HARTMANN *approaches* COLONEL) Colonel, your hand. How you find yourself? Oscar, my son, give me your hand also. My children—(*to the* GIRLS)—I shall not ask your hands, but I shall ask your foreheads (*kisses them*), and we will have our little lunch upon this sword?

COL. (*puzzled*) Upon this sword?

HART. Eh! Yes, yes, upon de grass—upon de herb. (*to* OSCAR) Oscar, my boy, a week to-day, and all shall be over. You shall be gone, and Lottchen shall be gone, and (*turning to the* COLONEL, *and taking his hand*)—and we two old men—we shall remain here to mourn.

COL. Yes; it is sad, but it is bright. (*taking him apart from others*) Is there any news this morning?

HART. Diplomacy, diplomacy, always diplomacy.

OSCAR. (*sorrowfully*) There is no fear.

HART. What! you like to fight, you?

COL. His profession, his father's, and his father's father's; we are soldiers by birth.

HART. I was just the oder thing. I was intended for a doctor, and passed through some of my examinations, when my father died, and I am compelled to be a merchant. But still, I have fought for all dat. In '48 I take de musket, and when de liberty—but dat is nothing now. But it is a fine thing—de liberty.

COL. So is glory.

---

* This part to be played with a slight German accent, and not to be made wilfully comic. Herr Karl Hartmann is to be a perfect gentleman, with a touch of the scholar and pedant in his manner—but always a gentleman.

OSCAR. And the truest glory is the glory of war.

HART. No, no, no. De glory of peace—dat is ten times greater. (*during this conversation table is laid and chairs arranged*) But come, de luncheon is ready. (*looking round*) But where is Captain Sound? Agnes, where is your fader? We must wait for Captain Sound.

(*bell heard*)

THE GIRLS. Here he is.

Enter CAPTAIN SOUND,* *door at back, carrying a case.*

CAPT. How do do, Lotte, my darling—my dear god-daughter? Agnes (*kissing her*), you are looking fresh as a daisy. How are you, Hartmann? and you, Colonel? and you, Oscar, my happy man, the happiest fellow in the world? (*to* BLANCHE *and others*) I have to apologise for not being here before, but, somehow, I missed the train from Dover. (*to* COLONEL) I have brought the London papers as I have come along. But there will be no fighting——

COL. No need for it.

HART. No, no; diplomacy will settle all that.

CAPT. All the better.

OSCAR. I don't know that.

CAPT. Well, it is bad for promotion; but then, you know, I am an old man, and can never think about a higher grade. But that's no matter—we can't be all admirals, can we, Colonel?

KATIE. (*to* CAPTAIN, *pointing to case*) What's that?

CAPT. This—this is the godfather's present to his god-child; and I think I have shown consummate choice. You see, Lotte is German—Germany is celebrated for its wines.

OSCAR. France is also celebrated for her wines.

CAPT. And England is celebrated for—being an island—and so my present is—what? You'll never guess; so I'll tell you. It is a silver boat to put your bottles in. (*opening case, and bringing out silver boat, which he shows*) You see it's a lifeboat, and fixed on a cradle that runs on wheels. You can put the Rhine wine there, and the Burgundy there,

---

* Captain Sound is not to be dressed in uniform, but in the morning dress of a gentleman. His manner is to be hearty, but not rough; in every respect that of a captain of a man-of-war, and not of the master of a halfpenny steamboat.

and it rolls all round the table beautifully.   The sound of
its rattle is enough to make you thirsty.

During this conversation the GIRLS *have looked at
the contents of the table, and express great admiration at them.   All sit down.* LOTTE *returns.   See
diagram.*

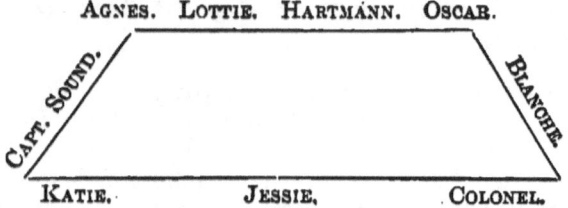

AGNES. LOTTIE. HARTMANN. OSCAR.

CAPT. SOUND.   BLANCHE.

KATIE.   JESSIE,   COLONEL.

HART. Open de wine.   (*two female servants open wine*)
There is nothing but pastry and fruit.   It is a lunch for de
young ladies and de lovers, Colonel (*looking towards him*)
For old men, like you and me, we can revenge ourselves at
dinner.   Colonel, you take wine?   Burgundy or hock?

COL. I thank you—the German wine for me.

OSCAR. And for me.

HART. (*rises and fills their glasses*) For me, de wines
of Vrance.   The Bordeaux—what de English call claret.
It is good, I can tell you.   This Bordeaux (*holding up a
glass filled*) comes from my brother at Berlin.   De young
ladies shall take Moselle.   I know their tastes.   It is
sweeter, and more nice with fruits, as they think.   (*a pause,*
GIRLS *whispering and nodding to each other, as if each bade
the other to say something*) What is all this signalling about?
You want some ice?   (GIRLS *signifying* No)   Some fruit?
(GIRLS *shake their heads*) No!   Then what is it?

BLANCHE. It is this——

THREE GIRLS. "Hear, hear, hear!"

BLANCHE. When men go to public dinners, they make
speeches.   I know they do, because we read them in the
newspapers.   I don't read them, because, generally, they
are so bad;-but I hear all about them; and, as this is Lotte's
betrothal, as they would say in France or Germany, and we
have no betrothals here in England——

THE GIRLS. More's the shame!

HART. You girls want to make a speech?

JESSIE. We want to drink Lotte's health.

AGNES. And prosperity.

KATIE. And happiness.

COL. ⎫
OSCAR. ⎬ Good, good, good ! Hear, hear, hear ! &c.
HART. ⎪
CAPT. ⎭

BLANCHE. Now, I'll begin.

THE GIRLS. Let's all begin together,
(*all this to be very gay and lively*)

BLANCHE. Mr. Chairman—my Lords and Gentlemen——

JESSIE. No!

BLANCHE. Don't interrupt. Mr. Chairman and Colonel——

AGNES. And the bridegroom——

THE GIRLS. Of course, the bridegroom.

BLANCHE. Though unaccustomed to public oratory, except during the time of the breaking-up of school——

JESSIE. No, that's wrong—it is before vacation.

KATIE. Yes, that's right.

AGNES. Katie, don't interrupt.

BLANCHE. I rise——

JESSIE. No, we rise.

KATIE. Yes, we all rise. (*they all rise*)

BLANCHE. To propose the health of——

JESSIE. And prosperity——

AGNES. To the young married couple.

HART. ⎫
COL. ⎬ Hear, hear, hear !

JESSIE. To Miss Hartmann.

AGNES. To the bride.

KATIE. She's only half Miss Hartmann now, and she's only half Mrs. Oscar.

BLANCHE. We all went to school with Lotte.

JESSIE. And we love her dearly.

THE GIRLS. Dearly.

BLANCHE. We know too little——

JESSIE. No ; too much.

COL. More's the pity.

BLANCHE. Of Monsieur Oscar de Rochevannes — we have not seen much of him lately——

AGNES. More's the pity.

BLANCHE. But he appears to us to be a young man worthy of being married, and even worthy of our Lotte.

EVERYBODY. Hear, hear, hear !

BLANCHE. I, therefore, with your permission——

JESSIE. No, that's not right.

BLANCHE. Yes it is.

AGNES. Don't quarrel.

BLANCHE. She puts me out.

JESSIE. No, I don't.

AGNES. Don't dispute.

KATIE. (*coming to the rescue*) Now, girls!

(*Moselle opened. All the* GIRLS *take their glasses*)

THE GIRLS. We drink the health of the bride and bridegroom.

HART.
COL. } Bravo! bravo! Capital!

HART. I am afraid that the girls will take too much wine. The Moselle soon gets into their heads.

OSCAR. (*rising*) Ladies, let me thank you for myself and wife.

THE GIRLS. Hurrah! Hurrah! Hurrah!

OSCAR. You are most kind, but you are anticipating. They do not drink the bridesmaids' health in England, I think, until the wedding breakfast.

HART. Some Rhine wine, Colonel; and pass the Bordeaux to me.   (GIRLS *pull crackers*)

COL. Ah, vive la joie. The sound of these fresh young voices makes me young again! I have once more nineteen years. Mr. Hartmann (*addressing him*), before I was sous-lieutenant, I used to pass some time with my friends the students, and I used to sing—it is more than thirty years ago—a little chanson with a pretty little chorus. If you please, I shall sing you that little song now.

ALL. Bravo! bravo!

COL. (*clears his throat, and sings*) You shall forgive that the voice is not sweet, I have slept too often in full air and on wet grass.

Gais enfants de Bacchus, vrais amis de la table,
　　De notre courte vie, egayons le chemin.
Que le sombre chagrin jamais ne nous accable,
　　Aussitôt qu'il parait, noyons le dans le vin.

　　Loin de nous les grandeurs, la fortune, et la gloire,
　　Il est plus doux d'aimer, de chanter, rire et boire.
　　Toujours gais et dispos, voltigeons tour à tour,
　　De l'Amour à Bacchus, de Bacchus à l'Amour.

(*chorus, repeated by everybody*)

Amis! pour bien mourir, il faut que bien l'on vive,
    Puis que on ne voit la bas, ni cabaret, ni vin,
Quand il faudra passer hélas! sur l'autre rive,
    La mort doit nous trouver, la bouteille à la main.

          Chorus—Loin de nous, &c.

Sans doute il est bien beau d'être à l'academie,
    Ou membre de l'Institut, ou même un Senateur,
Mais on est plus heureux au près de son amie,
    Vieux vin et jeune amie voilà le vrai bonheur.

          Chorus—Loin de nous, &c.

            (*everybody applaud*)

OSCAR. Now, papa—my Rhenish papa, you must sing us a song too—a German song.

HART. I was once like de Colonel—a student, but it was of medicine, and I will sing you a little song which we used to sing over our lager beer and pipes.

EVERYBODY. Bravo! Good! &c.

KATIE. A song in German!

HART. For de convenience of de ladies who not speak German, de chorus is in Latin.

GIRLS. Oh!

HART. (*sings*)

      Ça ça, geschmauset
         Lasst uns nicht rappelköpfisch sein
      Wer nicht mit hauset
      Der bleib allein!

   Chorus—Edite, Bibite, Collegiales,

         Post multa secula pocula nulla!
      Der Herr Professor
         Liesst heute kein Collegium
      Drum ist es besser,
         Man trinket eins "rum."

          Chorus—Edite, &c.

      Knaster, den gelben
         Hat uns Apollo præparirt
      Und uns denselben
      Recommandirt.

          Chorus—Edite, &c.

At the end of the song the gate bell is heard. A
SERVANT *brings on letters, which she gives to*
COLONEL *and* OSCAR. *They read them. The*
gaiety of OSCAR *and the* COLONEL *immediately*
gives way to anxiety and thought, and they sit at
the table, all their mirth gone, while the GIRLS
continue the chorus. Stage a little darker.

BLANCHE. How dark it's grown !

CAPT. Sudden squall.

HART. Colonel, de bottle stands with you. Oscar my
son——

LOTTE. (*seeing the expression of* OSCAR'S *face*) Oscar,
what's the matter ?

OSCAR. (*rising*) Nothing ; that is—news which——
                                    (*looking at his father*)

COL. News which—(*passes his letter over to* HARTMANN)
La Guerre.

HART. (*reading letter*) Krieg !
                          (*hands the letter over to* SOUND)

SOUND. War !   (*the four* MEN *rise*)

COL. (*after having read* OSCAR'S *letter attentively, rises.*
To LOTTE) My child ! It grieves my heart to tell you, but
here is an order for Oscar to quit England, and to rejoin his
regiment at Paris.

LOTTE. (*rising*) Oscar leave me ;—and the marriage——

OSCAR. (*heartbroken*) Must be put off till I return.

THE GIRLS. Put off ?   (*all rise*)

LOTTE. Oscar !

COL. The order is imperative. We must go at once.
We are but a short time from Dover, and must depart by
to-night's boat.

HART. But, my child—my child. Oscar must go ; but
he will come back soon.

CAPT. War is declared.

KATIE. But can't they put the war off until after the
marriage ?

COL. My child, the glove is thrown down.

HART. (*to* COLONEL) Yes ; you have thrown it down.

COL. Pardon, it is you ; it must be taken up.

Bell heard ; SERVANT *comes on with a telegram,*
which she gives to HARTMANN.

LOTTE (*to* GIRLS) Go ; I—I—I wish to be alone.

BLANCHE. Good-bye, Lotte, dear.

AGNES. Good-bye, Oscar.

KATIE. }
JESSIE. } Good-bye, good-bye!

HART. (*having read the telegram*) Lotte, from my brother at Berlin. War is declared, and his son, my nephew, your cousin, is forced to leave his father, to go and fight for Vaterland.

LOTTE. My cousin Fritz?

COL. What nobler duty than to fight for his country—to perish for his native land!

HART. And the father and the mother that he leaves weeping, and the heartstrings that are strained for the gratification of ambition!

COL. Of ambition?—of glory!

HART. Glory! War is an accursed trade!

COL. Trade! Pardon me, Monsieur Hartmann, war is chivalry—war is honour.

HART. (*catching his hands, and pointing to* LOTTE, *who is weeping on* OSCAR'S *shoulder*) See what is war!

COL. (*impatiently*) But more, much more——

CAPT. (*interfering*) Don't differ. It is bad enough as it is. Let us take a turn in the garden, and think what is to be done.

COL. (*to* HARTMANN) But France? }
HART. But Germany? } · (*together*)

CAPT. My dear friends——

COL. War is the most noble of professions.

HART. (*to* CAPTAIN) The greatest curse. Is not that your opinion?

CAPT. Well, you see, they are going to fight on land; I belong to the other element. Come, let's walk in the paddock.

Exeunt CAPTAIN, COLONEL, *and* HARTMANN, R.H. 2 E.

BLANCHE. God bless you, Oscar.

JESSIE. You are going to fight.

KATIE. }
AGNES. } We hope soon to see you back.

BLANCHE. To marry our dear Lotte.

KATIE. Yes, come back to marry Lotte.

THE GIRLS. (*all very tearful*) Good-bye, good-bye!

Exeunt GIRLS *into house. A pause.*

OSCAR. Lotte!

LOTTE. Oscar, you must leave me!

OSCAR. Yes, Lotte.

LOTTE. And, I shall never see you more.

OSCAR. Oh, yes, many, many happy days are yet in store for us.

LOTTE. It seems too strange, too sudden, too terrible. I can't believe it; I can't believe that you, my Oscar, who, six days hence, were to be my husband, are now to leave me to go and fight, perhaps to—to die.

OSCAR. (*cheering her*) Lotte!

LOTTE. We might as well have lost our wedding-ring; it will be useless now.

OSCAR. Not so. (*producing it*) I will wear it next my heart, beneath my cross, until I see you again, and I place it on your finger.

LOTTE. Never will that day come; I feel—I know it (*a very distant peal of thunder is heard*) Blighted! blighted!

Re-enter CAPTAIN SOUND, HARTMANN, *and* COLONEL.
The COLONEL *and* HARTMANN *are in anger.*

COL. I tell it above all—above arts, science, literature— above the base thing you call commerce, there is glory! Glory to a nation is as honour to a man; without glory a nation is valueless, as without honour a man is beneath contempt.

HART. And I tell you that glory is a delusion, a snare, a cruel lie? It means burnt homesteads, ruined villages, abandoned homes, desolation, and despair! What say you, Captain?

CAPT. I say I hate war; but when once you begin to fight, fight it out—you're better friends after.

HART. And my nephew, my brother's only son, torn from his home to be a soldier!

COL. And my son, who glories in his duty. Come Oscar, I will go with you. I go to offer my sword to my country. Where a grey head leads, young men will follow—as soldiers crowd after the white plumes in a field-marshal's hat.

HART. Lotte (*placing her in chair*) we will go to Berlin to console my brother, and to help him in his affliction.

COL. To-night, Oscar, to Dover—thence to Paris.

HART. To Berlin, Lotte. (*she is senseless*) Why, she's cold!

OSCAR. (*turning round*) Cold!

HART. She has fainted. Lotte! Oscar!

OSCAR *about to step towards her ; his father arrests him.*

Col. It bleeds my heart, my poor boy ; but we must go at once.

Oscar. Lotte, Lotte ! She cannot hear me ! Farewell ! my wife !

Hart. My child !

Col. My son ! For France and honour ·

Captain Sound.

Colonel.

Lotte   Oscar.

Hartmann.   in Chair.

Tableau.

ACT II.*

SCENE.—*Near a battle-field.* R.H., *a church. The church has just been shelled, and bears marks of cannonade. One side has been shot away, so that the interior is seen. A heap of rubbish—bricks, stones, &c., that have fallen,* R.C. *Grass plat before church, and trees. Trees at back, stretching away into the far distance. Night. Stage dark. See diagram.*

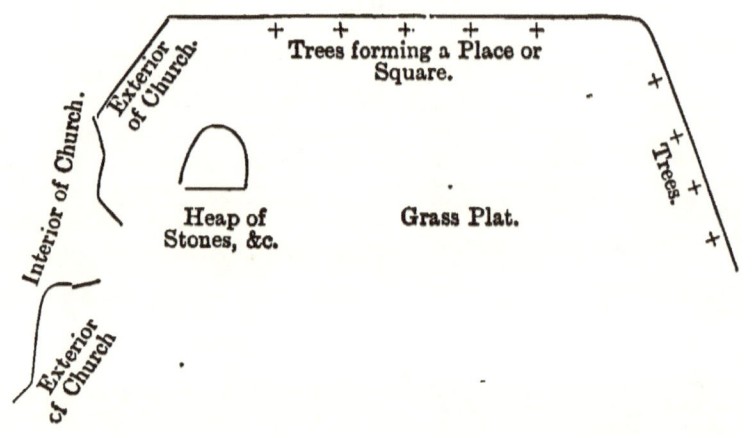

Discovered, R.H., *the* COLONEL *and* OSCAR, *forming— allowing for the difference of uniform—the picture from Horace Vernet's "Retreat from Moscow."*

OSCAR. (*lifting up his eyes*) Father!

COL. My boy!

OSCAR. Where are we?

COL. Behind the church.

OSCAR. Near which we met the foe?

COL. Yes; I brought you here for shelter; but you fainted, and I dared not to move you.

OSCAR. Is any one in the church?

---

* Anything like uniform or accoutrement seen in this Act must be stained, dusty, muddy, and exhibit the signs of severe use. Nothing sparkling, tinselly, or patent-leathered.

Col. Yes; I see lights there, and there are wounded men inside.

Oscar. Our wounded?

Col. Ours and the enemy's. All is not lost, my son— we have not lost honour!

Oscar. (*grasping his father's hand*) No, not honour; we cannot lose that. You are wounded!

Col. Slightly, a sabre cut (*pointing to his head*); but you, my boy, are wounded dangerously. Are you in pain?

Oscar. No, not much pain; but I am faint and thirsty. Give me some water.

Col. (*rolls up a military cloak, and places it under* Oscar's *head*) It is so dark, Oscar, I fear I shall not find the stream.

Oscar. Don't be long from me—don't be long from me, father.

Col. I'll fetch some water. (*taking up a helmet*) I'll be back directly.

As Colonel *is going off, one or two* Peasants, *carrying baskets and bags; two or three* Sisters of Mercy, *carrying sacks, bales, &c., cross the stage from the left, and enter the church. Enter* Hartmann, *l.u.e. He is dressed in a costume of the Ambulance Corps, and wears the red cross.* Colonel *is resting exhausted against the heap of rubbish. They do not recognise each other.*

Hart. (*approaching* Colonel) My poor fellow, are you wounded?

Col. No. When you have assisted your countrymen, I will thank you to look to mine.

Hart. De wounded are all of de same country, and we try to assist all alike. Pardon a moment, I go to fetch de lantern. *Exit* Hartmann, l.h.

Col. (*returns to* Oscar) Oscar! Oscar!

Oscar. (*wakes up, as if out of a swoon*) Who is it?

Col. Help is near—the ambulance has arrived.

Oscar. Don't let them move me—let me die here.

Col. Do not talk of dying. Think, boy—we are prisoners; but we shall be exchanged. We shall live, and fight again for France.

Oscar. France! (*with animation*)

Col. The ambulance.

He rises, and goes to meet Hartmann, *who re-enters, l.h., with a lantern and a jug-ful of water.*

HART. Here is some water. Drink.

COL. It is not for me.

> *The light of* HARTMANN'S *lantern falls upon him as
> he takes the jug.*

HART. Colonel !

COL. Hartmann ! (OSCAR *does not hear this*) Great
heaven !—you here ?

HART. My poor friend—and do we meet again, thus ?
You are wounded !

COL. No matter for me ; it is but slight.

HART. Lotte !   (*calling off,* L.H.)

COL. Lotte !

HART. (*to* COLONEL) She is here !   I will not tell her it
is you ; it will shock her too much.   Where is the poor
man who——

COL. (*pointing*) There, but——

> COLONEL *is about to speak, when* LOTTE *enters,* L.H.U.E.
> *She is dressed in a travelling dress, black and
> white—the Prussian colours—and wears the red
> cross on her arm.*

HART. My child see dere—(*holding the lantern*)—see
dere is one who needs your assistance.   Go to him—give
him help.

COL. But——

HART. It is her duty.   She will do it well for duty's
sake—as for de sake of him to whom she was betrothed.

> LOTTE *takes the lantern, and goes to* OSCAR.   *She puts
> the lantern down on stage, and kneels beside* OSCAR,
> *not recognising him.*   COLONEL *and* HARTMANN
> *go up stage,* COLONEL *explaining to* HARTMANN.

LOTTE. My poor friend, are you hurt ?   Can you hear
me ?   If so, don't speak, but point out where is your pain,
if you can.   Where is your wound ?   (OSCAR *raises his head
at the same moment that* LOTTE *disposes the lantern so that
the light shines upon his face and upon hers*) Oscar !

OSCAR. Lotte !

HART. Oscar !   Your son !

> (COLONEL *and* HARTMANN *advance,* L.H.   *Picture*)

LOTTE. Dying !

OSCAR. No ; not dying now that you are here, Lotte—
not now.   I shall live for you.

COL. For you, Lotte, and for his country!

HART. (*to* COLONEL) But how is it we find you here?

COL. Where should I be? We are soldiers—we have fought—we are prisoners. Let me put back the question. How is it that you and Lotte——

HART. When we arrive in Berlin, where we go to see my brother, I find the army wants surgeons. I was educated as a surgeon, so I volunteered, and Lotte accompanies me. This is our first battle, and Lotte finds her husband on the field—and this is war—and this is glory!

LOTTE. Father, he is fainting!

OSCAR. No, no! Don't leave me. Let me feel your hand. Do not go from me.

LOTTE. For one moment.

OSCAR. Only for a moment.

> *She goes into church, and returns again directly.*
> *Two or three* SISTERS OF MERCY *cross the stage,*
> *from church to* L.H.

HART. Have you been here long?

COL. I know not how long—since sunset. We were surrounded with a murderous fire—it hailed bullets—a sudden shock struck me to the ground, stunned; but only for a moment, as I think. When I woke up, I found myself by his side. (*During this,* LOTTE *bathes his brow with essences that she carries, and* OSCAR *has kissed her hand*) If he dies, he dies for France! (*with intense fervour*) The two loves of my life—the soil, the native land, the ground beneath me, trodden by the invader!—my son's blood spilled by his hand, and I without a sword to avenge him—without power to smite one foe!

HART. You are wounded—your head——

COL. (*tearing off the bandage*) It is nothing.

HART. My friend—let——

COL. No; your heart is a friend's, but your hand is a foe's. (*goes up the stage, followed by* HARTMANN)

OSCAR. Did you not say you had a cousin who was pressed to fight?

LOTTE. Yes, dear.

OSCAR. And I may have received this stroke from him. Lotte! Let my ears drink in your voice! Oh! it is hard to leave you—hard to leave my father—hard to quit fighting by his side until our flag is again victorious! Lotte, grant me one request.

LOTTE. (*on her knees, and kissing his forehead*) What is it ?

OSCAR. The church is near—the priest is near. If I am to live, let me know that, when the war is over, I can claim you as my wife. If I am to die, let me die with your hand in mine. Lead me into the church, Lotte ; let us be married there now, at once, while life remains in me, while my head is clear, while my heart is beating !

> *During this,* COLONEL *and* HARTMANN *have been up stage.* HARTMANN *has bathed the* COLONEL's *forehead, and attended to his wounds.* HARTMANN *advances.*

LOTTE. Father! (*she rises from her knees, and whispers to* HARTMANN)

OSCAR. Mr. Hartmann, Lotte's father, you will not withhold your consent ?

HART. No, no ; but the priest——

OSCAR. There are wounded in the church, and the priest is surely there.   (*the organ heard within the church*)

HART. But the witnesses ?

OSCAR. You, her father, and mine.

HART. But the necessary formalities for——(OSCAR's *head sinks.* LOTTE *looks imploringly at her father*) Be it as you wish.

LOTTE. (*taking his hand*) I will be yours in death, as in life. But think, you cannot bear being moved into the church.

OSCAR. Oh yes ; your love will make me strong.

LOTTE. My love—but we have no wedding-ring.

OSCAR. We have the wedding-ring I showed you at your father's—in your own home. I have worn it here, between my heart and the cross of honour.

> *He places his hand on his heart, and brings out the wedding-ring, encased in a small silk bag.*

LOTTE. (*taking out the wedding-ring*) There's blood upon it !

OSCAR. It is a soldier's blood—your husband's

LOTTE. But your father—we must ask his consent.

OSCAR. Don't go from me.

LOTTE. No, no ; my father shall speak to him.

> HARTMANN *understands ; goes and taps the* COLONEL's *shoulder. The* COLONEL's *back is to the audience.*

The stage grows a little lighter. Morning breaks. As the COLONEL *turns round upon him, the expression of his face shows that he is mad.*

HART. (*steps back*) Colonel!

COL. Yes—colonel—commander of the legion, who has fought and conquered, who will fight and conquer still! It is destiny!

HART. (*shocked, turns to* LOTTE, *and whispers to her*) His mind wanders!

LOTTE. Great heavens! Oscar must not know it. (*turning to* OSCAR) Oscar, can you rise?

OSCAR. (*rising*) Yes; your love gives me strength. My father——

LOTTE. Will follow us.

OSCAR. It is not far to the church. (*seeing it as he rises*) No; it is there—every stone is sacred—a shattered ruin, but still a church.

> *Organ heard.* LOTTE *and* HARTMANN *convey* OSCAR *to the church. They are received by* SISTERS OF MERCY, *and they pass out of sight.* HARTMANN *returns to* COLONEL. PEASANTS *cross the stage, and* SOLDIERS, *from left hand, into the church During all this the organ is heard.*

COL. (*advancing, quite mad, looking in the place where* OSCAR *had lain*) Where is my son? Where is Oscar?

HART. In the church.

COL. The church! What does he there? His place is in the front! Quick, men, to the front! These are our foes before us! Close up. We *must* conquer! The invader is before us! Every blade of grass should be a bayonet—every church a magazine—every house an arsenal —every man a soldier! Silently, men—silently, let not the horse's hoofs be heard upon the turf! We shall soon gallop out upon the open—we shall soon meet them, eye to eye, hoof to hoof, blade to blade! Tighten your belts!—the enemy, the foe is on the soil! Let every sword-stroke redden it! (*distant trumpet without*) The reinforcements have arrived. Oscar, keep close by me in the charge!

HART. My friend, let me conduct you to——

COL. 'Twas on this spot, Oscar, that our forefather's founded laws it is our duty to defend; on this spot they proclaimed the liberties we must reconquer! Well, boy, these laws, these liberties, these glories—prostrate for the moment

—shall rise again to the flame of our cannon and the flash of
our swords! Be the big heart of France heard in our
voices as we cry, "To arms!" We know for what we fight
—for the flag that flares above us—for the church-bells
that ring our women and children to the house of prayer.
Not only your wives, your infants, bid you draw the
sword, but more—your homes, your rights, your native land!
Draw, then! strike! strike, and spare not!

HART. (*with a concentrated self-contained enthusiasm—
not so demonstrative as the Frenchman's, but as deep and as
earnest*) Right, Colonel; and may the shame of a mother's
curse blight the coward who would refuse to fight when
called on by his Vaterland! Let the men rise armed from
the earth, as in the heathen fable. To the ranks! to the
front! all men that are men—men from the desk, the
counting-house, the workshop, and the plough! Vorvarts!
For your brides and your betrothed, for the grand past
and the bright future, Immer vorvarts! Recruit! enrol
battalions and brigades! March against the invader, whose
lusts are lands, and whose honour is ambition! Strike swift
and surely! for your faith and your freedom, for your blue
rivers and green hills, for Vaterland—Vaterland, home and
children! (*after a pause*) And when the fight is fought,
honour to the brave in misfortune, help to the fallen, and
be past hatreds dead and buried, as are the thousands of
heroes whose memories we weep! (*a pause*. HARTMANN
goes to COLONEL. *The stage grows lighter*. Look, Colonel;
it is morning. You can see the first rays of day
(*pointing*, R.H.) through the stained-glass windows of the
church. My daughter, your son—our children—are
married; and they come as in a hallowed light of the rich
purple and yellow glories the sun throws over them.

> *Effect of sun seen in the church.   Organ heard.*
> LOTTE *conducts* OSCAR *from church, and places*
> *him* L.C. *on the stage.* HARTMANN *arranges his*
> *military cloak.*

OSCAR. And you are mine—my wife?
LOTTE. Yes, dear; see, the sun is rising.

> (*distant cannonade is heard without*)

COL. And the battle recommences!
HART. But far from here.
OSCAR. Lift me up; let me see the sun rise—it may be
for the last time. Oh! what a beautiful world, Lotte, if

I were spared to it, gilded by the sun, lighted by your love !
Lotte—your hand ! Yes, I can see you in the lustre of the
day. (*to* COLONEL) Father !

COL. My boy !

OSCAR. Your hand ! Embrace me ! Hold me—keep
me firmer, yet. I fear that I——

> *His head falls upon his father's chest. Distant
> cannonade. Trumpets sound nearer. At the sound
> of the trumpet* OSCAR *raises his head, cries, "*Vive
> la France !*" and falls.* LOTTE *and his father over
> him.* HARTMANN *mourning,* L.C. *The coloured
> light from the stained-glass windows strikes upon
> the picture ; at the same moment female voices are
> heard singing hymn in church (only female voices,
> and without accompaniment)* PEASANTS *enter upon
> the stage, and behind the trees* SOLDIERS *are seen
> mustering.*

HYMN.

> " Death guards thy door, Eternity !
> Faith shall set thy spirit free ;
> Day shall dawn when past is night,
> Soul immortal, wing thy flight !"

ACT III.

SCENE.—*Same as Act I.—Autumn. Discovered*—LOTTE,
BLANCHE, JESSIE, AGNES, *and* KATIE. *They are working various things for the sick and wounded. A basket
at* LOTTE'S *feet, in which are various things already
worked.* LOTTE *in deep mourning. The* GIRLS *all
dressed soberly. Stage light and bright. A bale of
goods,* R.H., *near the shrubbery.* KATIE *reading a book.*

BLANCHE. (*reading a newspaper*) There is no news.

AGNES. No news ?

BLANCHE. That is, no news of any battle.

LOTTE. You read on, Katie, if you have done your
work.

KATIE. (*reading from book*—TENNYSON)

> " O father, whereso'er thou be,
> Who pledgest now thy gallant son ;
> A shot, ere half thy draught be done,
> Hath still'd the life that beat from thee.

"O mother, praying God will save
    Thy sailor,—while thy head is bow'd,
    His heavy-shotted hammock-shroud
Drops in his vast and wandering grave."

BLANCHE.
JESSIE.   } (*in a tone of remonstrance*) Katie!
AGNES.

LOTTE. Go on, go on.

KATIE. Are you sure you wish it, Lotte?

LOTTE. Yes; go on.

KATIE. (*reads again*)

"O, somewhere, meek, unconscious dove,
    That sittest 'ranging golden hair,
    And glad to find thyself so fair;
Poor child, that waitest for thy love!

"For now her father's chimney glows
    In expectation of a guest;
    And thinking 'This will please him best,'
She takes a riband or a rose;

"For he will see them on to-night;
    And with the thought her colour burns;
    And, having left the glass, she turns
Once more to set a ringlet right."

BLANCHE.
JESSIE.   } Oh, that's beautiful! (*pausing in their work*)
AGNES.

LOTTE. Go on with your work, and listen too.

KATIE. (*reading*)

"And, even as she turned, the curse
    Had fallen, and her future lord
    Was drown'd in passing thro' the ford,
Or kill'd in falling from his horse."

Oh, how dreadful!

BLANCHE. Don't read any more.

KATIE. (*looking off book. Half-a-dozen or so leaves
turn over. When she takes up the book, she begins,
unconsciously, in a fresh place*)

"I hold it true, whate'er befall;
    I feel it, when I sorrow most:
    'Tis better to have loved and lost,
Than never to have loved at all."

JESSIE. The words seem to fall like——

AGNES. Like rain.

BLANCHE. You mean like tears.

KATIE. Just as if the lines were printed in velvet.

AGNES. Black velvet.

BLANCHE. Black silk velvet.

LOTTE. (*repeating*) " 'Tis better to have loved and lost, than never to have loved at all ! " (BLANCHE *looks at her watch*) 'Tis time for you to go, girls, so leave your work. Will you be back by three ?

THE GIRLS. Yes.

LOTTE. I expect the carrier to call for this bale.

BLANCHE. And we'll take the basket into the house.

> *The* GIRLS *place their work in the basket.* BLANCHE *and* JESSIE *carry the basket off.* AGNES *and* KATIE *turn, and kiss* LOTTE *; they then go off into the house.* KATIE *has left the book on the bale.*

LOTTE. And the days pass, and pass, and pass ; and I feel still the same !   A widow, though no wife ; a maiden betrothed, and yet not wedded ! My lover, my husband— dead, and I not yet twenty-one ! But kings and emperors have willed it so, and statesmen are too cold and too proud to think of silly, weeping women ! The demand for glory must be satisfied, the desire for conquest must be sated, and it is we who pay the costs ! We, the sick at heart—the wounded of soul ! (*looking at the bale*)   My woman's life is over before it began, and he has gone from me—gone from me for ever ! O Oscar ! for one short moment of the past— for one return of the pressure of your arm against mine, as we wandered through this shrubbery—for one look into your eyes—for one breath of yours upon my cheek—for one half- painful strain to your strong heart—what would I give—what would I give ! No; the past is past ; it is not to return ! (*taking up the book unconsciously*) And how these lines echo my thoughts ! Strange, I know nothing of the man who wrote these verses, and yet I have thought and felt them—every syllable !

> (*opens the volume, haphazard. Reads*)

"Who broke our fair companionship,
    And spread his mantle, dark and cold,
    And wrapt thee formless in the fold,
And dull'd the murmur on thy lip,

"And bore thee when I could not see,
  ·Nor follow ; tho'·I walk in haste,
  And think that somewhere in the waste
  The shadow sits and waits for me."

(she goes off into shrubbery)

Enter COLONEL *and* HARTMANN *arm-in-arm, both dressed " en bourgeois."* COLONEL *seats himself on garden chair ;* HARTMANN *on the bale of goods.*

HART. A good walk, and a long walk—the longest we have taken yet.

COL. (*rising*) I fear too long for you, my friend. Your leg which was wounded—it cannot yet be strong.

HART. I only feel it now and then. The ball passed so clean through that it left but small mischief.

COL. (*looking round*) Where is Lotte ?

HART. I don't know.

COL. (*dropping his voice*) What does the doctor say ?

HART. All that is bad may be ; but nothing bad as yet. The seeds of consumption, but only the seeds. The great grief that she has passed through——

COL. (*taking his hand*) Yes, yes ; and what did the doctor say of me ?

HART. That you were as reasonable as he is, or as I am, or any other sane man ; but of a violent excitable nature ; terrible privations, and our loss, deprived you for some time of reason. Now, however, you are better—you have had perfect repose and quiet—·your mental tone is thoroughly restored, and you have no need to fear further hallucinations.

COL. (*vaguely*) No, no, no—no hallucinations ; but one I cannot banish—Hartmann—(*after a pause*) My son !—your son !—Lotte's husband !—I see him every day ! Every night, by my bedside, when I look into the square panes of glass of the window, he is there stretching out his arms to me—I hear his voice calling to me ; and, as the figure nears me, I feel his hot breath (*excitedly*) flicker on my face——

HART. My poor friend, you must not excite yourself ; remember what the doctor says. I am responsible for you. I will not say, do not think of him—that is impossible ; but I will say that when the room is dark, and your mind is highly excited—your fancy——

COL. Fancy ! Have these scientific men no belief? (*rising*) Last night—last night I saw him standing by my side !—saw him as plainly as—as (CAPTAIN SOUND *enters from the back. The* COLONEL *changes his tone quickly*)—as plainly as I see this good Captain Sound, who now comes to us.

CAPT. (*in a state of great perturbation, which he endeavours to conceal by his ordinary manner. He looks round frequently, as if fearing to be heard*) How d'e do?— how d'e do?—how d'e do? Better,—that's right. And you, Hartmann, you are well?—and Madame de Rochevannes, pretty well?

HART. Alas, no; my daughter still suffers.

CAPT. That's right—that's right. (*shaking hands with him for the second time. Then to* COLONEL) I congratulate you——

COL. Congratulate me!—on what?

CAPT. On looking so much worse—I mean better. Does he not look so much worse, Hartmann? So, so, so, so! I daresay, now, that you have received the good news?

COL. Good news! What good news can come to me?

CAPT. What good news? Why (*puzzled*), returning health. You are looking as though you had taken a new lease of life.

HART. What is the matter with you, Sound? You are talking nonsense.

CAPT. Am I? I daresay I am. I am a stupid old fool. I—I—I—I——

HART. Well, Captain, is it by accident that you have come here, or on purpose to speak to me? Is it that you want to say something to me alone?

CAPT. By Jove, Hartmann, you are a wonderful man! That is the very thing I came for.

HART. (*to* COLONEL) A little business, my dear Colonel; will you kindly excuse us a few minutes?

Enter LOTTE, *with book, from shrubbery.*

COL. Ah, Lotte, my child, good morning! Been for a long walk with your father; feel inclined to walk again; will you take me for a turn round the garden?

LOTTE. Oh, yes!

CAPT. My dear Madame de Rochevannes, good day; you are looking very well—I may say, hearty. I have seen a great deal of illness among seamen on the Gold Coast; but it is my honest opinion you will get over it.

HART. What is that old man talking about?

CAPT. I have a little matter of business to talk over with papa; and, as you and your other papa are going to take a stroll in the garden, I shall ask you when you come back to give me a hearing—I mean some lunch.

LOTTE. With pleasure.

3 E

CAPT. (*seeing book in her hand*) Reading? Ha! charming occupation. (*she gives him book*) "In Memoriam"; very clever, very clever. I have never read it, but I have no doubt it is very clever.   (*returns book to* LOTTE)

COL. (*aside, to* LOTTE) He has something—is it not?

LOTTE. I think so. Shall we walk?

COL. Let us go to the arbour, and there you shall read to me, will you? (*she assents. He touches the book*) Always the same, hein?

LOTTE. Always the same.   (*they go off,* R. 2 E.)

HART. Now, Sound, what is it? Is it about the railway which——

SOUND. No.

HART. Is it about Agnes going to Germany?

CAPT. No.

HART. Well then, what is it?

CAPT. I'll tell you.

HART. You seem excited.

CAPT. Not a bit, not a bit—I never am excited. You see, Hartmann, you are a learned man—you understand languages and medicine, and philosophy and mathematics, and music and the theory of thorough bass. I want you to tell me about your bringing back the Colonel here?

HART. I have told you.

CAPT. I want you to tell me again.

HART. When that I received the wound in my leg, I am sent back to Cologne, and the Colonel, who was at that time (*signifies "off his head"*) in my charge, and LOTTE accompanied us. We were in Berlin six weeks, and the Colonel having somewhat recovered, and received his parole, he was permitted to accompany us here.

CAPT. And Lotte came here with you?

HART. Yes.

CAPT. And her poor husband?

HART. You know we left him dead near the church. An attack was begun, and we were ordered to the rear, and were compelled to leave the poor boy's body. It was hard.

(*shrugs his shoulders*)

CAPT. Yes, yes, yes, yes; you left Oscar dead—quite dead, on the field of battle.

HART. On the field of battle.

CAPT. Quite dead—yes—just so.

HART. But why reiterate?

CAPT. Just so, why reiterate? Hartmann, you have a

nerve of iron, and a heart of gutta-percha; now listen. Last night, when I had just lit up my cigar, I was told that a gentleman wanted to see me, so I told them to show him in. The room was cozily dark, and the man was so muffled up that I couldn't tell who he was. He asked me if I was Captain Sound, and if I knew where you were? I said, Yes; I was Captain Sound, and I did know where you were. He asked me if you were in England? I said, Yes; at Sevenoaks. And then I thought he was going to faint, so I filled him a glass of port. As he took it I saw his face, and—(*looking at* HARTMANN)—it seemed to me to be a face I had seen before. (*a pause*)

HART. Yes.

CAPT. Well, then he asked after Lotte. I said, Do you mean my friend Hartmann's daughter, who is now Madame de Rochevannes? At this the fellow sprang up, and seized both my hands, and said, Yes. Hartmann—hold on—it was her husband!

HART. What? . (*staggering*)

CAPT. Steady, steady. Will you have some brandy?

HART. Brandy? No; go on, go on. (*agitated*)

CAPT. When I looked at him full in the face, I recognised him—it was poor Oscar. I was considerably knocked over. I told him that his wife was well, and that you were well, and that his father was here; and—and that knocked him over.

HART. And what did you do?

CAPT. I shook his hand, and—and asked him to have some dinner; and I ordered it up—but he did not eat. I asked him all about himself; and he told me that a German doctor, who was on the spot, finding the spark of life not entirely extinct, put him into a waggon, got into the waggon himself, attended him, and with him crossed the frontier. He was sent to Spandau—the bullet was extracted. He could not get any letters or news of his wife, whom he married under such extraordinary circumstances. Now, to make a long story short, he was exchanged, came over to Calais, and then—— (HARTMANN, *who has borne up, is seized by a sudden vertigo, and staggers into garden seat*) Steady, steady! (HARTMANN, *looking round to see that nobody observes him, bursts into tears*) Steady, steady! Don't cry. I can't bear to see anybody cry, but I dislike it especially in men, and women, and children.

HART. Mein Gott! Mein Gott! Returned—returned!

CAPT. Have you got any brandy about you?

HART. No.

CAPT. Then I have. (*takes out flask, and gives to* HARTMANN) Nothing, in extreme cases of happiness, or affliction, like brandy. It cuts both ways, and is a pleasant drink besides. You won't take some? (HARTMANN *signifies* No) Then I will.

HART. (*rising*) Oscar returned—returned!

CAPT. Yes; he had only fallen into a swoon, and was in a state of—of——I forget the word; in a state of insensibility. And, now, Hartmann, I have told you all.

HART. (*shakes* CAPTAIN *by the hand*) Where is he—where is he, Captain? (*looks round, and then whispers*) Now, the question is, how to break it to Lotte, his wife.

CAPT. And how to break it to the Colonel, his father?

HART. And the father mad, or half-mad!

CAPT. And the wife so delicate! The joy might kill her!

HART. The sudden news might drive his father——

CAPT. Good heavens, Hartmann! Taking it in that way, the boy's coming to life again will prove a misfortune, instead of a blessing!

HART. How to break it to them——

CAPT. Well, now, look here. Oscar and I sat up till about two this morning, and we considered the matter over, and to tell you the truth, Hartmann, though I appear a plain, bluff sort of fellow, I have a sort of genius for intrigue; in fact, I have all the talents for being a diplomatist, or a humbug! I don't know whether I'm most proud of it, or ashamed of it, but a brilliant humbug I am. So I proposed—it is my own idea—I proposed that we should break it to neither suddenly, but do it gradually and by degrees!

HART. Wonderful! You have a genius, indeed!

(*wiping his eyes*)

CAPT. Oscar saw it at once! So he brought a letter with him, ready written (*bringing out letter*) which I have here.

HART. And that letter——

CAPT. This letter—— (*Enter* COLONEL, R. H. 2 E. *To* HARTMANN) Stand by; he's here!

> As soon as the COLONEL comes on, HARTMANN *hums the refrain of the German song sung in the first Act, and walks about with an appearance of unconcern.* SOUND *looks at him, and endeavours to hum a tune.* COLONEL *watches both of them keenly.*

Col. Ah, you are gay, my friends; well, so much the better! Let us all be gay. I come to announce to you that lunch is ready. (*they both begin to sing, and walk about again*) What is it that you have, both of you?

Hart. I'll tell you, Colonel. The fact is, the Captain has received a letter——

Capt. (*getting nervous*) No, no, no.

Col. Has received a letter?

Hart. Yes! and the news has very much pleased him.

Col. So, so. I congratulate you, Captain!

Capt. For what? On the fact of my having received a letter which has very much pleased me? (*aside to* Hartmann) Hartmann, you must get me out of this. I really cannot——

Col. You have received news!

Capt. Yes—news.

Col. What is there that is in this news? Something of me, eh?

Capt. Well, well—yes. } (*together*)
Hart. No, no, no.

Col. You try to conceal something from me. What is it?

Hart. The fact is, we have received news of our poor Oscar's final resting-place.

Col. (*with exultation*) We left him—as a Frenchman—a soldier—should die—on the field, with the sky for his pall, and a church for his monument.

Capt. (*to* Hartmann) Take care, take care!

Hart. Well, the Captain has received news that his -resting-place has been found. Was it not so, Sound?

Col. Has been found——

Hart. And he has received the rights of sepulture and——

Col. Is there a cross to mark his grave?

Hart. A—a—a—a letter which Captain Sound got written last night——

Capt. Eh? No!

Hart. Which Captain Sound has received——

Col. Show it me—that letter! (Captain Sound brings out letter, which he hands to Hartmann, and which Hartmann hands to Colonel. Colonel crosses the stage to c.) You have received this letter, Captain Sound—(Captain signifies Yes)—about my poor boy, and you bring it on to me this morning? Thank you, thank you! Before that I open it, have you anything to tell me? (Captain offers him a chair, and signifies No. Colonel seats himself) My poor boy!

CAPT. (*passes at the back of stage, slaps his thigh, and says*) Why, Hartmann! we should not have given it him; it is in Oscar's handwriting.

HART. What shall we do?

CAPT. Take it from him   (*advancing*)

HART. No, no!   (*restraining him*)

COL. (*after an effort, summons up his fortitude and opens the letter, then looks at address*) It is like his writing. Oh, impossible! yet——(*opens the letter and reads*) "Mon Père——" Ah!

CAPT. I knew you would! it is your fault, Hartmann.

COL. (*recovering himself*) "Mon Père!"——(*tries to read it, his eyes filled with tears, then rising suddenly*) Then he is not dead?

CAPT. }
HART. } No.

COL. I knew it—I·knew it! I saw him last night. I touched him. It was not madness! Thank God! Thank God! (*he falls into a paroxysm. After he recovers, he hands the letter to the* CAPTAIN) But the letter! (*reading*) "My dear, dear father——" (*mastering his emotion*) "My dear, dear father——" (*to* CAPTAIN) It is not that I am mad, then?

CAPT. Mad be damned! You're as sane as I am (*with enthusiasm*) Continuez—allez vous-en, mon Colonel, le bon jour viendra!

COL. (*reading*) "I know not, as I write, when this shall meet your eyes; but when it does, let it assure you that your son—your little Oscar—is living, safe, and well; that he has recovered from his wound, and only awaits for the moment that he presses your kind and honoured hand for complete restoration. I have a long story to tell. For the moment, let it suffice that I have given my parole, and that I am again in France—again in France!" (*pauses for a moment, then resumes*) "I need not, my brave and honoured father, explain to you the emotions that fill my heart as I once more tread the soil of our beloved country. After all, the chief charm, the chief beauty of France is that it is always France—sunny, divine, incomparable." (*the* COLONEL *breaks down. He hands letter to* HARTMANN) Continue—continue—I can no more to see.

HART. (*reading*) "But to ourselves. I have heard—it may be untrue—that you left Germany in the company of M. Hartmann. My hand trembles as I write the name—Lotte! (HARTMANN *begins to be affected*) My wife! The wife who wedded a husband she believed to be dying. The chances of life are as the chances of war ; and I would give ten years of the happiness I look for to know that she is living. Does she still gild the earth ?˙ Has not Heaven robbed earth of such a treasure? If I could but see her——"

HARTMANN *breaks down, and hands letter to* CAPTAIN.

CAPT. My dear friends—my dear friends, you mustn't feel it so much. Be men ! be men ! To such men as you, who have seen battle, to break down like schoolgirls !

COL. } (*together*) { Continue.
HART. } { Go on.

CAPT. (*reading*) " If I could but see her, and you, and her brave good father—hear your voices—and feel the warm pressure of your hands, I think that I could die happy. If Heaven so wills it that such rapture should not be for me, I must resign my——" (*breaks down*)

COL. Give to me. (*takes letter*) Why, this has no address—no—— It has not arrived by post. How did you get it ?

CAPT. (*nonplussed*) I—I—I—it came with the letters.

COL. Ah ! do not deceive and trifle with me. You have seen him !

CAPT. No, no.

HART. Yes; he has seen him.

COL. When ?

HART. Last night.

COL. Here in England ? (*fixing his eyes—his rhapsody returning*) Oscar, my son, come back to me from the grave ! I can meet such happiness calmly—it shall not drive me mad ! Oh ! such a joy cannot to kill. Believe not those who tell it does. It is blasphemy to Providence. (*during this speech* OSCAR, *dressed " en bourgeois," has appeared in the archway of the shrubbery,* R.H. COLONEL *turns and sees him*) Why, there he stands—there— there ! No spectre, but real flesh and blood ! Oscar, my son, show your poor, old, mad father that it is no vision— no brain delusion—show him that you live ! (OSCAR *kneels for a moment, then darts forward to his father, who embraces him*) 'Tis he, as I have seen him, when they tell to me, those people of the world, that I have not my senses ! Oscar ! O my son ! to see you once again ! (*as if addressing Heaven*) Oh, Julie ! more like to you than ever !

OSCAR. My father, dear father ! (*crosses and shakes hands with* HARTMANN) And now tell me, Lotte——

HART. Mourns your loss.   We had feared consumption ;
but the sight of you——

COL. Ah ! yes, it shall restore her.

CAPT. Yes ; one young husband is worth ten patent
medicines.   A hearty cuddle is better than the most bracing
climate.

COL. You have recovered from your wound ? (OSCAR
signifies assent.   Bringing OSCAR *down, and looking at the
breast of his overcoat, on which there is no cross*) Et la croix ?

OSCAR. (*showing it in his undercoat*) Voilà !

COL. (*embracing him*) Mon fils.   C'est plus mon fils que
jamais.

> [*Where it is unlikely that the audience will understand
> French, the lines to run thus :*—COL. And your
> cross ?   OSCAR. (*opening his coat, and showing it*)
> Nearest my heart. · COL. (*embracing him*) My
> son—more my son than ever !*]

OSCAR. But Lotte—when shall I see her ?

HART. We must prepare her for your reception ; and
that reminds me.   Haste away quickly, for if she sees you
suddenly it might be too much for her.

CAPT. Hush !

> *A dead silence.   HARTMANN goes to the drawing-room
> window, motioning* COLONEL *and* OSCAR *to retire.
> They do so, to the shrubbery.   HARTMANN then
> opens the two windows, and* LOTTE *is seen in the
> drawing-room, her head on the table, and a book by
> her side.*

PICTURE.

OSCAR. (*whispering*) Lotte, Lotte, my dear wife !—I
must speak to her !

> COLONEL *keeps him back.   OSCAR is about to advance
> towards her again, when a motion from* HARTMANN
> *keeps him back.   LOTTE dries her eyes, and turns
> her face to the audience.   OSCAR starts.   COLONEL
> puts his arm round his waist, and darts off with
> him up the shrubbery.   LOTTE looks over the pages
> of a book listlessly, and puts a mark in them.
> HARTMANN sees that OSCAR and COLONEL are well
> out of sight, and is about to shut the window, when
> LOTTE requests him in action not to close it.
> HARTMANN advances towards CAPTAIN.*

HART. I am beside myself with joy. Oscar returned! Oscar returned! I could leap out of my skin!

CAPT. Don't do anything of the kind. Control yourself. In all these cases always show a profound calm, and set a good example to the men. (*excitedly*)

HART. I—I—I must do something.

> *Sings the chorus of the German song in the first Act.* CAPTAIN *joins in it.* LOTTE *comes from the room, down the stage.*

LOTTE. Why, papa, what good spirits you are in! Have you had some good news? Is there likely to be peace?

HART. Peace! (*going to* LOTTE *and kissing her*) My child, how very well you look! I have not seen you look so well for some time. She *is* looking well; is she not, Captain?

CAPT. She is indeed. I must wish you good morning, Madame de Rochevannes, for I have a little business to transact in town, and I must—(*looking at his watch*)—I must leave you.

HART. (*aside to him*) What for you leave me to tell her all by myself?

CAPT. Well, it rather frightens me to——

HART. You are so timid! Help me to break it to her.

CAPT. How are you going to do it?

LOTTE, R.   HARTMANN, L.C.

                                        CAPTAIN, L.

HART. I don't know. Yes, I do!

> (*with sudden inspiration*)

CAPT. Are you going to tell her now directly?

HART. Yes.

CAPT. Then, good-bye.

HART. What a coward you are!

CAPT. Yes, perhaps I am; but I don't like deceit. I can't bear to tell lies! (*going*)

HART. What, not to a woman?

CAPT. Well, that does make a difference. (*returning*)

HART. Back me up in all I say!

CAPT. I will. Don't lie more than is necessary.

HART. My child, I have good news.

LOTTE. Good news for us?

HART. Beautiful! I have a letter from your uncle.

LOTTE. From Berlin?

Hart. Ja. Your Cousin Fritz, whom we heard was wounded dangerously, is only wounded slightly.

Lotte. That is good news indeed !

Hart. Yes, indeed. But Fritz is not only wounded very slightly (*watching the effect upon her*)—he is not wounded at all —never has been wounded ; on the contrary, he has been promoted !

Lotte. Promoted !

Hart. Ja. He is now a Hauptmann.

Lotte. My brave cousin ! And is he still with his battalion ?

Hart. (*watching the effect upon her*) No ; he has gone back to Berlin, to his father.

Lotte. Discharged ?

Hart. Yes, discharged.

Lotte. Discharged—unwounded, and gone back to his father—to his home ?

Capt. (*aside*) If I could lie like that, I should make a fortune !

Lotte. But there have been no letters to-day. Who brought this news ?

Hart. (*puzzled for the moment*) Captain Sound. Sound, you brought the news, didn't you ?

Capt. Yes, yes, I brought the news. Very good news, too.

Lotte. But why did Uncle Fritz write to you, and not to papa ? He does not know you.

Hart. (*puzzled*) Yes, just so ; why did he write to you ? (*to* Captain)

Capt. (*aside to* Hartmann) Damn it, Hartmann, this is too bad ! (*aloud*) I suppose he knew that I was a friend of the family, and that I should be pleased to hear your cousin had been made a boatswain.

Hart. Hauptmann !

Capt. Hauptmann !

Lotte. But I can't understand——

Hart. Why then seek to inquire ? I have good news, and having good news, let's make the best of it. Your Cousin Fritz, whom we thought was dying, is not only returned to life, but to his home, so let us be gay. (*sings the chorus of the German song*) We will open a bottle of hock, and drink his health.

Lotte. Have you got the letter Captain Sound brought ?

Hart. (*boldly*) Yes—no, I have not. Sound, where is it ?

CAPT. I—I gave it to you. I gave it to you. (*aside to* HARTMANN) I can't go on lying in this way—not even to oblige a lady !

LOTTE. I should like to read that letter myself.

HART. (*gaily*) What more natural? Captain, she would like to read the letter herself. Give it her. What are you fumbling about ? Give her the letter to read.

LOTTE. But how could Captain Sound read it ? He cannot read German, and my Uncle Fritz does not write English !

HART. True, true, true! How was that, Captain?

CAPT. (*with desperation*) It was written in French.

LOTTE. Then give it to me.

CAPT. Bless my soul ! (*feeling for the letter*) I must have dropped it somewhere, and the dog must have run off with it. Phew !

(*mopping his forehead with his handkerchief*)

HART. (*taking his daughter's arm, and walking up and down the stage*) My dear child

LOTTE. My dear papa, and poor dear Uncle Fritz—how happy he must be !

HART. Yes, happiness is possible in this world; why should it not come to us?

LOTTE. Contentment, papa — resignation, but not happiness.

COL. (*who has advanced from the shrubbery during the last few words*) Ah ! my child (*taking her in his arms*)— and why not happiness for us? There are philosophes who tell that all here beneath this bright sky is but material ; that the mind, the soul, the higher, better nature exist but in conjunction with matter ; that if we see more than they see, hear more than they hear, and feel more than they feel —that if we have a distinct, higher, and clearer perception than is theirs—that we are mad. They not know everything, those philosophes. They will tell you that glory is a blatant vanity; that love of country is a foolish home-sickness; that love itself is a vain, passionate delusion. They not know everything, those philosophes. Those men of science think the heart can break with joy. It is not so. It may crack with grief. But, my child, the human heart is large enough to contain any quantity of happiness ! But I will not keep you longer to tell you that which have been already told to your father——

LOTTE. What do you mean?

COL. (*suddenly*) Oscar, my son, is not dead.

LOTTE. Not dead! (*noting the expression of the* COLONEL'S *face, then turning to her father, half afraid of* COLONEL) Has his malady returned?

COL. Ah, my child, do not fear me! My reason is not shaken. Oscar, my son, is living. I have strained him to my heart. I have seen him as I have seen him many a night since we left him on the cold ground near the church.

LOTTE. (*looking at her father.* CAPTAIN SOUND *looks at her. Going to* COLONEL) My poor, dear papa, you have seen Oscar?

COL. Yes; seen him last night in my dreams, and here to-day in the awakening sunlight. His first words were of you.

LOTTE. Of me?

COL. Yes. Ah! Grant me patience; she thinks I still am alienated. Lotte, I tell to you that your husband is here; that I have spoken to him upon this ground where I now stand, and so has your father and the Captain.

LOTTE. What am I to believe, father?

HART. (*hesitating*) My—my child!

LOTTE. (*turning suddenly to* CAPTAIN) Captain Sound, I have heard it said that Englishmen never tell lies.

CAPT. (*very uneasy*) I never heard of one doing so.

LOTTE. Upon your honour, then, as an English gentleman, and an officer, is this true or false? Have you seen my husband within the last twelve hours? (*imploring*) Oh, speak the truth! I am but a girl—a poor, weak, suffering woman—a widowed wife. My father turns from me, his father has delusions: I trust in you. Answer me by the love you bore your late wife—by the love you bear your living child. Have you seen him?

CAPT. (*after hesitating for a moment, and then taking off his hat*) I have.

LOTTE. You have!

CAPT. Yes.

LOTTE. Where?—where? (*falling into the* COLONEL'S *arms, her back to the shrubbery*) O Oscar! my love—my husband! Let me know that you are living—give me some proof of your presence!

> OSCAR *advances, takes the wedding-ring off her finger, and puts it back again. The* COLONEL *places her in* OSCAR'S *arms.* BLANCHE, JESSIE, AGNES, *and* KATIE *appear.* CAPTAIN SOUND *takes up his hat,*

goes up the stage to the door at back. He turns round to look upon the picture. LOTTE *and* OSCAR *in each other's arms.* COLONEL R. *of* LOTTE. HARTMANN L. *of* OSCAR. CAPTAIN *returns and shakes hands with* COLONEL *and with* HARTMANN, *and joins their hands at the back of the young couple. He then retires towards door at back.* GIRLS *group round.* KATIE *on her knees, hiding her head in* AGNES'S *skirts.*

CURTAIN.

PRINTED BY
SPOTTISWOODE AND CO., NEW-STREET SQUARE
LONDON